Cupid's Darts

A Sweet Hearts Collection

by

Susan Buffum

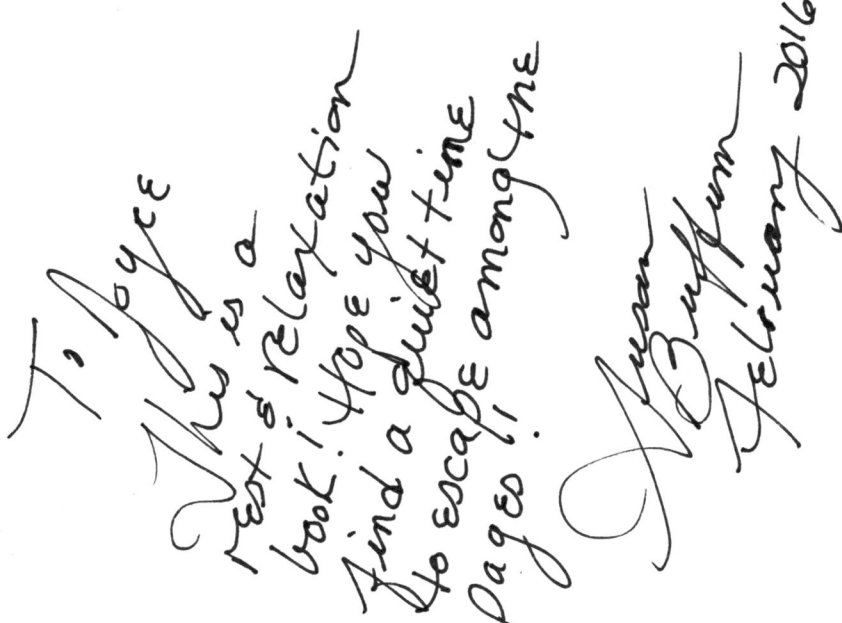

Susan Buffum

All rights reserved by the author. No part of this book may be used or reproduced by any means graphic, electronic, or mechanical, including photocopying, recording, taping, or by any information retrieval storage systems including file sharing, without the author's express written permission, except in the case of brief quotation embodied in critical articles or reviews.

Please contact the author at sebuffum415@gmail.com for permission.

Copyright January 21, 2016 by Susan Buffum

First Edition, January 21, 2016

This is entirely a work of fiction. All characters, names, incidents, organizations and dialogues in this publication are either the products of the author's imagination, or used fictitiously and are not meant to represent anyone currently living or deceased.

Printed by CreateSpace.com, an Amazon.com company

Dedication

To my late parents Theodore and Joan Adamcik who taught me what love is all about. To my husband John who doesn't always understand me but has always been there for me. To my daughter, Kelly, for whom I write these stories, who has been my greatest supporter and my biggest help when I have needed it (she's a tech whiz, I am not.) To Carol "Peech" Weeks my best friend from freshman year of college on. To Darlene Gogal, Gail Bevilaqua, Amanda Pothier and Kristina Sypek, my girl gang. And to my readers whom I appreciate more than I can say.

Titles by Susan Buffum

Miss Peculiar's Haunting Tales, Volume I

The Subtlety of Light and Shadow

My Magical Life

Miss Peculiar's Haunting Tales, Volume II

Love Me Knots

The Archetypes-First Generation

The Archetypes-Shockwaves

Miss Peculiar's Haunting Tales, Volume III

Auspicious Beginnings

Yuletide Stories

Always Christmas in My Heart

Together for the Holidays

Talon: An Intimate Familiarity

Talon: A Sense of Familiarity

Life Skills

Cupid's Darts: A Sweet Hearts Collection

Table of Contents

A Ray of Sunshine……………………………….7

Rebuilding a Life………………………………..25

The Best Man……………………………………61

Tangerine Twist…………………………………79

Secretary's Day………………………………..105

A Special Valentine…………………………...131

Lockout Rescue………………………………..139

Dragon and Butterfly………………………….161

Nine Innings……………………………………187

The Weeping Angel…………………………...233

Jack Cameron Takes a Bride………………..251

The Window Washer………………………….267

The Big Lemon………………………………...273

Coffee Connection…………………………….279

The Undertaker's Daughter…………………..285

A RAY OF SUNSHINE

He stood on the sidewalk looking at the plate glass window with its fancy gold lettering for some time being jostled by pedestrians, scowled at by others as they moved around him. Finally he shoved the sunglasses up on top of his head, grabbed the handle and pulled the door open. A bell jangled merrily. A few heads turned his way but quickly turned back to their sandwiches and soup as he walked to the counter where a pretty redhead was pouring coffee for an elderly man. He sat down beside the old man, resting his forearms on the counter. "Coffee," he said.

"Be right with you," the redhead replied, topping up the old man's cup. She dug some creamers out of her apron pocket, setting them on the counter beside the cup.

"Any day now would be nice," he grumbled.

The old man turned his head and gave him a look. The young man with the shaggy, raven-black hair gave him a dark look in return. Shelley set a cup and saucer down before the younger man and filled it. "Still take it black?" she asked, drawing his attention away from the man beside him. His dark eyes met hers. "Three sugars?"

"You remember," he said, his voice low. "That's a surprise."

"I have a head for trivial information." She slid the container of sugar packets closer to him.

"Is that all I am to you?" he asked. "Just a bunch of useless trivial facts?"

"Not useless. You have your coffee the way you like it, don't you?"

This was new, her talking back to him like this. She was more confident, more sure of herself these days. "You remember what I like to eat?" he asked next. Her hazel eyes began to slew away from his intent gaze. "For lunch," he clarified.

"Grilled cheese and bacon on whole wheat," she answered. "And tomato soup with a dollop of cream." This earned her a sardonic grin. "It's not on the menu but I know the cook."

"Is your old man going to kick me out of here?" he asked, stirring sugar into his coffee. Before she could answer he dropped the spoon, reaching across the counter to grab her left hand. His index finger and thumb massaged the faint indent of a wedding band that still lingered on her ring finger. "I heard a rumor about this," he murmured.

"It's not a rumor, it's a fact. He's not here anymore. I have a new cook."

"Is he just a cook or more than that?" he asked, his dark eyes rising to meet hers.

"Just a cook," she replied lightly. His finger continued to massage her finger a moment or two longer before he let go. "I'll go put your order in."

He watched her walk to the swinging door and go into the kitchen. She was still the prettiest girl in the Berkshires with her copper hair, now cut in a short pixie style that only emphasized her fox-like features. He'd been an idiot to let her slip away but he hadn't been ready for this sort of thing back then. He'd had a lot of wild oats to sow and she'd known it. That's how Tommy had stolen her away, offering her a version of the American dream that had satisfied her at the time. If he'd been around then he would have warned her about Tommy, saved her a lot of heartache. At least she'd gotten out of that marriage and he didn't have to worry about any assault and battery charges beating up that asshole who'd cheated on her every chance he'd had.

"You know Shelley?" the old man asked.

"Mind your own business."

Beside him the old man shifted on his cushioned stool. "She is my business," he replied levelly. "Shelley's my granddaughter."

He turned his head and looked again at the man. "I know her. We graduated from high school together eight years ago. We dated some in school. Her parents weren't crazy about that. I was from the wrong side of town."

"I know who you are. Recognized you the second you came through the door. You're that Sanborn boy. The middle one who went to jail."

"No," he said, shaking his head. "I didn't go to jail. Charges were dropped. There was no evidence that I robbed that gas station, primarily because I didn't do it. I was in Springfield at the time."

"Reve, that's your name, isn't it?" He nodded. The old man looked down into his coffee cup. "Things have never gone right for her. That damned son of a bitch she married, he cheated on her with every bimbo in town and the next towns over either side. He never treated her right. She was afraid to leave him."

"So what happened? How'd she get up the nerve to divorce him?"

"Finally took my advice and went for counseling. Met Caroline Shea. Good woman, that one. Took a couple of years but Shelley finally got up the nerve to kick his ass out of here. This is still the family business. It'll be hers as soon as I'm gone. Her father's not interested. He took off a year and a half ago. Moved out west someplace, Arizona, maybe? Her mother's got her real estate license now. Shelley's the one who's always loved this place. I'm leaving it to her. Won't be long now. I got liver cancer. It's spread here and there."

"Does she know that?"

"She knows that I been to doctors and the lawyer. She knows she's signed papers but I'm not sure she understands completely what it's all been about yet. I've taken care of her. She's always been a good kid. Smart. She could have done so much more with her life if she hadn't married that dumb ass womanizer."

"Shelley's always liked to cook and be around people. This is probably where she's happiest. She's worked here since she was fifteen, hasn't she? I used to come after school for a burger and a Coke. She'd be running around here taking orders, dancing to the music, chatting up everybody, laughing." He shook his head. "She's a regular ray of sunshine, she is."

"What are you doing back here? Thought you went to Connecticut or something."

"Rhode Island. Vermont. New York state. I've been around learning my trade."

"What trade would that be?"

"Classic car restoration, customizing cars." He added a bit more sugar to his cup, slowly stirring it in. "I have my own place in Lee. I'm doing all right." He turned slightly, nodding toward the window. "That's one of my custom jobs out there."

Mr. Colter turned on his stool toward the window. There was a black GTO with orange pin striping parked out front. Lots of chrome. "Nice," he said. "You sell a lot of cars?"

"I find old cars, restore them, customize them and then sell them at the shop or send them to auction. I make pretty good money on them."

Shelley came back with his grilled cheese and bacon and bowl of tomato soup. "Here you go," she said, setting the plate and bowl down in front of him. "Anything else you want?"

"Your phone number," he replied. Her eyes flicked to her grandfather and back. In the periphery of his vision he'd seen the old man give her a slight nod.

"Remind me before you go."

"Give it to me now," he answered, taking his cell phone from his hip pocket. "I may have to rush off. Bring me the check, too. I'm meeting someone at one thirty." She gave him her cell-phone number and then moved off to wait on a couple that had come in and taken the last available booth. "She seeing anyone?" he asked, stirring the cream slowly into his soup.

"She has dinner and goes to local hockey games with Pete from the post office now and again. No romance there, just friends. He eats here every day." Reve nodded. "You thinking of asking her out?"

Reve sampled the soup, nodding to himself. It was good. "Think she'd go if I asked?"

"She just gave you her number."

"I saw you give her the okay."

"She was always crazy about you. Never let anyone say anything bad about you. Still defends you if your name comes up and someone starts in on old history."

Reve's eyes rose as he followed Shelley who came back around the counter to go out to the kitchen with the order she'd just taken. "I broke her heart," he said.

"You can fix that quick enough. She ain't ever stopped loving you, you know."

"I didn't know." Reve ate half his sandwich. Shelley came to refill his coffee.

"Grandpa, you want a piece of that banana cream pie you love so much?" she asked.

"A small one, sweetheart. Watching my weight."

"Be right back. Reve, you still like chocolate cream pie?"

"Yeah, I do."

"I'll bring you a piece, on the house." She disappeared back into the kitchen.

"You see what I mean? She don't forget a thing, but she can forgive in a heartbeat."

"I don't deserve that kind of quick forgiveness. She's too good." He finished his sandwich, sipped his coffee and then got out his wallet. "How much do I owe you?" he asked her as she set their plates of pie down before them.

"Seven dollars."

He took out a twenty and a card, slid them across to her. "Keep the change. Keep the card." He stopped her from picking up the card. "Let me see your pen." She handed it to him. He flipped the card over and wrote another phone number on the backside. "That's my cell number. Hang onto it."

"I will," she said, her eyes meeting his. He winked at her. She smiled and blushed simultaneously and then looked at her grandfather who was enjoying his pie. "You good, Grandpa?"

"Yup. Thanks, sweetie."

"See you again?" she asked Reve.

"I like the food here. I'll be back," he replied.

"Good." She went to wait on a man at the far end of the counter who'd just sat down.

"Look," said Mr. Colter. "I have a '64 Mustang convertible in my garage. It was my mid-life crisis car. Needs work. You interested in it? Maybe making it a sweet ride for my little girl?"

"You asking me to make it cherry for Shelley?"

"Yeah, guess I am. What do you figure it'll cost me?"

"I'd have to see what you've got before I can give you a price." He ate the last piece of his pie. "What if I swing by on Saturday evening? Will you be home?" Mr. Colter nodded. "I'll take a look at it, make a list of what needs to be done and then work up some figures and get back to you by Wednesday at the latest. We changing the color?"

"Buttercup yellow." Reve winced. "She likes yellow."

"Okay. But I can't see myself tooling along the Pike in a bright yellow Mustang."

"Not even with a beautiful redhead behind the wheel?"

Reve ran his fingers up through his tousled hair. "I'd have to think about that for a bit." He stood up, held out his right hand. "Good seeing you again. You still out by the lake?"

"Good seeing you. Yup, still on Shady Cove Lane. White cottage with the bright blue shutters."

"See you Saturday about seven o'clock?"

"Sounds good. You drink beer?" Reve nodded. "We'll have a coupla beers and look that car over good."

Shelley came back through the swinging door. "You going so soon?"

"Have a meeting to get to like I said, otherwise I'd stay a bit longer. I'll call you in a day or two." He turned and walked to the door, pausing to glance back over his shoulder at her before he left. She was standing behind the counter watching him, and something about the way she was looking at him made him think that she was afraid he'd never come back. That told him what he wanted to know right there. He was pretty sure her grandfather would tell her what she wanted to know.

You awake?

Shelley reached over to the bedside table to grab her cellphone. She had been lying in the dark, unable to fall asleep. Reve had said he'd call her in a day or two but he hadn't called. Therefore she was surprised when she saw the text was from him. *Can't sleep*, she texted back. *Too hot.*

Want to go skinny dipping?

Her heart leapt into the back of her throat. Her finger hesitated over the keyboard. Taking a breath she quickly typed, *Where are you?*

Down by the lake.

Swimming?

Thinking about it. Want to join me?

She hesitated again and then typed, *Sure.*

His response came about thirty seconds later. *Put your suit on. Neighbors may be awake.*

She blew her breath out, relieved. *You want me to drive there?*

I'll come get you. Give me fifteen minutes.

I'll be out front.

Her legs felt wobbly as she got out of bed to rummage in her dresser for the two pieces of her tankini. It was eleven-thirty on a Thursday night and she was going to go swimming with Reve at the lake! It was insane! She had to be up at five to get to work for five-thirty to do some prep work, get the coffee started, the deliveries checked in.

She looked at the phone that she still held in her hand. She should text him that she couldn't go. She had to get some sleep, but her heart was going a million miles per hour. There was no way she was going to be able to get back into bed with any hope of sleeping. "This is sheer madness," she muttered as she tugged off her nightgown, pulled on the bottom of her suit. She slithered into the top of the suit and then flipped on the overhead light, searching the floor of her closet for her flip flops. In the narrow hall linen closet she grabbed a beach towel before hurrying to the front closet to get the tote bag she used for going to the lake. Groaning, she ran back to the bedroom, pulling on a pair of denim shorts. She stuffed a t-shirt into the tote bag and then threw her keys and a small bi-fold case with her ID and a twenty dollar bill into the bag.

She switched off the lights and then ran down the steep stairs to the sidewalk door. She had the front apartment above the café. There was some traffic as usual for a Thursday night. The bars were still busy. There were a lot of people at the lake this summer. As she waited in front of the café she wondered where on the lake he was going to take her? The public beaches closed at nine o'clock. Was he staying at a friend's?

"Shelley!"

A Jeep had pulled up to the curb. "Hi," she said, climbing into the passenger seat, stuffing her bag down by her feet. She buckled up as he pulled out into traffic. "Where are we going?" she asked. "The beaches are closed."

"Not the private ones," he replied. She glanced at him. "I just got back from Worcester at eight thirty. Had some things to do around the shop. Thought I'd take a swim before going to bed. I didn't wake you?" She shook her head. "Thought I might be. You must have to get up early. Didn't think of that when I texted you."

"I couldn't sleep. My air conditioner's not working right."

"You didn't leave it on, did you?" She shook her head. "Good. Don't want the place burning down if it's a shot compressor."

"I have the windows open and had the fans on."

He soon slipped out of traffic to follow side roads. She had no idea where they were going. She wasn't familiar with all the little roads and lanes around the lake itself, but he seemed to know where he was going. Still, her insides felt like wobbly jelly and she had to sit on her hands because they were shaking. It'd been a long time since she'd gone anywhere with Reve Sanborn alone like this. Her grandfather had told her he owned his own business, something to do with cars but she hadn't quite caught everything that he was saying as it had been during a rush of customers after Reve had left that day. If Grandpa had given him the nod then she should be all right, even though Grandpa was getting older and he had health issues now.

He pulled up in the yard of a two story beach house with a separate four bay garage with what looked like a small shop at one end. There was another building across the driveway, a bunkhouse, maybe? The main house had a deep front porch facing the lane they'd come in by. "Come on," he said.

She climbed out and followed him along the path beside the house. The rear of the house had a huge deck for outdoors entertaining. There was a balcony off the second floor rear with atrium doors that must provide an awesome view of the lake. "Whose house is this?" she asked as she jogged a few paces to catch up to him after goggling at the house.

"Does it matter?"

"We're not trespassing, are we?"

He laughed. "No. We're not."

The path led to a private beach. White sand had been trucked in. Quite a lot of it. It went all the way from the end of the path to the water. Reve was stripping off his t-shirt, kicking off his sandals. Her heart nearly stopped as he unfastened his denim shorts but he had a regular trunk-style bathing suit on underneath. She threw her bag down in the sand, tugged down her shorts. He told her to jump in before the mosquitoes drained her dry.

She ran down the sandy beach and splashed into the water. The lake bed quickly graded down and she found herself neck deep in the water. It felt cold after the heat of the apartment and the sultry night air. Reve dove in close beside her, startling her. She caught glimpses of him as he swam underwater. He swam like a fish. It brought back memories of high school days, hurrying home to do her chores and homework, make supper for her parents who both worked so they could eat when they got home, and then going to the lake with friends, seeing Reve there. They'd dated senior year for a little while but her parents had made a fuss about him. Then he'd been accused of robbing that gas station not too long after graduation and her parents had forbidden her to ever see him again. And Tommy had started pursuing her. She'd lost track of Reve in the hectic days that followed as she began working full time at the café.

She swam out a ways, felt something skim past her beneath the water and gasped. Reve surfaced a few feet in front of her. "You still swim like a fish!" she said. "I thought you were a shark!"

"No sharks in this lake," he said. "Just big fish."

She swept wet hair back from her face. "Are you a big fish?"

He swam toward her and she back paddled. "What did your grandfather tell you?' he asked.

She shrugged. "Not much. He said something about cars. You do something with cars. It was crazy busy after you'd left. He's been in Boston for tests the past few days. I haven't talked to him."

"I customize cars, restore vintage cars," he said.

"Oh, like on TV?"

"I suppose so."

"Who do you work for? Anyone I know?"

"You know him," he replied. He ducked under the water before she could ask him who. She screamed when he lifted her up and threw her over his shoulder. She came up a few feet behind him sputtering a little. "Come back here." She swam back to him. "Here, get your feet into my hands. You used to like to dive off my hands."

"I'm not seventeen anymore."

"You're twenty-six years old. You're not a decrepit old lady yet. Come on. Up you go." She got her feet into his hands, squealed as he lifted her up. She flew off his hands, diving gracefully into the water. He let her dive off his hands about ten times before he chased her, easily catching her. She wrapped her arms and legs around him like she used to as he treaded water. "At least he didn't beat the fun out of you," he said.

Her face was close to his. Her eyes met his in the moonlight and starlight. "No," she said. "He didn't."

"You divorced him?"

She nodded. "Grandpa helped me pay for a private investigator. He got enough evidence to prove in court that he was unfaithful to me. Tommy couldn't deny it. I got a lump sum of twenty-five thousand dollars before he took off. I haven't heard from him since."

"You're well rid of him." He touched her cheek. "I wish I'd been around to stop you marrying him in the first place."

"What would you have done? Barged into the church, marched down the aisle, ranting and raving about him not being good enough for me and then thrown me over your shoulder and carried me out to your Harley, roaring off into the sunset with me trailing seed pearls, bugle beads and baby's breath in our wake?"

"If that's what it would have taken, yeah, I would have done that."

She bent her head, resting her forehead against his, her eyes closed. "Where were you, Reve? Where were you when I needed a black knight to come to my rescue?" she asked quietly.

"Off trying to make a better man of myself," he replied. "I thought you'd wait for me."

"My parents put too much pressure on me. I broke. I crumbled." A little sob burst out of her. "I wasn't strong enough to chase my dreams!"

"Shh!" he said. "Don't cry, Shel. If you think about it, neither was I. I wouldn't have left you behind if I'd had any strength or sense back then"

"I nearly fainted when you walked through the door the other day. I never thought I'd see you again."

"I wasn't sure I'd ever be back, but things worked out better than I thought they would. When I had a chance to own my own business I was ready to go west, or south. Then one night I had a dream and you were in it. I woke up the next morning and started scouring the internet for any sign of you. I Googled the café and there you were. You and your grandfather, right where I'd left you eight years ago, except you had Tommy's last name."

"The site hasn't been updated. I took Colter back, got rid of the Birch. I'm Shelley Colter again."

"Just like you were when I left."

"Only older and wiser."

"We both are, older and wiser."

"Did you ever get married?' she asked.

He shook his head. "Had my share of girls. I'm no saint, Shel. I'll be honest with you about that. I had a lot of girls."

"You've always been a chick magnet."

He made a face. "Yeah, well, the only one I ever wanted I had to let go of." He brushed tears off her face with his wet hand. "Shelley, you agreeing to come swimming with me like this, does that mean you were just hot and unable to sleep and needed a diversion, or does it mean you…"

"Oh, stop already and just kiss me!" she cried. "I just want you to kiss me."

He did not hesitate. He caught her mouth with his and kissed her. Her arms tightened around the back of his neck and she kissed him back. Immediately he was eighteen years old again, kissing pretty little seventeen-year old Shelley Colter in the lake behind the canoe, amazed that such a sweet and innocent girl would even allow him to touch her never mind kiss her. He wanted to make love to her back then but knew he couldn't. He'd waited until a week before her eighteenth birthday before he brought her back to the lake one night and made love to her under the stars. He'd been her first lover, and he'd liked that. She'd waited for him. Two months later everything went to hell with the gas station robbery, his being arrested, her parents forbidding her to ever see him again. Even after he was acquitted they had not allowed him near her. In frustration, he'd taken off. After a year of living rough, barely surviving, he'd found Henry Fitch and begun to learn all there was to learn about classic auto restoration and customizing cars. He'd worked hard to learn his trade, had saved his money by living frugally. And dreaming about the girl he had loved and lost because of some rattled gas jockey's misidentification had led him back home, and to this very moment that he had never dared dreamed of. "Shelley," he said, his voice husky. "We need to get closer to shore. I need to put my feet on solid ground."

"Mm, sorry." She slid her mouth from his, tilting her head, trailing little kisses down his jaw, the side of his neck as she unwound her legs from his waist, sliding down his body, letting go of his neck. She sank beneath the water and he felt her circle him, brushing against him, not once, but twice, and then she was gone.

He swam after her, catching her near the shore, bringing her up out of the water. "Little fishy, I thought you were going to take the bait back there," he said.

"Whose house is this?" she asked. "Is the owner home?"

"The owner is home," he acknowledged.

"Oh, damn it all!" she cried.

"Why? What's the matter?"

"I don't want him calling the police, reporting lewd behavior on his private beach, trespassers. I don't want to get you in trouble. We need to go. Come home with me."

"To your hot little apartment? Why can't we just stay here?"

"Because we'll get in trouble!"

He suddenly laughed. "I've been in trouble before. I think I can get us out of this if the owner complains."

"Reve…" She seemed exasperated, anxious.

He decided to set her mind at ease. "Shel, this is my house. This is my beach. And you're my girl, aren't you?" She opened her mouth to response but no words came out. "You still think you'll upset the owner?"

"Are you serious?"

"You want to see the deed? I have it in a safe inside."

"Do you have the keys?"

"Of course I do."

"Where?"

"In my shorts pocket. Front right." He watched her march up the sand to where he'd stripped off his shirt and shorts. She grabbed his shorts, dipping her hand into the front right pocket, pulling out his keys. "What are you going to do with those?" he asked.

"I'm going to go inside. Nothing is worse than sand in your cracks and crevices."

He laughed as he strode up the beach, scooping up their things, following her to the back deck of the house. She was trying keys when he caught up to her. "There's an alarm system. It's the next key. Get the door open then let me go in first to disarm it before the cops really do show up." She opened the door and he slipped inside, going to the alarm panel. "All set. Come on in."

She couldn't see much of the house in the dark. He secured the door and then led her through a large room to a hallway and then up an open flight of stairs to the second floor to the bedroom with the balcony overlooking the lake. She really didn't see much of the bedroom either except shadowy dark forms and then the bed as he picked her up and tossed her into the middle of it. "I'm wet!" she cried.

"I hope so," he replied.

And that's all the talking they did for quite some time except for a few murmured words here and there as they relearned one another's geography. He was better at it then he'd been in high school from the sounds she was making. And she wasn't as shy as she'd been back then. She'd learned some things that surprised and pleased him and made him want her all the more.

It was after two o'clock when they finally fell apart, breathing hard, lying side by side, arms touching. "You okay?" he asked.

"Never been better," she replied, her voice a little raspy and breathless still.

"Think you can sleep now?"

"You taking me home?"

"No, I meant here, with me. Think you can sleep?"

"I have to be up in a couple of hours."

"I'll be up. I'll wake you up."

"At four? I have to get home, take a shower, get to work for five thirty."

"I'll get you up at four, we'll take a shower. I'll get you home for quarter past five. You can run upstairs and get dressed and then come back downstairs to go to work. I'll hang around, have breakfast, if that's all right with you."

"That's fine with me." She turned toward him, smiling. "Don't make me late."

"Okay, we'll make love in the shower to save a little time." She laughed. He liked how she laughed, how she smiled at him in the near darkness. This is what he'd missed all those years. This is what he'd wanted. He hoped it was what she wanted, too, that it would last. "Go to sleep, little fishy."

She turned onto her other side and snuggled back against him. "This little fishy has always been attracted to your bait," she said, sounding drowsy.

He put his arm around her, pulling her closer, tucking her head underneath his chin. She was going to be tired tomorrow and so was he, but it had been well worth every minute that he'd spent with her tonight. As her breathing evened out and slowed in sleep he let his mind drift to the 64' Mustang convertible in her grandfather's garage. Buttercup yellow. It wasn't a color he'd have chosen, but Shelley was like sunshine in human form. It suited her, he thought. He felt warm and illuminated just being close to her. "I love you," he whispered, practicing the words he had always wanted to say to her but never had. He had a good feeling that maybe this time they would finally get said and he'd hear her say those same words back to him after eight long years of waiting and wondering if she still cared about him as much as he still cared about her. "Goodnight, sunshine," he murmured as his eyes finally drifted closed.

REBUILDING A LIFE

The thunder had been booming for an hour already, the lightning flashing blue-white, strobing through the dark rooms with eerie flashes, giving me glimpses of still shrouded furniture. I had only arrived ten days ago to take control of my late great-great-aunt's estate, a wretched, crumbling, brick Second Empire mansion with wavy old glass in the windows and draughty rooms full of musty old furniture and acres of dusty artifacts collected from numerous, long deceased Talbot relatives and preserved here for lucky ol' me as I was the last of the line, my parents having died in a terrible tour bus crash just outside of New York City just over a year ago.

I had inherited the estate seven months ago from Theodosia Charlotte Talbot-Winters. She had been one hundred-four years old at the time of her death. I remembered meeting her when I was a child. She had looked like a mummy to me when she had probably been only in her early eighties. I was twenty-six now, all by myself except for my Golden Retriever, Buttercup, my boyfriend of two years having thrown me over for an actress he'd met when in New York City on business, or so he'd said. Whatever. My true feeling is that he bolted when he saw the deplorable state of the estate, foreseeing grueling years of renovations and restoration work before the place would be even remotely habitable. We'd only seen the exterior that day as the attorney handling the estate had forgotten the keys back at the office. Danny had bitched and moaned about the crumbling house and outbuildings all the way home and for days afterwards, deaf to my thoughts that the place might be different inside, that it might just need exterior and cosmetic work. Nothing I'd said had swayed him. We had argued bitterly, him pushing me hard to sell the place to a developer, to take the money and run. I refused, adamantly. And then, one day, he was gone.

Another crash of thunder literally shook the house, rattled the windows. Buttercup whimpered. I had worked my butt off over the past few weeks making a few rooms habitable. I liked this one, the old game room. It was casual and comfortable. There was a door leading out onto the patio with its broken brickwork, but I had a vision of that brickwork being repaired, the sunburst pattern restored. "It's okay, baby," I murmured, reaching down to pat her head reassuringly as I looked toward the door. I couldn't help it. I screamed. My scream sent poor Buttercup scrambling out into the hallway, yelping and whining while I sat frozen in horror. There was someone at the door! A ghost? A madman? I didn't know but there shouldn't be anyone out there. I was pretty sure I'd closed the gate earlier this afternoon when I'd come home with groceries and dog food. But had I closed it securely?

Lightning flashed again and then the person was banging on the door, yelling something. "Go away!" I shouted. "Get off my property or I'll call the police!" Where was my cellphone? Most likely in the kitchen on the charger, I thought, as I patted my empty pockets and looked around for it.

"I need help!" he yelled back at me, his palms against the glass. "I ditched my bike! I'm hurt! Let me in!"

He sounded like he was in pain, and desperate. I got up and walked to the door. "I have a dog!"

"Yeah, I saw her run and hide," he replied from his side of the glass. His dark hair was plastered to his head, hanging, dripping in front of his eyes. The side of his face was filthy, and there was a bloody handprint on the glass.

"You're not a mass murderer are you? An escaped convict?"

"Are you carding me to get into your house?" he asked, wincing as he tried to reach for something. His face was chalky pale. He staggered and fell against the door.

I quickly twisted the deadbolt, threw the straight bolt, twisted the key and wrenched the door open. He half staggered, half fell into the room and I saw how the outside of the left leg of his jeans was all chewed up, muddy, wet and bloody. "Oh, my God! I need to call 9-1-1!"

"No! Don't!" he cried. "I had my license revoked for the bike. I'm not supposed to be riding it." He limped to the couch and fell onto it with a groan, throwing his head back, grimacing. "Just…Christ! Just let me sit here for a minute."

"You're bleeding."

"Great observational skills. You got any Tylenol? Towels? Band-Aids? Percocets?"

"Whisky and hot water," I replied.

"Do I get to drink the whisky or do you mean you'll use it as an antiseptic?"

"Maybe both if I can't find any other alcohol around this place." As I turned I saw Buttercup had come to the doorway. "Her name is Buttercup. She's a sweetheart. She won't bite."

"Can't say the same about myself. My old man says I'm a real bastard. The cops agree. Just about everyone in town agrees. I'll let you form your own opinion. You're new around here, right?" I nodded. "Yeah, thought so. I've seen you around town. Heard you inherited the place from the old girl." He leaned deeply back into the couch, clenching his teeth. "Ah, shit! Go get that damn whisky. Vinnie needs some medicine bad!"

"Is that your name? Vinnie?"

"Yeah, Vincent Rose. Ain't that a pretty name? Do you know guys with pretty names get the shit kicked out of them on the playground, get their heads shoved into toilets in the locker room, and worse. I didn't like that much. I had to fight a lot of bad-ass dudes growing up." He raised his head and opened his eyes, looking at me. "Baby, I really need something for the pain or you're going to be picking up chunks of my tongue off the floor as I bite it to pieces to keep from screaming my head off like a girl." I just stood there staring at him. "Please," he added.

I had an idea that he was not the sort of guy who used the word please a lot. "I'll be as quick as I can. Try to get those pants off so I can see what I have to deal with."

"You're going to have a lot to deal with," he said through gritted teeth.

"Drop the tough guy act. If I find what I need you're going to be a whimpering baby. There's just you and me here. You behave yourself and I'll never tell a soul you cried like a girl. I promise you that." I turned and left the game room. If he decided he could go elsewhere, so be it, but if he wanted my help he was going to behave himself while in my home.

By the time I got back he was laying on the couch, his jeans and boots off, right arm draped across his eyes, face ashen. The outside of his left leg from hip to knee looked like ground beef. There was road rash on the side of his calf as well, and on his left arm. I put down the supplies I had found, old as they were, went to the kitchen and heated some water in the kettle, pouring it into an enamel basin. Grabbing some additional towels from the pantry dish towel supply, I hurried back to the game room. I pulled the lamp table out and over, illuminating the horror I was about to deal with, then a chair and a stool for the basin. "If you're waiting for me to pass out or fall asleep it ain't happening," he said without moving his arm.

"I realize that. Here. I found some of my great-great aunt's pain med in her bathroom. I think it's still okay. Take two."

"Give me three and I'll let you know if it is or not."

"That's not too much?"

"I think this'll go better if I'm pretty much knocked out, don't you?" he replied.

I shook three tablets into my palm. "Open up." He opened his mouth. I dropped the pills in and he swallowed them dry. "You want some water?"

"Whisky."

"Jesus, no! That just might kill you!"

"Just give me a shot glass full and stop worrying. If I die, get your damn dog to help drag my body out into the woods behind this place and let me rot back into the earth I crawled out of."

I went to get the whisky, gave it to him. He managed to lever himself up enough to bolt it down. His eyes were raw-rimmed, dark with pain as he lay back down. "This is going to hurt," I said.

"Thanks for the heads up." He closed his eyes but as I dipped the first wash cloth into the basin and then turned back I found him looking at me. "What's your name?"

"Charlotte."

"That's an old-fashioned name."

"I was named for my great-great aunt. Maybe that's why she felt compelled to leave me her estate."

"She leave you just the house, the property and all the crap inside?"

"No, she left me everything," I replied, not elaborating as it was none of his business that I had money. I'd probably already said too much as it was.

"Lucky you," he murmured, his eyes, hazel in color now that I could see him in better light, closing, his mouth a grim line.

He made a few sounds as I carefully washed the blood off his arm. I figured I'd start at the top and work down as the medication would kick in by the time I got the arm under control so I could work on the leg without him knocking me on my butt or kicking me in the head. "Where's your bike?" I asked as I worked.

"In the woods behind the house."

"You were on the back road?"

"Yeah."

"That road's in pretty poor condition."

"Yup."

"Anything I need to go sweep up after I take care of you?"

"Mmm, probably the broken mirror, chrome bits, bloody chunks of flesh and scraps of leather."

"That ought to be fun in the rain and mud."

"Nobody drives back there."

"Except you."

"Except me." He moaned softly then added, "Back gate's busted, by the way."

He fell silent after that. Buttercup came in and lay down beside the couch while I worked. I had to keep getting up to go to the kitchen to change the water in the basin, heat more, but I was making progress. At nine o'clock Vinnie was out cold on the couch and I was out of supplies. I decided a quick trip downtown to the pharmacy was in order. I left Buttercup to guard the house and the injured young man and then hurried out to run my errand of mercy.

The salesclerk gave me a strange look at the amount of antibiotic ointment, wound cleanser, gauze pads, bandage rolls and bandage tape I was buying. I also threw in a huge bottle of ibuprofen. "Are you a nursing student at the college?' she asked.

"No. I'm doing a lot of remodeling at the house I inherited. Accidents happen so I want to be prepared."

"Oh, well, that's probably a good idea, to have lots of supplies on hand in the first aid kit."

"Yes. It was full of old stuff from around the fifties, all yellowed with age." The girl wrinkled her nose at that as she bagged my purchases.

"Good luck!" she called after me.

Back at the house things were as I'd left them. The thunderstorm had passed or we were in a lull between storms. I reheated the water and went back to work, groaning inwardly at the mountain of laundry I'd be hauling to the laundromat tomorrow, or else I would have no decent towels in the house.

Vincent, I couldn't help but notice was lean with sinewy muscles. He still retained a lot of summer tan on his arms and legs. I spent a long time tweezering gravel from the side of his knee and the outside of his calf, scrubbing the wounds with Betadine solution. He never stirred. Finally, I applied an entire tube of antibiotic ointment and did my best to dress and bind his leg in a mummy-like fashion.

By the time I was finished I was exhausted but I got one more basin of hot water with which I washed his face and hands before covering him with a quilt that I brought down from my bedroom. I also brought him a pillow that I tucked under his head. I moved the table and lamp back into place, moved the chair and stool, washed the basin, shut off the lights and trudged up to bed.

"Charlotte!" The sound of my name echoing through the house woke me from a dead sleep in the early hours of the morning. I threw the covers aside, and ran barefoot to the main staircase, thumping down the dusty carpeted stairs to the front hall. "Charlotte!"

"I'm right here!" I ran down the dark hall to the game room which was also dark and nearly tripped over Buttercup who was pacing anxiously in the doorway. "What is it? Are you in pain?"

"Hell yeah! I'm in serious pain!" he snapped. "But that's not why I need you. Christ, I need to take a piss something fierce! Help me up!" He was trying to lever himself up but his injured limbs had stiffened up and were obviously giving him a lot of pain.

"Hold on! Just stop struggling! There has to be a better way to do this!"

"I could pee the couch but I don't want to lie here in cold piss."

"Just hold on!" I snapped, slapping on the light switch, making him groan and throw his arm across his eyes. "Just stay put and be still for two minutes!" I ran to the kitchen and then into the pantry, pulling open cupboards and cabinets until I spotted a stainless steel water pitcher. It would have to do. On my way out I grabbed a couple of the rattier old towels and brought everything back to the game room. "Here, pee in the pitcher, you know, like down the spout."

He opened his eyes and looked at me, then at the pitcher. For a long moment he was silent, then he held his hand out and I gave him the pitcher and the towels. "Get lost. I'll let you know when I'm done."

"Put the towels down…"

"I can handle this, okay? I won't piss on your couch."

"Come on, Buttercup. I'll let you out."

I took my dog to the kitchen, into the back service hall and let her out onto the back porch, standing there in the gray light of dawn listening to the wind rattle the dead leaves still clinging to the branches high up in the oaks. Buttercup ran down the wooden steps and raced into the yard, burning off stress and energy before squatting to relieve herself. I decided to let her stay out for a bit as I went back into the kitchen and started the coffee maker. Soon the kitchen was fragrant with the aroma of brewing coffee.

"Charlotte!" I rolled my eyes, walked back to the game room. The pitcher was wobbling as he held it out to me. It was heavier than I thought it would be. "Sorry, had a few too many beers last night."

"Just a few?" I commented as I carried it out of the room to the lavatory in the back hall, dumping the contents into the toilet and flushing. There was no blood in his urine so I guessed he hadn't injured his kidneys, which was good news for him.

I rinsed the pitcher and brought it back to him, telling him he'd have to use it until he was ambulatory. "I'll be up before the end of the day," he predicted. "Baby? You got any more of those pain pills?"

"You can have two with breakfast."

"I need them *now*."

I gave him two ibuprofen with water. He said he'd eat some scrambled eggs and toast, have some coffee. I went upstairs, put on my robe and slippers because I had noticed that he had noticed that I was just in my thermal shirt and flannel pajama pants.

Back downstairs I found a bed tray in the pantry that would work for him. I scrambled some eggs, adding bacon bits and a dash of pepper as I cooked them. I buttered and spread orange marmalade on wheat toast, cutting them in triangles. I carried the tray in to him. He managed to push himself upright against the arm of the couch so I could set the tray across his lap. He told me how he took his coffee, so I went back and made him a mug and then brought that and my own breakfast in.

 I called Buttercup in through the game room door, took her to the kitchen and fed her. Then I returned to the game room, sat down in the wingchair and tackled my own breakfast. "You're a decent cook," he said, shoveling more egg into his mouth.

 As we ate, the sun rose and he came into better view, sleep tousled and scruffy-jawed. He was a nice-looking guy. No, he was actually gorgeous and I felt my heart flutter at this realization. "What do you do for work?" I asked him as he sipped his coffee. "You'll have to call out sick today."

 "I'm out of work at the moment. I do whatever odd jobs I can get. I worked for my brother-in-law for a while in construction but he fired me because I showed up for work drunk five times too many times." He shrugged. "I don't drink anymore."

 "Except for a few beers, like last night."

 "I drink beer occasionally but I quit the hard stuff." He finished his coffee. "What about those pain meds now?"

 "Okay." I took his mug, went to the kitchen, shook out two tablets and brought them back with a half glass of water. "I'll check your injuries later. Just lie there and rest for now. I need to get dressed and then go do some laundry and grocery shopping. Is there anything you like to eat?"

 "Pork chops. Thick ones. Broiled. With applesauce on the side."

 "Well, you're not shy about asking for exactly what you want."

 "I didn't say T-bones and lobster, did I?" he pointed out, wincing as he eased himself back down.

 "I'm leaving Buttercup here with you."

"Yeah, no problem. I won't be looting the place while you're gone. Maybe tomorrow, if I can get my ass off the couch, I'll tie you up and steal the best silver." He gave me a wry grin.

"Then I'll have to grab that old baseball bat I saw in the closet and whack you with it a few times."

He chuckled as his eyes closed. "It's true what they say about redheads then, hotheads, ever last one of them."

I thought I was pretty even-tempered but I didn't say so. I merely tucked him in snuggly, adjusted his pillow. "Have a nice nap." I didn't know if he was asleep already or not but he didn't respond.

I nursed him for three days, giving him ibuprofen for the fever he developed, checking him twice a day for signs of worsening infection, but it was primarily his body struggling to repair the damage. He was still in pain but I doled out the few remaining pain pills slowly, supplementing them with the ibuprofen and shots of whisky, managing to get him through the worst of it. On the fourth day he struggled up off the couch, using my great-great uncle's cane to help him balance. He hurt but he made himself walk to the lav to take care of business himself, much to my relief.

I was in the kitchen cutting the meat off of soup bones that had been simmering for hours for the soup I was making when he limped into the room, cane thumping on the old linoleum. "Smells good in here," he said.

"You should go sit down. You're wobbly."

"I'm cold and I need clean clothes."

"Which are where?"

"At my trailer."

"You live in a trailer?"

"Yeah, is there something wrong with that?"

"No."

"Well, it's actually an RV parked on my sister's property."

"The one who hasn't called to find out what happened to you?"

"Oh, you found my cell?"

"In your jacket pocket. I've charged it. You haven't gotten any calls."

"You my secretary now, too?"

"Vinnie, you've been laid up here nearly a week and no one has been looking for you. Don't you find that a bit odd?"

He laughed. "No. No one gives a damn about me, Charlotte. I'm nothing but trouble."

"No, you're like the invisible man. Want to be honest with me and tell me exactly what sort of trouble you are exactly? Why has no one been concerned about your having gone missing?"

He dragged out a kitchen chair, carefully eased himself down into the seat, leaning his forearms on the table, wincing as he did so. "I'm between jobs. My sister is out of town. Her husband is in New Hampshire working on a construction project. She went with him. She never calls me. She doesn't exactly like me and just lets me use the RV because I have no place else to live. I have a couple of friends but they're not close friends. They're drinking buddies I meet up with in bars occasionally. Nobody's looking for me because I don't matter to anybody enough for anyone to care if I disappear or not."

I dumped the cut up meat back into the stock pot, stirred the contents and then set the lid on the pot to let it simmer some more. Turning, I leaned against the counter, looking at him. "Are you as big an asshole as you're making yourself out to be?" I asked.

"Probably."

I nodded as I pushed away from the counter, going into the pantry for bowls and soup spoons. I brought them out to the counter. "Think you can keep your drinking and whatever else you do under control enough to work hard?"

"I've done it before."

"You know how to fix things?"

"Fix things? Like what kind of things?"

"Houses. If you haven't quite noticed it yet this house is a mess. A lot of it is exterior but there's enough work inside the house to keep us busy all fall and winter. We can start tackling the exterior in the spring."

He sat looking at me, obviously surprised by the offer of work, steady work at that. Hard work. "You say 'we', as in you and me?" I nodded. "Um, baby, you do realize that I can't single-handedly do all the exterior work. You're going to have to hire a contractor who'll subcontract a mason to fix the foundation, a bricklayer to work on the exterior brickwork, a roofing guy to fix the slate roof, an ironworker to fix the ironwork on the tower." He took a deep breath and blew it out. "How the hell much money did you inherit?"

"Enough," I replied, not comfortable telling him the exact figure.

"If we do this together we're taking no shortcuts. We're not going to do a half-assed, shoddy job of it. You plan on living here afterwards, right? Not selling the family estate and moving to California or someplace?"

"No, I think I want to live here."

He nodded. "Yeah, okay, what the hell. I'm in. I've got nothing better to do. But," he added, "I'll need a room. Weather's getting colder and I need a warmer place to live."

"If I let you have a room here you're going to have to obey the house rules."

"You making up the rules or are they already in existence?"

"I'm making them up."

"Okay, can I have some input into that? I mean, I have some basic needs I like to fulfil now and then, you know, like," and here he shrugged, "sex, for instance. I like sex. I'm not enamored of myself so I pick up a girl here and there, get it on with her and…" Here he held up his hand to stop me as I opened my mouth to respond to that, "then she usually leaves pretty quickly, never comes back for a second go at it with me. I repel women as regularly as I repel most everyone else."

"I guess I could live with that as long as she's not the jealous, scratch-a-girl's-eyes-out-for- looking-twice-at-you type of girl."

"I'd let them know I was living with a girl but not in a relationship with her, except for, you know, stuff related to the house."

"Okay. What else?"

"Beer. I drink it. Not daily. I might go on a little binge here and there. I'm not a freakin' alcoholic. I quit the hard stuff, like I said. I don't crave it. I smoke a little pot, but if you want me to do that elsewhere I will. I don't do drugs."

"Pot's a drug."

"Do you want to kill me?" he asked.

"No. If you're going to work for me and we're going to do this right then I need for you to be clear-headed and focused. I'm not going to pay you good money just so you can let it all go up in smoke."

He sighed, running the fingers of the hand he could get up to his head through his tangled hair. "Okay. No pot. Take away all my vices, why don't you?"

"I'm not saying you can't. I'm just saying that when you're working I don't want your brain foggy. I love this house." I grabbed a bowl, plucked off the cover of the stock pot and ladled soup into the bowl, carried it to the table and set it down in front of him. I brought the plate of bread I'd already sliced and set that on the table. I brought him a spoon and some napkins. I filled my own bowl. "I drink milk when I have this soup. It's comfort food for me."

"Sounds good," he said.

I poured two glasses of milk, set them at our places and then sat down to eat. He ate as if I had been starving him since his arrival. I filled his bowl twice more and he ate every bite before leaning back in his chair with a satisfied sigh. "I'll go get your clothes. You can't go riding around in my car half-naked."

"I've been more than half-naked in cars before," he replied.

"In this weather?"

"In all kinds of weather. Two bodies in motion can generate quite a bit of heat. It's physics. Look it up." His eyes were issuing me a challenge.

"I'm well aware of that fact," I replied crisply, carrying the bowls, spoons and glasses to the sink.

"I ain't seen a guy around this place yet. Where is he?"

"None of your business."

"He's not going to be jealous of my being here, is he?"

"Hardly."

"What is he? Dead?"

"He's shacked up with an actress in New York, if you must know," I snapped in response, telling him more than he needed to know.

He was silent, struggling up from the table, hissing a bit with pain and stiffness. "He's an asshole," he muttered, as he limped out of the room, cane thumping hard against the floor, Buttercup's nails clicking on the linoleum and then wood floor as she followed him back to the game room.

I basically hauled all his stuff, some of it rather disgusting, from the RV at his sister's house to my house in five carloads of various amounts of stuff. His wardrobe appeared to consist of several pairs of faded and frayed jeans, around ten t-shirts, a couple of flannel and denim shirts, a denim jacket, two leather jackets, and underwear and socks that had all seen better days. He had a stereo system, stacks of CDs, a 42" flat screen TV and an assortment of DVDs, stuff I'd never watch even if you paid me. And tools. He had tool boxes I had to half empty before I could strain to carry them to my car. He wanted all his tools put in the back service hall. I glared at him. He patted his injured leg, said he'd help me if he could and then shrugged.

I spent a whole day cleaning a room on the second floor at the back of the house for him to use, and its private bathroom. I screamed when I disturbed a nest of spiders. Buttercup scrambled up the stairs to come to my rescue. I was surprised to hear Vinnie stumping up the back stairs as quickly as he could move. "Sorry!" I called. "Freakin' spiders!"

He continued up the staircase, tracking me down, surveying the eight-legged carnage spread all across the bathrooms floor. "That one's still twitching," he said.

"Where?" I cried, jumping.

He laughed. "Just kidding." He leaned against the doorframe, studying the antiquated bathroom fixtures. "Well, this is different."

"Not the luxurious living conditions you've been used to in the RV?"

He blew air out his nose. "No. It's actually a hell of a step up from a chemical toilet and hauling five gallon jugs of water into the RV every two minutes. You've elevated me in status."

"I'm not sure how comfortable the bed is."

"Want to try it out?" he asked, giving me a sideways glance.

"No."

"Gotta be better than the couch although I can sleep just about anywhere." He turned, limping around the bedroom, checking out the furniture. "You do all this cleaning for me?"

"Yes."

"Man, can I hire you to keep my room clean?"

"No."

I carried the mop and pail out of the bathroom. He was standing beside the bed, watching me. "What's with the one word answers? You pissed off at me about something?"

"No."

"There you go again," he pointed out.

"I'm tired."

He patted the bed. "Come lie down and take a nap."

"No." I continued out of the room, into the hall, and down the back staircase.

I left him to his own devices, running to the store to buy him decent underwear and socks. From moving his clothes over I knew he liked boxer briefs and calf-high sweat socks. I knew what size jeans he wore and added a new pair of Levis to the cart. I'd also determined he wore a size ten boot, so my next stop was to the shop that sells work gear for a pair of nice steel-toed boots. I got him several pairs of work gloves too, figuring him to be a large.

I picked up a few groceries and went home, carrying an armful of bags to the back porch, dropping the box with the boots that I'd tucked under my arm as I tried to open the door. It made a solid thump. I bent down to grab the box, but couldn't get my hand around it. Standing up I found Vinnie standing in the back hall looking at me. "You need a hand?" he asked.

"That would be nice."

He opened the door, grabbed the boot box from the floor, held the door open for me so I could carry everything else in. "You get these for me?" he asked, holding the box so he could see the picture on the front.

"Yes."

"Sweet."

I dropped three bags on the floor so I could heave the bags of groceries up onto the table. "Those are for you too," I said, indicating the bags on the floor.

"What else did you get me?" he asked, limping over, setting the boot box on the table, bending slowly and picking up the bags, opening them, peering inside. His eyebrows rose. "Jeez, Mom, you're supposed to wait and buy me new socks and underwear for Christmas," he said. I don't know why, but I suddenly burst into tears. "Hey! Hey, what's this all about?" he asked worriedly. "You're not having second thoughts about having a kept man in the house, are you?"

"I'm just tired!" I sobbed. I was. I had been taking care of him, shopping, cleaning and trying to cope with the overwhelming amount of work I had to do in this house before we could even start tackling repair work indoors. I had moved a ton of stuff from the rooms I had managed to clean so far, and all that stuff needed to be gone through. "I need to order a dumpster! A big one!" I cried.

"Let me handle that. I'll get right on it."

"I need to call the plumber!"

"I can do that. What's leaking?"

"Everything!" I sobbed. "And I need to make lunch!"

He set the bags down on the table, limped around to where I was clearly having a breakdown and tried to touch me. I pulled back. "No, I just want to turn you around. I'm not going to molest you or anything, just turn you around."

"What for?"

"Here. Look." He turned me around. "I made chicken soup for lunch from the leftover chicken."

"You made chicken soup!" I cried almost hysterically.

He turned me back around, pulled me into his arms and held me, held my head against his shoulder. "It's going to be okay, Charlie," he said quietly. "You're the boss around here. You just need to learn to delegate. If you run errands then you say, Vinnie, throw something together for lunch I'll be back at such and such a time. I can cook a little. You like mac and cheese? Hotdogs? Burgers? American chop suey? Chicken soup? I can cook basic stuff. I haven't died from my own cooking yet. You're running yourself ragged. I'm okay to do some stuff around here. I need to move around. I'm stiff as hell. I need to get the use of my leg and arm back. Delegate, damn it, okay?"

"Yeah, okay," I said, nodding, getting the message.

"We're like partners here in this project palace. Let's sit down now and have some lunch. Have some nice hot chicken soup. Then we're going to find some paper and start making a list of the top priority shit we need to tackle here first. We can start a second list for stuff we can do once the big stuff is done. Plumbing is a top priority. I'm not going back to crapping in a chemical toilet and having to empty it out. Believe me, I've evolved higher than that." He tilted my head back, looking down into my eyes. He had amazing hazel eyes—brown, gold and green. Long lashes. "Agreed?"

"Yes."

"One last thing," he said.

"What?"

"Speak to me in sentences. One word sentences and responses make me feel like I've done something wrong."

"You haven't done anything wrong," I said quietly. "You've been nothing like what I first expected you'd be like."

"Yeah, well, we've really only just hooked up. Wait a little longer before you start thinking I'm a decent sort of guy. I'm not. Not really."

He sat me down at the table, put away the groceries as quickly as he could limp around and then he got out bowls and filled them with the soup he had made—chicken noodle to be precise with diced up carrot and celery. He cocked an eyebrow at the fridge and I nodded. He poured milk. More comfort food for two souls who had more than enough woes to fill a book.

"I gave Buttercup some chopped up chicken. Is that okay with you?" he asked.

"That's fine. Good. She likes chicken."

"That's better. One, two and three word sentences all in one breath." He smiled at me across the table, his left hand going down to stroke Buttercup's head as he did so. They had apparently become fast friends when I wasn't looking. Or maybe it was the chicken they had shared. "How's the soup?"

The soup was delicious. "It's good. Nice." I frowned, shook my head. "No, the soup is delicious. Thanks for thinking to make it while I was out."

"Bravo, Charlotte!" he said, his smile widening. "You're welcome."

He cleaned up while I went to the study to find a notebook and a couple of pens that worked. When I got back we sat at the table again and started making two lists— Top Priority and Also Important Stuff To Do. Plumbing and electrical upgrades were on the first list along with a new multi-zoned heating system and multi-zoned central air. He put ceiling fans on the Top Priority list. "The boxes can be put in with the wiring upgrade. It'll be too expensive to use central air all the time, and it's nice on some evenings to lie in bed with the ceiling fan rotating overhead moving the air around gently."

"O...kay." He winked at me and I smiled. "All right then. Moving on."

"I'm just teasin' you, you know."

"I know," I replied, although somewhere deep inside of me something shifted, opened a crack and let a shaft of light touch my heart.

A short time later I left him to the list making so I could run to the laundromat again to wash all his new clothes and the current laundry. When I got back I found him sound asleep on the couch in the game room, Buttercup stretched out beside him. I went up to the second floor, made up his bed with fresh sheets I'd bought and laundered this afternoon, a couple blankets and a down-filled comforter. I'd gotten him a couple new pillows. I'd also bought blue bath mats and blue and gray plaid towels for his bathroom. I still needed to go out and get him some personal items, or maybe he was ready to try a drive to the pharmacy with me. I'd ask him when he woke up.

I put my own laundry away, went down the back staircase and glanced at the lists on the table. He had added quite a bit. On the Top Priority list he had added— Fix up Master Suite for the new Queen of this castle. I was oddly touched, but I certainly didn't feel like a queen.

I set the new crockpot I had bought on the counter, took the bag of groceries I'd just picked up out of the fridge and set about making pot roast for dinner. A cool front had come in. Perfect weather for pot roast.

While that started cooking I went to the study and began going through the desk. About a half hour later a loud metallic thud from outside startled me. I got up and ran to the opposite side of the house and looked out the window. A huge dumpster had just been delivered! Well, Vinnie was a man who could get things done when he put his mind to it.

"What the hell was that?" he asked, limping out of the game room, looking half asleep.

"The dumpster was just delivered." He looked at me somewhat warily. "Thanks."

"Yeah, hold that thanks until after you see the bill."

"It doesn't matter. I have to start cleaning stuff out of here. She was a pack rat of sorts. There's family history stuff I want to hang onto, but old receipts, magazines, catalogs, tax records and so on, that can all get thrown out."

"Maybe you need to get a paper shredder too."

"Mm. This stuff is old, but some of the accounts may still be active. I just don't know. Good idea. Get on it."

"Aye, aye, Captain." He gave me a quick salute. Then he stopped, his face sobering as he sniffed the air. "What's that I smell?"

"Pot roast."

"Wow. I haven't had that since I was a kid."

"It's cold out."

"Yeah, house feels chilly." He scratched his head. "Look, I need to go up and hit the shower. Go add chimney sweep to the top priority list. I can cut some wood in a week or so and we can use the fireplaces for additional heat."

"I'll go do that."

"Come up in twenty minutes to check my injuries."

"You'd better be wearing a towel."

"Yeah, I will be. You know I'm a shy guy." He chuckled as he made his way to the back staircase.

Twenty minutes later he was standing in his bathroom, a plaid towel tucked around his waist. I sat on the closed toilet and carefully looked at his arm and leg. There were a lot of scabs, a lot of red rashy looking places, but no further sign of infection. I looked up into his hazel eyes and smiled. "I think you're healing, Vin." He smiled, put his hand on the place where the towel was tucked. "Uh, get dressed. Meet me downstairs. We're going for a drive."

I got up quickly and left the bathroom, heading downstairs.

I drove him to the pharmacy. He groaned a bit climbing in and out of my Toyota Corolla. "Go crazy," I told him, handing him a hundred dollar bill. He winked at me, went into the pharmacy by himself. I stayed in the car and waited.

When he came out we both started talking simultaneously. "We need to…" We stopped. We looked at one another.

"You go first," he said.

"We need to buy a new car. A pick-up truck or an SUV. Which would be more practical?" I asked.

"How about an SUV for you and a pick-up truck for me?"

"I suppose we could do that. You own anything other than the wrecked bike to trade?"

"No. I had a truck but it got repossessed. I have piss poor credit. Sorry. I didn't know it was going to ever really matter."

"It doesn't matter. Not right now anyway. I have excellent credit." I started the engine. "Now, what were you going to say?"

"We need to swing by the package store." He saw my expression. "I want to buy us a bottle of wine to have with dinner tonight," he continued.

"Oh, all right." I drove to the liquor store. As he opened the door to get out I said, "Vinnie, do you have enough money left to buy yourself a case of beer?"

"Yeah, but I'll just get a six pack."

"Get two. I can be difficult to live with at times."

"Oh, really?" He quirked me a wry grin, winked and got out.

He was arguing with a guy around his age when he came out carrying two six packs and a bottle of wine. I was about to step out of the car and mediate to the best of my ability when he handed over the beer, turned and stalked to the car. He eased himself into the passenger seat, cursing under his breath. "What was that all about?" I asked.

"Asshole said I owed him some beer. Wouldn't take no for an answer. I don't remember owing him anything."

"You were probably drunk." I had my hand on the gear shift lever but stopped. "Stay put," I said. I got out and went quickly into the store. "I want a case of the beer the tall guy with the leather jacket just bought." He fetched it for me and I lugged it out to the car. "Pop the trunk!" Vinnie gave me a look before reaching over and popping the trunk open for me.

I pulled out of the parking lot, heading toward the Toyota dealership in nearby Tufton. "You didn't have to do that," he said.

"I know, but you've been an okay unexpected house guest, and now we're sort of partners in fixing up the estate. I can let you have the beer if it's that important to you."

He was quiet after that. At the Toyota dealership the salesman assumed we were a couple but Vinnie soon had him understanding that he was my employee and I was there to buy a Tundra with an extended cab and a hybrid Highlander, both new, both black. He wanted top of the line in both vehicles. I just nodded. I didn't know much about cars so I allowed him to hash out the details. I traded in the Corolla, wrote a humongous check and we drove off the lot about two hours later in the Highlander because it had been in stock. The Tundra would be delivered in a couple of days. They had to get it from another dealership, get it registered. The Corolla registration was being transferred to the Highlander.

We had our celebratory dinner in the dining room at seven o'clock that night— pot roast, the meat so tender it fell apart at the touch of our forks, and a nice deep red wine that complemented the meal perfectly. While I cleaned up Vinnie took Buttercup out into the yard. They came in about fifteen minutes later. "Drizzling out," Vinnie announced.

"Gotta love New England."

"You decorating the place for Halloween?" he asked.

"Doesn't it look spooky enough?" I replied.

"Needs more cobwebs and some jack o'lanterns. I'm actually a whiz at carving pumpkins."

"Are you?"

"Sure. Me and Pumpkin Masters go way back."

"Then we'd better go get some pumpkins, a carving kit, some fake cobwebs and a ton of candy tomorrow."

He picked up the wine, and the glasses I had just washed. "Come with me." I followed him to the game room. "Sit with me for a bit." He eased himself down onto the couch. I sat down at the other end. He filled the glasses, set the bottle down on the end table beside him. "To my partner," he said, reaching over to touch his glass to mine.

"To my partner," I repeated.

He switched the light off so that we were sitting in the dark. Buttercup whimpered a bit, but then settled down at our feet. We sipped wine. "Close your eyes," he said.

"Um…why?"

"I want you to imagine the future." He laughed softly. "Don't worry. I'll stay here at my end of the couch. I won't touch you."

"Okay. Eyes are closed."

"Imagine what this house looked like back in the day when it was brand new and your great-great uncle carried his blushing bride across the threshold and set her feet down on the black and white marble tiles in the reception hall for the very first time. What do you see?"

What did I see? I pictured the hallway just inside the entry vestibule as it looked now, marble tiles dulled with age, scuffed, the white somewhat yellowed. I saw horrible fifties wallpaper curling away from the high moldings at the top of the hall walls, the paper dated and grungy with age. I saw the beautiful mahogany woodwork covered over with several layers of paint, chipped and peeling in places. But then I saw the grand staircase, the wood polished to a sheen, carpet runners with brass rods going up the stairs, not the current cheap carpet tiles. I saw a bronze winged figure holding a flickering torch atop the newel post at the foot of the stairs. Where was she now? "It was beautiful," I replied finally, remembering some pictures I'd seen, taken around the turn of the century, my great-great aunt posing at the foot of the stairs, beautiful, and oh so young, smiling happily. "There was a bronze angel holding a torch on top of the post at the end of the stairs. In a picture I have, my great-great aunt has her hand on the figure's bare foot. The woodwork is breathtaking. It glows. There's dark flocked wallpaper on the walls, a chair rail, dark moldings. Everything was crisp and pristine."

"That's what we're going to recreate here, Charlotte," he said. "I'm going to help you restore this house to its former glory, or die trying."

"Well, you don't have to go that far."

"The place is starting to grow on me now that I can get around. It was pissing me off being stuck in this room for days on end but, now that I can walk around I'm seeing a lot of things I like. And a hell of a lot of things that I don't like that we need to fix."

"I know. It's overwhelming to sit here thinking about all the work ahead of us."

"Drink your wine."

"I am."

"Need a refill?"

"Not yet."

He was quiet. Buttercup snuffled and shifted on the carpet at our feet. I sipped some of my wine and then leaned my head back and closed my eyes again. Vinnie remained quiet but I heard him refill his glass. I hoped he wasn't getting drunk, then remembered he was a drinker whereas I was not. He probably could drink wine and only get a mild buzz from it. I was feeling a little dizzy, a little giddy. "What are you going to dress up as for Halloween?" he asked.

"What?" I'd been thinking about the house and the wine, not Halloween.

"You should dress up. Give the kids a bit of a scare."

"They'll probably be scared enough just walking up to the door."

"It's Halloween. You should be a witch."

"Okay, if I dress up as a witch then you have to dress up as a vampire or something."

"I'm more of a zombie type guy."

"I don't have trunks full of zombie clothes in the attic, but I do have trunks full of old fashioned dress clothes—suits, tuxedos, opera capes. I prowled around up there when I first got here."

"With all the spiders?"

"Yes, wasn't that brave of me?"

"Yeah, considering the freak-out you did not too long ago in my bathroom."

"Truth is I didn't even think about spiders until I was already up there. I killed a dozen or so, whatever ones I saw. A lot of daddy longlegs."

"Maybe we should add exterminator to the list. There're signs of mice too."

"I've heard them in the walls."

"They do a lot of damage. Squirrels too. We don't want rodents in the walls or attic." He sighed, set his glass down. "I'll make some calls tomorrow, if that's okay with you?"

"Yes. That's fine."

"We spent a big chunk of change on new vehicles today."

"Yes. We did. But that's all right. We'll be hauling materials. And Buttercup, well, she pretty much filled up the back seat of the Corolla. I needed to get a new car now that she's full grown."

"She'll have plenty of room in the back seat of the Highlander, and the Tundra, too, if we take her along to the home improvement stores and lumber yard."

I was quiet for a long time, sipping my wine, finding I'd finished it and setting the glass down on the table at my end of the couch. I had been scared half to death when Vinnie had come pounding on my door during a thunderstorm all muddy, bloody and chalky-white faced. But he'd really been a blessing in disguise.

I was just about to mention that I was glad he was here when he said, "I may be here for like two years or maybe a little longer working on this place, but when I move on, this house is going to be your private palace. It'll be just like it was back in the day." He sighed. "And I will have the satisfaction of knowing I actually accomplished something in my life. That I saw something through from start to finish."

"I'll write you a glowing reference."

"Thanks, Charlie. I knew I could count on you."

I leaned forward, elbows on my knees. "Have you ever been to jail?"

"Jail? Just once. Drunk and disorderly when I was like twenty-one years old. Judge fined me and sent me home the next morning. Told me to stay sober, get a job and grow the hell up. It took me seven years but I think I'm finally getting there."

"Ever been to prison?"

"No, and I don't plan on going. I'm not going to be anybody's prison girlfriend!"

I smiled. "Tell me again why you can't hold onto a girl?"

"Honest truth? I'm a freakin' loser. What have I got to offer a girl? I can't hold a job. I didn't go to college. I have no money. I spend too much time in bars."

"Did you finish high school?"

"Yeah, I managed to do that."

"We should discuss a salary I can pay you for the work you'll be doing around here."

"You're covering room and board, aren't you?"

"You'll need medical insurance."

"I've got state insurance for that at the moment."

"Is that based on income or lack thereof?"

"Yeah."

"I'll pay you sixty thousand a year, does that sound fair?"

"Why so much?"

"You're going to be working your ass off."

"Oh, well, okay then. Sounds good to me. It's the most I've ever earned in my life."

"You really are going to earn it. You've seen the house. But you haven't looked in the carriage house yet, or the gatehouse, or the pool house."

"Jesus, I could grow old and die here and never be finished."

"Already discouraged?" I asked. "Imagine how I feel." I got up, carefully skirted Buttercup who lifted her head and watched me walk to the door and look outside. It was raining again. No thunder and lightning at least.

I heard Vinnie moving around and then I sensed him standing behind me. He put his hands on my shoulders. "You worried that it'll be too much for me, that I'll bolt?"

"I just can't get past the this is all so overwhelming phase."

"You can't envision it all as one project, Charlie. You have to see it as a long series of small, medium and large projects, some going on at the same time, but all leading toward a finish point." He massaged my tense shoulders a bit and I began to relax. "Tell you what, you handle the cleaning out of the junk and the boxing up of your family history stuff, and the check writing. I'll handle the small projects and the medium projects inside the house, and arrange for the big projects to get done by the best people I can find for the money. You and I have to trust one another completely. We're going to be in this up to our eyebrows for a couple of years at least. We're going to argue and fight, have humongous disagreements, hate each other some days, probably cry together when something goes horribly wrong other days."

"Something like a marriage, right? Ups and downs, good times and bad? For better or worse?"

"Yeah, like that but with no honeymoon period and no sex to relieve the stress."

"I told you that you could bring girls in as needed."

"I know you did. But..."

"But what?"

"It would be like I was being unfaithful to you."

"But we're not..." And here he turned me around and took me in his arms, ducked his head and kissed me. I tensed, not having expected this from him, but then I realized that I had been wanting him to kiss me like this. I had lain awake at night imagining such a scenario as this, and here it was actually happening. He was not the kind of guy I had ever imagined myself being with, but I had also never imagined myself inheriting a decrepit old estate and a ton of money. My life was all about new experiences these days, uncertainties, pushing forward into the unknown. Isn't that what a new relationship was also like?

"No, we're not," he said quietly. "Not yet, anyway." I could just see him in the ambient light from the hall. His eyes met mine, were searching mine for something, some sign.

I reached up, took his face in my hands and pulled him back to me, kissing him. Tasting him. He tasted like wine, and I probably tasted the same way to him. It had been a very good wine. Sweet. "Not yet, but…maybe one day?"

"It's a little too early in our relationship for you to be proposing to me," he replied. "Let's just take it one day at a time, see how it goes. We both have questionable track records…"

"Danny was a jerk."

"I'm sure my former girlfriends all said the same thing about me."

"I'm sure you can be at times, but for the past few weeks you really haven't been." I kissed him again and he pulled me closer, letting me know he was aroused. This sent jolts of heat through me. It had been awhile since I'd made love but I thought it might be worth trying with Vinnie. "Maybe we should go upstairs," I murmured.

"Are you drunk?" he asked.

"No, just mildly buzzed."

"I don't want you waking up in the morning accusing me of taking advantage of you."

"Are you going to accuse me of taking advantage of you?"

"You can't take advantage of a guy who wants to get in your pants," he replied. "That would never hold up in court."

"You're so funny sometimes."

"Just don't laugh at me in bed. You'd hurt my feelings."

"Do we need to go to the pharmacy?" I asked as he kissed me by my ear, down the side of my neck.

"Nope, bought some condoms today to have on hand, in case I met a girl willing to jump in the sack with me."

"Were you a boy scout?"

"Never."

"But you're always prepared."

"Not always. I just happen to be tonight."

"I need to lock up the house."

"You go upstairs and wait for me. I'll let Buttercup out one last time, lock up, turn out the lights and be up as soon as all that stuff is done." He kissed me dead center on my forehead. "Don't fall asleep waiting for me."

"Don't take forever."

"If I could accomplish everything in one minute or less I would. See you in two." He turned away, calling for Buttercup to get up and follow him as he left the room. She did. My dog had grown quite fond of him, too.

I checked the patio door, closed the drapes, and headed upstairs, running my hand along the bannister. It probably needed to be sanded and varnished, or polyurethaned, whatever the best process would be to return it to its burnished luster. It would be nice to walk down this staircase and feel the satiny finish beneath my hand. It would be nice to come downstairs and find Vincent standing there watching me, admiring me. He would be dressed up in a suit, looking like a movie star and I would be in a dress, ready to go out to dinner to celebrate our fifth wedding anniversary. There would probably be work still going on here on the estate, the outbuildings and gardens. Buttercup would be standing by the door, wanting to go for a ride in the SUV. We'd promise her we'd bring her home something, let her eat it in the drawing room where we'd have some wine in front of the fire before going up to the bedroom to continue the celebration.

Maybe it would all work out like that. Maybe not. Maybe he would bolt, feeling trapped by the work and a steady girlfriend. I kind of hoped that he had sown all his wild oats, that he was ready to commit to a house and a real girlfriend and a ton of responsibility. That he wasn't just sucking up to me for a free ride.

"Charlotte!" he called from the foot of the main staircase as I reached the bedroom door. "Hey! Charlie!"

"What's the matter?" I called, walking back toward the stairs.

"Buttercup got skunked! Damned skunk is holed up under the back porch and it got her! Sorry. Sex is on hold. I've got to give her a bath! We got any tomato juice?"

I started down the stairs, already smelling skunk. "We'll have to use ketchup and tomato sauce diluted with water. Where are we going to do this?"

"The tub in my bathroom would probably be best," he replied. "Go run some warm water. I'll wash her face again, grab the ketchup, open the sauce then herd her upstairs. He gave me a wry look. "Sorry about this. A skunked dog is hardly romantic."

"It's early still."

"We're both going to reek of skunk."

I looked at him and then said, "I think there's an extra big bottle of ketchup in the pantry. Grab that too and we'll deskunk one another after. Think that'll work?"

He grinned. "Yeah, we can give that a shot. Your bathrocm though. We'll disinfect them both tomorrow and then run out to get some dog shampoo or whatever we need to get Buttercup smelling like a rose again. And we'll have to do more laundry. Got any more old towels?" I nodded. "Grab them. I'll be up in a few minutes with her."

We both set off on our separate missions. Bumps in the road, I thought, as I raided other bathrooms on the second floor for whatever towels I could find and then hurried to fill the tub in his bathroom. Every life had bumps along the way. It was how people dealt with them that indicated how well they would work as a couple.

Vincent and I worked well together. We made a good team. Hopefully, we'd make a good couple too.

Only time would tell.

THE BEST MAN

"I've known Dave my entire life. We grew up living across the street from one another. We rode our bikes as kids making believe we were on motorcycles while making loud pretend engine noises as we circled the block. We rode the bus together, went to school together, played on the same teams, thought girls were stupid." He paused here to look at the bride. "Sorry, Becky, turns out we were both wrong about that." She smiled in a forgiving manner and he continued. "Our families vacationed at the same beach. We hung out together ogling bikini-clad, flat-breasted girls with narrow hips and no asses like we were a couple of cool dudes, and staring like slack-jawed Neanderthals at the older girls with the big boobs and nice asses. Dave and I survived adolescent angst and faces full of zits in middle school and into high school. We survived surging hormones and the embarrassment of buying condoms from the druggist who sold our Moms diaper cream for our rashes when we were babies. We played Varsity baseball and won some trophies for the high school. We double dated. We got lucky occasionally. And then we went off to college. Dave hightailed it to the west coast. I stayed here on the east coast. He had great weather, lots of sunshine, lots of beautiful girls. I had snow and ice, clouds and gloom and pretty girls all bundled up in sweaters, sweatshirts and corduroys. We graduated and Dave moved back east, got a great job, met a great girl." Here he gave a nod to Rebecca. Dave squeezed her hand, kissed her cheek. "Yeah, I don't need to tell you the rest of that story because you're all sitting here witnessing this chapter being written today. Dave's a lucky guy.

Becky's a very lucky girl. And I'm out a hundred-seventy bucks in rental fees for this monkey suit. The rose fell out of my buttonhole someplace, probably in the men's room, but let's not all go rushing to look for it at once. And today I get to dance with my….drum roll please…..sister who happens to be Becky's best friend and her maid of honor! Who doesn't want to dance with his sister at a wedding? But I'm not complaining. She's the one who'll suffer from my total lack of grace and two left feet. Sorry, Virginia. You might want to go change those sexy shoes for combat boots after dinner." He sighed then arranged his face in a more sober expression. "Today I stand before you and offer this toast to my lifelong best friend and his amazing new bride. I wish them both a lifetime of happiness, prosperity, and best wishes in everything they do as a couple from this day forward. I love you both, and I hope you'll invite me over for the World Series and the Super Bowl so I don't have to go sit alone in a bar someplace and watch the games on a crappy TV with poor sound quality while eating Cheetos and Chex Mix from a community bowl with guys who probably don't wash their hands after…"

Dave grabbed his arm and he looked down into his friend's face. "Don't worry, Drew. She'll go shopping with her friends who don't care about sports either on game days. And we'll have sanitary snacks, ice cold beers and some fun, same as we've always had."

"Thanks, Dave." He raised his champagne glass. "Ladies and gentlemen, to the beautiful bride and her very fortunate groom!"

Dave looked up at him and then gave his arm a tug. "Great toast, Drew, you can sit down now."

"Oh, right." He dropped down into his seat, placing his empty champagne flute on the table.

"How much have you had to drink?" Virginia hissed from his left side.

"Not enough if you still have this ability to annoy me," he replied.

"Oh, just behave yourself!" she warned.

"I've been behaving myself now for twenty-six years," he replied. "And exactly where has that gotten me?" Dave elbowed him and he turned toward his friend. "Yes, is there something I can do for you? Buy you a drink, maybe?"

"What's the matter with you?" Dave asked, his eyes searching his friend's face worriedly.

"Nothing. I'm fine. I'm not even drunk. Imagine that!"

"Are you the fish or the prime rib?" a voice asked from behind his opposite shoulder.

He turned to look at the server who had come up behind him. "Do I look like a fish to you?' he asked.

"No, sir."

"Then I must be a prime rib." She made a note on a card she held in her hand. "Are you our server?" he asked.

Her large caramel-colored eyes rose to meet his hazel eyes. "Yes, sir," she replied.

He leaned back in his chair and said, in a conspiratorial tone, "Look, this is real food right? Not just frozen food reheated in a microwave and arranged nicely on a heated plate?"

"Um…I'm pretty sure the chefs in the kitchen are cooking the food fresh as we speak."

"Good, because I know Becky's folks laid out a ton of money for this shindig. One of my duties as best man is to make sure they don't get ripped off."

"Are you harassing the help?' Virginia asked, slapping his arm. "Leave her alone and let her do her job."

"I was just checking on things," he said. He turned in his seat as the server moved behind his sister to ask if she was having the fish or the prime rib. "Look at her pouty mouth," he said. "Doesn't she look like a fish?"

"Drew, stop it! You aren't funny! I am having the fish, but it's not because I look like one!"

"Hey, serving girl, are we getting fruit cups?"

"Yes, sir. They'll be coming out shortly."

"Can you put double cherries on mine?" Her eyes met his and he saw that she looked flustered. "If it's no trouble," he added.

"I'll see what I can do, sir." She started to move past Virginia, but turned back and added, "Seeing as it's for the best man."

"Thanks, I may be the best man but you're the best!"

"You are so immature sometimes! I don't know how Dave has put up with you for so many years!" Virginia said. "God only knows I can't take you for very long."

He ignored her. He was, if truth be told, incredibly bored. His eyes searched the room for familiar faces. All of his and Dave's mutual friends were present with their wives or girlfriends, chatting and laughing at the crowded tables. He resented having to sit at the head table beside his sister. He had no one to talk to. Dave and Becky were busy kissing every time someone struck their glass with a utensil. He was uncomfortable in the rented tuxedo, although relieved that it was black and not some horrendous color, like powder blue. As soon as he'd eaten, the damn bow tie was coming off and he was unbuttoning his collar. He slipped his feet out of the rented shoes and sighed. He wished he'd brought sneakers. All he had in his car was a pair of sandy flip flops from the beach the other day.

His eyes fell on the server. She was making her way across the crowded room toward the kitchen. She was shorter than the other female servers, probably just a couple inches over five feet tall, and very slender. He didn't see how she'd be able to lug one of those huge heavy trays around. The trays probably weighed half as much as she weighed.

His stomach growled. Sipping some water, he wished he had a beer instead, thought about going to the bar but knew he needed to behave today, and not get roaring drunk like he had at the bachelor party. He really hated hangovers with a passion, was sick of them, actually. He was determined not to wake up tomorrow with a raging hangover.

The kitchen doors were swinging busily as servers came out with trays laden with fruit cups. He watched for the head table server, spotted her by her lack of stature and her cute, pixie-cut red hair. Her red hair was without a doubt real. Most of the rest of the redheads in the room had dyed their hair and none of them looked quite like this little cutie.

She served the bride and groom first and then set his fruit cup down before him. "Double cherries," she murmured before moving to his other side to serve Virginia her fruit cup.

He tried to catch her eye but she was concentrating on serving the fruit cups to the head table and then to the parents and grandparents at their table. He found himself watching her instead of eating. Virginia elbowed him. "Stop daydreaming and start eating," she said.

"Will you stop telling me what to do!" he snapped.

"You're twenty-six years old!"

"I think I'm aware of that. But thanks again for reminding me."

"Loser," she muttered.

He popped a cherry into his mouth, savoring it and then ate the rest of his fruit.

Salads came out next. He asked the server for extra Thousand Island dressing. She gave him a look but didn't say anything. When she was finished serving the salads she took her tray back to the kitchen and then returned with an extra cup of dressing which she set down beside his plate. "Thanks, very much," he said. "Hey! What's your name?"

She pointed to her name tag. "My name is Daisy."

"Are you serious? I thought maybe you had someone else's name tag on by mistake. You don't look like a Daisy at all. You look like a Poppy." He glanced at his salad plate. "No, you look more like a chile pepper. I think I'll call you Pepper."

"Okay, whatever," she replied before walking away. He leaned back in his chair to watch her. She had a sweet little butt in her snug black pants. She had on a long-sleeved white blouse and a black vest, black shoes. He wondered how she could rush around so much dressed like that and not be sweating buckets. He was roasting in his tuxedo, wanted to take off the jacket and roll up his shirt sleeves.

"Will you stop bothering the waitress," Virginia said, scowling at him.

"Be careful, your face might freeze like that," he warned her.

"I don't care. They've already taken the formal pictures," she said.

He shrugged as he drizzled the extra dressing on his salad. The vegetables were cold and crisp but he didn't eat it all. It got rather soggy with the extra dressing on it.

Daisy, or rather Pepper as he preferred to think of her, next brought baskets of warm bread to the tables, dishes of single-serve margarine. "Excuse me, Pepper? Can I get some real butter?" he asked. He thought she was going to say something but she just nodded and walked away.

"Why are you annoying the waitress?" Dave asked, leaning toward him.

"She's cute and I'm not enjoying sitting next to my sister."

"If you'd managed to hold onto a girlfriend Becky would have let her be a bridesmaid. Why the hell can't you keep a girl for more than three months?"

"Must be because of my friends," he replied, making Dave scowl and turn back to Becky. He really didn't know the answer to that question. He had a great job, made good money, had a nice condo, an SUV, loved sports, fishing, hiking, going to the beach, swimming, woodworking in his basement shop. He didn't like dancing, shopping, or going to endless parties. He didn't mind the occasional movie, but he just couldn't sit through a stupid chick flick without his eyes rolling up into the back of his head. He was pretty damn good in bed, or so he'd been told. But evidently, he wasn't good enough at everything the girls he had been with were looking for. Or maybe he had been dating the wrong sort of girls? Maybe they weren't looking for commitment, just casual sex and good times. But where in the world did a guy go to find a keeper like Becky?

"Prime rib, medium well." A plate was set before him, the stainless steel cover whisked away. "Baked potato, two sour creams and three real butters on the side, green beans." She paused then asked. "Is there anything else you'd like?"

He tilted his head back to look at her. "Who told you this is what I wanted?"

"You did. It was on your request card."

"Then why did you have to ask me what I'd wanted?"

"I was just verifying orders for the kitchen."

"I see." He straightened up, picked up his knife and fork and began to eat as she served Virginia her fish, rice pilaf and steamed vegetable medley. She was three seats down the table when he said, "Excuse me! Pepper! If it's not too much trouble, can you bring me some gravy?" Her back stiffened slightly before she served one of the bridesmaids her meal, then she turned back and her eyes met his. "Please."

"It's no trouble, sir."

"Will you stop it!" Virginia fairly growled at him. "I am so fed up with you acting like a child!"

"I'm not a child. I'm a man who knows what he likes and doesn't like when it comes to food."

"You are being a pain in the ass and an asshole at the same time."

"Some trick, eh?" She sniffed, turning away from him.

"Gravy." She had come up to the front of the table with a small gravy boat and set it in front of his plate.

"Thank you, Pepper. I will not forget you when I leave a gratuity."

"Um…you can't leave tips. It's not allowed."

"How on earth do you manage to make ends meet?"

She flushed. "The gratuity is included in the price of the meals that have been ordered." She glanced over her shoulder. "Really, I can't talk to you. I'll get in trouble."

"I realize that. That's why I'm asking you for double cherries, extra dressing, gravy…" Her flush deepened and she looked as if she didn't know how to respond to that. "I'm serious. This is the weirdest way I've ever hit on a girl, asking her for condiments and sauces."

"Please stop. My supervisor is watching us." She ducked her head and walked away.

He picked up the gravy and poured some over his prime rib to show that supervisor that she had performed her job diligently, providing for the customer's needs.

Before long it was time for Dave and Becky to cut the cake. He sat in his seat idly watching them smush cake in one another's faces thinking that if he ever got married he would feed a dainty bite to his bride, maybe smearing a little bit of sweet icing across her lower lip in the process, but not smashing cake in her face like Dave had. That way he could kiss her and lick the icing from her lips and it would be very romantic, not slapstick farce.

The cake was whisked off to the kitchen to be portioned out. Pepper served coffee and tea. In the meantime, Dave and Becky had a first dance, then Becky danced with her father and Dave with his mother, and then Becky danced with Dave's father and Dave danced with Becky's mother. Andrew glanced at his watch and sighed. The dancers returned to their seats as the servers came out of the kitchen with wedding cake and ice cream.

As his plate of cake and ice cream was set down before him he said, "I thought I'd ordered the parfait." He was rewarded by a quickly stifled laugh. Virginia kicked him under the table.

Dessert was eaten and the band began to play. Couples moved out onto the dance floor as the servers scurried about to collect plates and silverware, serve last cups of coffee. Andrew remained in his seat, refusing to dance with Virginia who left the table in a huff to dance with Dave's brother Rick.

"Coffee refill?"

"Yeah, thanks." She filled his cup, set four creamers down beside it. So, she had been observing him and knew he liked his coffee very light and sweet.

"You don't dance?" she asked as she loaded cups, saucers, water glasses and linen napkins onto her tray.

"Not with my sister."

"Oh, that's rather awkward, being paired with your sister."

"Tell me about it."

"Well, I'm sure you'll find someone else to dance with. There're lots of pretty girls here tonight."

He looked around the room. There were, she was right, but all the pretty girls had husbands, or boyfriends. "I'll be the wall flower tonight," he said.

"You don't seem to be having a very good time at your best friend's wedding."

"I would have a much better time if you'd put on a dress and dance with me." She flushed, moved down the table to gather more glassware. "Seriously, what time do you get off work?" he asked.

"I shouldn't be talking to you."

"But I really do want to dance with you, Pepper. When you get off work, run home, put on a dress and then come right back and we'll dance. I mean it." He watched her. "Please. I'm inviting you to be my date for this wedding. I know it's way beyond last minute. I should have said something sooner, but the truth is, I hadn't met you yet."

"You'll be drunk and dancing with all the other girls by ten o'clock."

"No, I swear to you, I won't be drunk. I've only had one beer, and three cups of coffee which negated that beer hours ago. And I won't be dancing. I'll be sitting here waiting for you to come back looking like a dream." She shook her head, heaved her heavy tray up and walked away. He watched her go. He had given it his best shot. He'd been sincere. He could only hope that she'd taken him seriously, but he doubted that she had. She probably got hit on fairly regularly by drunken assholes at weddings. Only, he wasn't drunk. He was just attracted to her although she wasn't the size and shape girl he usually went for.

Dave bought him a beer and Rick bought him a beer. The bottles sat untouched on the table until Greg and Carl came along and asked if he was going to drink them or not. He shook his head. "You feeling okay?"

"Yeah, I'm good. Just watching everybody dance and doing some thinking."

"Look, go dance with Jennie. She'd love it. She's always had a crush on you."

"No, really. I'm happy where I am."

He went to the bar, got himself a Coke, drank it as he wandered about the room. He talked to his father a bit. His father was disappointed in him because he hadn't danced with Virginia. He excused himself, went to use the men's room. As he washed his hands he checked the time. It was after ten-thirty. The reception would end about eleven-thirty or twelve at the latest. Dave and Becky had to get up early to catch a plane tomorrow morning.

Some people had already left the reception but there were still quite a few remaining. There were little groups talking, some couples still dancing. He returned to the head table and sat down, folding his hands on the table top and watching the dancers. Dave and Becky were on the floor again, Dave staggering a bit and Becky clinging to him. She had taken off her shoes, he noticed.

And then the couples on the floor seemed to part. In the corridor that opened across the dance floor he saw a petite figure with flame-red hair. She was wearing a buttery yellow, ankle length dress, the sheer overlay floating a bit in the breeze created by the ceiling fans. The dress left her shoulders exposed. She had creamy skin. His heart skittered across several beats and then began to beat rapidly. Her eyes met his across the room as he stood up.

Coming around the head table he walked toward her. She came a few steps further into the room. "Pepper, I'm glad you could make it. I've been waiting all night for you to get off work so you could come and join the celebration." He smiled at her. She smiled a bit shyly back at him. He took her hand. "Can I buy you a drink before the bar closes?"

"No, thanks. I'm good."

"Why don't we dance then?" The band was playing a slow number. He drew her close, put his arm around her. "I have to warn you, I was the one my mother didn't waste her money on sending for dance lessons. She knew better."

"You'll be fine, I'm sure," she replied.

He gazed down into her face. "You look beautiful," he said. He liked how she blushed.

"You look very handsome." He had untied the bow tie so that it hung loosely around the unbuttoned collar of the shirt. At this hour of the night he was a bit scruffy looking with the five o'clock shadow and his longish hair curling over his collar.

"I feel like an idiot in this monkey suit."

"Maybe so, but you're very dashing nonetheless."

"Andrew, who's this young lady? This is the first time I've seen you on the dance floor all night," his mother said as she came up to them.

"This is Daisy, but I call her Pepper. Pepper, this is my mother, Mrs. Shaker."

"Hello, dear, it's a pleasure to meet you. Are you a friend of Andrew's?"

"Um, yes," the girl replied.

"Have you been here all night?"

Pepper and Andrew shared a look and seemed to come to a silent agreement between them about the story they would tell. She had served his parents their meals tonight, and Mrs. Shaker hadn't even recognized her. "No, I'm afraid I had to work. I couldn't get out of it."

"So I asked her to just meet me here after she got off work. And, here she is."

"Have you known Andrew long?'

"No, not that long." She shrugged. "Just a little while."

"Well, you're a lovely young lady. I'm glad you made it to the reception. He's been looking so glum and restless all evening. You two go dance and have a bit of fun. I'm afraid the party's starting to wind down now." She reached out and squeezed Daisy's hand. "Will we see you again?"

Daisy looked at Andrew. "Of course you will, Mom. I'll bring her to Dad's birthday party next month."

"Oh, Andrew! Don't be ridiculous! Bring her to dinner sooner than that! Dad and I would love to get to know her better. You can be so secretive sometimes!"

"All right. I'll bring her to dinner soon. We'll compare schedules and let you know when we're both free. Okay?" He watched his mother happily head off to join his father who was talking to Becky's parents. "I guess I'm going to need your phone number," he said, taking his cellphone from his jacket pocket. She gave him her number. "When I call you, you'll have mine, or do you have your phone hidden on you somewhere?"

She made a face. "No, I forgot it at home. I had to peel off my clothes, jump in the shower, get dressed and rush back here. But I made it." She looked at him again, marveling that she'd had the courage to take a risk like this for this man. There was just something about him. He hadn't been maliciously teasing her. He'd only been trying to get her attention, and he'd succeeded.

"Dance with me again. I like holding you close."

"I can't believe she didn't recognize me," she said.

"That's because she didn't notice you like I did. To her, you were just a server doing her job, practically invisible. But to me, you were like a torch that lit up the room."

"Is this how you always pick up girls?" she asked.

"No. I'm actually not very good at picking up girls. And besides, this isn't just a wedding reception pick up. I'm really interested in getting to know you better."

"I guess I can say the same."

He looked around the room, toward his parents. "We should have a few dates between now and Mom's invitation to dinner."

"That would probably be a good idea."

Dave and Becky came up to them. "Drew, who the hell is this?" Dave asked.

"This is my date. Daisy, this is the groom, Dave, and this is the bride, Becky. Dave. Becky, this is Daisy."

"Did I invite you?" Becky asked.

"I invited her. I RSVP'd and put two guests on the response card, right? Here she is. She had to work earlier, just managed to get here in time for a few dances with her man."

"Well, that's good," Becky said. "Nice to finally meet you, Daisy."

"Do I know you? Did you go to Montague High?" Dave asked.

"No, I'm from Brenton, two towns over."

"How in the world did you meet Drew? He's practically a recluse when he doesn't have Dave dragging him around by the ear."

"Um, I met him at a wedding," she replied.

"Whose wedding?' Dave asked.

Daisy looked at Andrew who replied, "A girl I went to school with. She invited me to her wedding." He shrugged. "Now, if you don't mind, I'd like another dance with my girl before it's time to shut this party down."

"Go for it. Look, when we get back from our honeymoon you guys have to come over. We want to get to know Daisy better. We'll have a cookout!"

"Sounds like a plan." Andrew took Daisy back in his arms and danced with her.

"I thought you said you had two left feet," she said.

"I do."

"You're doing remarkably well. Do you have a prosthetic right foot on tonight by any chance?" He laughed. She was funny. He liked a girl with a sense of humor.

"No, just two damn uncomfortable shoes."

"Let's be daring and kick our shoes off and dance in our stocking feet," she suggested, a mischievous light dancing in her eyes.

"I like the way you think," he replied. They kicked off their shoes and danced some more.

Mr. Shaker frowned as he watched his son dance with the petite redhead. "Who's that girl, did you say?" he asked his wife.

"Oh, that's Andrew's new girlfriend. Her name is Daisy. He's been keeping her a secret from us. I guess, with his track record with the girls, he's been reluctant to introduce us to this new one."

"They're both smiling. That's a good sign."

"They look good together, even though she's on the short side. And she's very sweet. Much nicer than those bar pick-ups he's brought home in the past."

"Crazy kids! Look at 'em dancing without their shoes." He chuckled.

"Oh, Lord, my feet are killing me!" She looked at her husband. He looked at her, cocking an eyebrow. They kicked off their shoes and then stepped out onto the dance floor. "If anyone asks, the bride started it when she took off her shoes earlier!"

"I hope this is the one. He's a good boy. Never gave us too much trouble."

"He had his moments, same as most boys do, but I think he's ready to settle down now that Dave has gotten married."

Mr. Shaker looked again at his son and the petite redhead he was dancing with. "She looks familiar but I can't place her."

Andrew walked Daisy to her car, a red Toyota Corolla, at ten past midnight. They had just seen Dave and Becky off in the limousine. People were getting into their cars and heading home. The lot was emptying quickly. His parents were already gone. "Thanks for coming back. I really didn't have much hope that you would."

"I wasn't going to, but then I thought, well, he asked me so I'll accept, and if he's horrified that the waitress has come back to dance with him, well, then I'll just go home again."

"And have a good cry into your pillow? I wouldn't do that to you." He lightly caressed her face, cupped her chin in his hand, tilting her face up to his. "You have gorgeous eyes." They looked into one another's eyes for a few long moments. "Is it too soon to kiss you goodnight?"

"I don't think so. I mean, we've been dating for an hour and a half already."

He smiled. She smiled. And then he kissed her. "I might have to crash a few receptions," he said.

"Once the receptions get going no one would even notice, probably. You'd just be a late arrival, a friend of a friend." She shrugged. "Or you could just come see me, or I could come and see you."

"That might be better. I wouldn't want to risk getting you fired." He opened her door for her. "Be careful driving home. I'll call you tomorrow night?"

"Okay. I'll be around."

"Are you working?" She shook her head. "How about if we go out tomorrow night then?"

"Why don't you just come over and I'll cook dinner for you and we can, you know, talk."

"Sounds good to me."

"Do you like spaghetti and meatballs?"

"That's one of my favorites. You cook, I'll bring a loaf of Italian bread and a bottle of wine."

"You've got a date. Call me in the morning, but not too early. I'm exhausted!" She pushed herself up onto her toes to kiss him. "Goodnight, Andrew. Thanks for a lovely evening."

"Goodnight, Pepper. See you tomorrow. I'll call you around ten to get directions to your place." She nodded, slipped into the driver's seat. He leaned in, gave her another kiss and then backed out and swung the door shut.

He stood watching her drive away. He had a good feeling about Daisy. She had come to the reception at his invitation after getting off work. She had danced with him and they had smoothly created an illusion of already being an established couple as if they had rehearsed it all for weeks. They had easily passed the Mom and Dad, best friend and his new wife test. His mother had obviously accepted Daisy and given her approval by insisting that he bring her to dinner soon. His father had just smiled a lot at her. Dave and Becky wanted to get to know her, too. He, himself, was anxious to get to know her better. He was pretty sure he was going to like her, that he would probably find himself hopelessly in love with her in no time.

He smiled as he walked to his SUV, and then he glanced back at the reception facility. If things worked out, maybe they would be holding their own wedding reception here in the future. And then he laughed. He liked calling her Pepper, but he might have to change that and call her by her real name. After all, he couldn't go around introducing her as his wife, Pepper Shaker—but then again, maybe he could.

She'd probably find that as funny as he did.

TANGERINE TWIST

Beaman Rhys' Uncle Arlys had been a true eccentric. He'd suffered from agoraphobia so had not left his home, a crumbling cement mansion circa the 1920's that he'd inherited from his great grandfather who had liked him better than he'd liked his own son and grandson, his grandson being Arlys' father Weylin, in ages. Arlys Rhys had also been OCD and a collector of weird shit, something akin to a true Victorian with their cabinets of curiosities stuffed full of bones, fossils, flora, taxidermied three-headed mice and whatnot, only according to Beaman, the entire house was chock-a-block full of this stuff, most of it having been purchased online and shipped to the house over the past three decades. He was also a hoarder. Beaman had been frustrated all throughout high school with the state the house had been in, worried that it was going to burn down and he'd be trapped deep in its bowels, unable to find his way through the wending narrow paths, through the towering mountains of crap his uncle had not been able to let go of. He, Beaman, his uncle's caretaker, had managed to carve out a decent two rooms for himself at the back of the second floor, keeping the servant's staircase clear for an emergency exit and a rope ladder under his bed that he could tie to the radiator and fling out the window to climb down in case of fire blocking his escape down the staircase.

The Rhys's were and still are filthy rich. Beaman had an older brother, Benes, but Benes had decided to circle the globe alone in a sailboat almost three years ago and no one had seen him nor heard from him in thirty-three months. Beaman, I'd heard, was rather nonchalant about his brother's disappearance saying, "He'll either show up one day or he won't. In seven years he can be declared legally dead. It would be just like him to show up the next day with the ink not quite dry on his death certificate."

Beaman's grandfather was in a nursing home, more or less consigned there by Beaman's old man who was a bitter alcoholic addicted to pain medication since the car accident that had killed Beaman's lovely mother, Larina Butterfield-Rhys six years ago. I still remembered going to their house, a stucco and timbered mansion with leaded, diamond-paned windows one might have found Shakespeare burning the midnight oil behind when I was in grade school for a birthday party for Beaman's Persian cat Sophie. My mother had dressed me in a frilly, scratchy, pink party dress, white ankle socks, pink Mary Janes, tying my then waist length red hair back in a lush ponytail with a pink satin ribbon. I looked hideous in pink. It clashed with my hair. She'd powdered my freckles and I'd been horribly congested during the whole party, me and the cat sneezing every two minutes. The worst part of the party had been my being pushed into the kidney-shaped pool by Scott Farnham and Francis Sawyer and then being pulled out by the Rhys's pool man, Javier Fuentes, looking like a drowned pink rat. The best part had been that the powder had been washed off my face and my nose had cleared up so I'd stopped sneezing *and* Mrs. Rhys had wrapped me in a huge fluffy white Egyptian cotton towel and then hustled me inside, stripping me naked in her personal dressing room, drying me with the towel and then dressing me in one of her exotic caftans, using a gold cord from her wardrobe closet, a belt, I guess, to tie around me so I wouldn't fall out of it. She'd used pinking shears to cut the skirt of the caftan all around so that it was ankle length on me. I had been horrified that she'd destroyed her own clothing for my sake when I could have just been wrapped in a dry towel and my mother called to come and get me. Instead, I had been invited to stay for supper. All the other guests had left with their shopping bags full of party bling and plates of leftover cake while I had lounged on the sofa in the massive family room catnapping with Sophie who'd been worn to a frazzle by the party. Beaman had pretty much ignored me that day, although he had passed me the peas twice at dinner, giving me a weird look because I actually *liked* peas and was taking a third helping. I hadn't known what the entre was—some sort of fish stuffed with herbs, green slimy stuff and lumpy grayish stuff. I'd picked at the fish and it had been okay—delicate, white and flaky—but the stuffing had not been appealing to me in the least, therefore I had overdosed on the tiny, bright green peas and gone home with a wicked stomach ache.

    Now, here I was at age twenty-four attending Beaman's Uncle Arlys' funeral feeling like a street person who had wandered into a high society function. He had already noticed me primarily because I stood out like a sore thumb with my spikey, short, flame-orange hair, multiple ear piercings, the little diamond stud glittering in the hollow on the left side of my nose; my attire a black satin vest with antique silver buttons worn over a red bra, with black spandex capris that emphasized how thin I was, and sweet little black ankle boots with a rolled cuff at the top and silver buckles that reminded me of the kind of boots a totally Goth Peter Pan might have chosen while stalking around Neverland full of attitude. Of course this outfit showcased my assorted tattoos, most of them only temporary ones because I was a big chicken when it came to needles and pain. The small ones were real— like the weeping rosebud on my right shoulder, the raven perched on my collarbone, and the shooting star on my left wrist. I had a little silver ring piercing my navel that was visible when I lifted my arms. The capris rode low on my narrow hips.

Beaman was standing with his Aunt Lucine and his other aunt, whose name I couldn't recall at the moment, as I approached them. He looked so hot in his fitted black suit that I was afraid I'd start panting and slobbering. I'd always had this sort of reaction to him, like Pavlov's dog drooling over reward kibble. It was embarrassing, to say the least. I couldn't even make eye contact with the guy without my knees turning to Jell-O and my heart wobbling in my breast. The last I'd heard he'd gotten engaged to Ella Fayre, the drop dead gorgeous blonde who'd been the bane of my existence since the beginning of time. She'd never missed an opportunity to badmouth me to whomever would listen. It had always been a mystery to me why she'd never been invited to Sophie's birthday parties while I had been. Maybe that's why she'd always been so hostile toward me. I'd probably been invited primarily out of a sense of charity. Beaman's mother had always been charitable, a true philanthropist. I surreptitiously glanced around to try to spot where mine enemy lurked but I didn't see her among the many familiar faces of former classmates.

I paused to bow my head at the gun metal-gray casket containing the mortal remains of Uncle Arlys. In a sudden lull the crack of my gum sounded as loud as a shotgun blast. Heads turned in my direction. I feigned a limp, as if it had been my knee joint popping but Beaman's narrowed eyes told me that he, for one, hadn't been fooled.

I murmured a soft, "So sorry for your loss," to each of his aunts, who both hesitated before offering me their hands to press with my own little paw with my black-painted nails and fingers encased in an assortment of metal bands etched with esoteric symbols and signs. When I reached Beaman my vocal cords locked up.

"What's the matter? Choking on your gum?" he asked, his voice low. "You need me to do the Heimlich on you? Just nod your head if you do." I shook my head. "Good. I really didn't think you were choking since your face is white not blue." I tried to sidle away but he reached out quickly and grasped my wrist. "Cat got your tongue?" he asked. I shook my head. "Just can't muster any sympathy for my loss?"

"Don't be absurd," I hissed, finding my voice at last. "I'm sorry he's gone." I willed myself to raise my eyes to meet his gaze. He had the most amazing hazel eyes I'd ever seen. His irises were like kaleidoscopes that had captured all the colors of autumn, except the reds and oranges. The browns, greens, and golds were all there spraying out from the black pupils like sunbursts. His eyes complemented his longish, dark-blonde hair. "I…" I completely lost my train of thought.

"Nice of you to dress up for the wake," he said. "Are you wearing a red thong to match that bra?"

I gasped and nearly did inhale my gum. "You can't ask me that!" I cried, loud enough to cause heads nearby to turn. My cheeks suddenly burned.

"I'm just curious," he replied. "I honestly didn't expect to see you here. I thought you'd moved out west."

"No, I'd thought about moving out west but I went to New York City instead."

"You came all the way from New York City for this?" He'd begun to look incredulous.

"No, I came all the way from Camden, Massachusetts for this."

"So you're back in town?" I nodded. He seemed to be mulling that bit of news over as he looked around the room at all the people who had come to commiserate with him over his loss. I began to drift away but he caught my wrist again. "Tangerine, are you coming to the funeral tomorrow?"

"I don't know." No one had called me Tangerine since he'd started doing that in middle school.

"Ella's in Europe. I know she despises you. I…I'd like you to be there."

"Fine, I'll work it into my busy schedule. What time is it?"

"Ten o'clock at St. Mark's. Nine o'clock here."

"I've been here already. I'll be at the church for ten." I started to move away again only to realize that my arm was not following me. He was still gripping my wrist, rather hard. I frowned slightly. Beaman had never been clingy before. What was with this? "Can I have my arm back?" I asked.

"Will you dress decently?"

"For your Uncle Arlys? Or for God in His house?"

"Neither. For me."

"I'll run right home and examine my wardrobe but I can't guarantee I have anything better than what I'm currently wearing."

"Go buy a dress and some normal shoes."

"I suppose next you'll be reminding me to buy pantyhose to go with that get-up."

He suddenly flashed a quick grin but got it under control. He leaned down, touching his warm cheek to my hot cheek as he whispered in my ear, "I'd prefer that you wear thigh-high black stockings, black bikini panties, a black push-up bra, strapless, and a minimum of a two and a half inch heel."

"Oh, really? And what will you be wearing while I suffer through that ordeal?"

"A secret smile and a hard-on." Well, that left me absolutely speechless. "Thanks for coming to the wake, Orange Crush." He released my wrist, but his fingertips brushed the back of my hand in doing so and it felt as if electric currents were shooting up my arm, jolting my heart. It was beyond my comprehension, but I think the great Beaman Rhys had just made a pass at me! My brain was spinning as if he had stood it on end and given it a quick flick with his forefinger and thumb.

At the door I glanced back. His Aunt Lucine was watching me, her expression ponderous and inscrutable. Had she overheard our not so respectful repartee? What in the world did she think of me? I suddenly felt like the hired slut at a ritzy bachelor party. I quickly put distance between myself and the wake attendees, especially Beaman. He should not have been saying such things to me when he was engaged to snooty Miss Fayre!

It was as if I were in an hypnotic trance as I walked the aisles of Marshall's that evening, looking for a decent dress. It really didn't surprise me when I found it just hanging there as if it had been patiently awaiting my arrival to purchase it. It was simple, understated yet had an adorable sweetheart neckline that belied the saucy thigh-high slit up the left side of the skirt. It fit me to a T. In the shoe department I found the requisite two and a half inch high spiked-heel black pumps. A quick rummaging around in the foundations department scored me a black strapless bra that might squash and lift what little I possessed in the mammary department, a pair of black bikini panties and even the suggested thigh-high black stockings. I even prowled through handbags and came up with a little black shoulder bag that would hold my cellphone, my keys, a condom packet, a breath mint, a few dollars and not much else. It all cost me nearly a hundred fifty dollars, a staggering sum of money to limited budget me. It was the handbag that did it, but I needed it since the dress had no pockets and I couldn't lug around a mini messenger bag or a black leather backpack at a funeral like a reliquary salesman.

    On Thursday morning I took a leisurely shower and then combed my hair out without gelling it to death. Uncontrolled, it lay in a simple chin length pageboy. I applied a hint of smoky eye shadow, a tiny bit of umber mascara, and clear lip gloss. I tended to flush easily so didn't even own blush. I got dressed and then walked out into the bedroom to stand before the full length mirror hanging on the inside of my closet door. I looked like an alien being to my own eyes. To the normal person I probably would appear to be a girl-next-door-pretty young woman appropriately dressed for a funeral, although my freakin' shoes were a little too high, but I was only five three, so this boosted me to nearly five six. I hoped I wouldn't get a nosebleed tottering around at this altitude. I didn't have room for a single tissue in my tightly packed purse.

    I had to lose the shoes to drive to the church, wearing my moccasins instead. The funeral procession had not yet arrived so I milled about on the front walk with other church-only mourners, mostly senior citizens who looked as if they had all just wandered over in a group from the Alzheimer's facility on the next block. I was relieved when the stately, somber, black livery vehicles began pulling up the long, curved driveway. The funeral director and his assistant were in the lead car, followed by the hearse, then the flower car, and finally the black limousine in which Beaman and his aunts were riding. A black SUV pulled up next, driven by Beaman's cousin Piers who had not been at the wake last evening, at least not while I'd been briefly present. I was surprised that I remembered his name, but it popped into my brain the moment he stepped out of the SUV and adjusted his distinctively striped tie. Piers was basically an idiot. I was surprised that he had a driver's license. I hadn't thought he'd ever passed a test in his life, but he'd evidently passed the driver's exam—written *and* road. Holy shit! This elevated him ever so slightly in my opinion.

    Beaman got out of the limo and stood looking around. I felt it like a body slam the moment his eyes landed on me. Slowly I raised my eyes to meet his only to be stymied by the dark glasses he was wearing. I couldn't really read his eyes, but the corners of his mouth twitched. I didn't know if I'd met with his approval or not, but when he tripped on the church steps because he was looking back at me over his shoulder as he escorted his Aunt Lucine I figured I had aced his challenge. I turned ever so slightly to allow the breeze to flutter the slit of the skirt, flashing the lacy top of the thigh-high black stocking on that leg. If this had not been a solemn occasion I was pretty sure he would have ditched his aunt right then and there and come loping down the stairs like a wolf. It kind of blew me away that I had this sort of power over him. It was unexpected and gave me something to mull over as I sat in a creaky pew with the smell of musty missals and hymnals fluttering against my nostrils, tempting me to sneeze. I kept pinching my nose to fend off the sneezes since I had no tissues on me.

    I was squirming by the time the service ended. I should never have had a large coffee on the way to the church. I didn't know this church so had no idea where the ladies room was located. The priest had made his final gestures and concluded the service and was announcing a reception immediately following the burial at the Silver Maple Country Club. Those not attending the burial were welcome to head over to the club where there would be hors d'oeuves and champagne.

    I caught Beaman looking at me as he followed the casket up the aisle with an aunt on each arm. I tried to look properly somber but I was flushing again at the way his eyes were literally devouring me alive. What was with him? And where was Ella the Disemboweler? I wondered as I craned my neck to check out the retreating view, nearly falling into the aisle, unused to the wretched high heels. I felt like a novice circus performer trying to learn a balancing act on stilts. I thought I might be lucky if I only had a sprained ankle by the end of the day.

    I sped to the country club, bolting for the ladies lounge to seek blessed relief from a distended bladder. I literally moaned with relief. Upon leaving the stall I caught an elderly woman scowling at me as if I had been having sex in the stall with a man I had snuck in there. I wanted to swing the door open to show her that I had been quite alone but she turned away and huffed out like the little engine that could. I carefully washed my hands, upon which I wore only two rings today, my other fingers marked by the indents of the absent rings.

    I went to the designated function room where I was immediately handed a flute of champagne and offered hot something-or-others on a tray. I declined the unidentifiable bacon-wrapped foodstuffs, sipped the champagne and wandered over to a round table upon which sat platters of recognizable fruits, crackers and cubes of assorted cheeses. I filled a small plate with grapes, strawberries, melon chunks, cheese cubes and pale round crackers. Then I walked around juggling the plate with unstable contents and the champagne until I realized that there was no designated seating plan. I chose a seat overlooking the patio where golfers in pastel outfits were already enjoying a light lunch and cocktails under colorful umbrellas. There was a koi pond in the middle of the patio. I'd have to check that out later because I was a sucker for koi.

    I had been offered a second flute of champagne and could not refuse it. I'd eaten everything from my little plate so it had been whisked away by an efficient waiter who didn't have a whole helluva lot to do at the moment since the room was very sparsely populated. I got up and went to check out the new hot treats that had been set out. I chose a couple meatballs and returned to my seat.

There was a stir in the room as an influx of mourners arrived. Cousin Piers filled a plate, grabbed some booze and made a beeline to the table where I was sitting by myself. "I haven't seen you in a dog's age, Jennifer," he said.

"My name's not Jennifer," I politely informed him.

"You look like Jennifer."

"Poor Jennifer," I murmured.

He ate some food and then tried again. "So, is your name Daisy? Seems I knew a redhead named Daisy once, although Poppy would have been a better name for her, don't you think?"

"Mm."

"Were we in school together at least?"

"Uh, no. I think you went to Faulkner Prep. That tie gives you away. I was at the public high school with a slumming Beaman, only a couple of grades behind him."

"Oh, then maybe I saw you at the house once or twice?'

"Possibly." I really couldn't remember exactly how I knew him. The meeting had evidently not been a memorable moment.

"One of those stupid birthday parties for that damn cat?"

"Quite likely."

"Okay, clue me in since I'm drawing a blank. What's your name?"

"I reveal my name only on a need to know basis," I replied. "And I don't think you need to know."

He looked startled by my response and then confused. Finally he settled on pissed off. "Bitch," he muttered as he grabbed his plate and stood up. I was so not going to be his funeral pick-up date. He couldn't think of anything more profound to utter so he just stalked off in search of liquid consolation.

Beaman arrived with his aunts, looking all around. He spotted me but stayed with his aunts for the time being. A few former classmates came over and filled in most of the table where I was sitting, but no one sat on either side of me as if I radiated some sort of force field that repelled them and kept them at a chairs width distance.

The priest from the church arrived and after talking to Beaman and the aunts for a while he made his way to a podium and tapped the microphone, making everyone cringe at the shrill squeal of feedback from the speakers. "I guess it's on," he said, more to himself than to us although his comment was broadcast over the PA system. He took out some crumpled papers from his black jacket pocket, smoothed them noisily out on the podium, then cleared his throat, adjusted his reading glasses, then peered out over the tops of them at all of us. Most everyone had taken a seat knowing that his little speech was forthcoming. No one wanted to be caught falling asleep on their feet and crashing to the floor.

His speech was mercifully brief. There really wasn't a whole lot anyone could say about an eccentric recluse with a mental disorder. I figured he was hungry because his eyes kept drifting from his notes to the staff hauling out the massive buffet, arranging it all on several sturdy tables from which the mourners could help themselves from either side of. "Amen," he said, startling us all into hastily echoing his concluding sentiment.

Beaman got up and walked to the podium, shook the priest's hand. Then he took his place at the microphone and gave a brief thank you to all of us who had come to pay their respects at the passing of his Uncle Arlys. He said he appreciate our taking time from our busy lives to be with him, his aunts and cousin today. Then he motioned toward the buffet tables. "Enjoy."

I got up and walked behind the people from my table to the buffet, taking a plate and some silverware wrapped in a real linen napkin. I was going through the line when someone directly behind me laid a hand on my ass. I snapped my head around to snarl a threat to remove the offending hand or lose it but the threat became null and void due to the shock of finding that it belonged to Beaman who was behaving boldly and totally out of character. "What do you think you're doing?" I hissed, my eyes meeting his, which almost made me topple over. He moved his hand to my waist to steady me, trying to help me regain my balance which was now totally off kilter.

"Getting some food. I'm hungry," he replied. "What about you? Are you eating these days? You're thin as a rail."

"I've always been naturally slim," I responded.

"I was just checking to see if you'd grown a real ass yet. There's a little something there."

"You touch me anywhere else and they'll be calling the paramedics while people crawl around on the floor looking under their tables for your severed hand."

"That's what I've always liked about you, Tangerine, your sweet and charming nature. It gives me the warm fuzzies."

"You have a pair of warm fuzzies on you all right, but you didn't get them from me."

"Can you lighten up on me a little today? I'm in mourning, if you hadn't noticed."

"Yes, I noticed you're wearing black."

He helped himself to a piece of grilled chicken and then landed a piece on my plate. "Eat that." I scowled at him. "I saw the stocking," he said, sending a shot of heat straight down my spine.

"I don't know why I bothered dressing to your specifications. I must have my own psychiatric issues."

He leaned close and whispered in my ear, "No, it's because you're anticipating my removing each item piece by piece later on. Admit it. You've been waiting for this, the moment you had me wrapped around your little finger. Damn it, Mila…I never saw this coming until I saw you walk into the funeral home yesterday. All of a sudden it was like I'd swallowed a lust pill."

He had reached around me to steady my plate which had once again begun to tilt alarmingly toward dumping its contents onto the carpet at my feet. "Are you sure you didn't mistake your vitamin for one of your late uncle's Viagras?"

"When the hell did you transform from a freak into a femme fatale?"

"I don't think I actually have. When was the last time you had your eyes examined? Or maybe it's your head you need to have examined because if I'm recalling the past correctly, you never really gave a rat's ass about me. It was your mother who kept inviting me to Sophie's parties. She had some sort of weird obsession with me, didn't she?"

He added a spoonful of roasted red potato chunks to both our plates. Why he thought I could not serve myself was beyond me. "She felt sorry for you. You were like her pet project. She desperately tried to normalize you. The rest of us knew it was a lost cause."

"Mm, well…at least she was nice about it." I stopped him from putting green beans on my plate. "I'm having salad."

"You should eat a lot of vegetables."

"I'll be eating lettuce, tomato, cucumber, celery, carrots, radishes, with tiny green caterpillars as added protein. I don't want soggy green beans."

"Will you sit with me and my aunts?"

"No."

"Please."

"Oh please, Beaman, don't beg. It's just not like you. You'll give me nightmares."

"Mila..."

"Stop calling me that!"

"Tangerine!" I bent my head and shook it. "I've been an idiot my entire life," he said.

"Just realizing that now, are you?"

"Unfortunately, yes."

I set my plate down so I could fill a glass bowl with salad. I heaped it high because I liked salad. Then I drizzled Ranch dressing all over it. "Why do you want me to sit with you? Where's your fiancee? I'd really rather not piss her off. I might be able to return this dress I will never wear again if I can manage not to have someone throw something on it."

"Ella dumped me," he replied quietly. It did something to me to hear the naked wound pulsing in his voice. She had torn his heart out. I had a crazy urge to rip his shirt open and gape at the hole in his chest but I restrained myself. My brain was running on two tracks at the moment—one the sadistic little train of satisfaction that his perfect fiancée had not been so perfect after all, and the other the little tugboat of sympathy that wanted to pull the shipwreck of his soul to shore where I might be able to work some kind of magic on it to fix the damage it had taken. "There, you were right all along. I am a loser," he concluded.

"I never called you a loser," I said.

"You didn't have to say it aloud. Every look you cast my way broadcast that loud and clear."

"You're being uncommonly melodramatic, putting unsaid words into my eyes instead of my mouth. Really Beaman, pull yourself together here. I wasn't the one who dumped you at the altar of rejection. I'm the one who went shopping last night and bought this whole get up to…to…oh, my God…" I said in shock, my eyes wide, my jaw practically unhinging.

"What's the matter with you?" he grumbled.

"I just realized that I'm very ill."

"You look fine to me, except for your face."

"Beaman, I went shopping. I spent money that I couldn't afford to spend on clothes that I'm only going to wear this one time. I bought everything you told me to buy and I'm wearing it right at this moment. What the hell is wrong with me? Please, get out your phone and call the paramedics right now. No, you'd better call the medical examiner because I think I'm going to drop dead from the shock of it all right here."

"You did do that, didn't you?"

This reminder that I had done exactly as he'd asked perked him up. He picked up my salad bowl and handed it to me, grabbed my plate and nudged me ahead of him toward the table where his aunts sat picking at small portions of food they had selected at the other buffet station. They looked up like twin budgies as Beaman set my plate down, pulled out a chair for me and then set his own plate down at the place right beside me.

"Hi," I said as I sat down.

"Aunt Lucine, Aunt Rose, do you remember Mila Talbot? She was two years behind me in high school but Mother used to invite her to all of Sophie's parties."

"Yes, the little redhead girl whose mother dressed her in pink all the time. I do remember her." Her hawk's eyes landed on me with a predatory appraisal of my menial existence. "That was some outfit you were wearing last evening," she commented.

"I'd just gotten out of work."

"Exactly where do you work that they allow you to dress so…provocatively? This isn't the Vegas strip."

"I'm actually self-employed. I was doing some film editing at Penn and Silver Studios. I make documentaries. I can pretty much wear whatever I want to. I don't enforce a particular dress code for the volunteer techs and myself."

"Mila is artistic and creative. That gives her license to be different, to express herself whatever way she pleases," Beaman explained.

"Well, I for one have never actually seen a red brassiere before."

"Walmart sells them," I informed her, in case she wanted to run out and buy one.

"So does Fredericks of Hollywood," Aunt Rose added. "I've seen the catalog at Arlys' house," she explained to her sister.

"Actually, they're pretty common nowadays. If I remember correctly, Rhett Butler gifts Mammy red taffeta pantaloons in *Gone With The Wind.* Red underwear is not just for harlots and assorted other loose women anymore."

"I thought she looked pretty damn hot."

"It was rather warm in the room with so many people crammed together," Aunt Rose agreed. I wondered if she was trying to mellow the tone of the conversation or if she had totally missed Beaman's point. "What are you currently working on, dear?" she asked me.

"A documentary on invisible children." Her eyebrows shot up as she looked around the room as if there might be any number of invisible children hiding in the corners, sticking their dirty fingers into the desserts stacked high on a third table. "Kids who have fallen through the cracks of society. Homeless kids, kids who have been kicked out of their homes or abandoned by their parents or who have simply run away from home. They're out there. It takes some legwork to track them down but I found several and I've been filming them for a few months. This documentary is going to make a lot of people uneasy."

"Are you an agitator?" Aunt Lucine asked.

"Probably," I admitted. Why deny it? I didn't stick my finger in the pot just to hold it still. I liked to stir things up.

There was a brief silence as we began to eat but then Aunt Rose said, "We thought there would be a wedding at the end of the summer, but alas, that has fallen by the wayside." She cast a woeful look at her nephew who suddenly turned and asked me what he could get me to drink from the bar. I replied I wanted tonic water with a twist of tangerine. He got up and walked away from the table like a man on a mission, primarily to avoid what was coming from the mouths of his aunts.

"He would have had it all with Ella," Aunt Lucine remarked when he was barely out of hearing range. I was trying to figure out why on earth any man would be considered to have it all with a nasty little two-faced bitch in his bed. It didn't make sense to me. "She's inherited a fortune from her maternal grandparents, that girl has."

"Isn't Beaman rich?" I asked with a total lack of couth and utter impropriety.

"Well, of course he is, even more so now that Arlys has passed. He stands to inherit the house and everything, unless Arlys suddenly found a reason to favor Piers, poor fellow."

"I'm not sure I remember which one of you brought him into the world," I said.

"Neither one of us. It was Bela who gave birth to that boy." I didn't remember Beaman having an Aunt Bela and must have looked blank because she rolled her eyes and continued, "You know, the one who leapt off the roof of the SkyLiner Hotel downtown in the mid-nineties?" Oh, that Bela. She had been stark naked and zonked out on pills or something. A society girl who had reached rock bottom. Or maybe it was just because she had given birth to Piers, a dismal achievement in a life studded with glittering parties, galas and balls. I believe she had been an equestrienne in her youth. I also vaguely recalled a whispered story of her having been raped on the grounds of this very golf course when she was fifteen years old. And suddenly I was doing the mental math. Beneath the sum total line I found the name Piers which startled me so much that I dropped my fork with a clatter loud enough to cause heads to turn. Piers had been the result of that rape. The hastily arranged marriage on Bela's sixteenth birthday to a man my father's age, who was rumored to be quite a Lothario, was to shield her from social ostracism. It was weird how one remark could suddenly free an old scandal from its careful packaging to reveal the ugly truth and the tragic players in their most disquieting rolls.

"Mila doesn't need to hear old stories," Aunt Lucine muttered, giving me a warning glower, like I would suddenly stand up and shock the room with the revelation that I'd just experienced. "Why is Beaman suddenly so close to you?" she asked, effectively changing the subject.

"I have no idea. I hadn't seen him in years until last evening."

"It was like you shoved a roman candle up his behind and lit it up," Aunt Rose said, causing Aunt Lucine's mouth to twist in an ugly manner. I'd thought she wasn't so sharp but she didn't miss the warning look from her sister. "He lit right up, you can't deny that," she argued. "He's been so down in the dumps since Ella sent him the Dear John letter from the Riviera."

"Maybe he's just having a delayed reaction to the happy news that she's left him."

"Why would he be happy about being thrown over for a Frenchman?"

"You'd met her, hadn't you?" I countered. "I've never liked her. She was such a phony in school."

"Maybe you were jealous," Aunt Lucine suggested somewhat cattily.

No. I was never jealous of her. I was often disgusted by her behavior, her honey-blonde superiority and syrupy disdain for the likes of me. "No, I don't believe so. I was jealous of Emma Adams because she was so artistic I swear she had to have had India ink flowing through her veins. I always wanted to be able to draw like her."

Beaman returned just then setting down a tall, narrow glass of clear bubbly liquid with a spiral of tangerine rind dangling in the soda water at my place, a bottled micro-brewed beer at his own seat and gin and tonics at his aunt's places. Simultaneously, the older women lifted their glasses and drank deeply, probably to wash the taste of me from their mouths. I can't imagine I was a flavor they were enjoying. "I hate funerals," Beaman said.

"I don't think we're meant to enjoy them," I murmured just as a burst of laughter came from the table where I had first been sitting. I slewed my eyes in that direction and saw everyone seemed to be looking at me and Beaman and the aunts but they all quickly looked away and another burst of laughter came from that direction. "Great," I muttered. I loathed being the butt of other people's jokes. "Beam, I really should go," I said, setting my fork down. "I have some stuff I need to do."

He turned his head and looked at me as if I had just stuck my butter knife into the hole in his chest and given it a hard twist. "No, you can't go, you haven't even finished eating yet."

I shook my head. "I do have to go." He had to know I was the triangular peg here among the squares and circles. "I'm sorry for your loss," I said as I stood up, grabbing my bag, slinging it over my shoulder.

I was already in the lobby when he caught up to me. "Let me walk you to your car," he said.

"I can manage to find it on my own." That didn't deter him from moving past me to open the door for me although there was a doorman and at the bottom of the curved stone steps a valet who would retrieve my car if I handed him my key. "Go back inside where you belong," I hissed at him as he followed me down the stairs.

He was like a stray dog hoping for a treat or a pat on the head, some sign of affection and acceptance. By the time we reached my car, an old Toyota Corolla with some missing paint, I had tears blurring my vision. "I can't fix you!" I cried as I tried to unlock the door with the key I'd fished out of my tiny bag. The fob thingy no longer worked so I had to insert the key. I kept missing the lock.

Beaman took the key from my hand and stuffed it into his pocket. "You already have," he replied but I shook my head. "Just seeing you again has changed my life in ways I never could have imagined. I didn't sleep last night. All I could think about was you." He shook his head, suddenly laughed. "My God, Mila, you went out and bought clothes to wear to this funeral. Not just any clothes, but the exact clothes I asked you to wear. What does that tell you?"

"I don't know!" I cried, flooded with confusion. "That I'm crazy?"

"No! It tells me that you do care about me and you wanted to make me happy on a day when I'd be feeling kind of lost, sad and defeated."

"Oh, Beam, you've never been defeated. You've always manage to come out on top in everything."

"No, not in everything. I'm a big time loser in love."

"Well, yeah, that was a huge misstep on your part. Really, you should have talked to me and I'd have told you what she was really like."

"I had no idea where you were or I would have. I had to wing it without my spirit guide." I chuffed a soft dismissive snort through my nose. "Tangerine, you've always been on the periphery of my life like a little orange moon circling the planet I live on. There's always been this gravitational pull toward you. I should have paid more attention to it years ago."

"You make it sound like we're a couple of old farts, Beam. I'm only twenty-four and you're like, what? Twenty-six?" He nodded. "God, we have so many years ahead of us in which to screw up our lives some more."

"I'd rather avoid the screwing up stuff. I've done enough of that lately." He leaned against the car in his black suit. I knew his jacket would be covered with pollen and road dust when he moved away. I wanted to tell him he was ruining his suit but I couldn't seem to speak at the moment. "I get the house, the property and everything else. It's a nightmare. He never let me throw anything out. It's going to take half a century to go through everything and sort out what can go to auction, what gets trashed, what should go to whomever. Jesus, I'll be an old man before I'm done."

I nodded and then said, "I should come over and film the house and do some sort of documentary on OCD behavior and hoarding. It would be impressive from what I've heard about the way it is inside."

"Sure, bring your camera and crew and have at it."

"It's just me. I pretty much do it alone."

He hesitated a moment and then said, "That's a sad thing, doing it alone. But that's how it is with me too these days." I wasn't so sure if he was talking about our day to day lives or our private nighttime activities. Either way, he was spot on. It was sad. "Look, what are you doing the rest of the day?"

"Changing my clothes and then…" I shrugged. I didn't know. I had no set plans.

He dipped his hand into his pocket and pulled out a key ring, worked a big key off of it and held it out to me. "Go grab your camera and stuff. Go to the house, let yourself in, wander around a bit, if you're as brave as I think you are. Get a feel for the place, start filming. It's creepy in places. Don't be afraid. No one's there. I have to stay awhile longer and then I'll be home." He looked at me. "Don't change your clothes, but you'll have to put on comfortable shoes. Bring the ones you have on now though, for later. And bring whatever else you'll need. You know, something you can be comfortable in later, your toothbrush…"

"You want me to start work on the documentary today?"

"Yes, absolutely." I stared at him. "And I want us to start working on our relationship today."

"Do we have one of those things going? A relationship?"

"You dressed up for me. That's a good sign that we might be developing one, right?" There was hope glimmering in the depths of his amazing eyes that gave me a sudden warm aura around my heart.

I decided to throw this stray pup a bone. "Right," I agreed.

He took my little purse and opened it, poked two fingers inside and pulled out the condom packet. "I noticed this when you took your key out and hoped it wasn't just a wet nap." I flushed, caught like a fish on his line. "Were you planning on picking up some guy here at the funeral today?"

"No."

"My cousin Piers perhaps?" I hit his arm, shaking my head. "Me?"

"I just like to be prepared. One never knows."

He stuck the packet back into my bag and snapped it shut. Then he dug out his wallet and handed me a couple of twenties. "Do me a favor, swing by the pharmacy and buy some more. Buy a couple of boxes." My eyebrows must have shot up to the top of my head. He laughed. "We won't use them all up today. We'll keep some in reserve." He pulled me into his arms and hugged me, resting his cheek atop my head. "Mila, when you walked into the funeral home last night you suddenly changed the course of my life. I'd had no hope of ever finding you again."

"You could have Googled me. God, Beam, don't you get out? Don't you use social media? I've been around downtown running errands and stuff. I live over the damn pharmacy."

"How would I have known that? I thought you were still out west."

"I never went out west! Why were you so out of the loop?"

"Ella," he answered.

She had suppressed all information in regards to me, kept him in the dark. The conniving bitch! "Well, I'm glad I bought a newspaper the other day and saw the obit or else this never would have happened."

"Fate works in weird and unfathomable ways."

"Your aunts don't like me," I said.

"Are we going to let that be a stumbling block to our future?" I shrugged. "Well, for what it's worth, I like you and that should be good enough to start with."

"I suppose it should be."

He nudged my chin up, looking down into my eyes. "I remember you sleeping on the couch with Sophie. You were like something out of a fairy tale in my mother's hacked up caftan with the gold cord belt and your hair all fiery and loose. You looked so sweet and ethereal with your feline familiar. A little flame-haired witch. You enchanted me way back then."

"I'm not a witch."

"No, you're something else entirely." The way he said it made me smile. "You're beautiful," he said, and then he kissed my cheek. "Go on. I'll see you later."

"See you, Beaman." He unlocked the door of my car, laid the key in my palm on top of the twenties and his house key. "Don't drink too much."

"I won't. I want to be sober when I take you to bed this evening."

"Okay, although it might be better if you *are* a little drunk then."

He shook his head. "No, I don't think so. Go on before I jump into the passenger seat and shock the hell out of the aunts." He closed the door but then opened it again, leaning down. I turned my head to see what he wanted and realized that he was going to kiss me. My heart did a cartwheel. I kissed him the exact same way he kissed me, as if we had been kissing one another all of our lives. He looked like a man who had taken a miracle cure as I backed out of the parking space and waved to him. He raised his hand and waved back, sending little sparklers throughout my body.

When I unbuttoned his shirt tonight I imagined I would not find a gaping hole in his chest, his heart torn out. Instead I would find a perfectly wonderful chest with a strong heart beating within it. It would give me a mighty powerful feeling knowing I had restored that damaged heart—especially when I hadn't yet given him but a tiny iota of the love I had for him within my own heart.

SECRETARY'S DAY

"Charlotte! I need you to call Palmer Travel." There was a pause and then from the office he called, "Charlotte! I need to speak to a Mrs. Yardley there and only to her."

"Yes, Dr. Fox." I grabbed my three pound Rolodex, paging through it until I came to Palmer Travel Agency. I punched in the number on my phone, adjusting the headset that I wore. "Good morning, this is Charlotte from Doctor Fox's office. Is Deborah in today?" She was. As I waited for her to pick up her extension I glanced at the screen on my computer. The reports on Mrs. Tompkins were still downloading from the hospital in Kenton. "Hi, Deb, it's Charlotte. Can you hold the line for Dr. Fox please? Thanks!" I put her on hold then used the intercom feature to let the doctor know that Mrs. Yardley was on line 3 for him.

"Thank you, Charlotte!" he called through the door of his office that stood ajar.

I shook my head. He was so hopeless sometimes. I got up and went into the little break room, poured him a cup of coffee adding a splash of half and half and two sugars. After working for him since graduating from college five years ago I knew quite a bit about the doctor, his likes and dislikes. He had obtained a divorce from his first wife, Ashley, the week that I was hired. I hadn't known her except from rumors. Evidently she had agreed to stay home and be a mother, but then she had gotten her real estate license and refused to give him children. A year after his first divorce was finalized he'd married Olivia whom he had met in a singles bar. I never liked her. She had been very condescending when she'd visited him at the office, talking down to all of us on the phone. Sultry and gorgeous she may have been, but she was not a nice person. We'd all heaved a sigh of relief when he'd ousted her from his life fifteen months ago. He'd been working long hours ever since, paying alimony to two ex-wives, but two months ago his fortunes had changed as both exes had landed new big fish from the small pond of available bachelors with money. His bank accounts were far less anemic lately so I guessed, at the ripe old age of thirty-three, he was treating himself to a much overdue vacation with this call to the travel agency. He hadn't asked me to block any vacation time in his appointment book yet so maybe he was just information gathering?

 I nudged his door open with the toe of my shoe. He was still on the phone. He glanced up at me as I entered, smiled when he saw the coffee mug in my hand. He was a nice looking man with sandy brown hair worn a bit too long so that it was always curling over the collar of his shirts, and warm hazel eyes. His patients all adored him. He hadn't become jaded as many physicians do when dealing with life and death, sickness and disease—putting themselves above all of it by being nice to the patient's face and then disparaging them behind their backs. He truly cared about his patients and often stayed late researching symptoms and diseases to try to find the optimal way to treat a patient who presented with puzzling issues. I set the cup on the coaster on his blotter. He mouthed, 'Thank you!' I nodded, turned and went back to my desk.

 I had the reports from the hospital tucked into Mrs. Tompkins' chart when he came out of his office. "Charlotte, have you seen my stethoscope?" he asked.

I looked up. He was a brilliant physician but he was more or less clueless at times. "Would that be the stethoscope draped around your neck?" I asked, giving him an inquisitive look.

He reached up, grabbed it and pulled it down, tucking it into the pocket of his white coat. "That would be the one. Thank you." He strode toward the door.

"Doctor!" I called and he stopped. "You might want to take Mrs. Tompkins chart with you. Her hospital records from Kenton are there."

"You're an efficient and hard-working secretary," he said. "I really ought to give you a raise." He came and took the heavy chart. "Remind me tomorrow."

"I've also downloaded the reports to the electronic records so you can access all her labs that were done there, and any x-rays, CT scans, EKGs or MRIs she may have had while hospitalized. I scanned in her last report from the pulmonologist too."

"Good job," he said, nodding as he turned and left the office area.

I checked the schedule for tomorrow. We had mostly gone to electronic records but the doctor still liked to have the paper charts to refer to and jot notes in. He didn't like sitting in the room paying more attention to his typing than to the patient. He felt he was too distracted while attempting to not misspell anything. He didn't trust the digital voice recorder programs that translated his dictation while in the room with the patient. He had found too many errors in the reports as the computer had misunderstood some of the medical terms—for instance, instead of saying the patient needed a physiatrist, for pain management, the records had said the patient needed a psychiatrist. The names of medications were also confusing to the program. So, I'd pulled the charts for the next day and was now checking to make sure I had them all.

While he was in with Mrs. Tompkins and our medical assistant Irina I checked insurance eligibility for about half the patients, making sure the ones we hadn't seen in a while still had Dr. Fox listed as their primary care. Sometimes, even though they still had the same insurance, they may have accidentally let it lapse and then resumed it. Often, when resuming, if they didn't name a primary care the insurance assigned one and people came in thinking everything was the same when it wasn't. I liked to be sure our patients were still our patients on the day of their visits.

"Charlotte?" I looked up. He had his head around the door. "Can you see if Dr. Owens has time for a consult with Mrs. Tompkins this week? The diagnosis is new onset afib."

"I'll call Cecile and find out." I picked up the phone and keyed in Dr. Owens number from memory. "Hi, Cecile, it's Charlotte at Dr. Fox's office. Doctor is wondering if Dr. Owens has any openings this week for a new patient with new onset afib?" She checked the schedule and found a slot on Thursday at eleven-thirty. I gave her the patient's name, address, telephone number, insurance information and said I would fax over copies of her EKG, chart notes and her med list before I left this afternoon. After disconnecting, I wrote an appointment card for Mrs. Tompkins, went to the exam room door and knocked. Irina opened the door and took the card. I heard the doctor call, 'Thank you, Charlotte,' as I turned and went back to my desk.

Fifteen minutes later he came back into the office area. "Charlotte, will you drop my suit coat at the cleaners on your way home this evening?"

"Yes. Just leave it on that chair," I said, indicating the visitor's chair on the other side of my desk. He nodded and carried Mrs. Tompkins chart into his office, swinging the door closed, but not all the way. The dry cleaner was in the direction that I traveled home. He traveled in the opposite direction. It was something I often did for him as it really wasn't a big deal to pull in, drop off the jacket, tie, shirt— whatever— and then pick it up two days later. He always reimbursed me.

"Charlotte! Could you refresh my coffee?"

I went to get his mug. It had barely been touched but was now too cool. I took it to the kitchenette, dumped it down the drain, rinsed the cup and prepared a fresh, hot cup, taking it to him. He looked up from the chart notes he was handwriting and gave me a smile. "I don't know what I'd do without you. You're my right hand…uh…woman."

"Oh, you'd find someone else who'd do the same things I do. Secretaries are a dime a dozen in this world." I went back to my desk and called the answering service to let them know the office was closing. Rebecca said, "Hey, have a great Secretary's Day tomorrow!"

"Yeah, right. Does any employer even know that day exists?"

"Oh, sure! Lots of bosses buy their secretaries flowers or candy, or treat them to lunch or just, you know buy them a coffee or something, maybe give them a card."

"I don't work for one of those bosses," I said. "Goodnight!" I hung up the phone, got up and went out into the waiting room to straighten up the magazines, toss away the trash the patient's left behind on the tables and chairs, and sometimes the floor. Occasionally I found a pair of glasses, a scarf, an insurance card or a pair of boots someone had left behind. I had a lost and found box in the office. There were still quite a few items in it. How could someone lose a cane and not remember where they'd left it? I had three propped in a corner behind my desk beside a file cabinet.

Irina had finished cleaning the exam rooms. Stripping off her pink gloves she stuck her head around the door and said goodnight. I wished her a goodnight and then went back out into the waiting room to make sure the door was locked. Returning to my desk I found Mrs. Tompkins chart on my blotter, Dr. Fox's suit coat on my chair. I could hear him moving about in his office, getting ready to leave for the day. I opened the chart, grabbed the chart notes, EKG readout and med list and then faxed them to Dr. Owens' office with a note. I put all the paperwork back into the chart then set it aside to post tomorrow morning.

Dr. Fox came out of his office. He had rolled up his shirt sleeves, loosened his tie. His sunglasses were propped on top of his head. "Not a bad day, Charlotte. Do you have plans for tonight or are you just going home for a quite dinner and some relaxation?"

"I don't have any plans. I'll probably just reheat last nights' leftovers, run to the grocery store to get a few things for the rest of the week, and then go back home and read."

"I think I'll head over to the country club for dinner, see if anyone's around who might want to play nine holes before it gets dark."

"All right. Got your pager on?" He patted his belt and nodded. "Cellphone?" His hand went to his front pocket where I could see the outline of his phone against his thigh. "Keys?" He gave me a wry smile, held up his key ring. "You're good to go. Goodnight, Doctor."

"I have a first name, you know," he said.

"Yes, I'm aware of that." His first name was Andrew, but a lot of people called him just Drew. I guess he preferred that to Andrew. "Goodnight."

"Goodnight, Charlotte. See you tomorrow."

He left. I watched through the window to make sure that he closed the door completely behind him. One night he hadn't and some weird guy had wandered in and it had been both scary and frustrating as he hadn't wanted to leave. I'd had to call the security guard up from the lobby to remove the man, who had mental issues, from the office. It had left me pretty rattled. You never knew these days.

I finished up a few things, shut down the computer and then gathered up my shoulder bag, lunch bag, my sweater and the doctor's jacket. Glancing at the clock I groaned. I would have to rush to get to the cleaner's before they closed at six.

Wednesday morning came too early, as most weekday mornings have the habit of doing. I unlocked the office, switched on the lights and air conditioning, booted up the computers, got the sound system running with some nice soothing music. I made sure the charts were in order, and then started the coffee maker. I noticed the doctor had spilled some coffee on his white coat so I stuffed that one into the laundry hamper that the laundry service picked up once a week and got out a crisp, clean coat from the closet and hung it on the hook behind the door.

Irina straggled in with her extra-large espresso and a giant muffin. She sat hunched forward at the small table in the kitchenette munching her muffin while listening to tunes on her iPod. I checked the faxes that had come in, initiated a prior authorization for a procedure for Mr. Noonan. Irina trudged through carrying the remains of her coffee, not looking anymore wide awake than she had when she'd first walked in. I fixed myself a cup of coffee and then sat down behind my desk.

Dr. Fox was ten minutes later than usual. He seemed somewhat distracted as he passed my desk and didn't even say good morning. I thought perhaps his golf game had gone poorly last evening. I got up and went to fix him a cup of coffee. As I turned I saw he was standing at my desk, a confused expression on his face. "Is something wrong, Doctor?" I asked.

"Uh…no. Well…yes…but I'll take care of it." He started for his office, stopped looked back at my desk, saw I had a cup of coffee there, and then looked at the cup in my hand. "Is that for me?"

"Yes."

"Thank you, Charlotte." He came and took it from me then went into his office and closed the door completely, something he rarely did unless he took a patient in there to give them bad news.

I sat down at my desk, picked up a pen and sat there tapping it on the blotter, thinking. Irina came and stood before my desk, rapping her knuckles on the wood as I had been lost in my own thoughts evidently. I looked up at her. "You want me to unlock the door so the patients can get in, or what?"

I glanced at the clock and saw that it was a few minutes to nine. How on earth had ten minutes passed so quickly! "Go ahead," I told her. "I was just thinking about someone."

"Got a new boyfriend?" she asked, giving me a half grin.

I shook my head. My last boyfriend had been a disaster as had been the two prior to him. I had seriously been thinking about remaining single, adopting a dog. Men my age were impossibly immature and seemed to only be interested in sex, not really the woman they were with, just what she could do for them in the bedroom, or wherever else they felt the urge. I was tired of being viewed as one dimensional and worried about anything I might agree to do showing up on social media for all the world to see. I liked my private life to be exactly that, private. Guys seemed particularly enamored of their cellphones these days.

A rap on the glass window startled me. It was Mr. Grant, checking in for his nine o'clock appointment. I checked him in, made sure everything in his chart was in order, let Irina and the doctor know the first patient was here. Irina came and got the chart, called the patient in. Doctor Fox came out of his office tucking his hands into his white coat pockets. He had on an orange sherbet colored shirt today, a tie with silver, orange and navy blue stripes. He had matched it up with khaki slacks. "Charlotte? Have you seen my prescription pad?" he asked, pulling his empty hands from his pockets, turning them palm up to show that he had not found it.

"I saw it on your desk last night. It's not there?" I got up and walked toward his office. He stepped aside so I could go through. His prescription pad was exactly where I had seen it last night. I walked to his desk, grabbed it and turned toward the door, but I'd seen something else on his desk that made me turn back, a puzzled expression on my face. There was a card in a pale green envelope propped against his coffee mug. The envelope had my name scrawled across the front. "What's this?" I asked.

"I guess that's for you," he replied. He had come partway back into the office, his hand extended for his prescriptions. I absently handed him the pad. "It's Secretary's Day," he said.

"Oh. Right." I picked up the envelope and his cup. Turning I saw he was looking at me. "It's just, well, you've never gotten me a card before."

"No, I never have," he admitted. "I really had never thought about it and I apologize for that. You're a damn fine secretary and I appreciate everything you do."

"Well, thank you." I walked past him since he didn't seem inclined to move. He followed me out into the reception area.

"I couldn't imagine this office without you."

"Are you worried that I might leave?" I asked. "Did someone at the club tell you Doctor Urbanski is looking for a new secretary and now you're worried I might apply?"

"Will you? Apply?"

"No. Why would I even consider that? I'm happy where I am."

"Are you happy?"

I gave him a look. "You know, Mr. Grant is in there waiting to see you. I said I was happy. Now go make him happy. His reports came back negative." I waved him toward the examining room. "Go! Do your job."

He started for the door, but hesitated again, turned back. "Charlotte?"

"What?"

"Can you book a reservation for six-thirty tonight at Luigi's?"

"For how many?"

"Just two."

"Six thirty, all right. Your usual table?"

"Yes," he replied, and then he was frowning, shaking his head. "No, not the usual table. I'd like one…uh…a quiet booth. Something more…" He shrugged and some pink flared in his cheeks. "Something more intimate this evening."

"All right then. I'll take care of that for you."

"Thank you, Charlotte." He quickly went into the examining room and I heard him cheerfully greeting Mr. Grant as he swung the door closed.

Now I was beginning to understand his peculiar behavior this morning. He had met a woman at the country club last night. She must be something else if he was asking for an intimate booth at his favorite Italian restaurant for tonight! I looked up the number in my Rolodex and jotted it down on my To Do list pad as the restaurant wouldn't be open until ten. I sat there staring at the number, hoping that he hadn't picked up some trolling bimbo like his last wife, someone who would spend his money and make him miserable. He hadn't mentioned that he was seeing anyone, hadn't acted like he was until this morning, so he must have met her only last night. My stomach sort of clenched at the thought that someone else was going to take advantage of a very nice man who deserved so much better than what he'd had in the past. He didn't seem to have much luck in the romance department. But then again, neither had I.

At ten o'clock I booked a secluded booth at Luigi's for six-thirty for Dr. Fox. At ten-twenty a rap on the glass window surprised me. It was a floral delivery man and he had a crystal vase of beautiful flowers in shades of yellows, purples, deep blues and white. "For Miss Charlotte Redding," he said.

"That would be me," I replied, although I had no idea who would be sending me flowers.

"Have a great day!" he said as he turned and quickly left.

There was a card with the flowers. I put the vase on my desk, plucked the little white envelope from the plastic trident tucked into the flowers, sat down and pulled out the card. 'Happy Secretary's Day to the best secretary ever, Drew Fox' Well, a card and flowers this year! He must have overheard some men discussing Secretary's Day last evening at the club and realized he had a secretary after five years—and actually remembered to swing by a drug store and buy a card on his way in. But when had he ordered the flowers? Is that why he'd closed the door to his office this morning? To order them? That was a pretty fast delivery if they had gotten here in just over an hour. No—he had to have ordered them yesterday at the very least. He had to have been thinking about this for a day or two, and that made me feel an odd warm sensation in the vicinity of my heart. He had put some thought into Secretary's Day this year, but I still didn't know what the catalyst could possibly have been.

When he came out of the examining room after seeing Mrs. O'Brien his eyes fell on the vase of flowers on my desk and again color stained his cheeks as he glanced at me and then looked quickly away. "Thank you," I said. "They're beautiful."

"Glad you like them," he murmured as he went through into his own office.

This was turning out to be a very unusual day. A card, flowers and now it was as if he was suddenly uneasy being around me, almost as if he was shy and uncertain! I shook my head, got up and went to the kitchenette to fix him a fresh cup of coffee. Tapping on his door I heard him say I could enter. He was at his desk handwriting notes in Mrs. O'Brien's chart. I exchanged his empty cup for the full one. He kept his head down, busily writing. I turned and walked back to the door. "Charlotte?"

"Yes, Doctor?"

"Were you able to make that reservation for this evening?"

"Yes. You're all set for six-thirty." I heard him murmur a quiet thank you as I pulled the door shut behind me.

He continued to behave strangely for the rest of the morning and that began to make me uneasy. I normally eat lunch at my desk, but today, I left the office and treated myself to lunch at the café on the corner. The counterman, Johnny, flirted with me a bit as usual. He liked redheads, he'd told me the first time I'd eaten lunch there five years ago. Today he told me I was the prettiest redhead he'd ever seen. Flattery would get him nowhere. He was at least fifty-something years old to my twenty-seven. I didn't mind a man up to ten years older than me, but thirty years older was a bit out of my dating range. I thanked him for the compliment, left him a nice tip and returned to the office.

I found a wrapped package on my desk. It was a one half pound box of cherry cordials, my favorite candy. At Christmas I usually treated myself to a box and left it on the corner of my desk where Irina and the doctor could help themselves. They didn't last long. I opened this box and put it at the corner of my desk after helping myself to one. By now I knew who they must be from. He really was trying to make up for five years of neglecting me on Secretary's Day!

When he returned from lunch he walked past my desk and went into his office. I got up and rapped on the door frame as he'd left the door open. He was exchanging his suit jacket for his white coat, but glanced at me. "You're spoiling me today," I said. "Thanks again."

"I just want you to know how I feel about you," he replied, not meeting my eyes.

"I've gotten the message." I turned, and said, "I'm not leaving you, okay? You're stuck with me for the duration."

"Glad to hear that," he replied.

And that was all he said to me that afternoon, except for the usual, "Charlotte, can you do this," and "Charlotte, can you do that." Things seemed to be getting back to normal now that his gift giving was complete.

His appointment with Mrs Stephens, a notorious hypochondriac, ran overtime. Irina looked annoyed as she had to stay in case the doctor needed her. I had to stay as well, to lock up the office. I wasn't as annoyed as Irina, who had a date, because I didn't have a date and was just going home. There was really nothing there that urgently required my presence. At five forty-five Irina came breezing through. "He's done. I'm outta here!" She grabbed her bag and flew out the door. I could hear the doctor and Mrs. Stephens exchanging a few more words and then she came to the window to schedule a follow-up appointment, and he went into his office. I got her appointment booked and saw her out, closing and locking the door behind her. I straightened up the waiting room, peeked into the examination room. Irina would have to be in early tomorrow to straighten it up. That wasn't my job. I switched off lights, closed the door, returned to my desk, shut down my computer and then went into the kitchenette to dump the coffee carafe and wash it.

At six-ten I was ready to call it a day. I gathered up my things and had just bent to give my flowers a parting sniff when Dr. Fox came out of his office, adjusting his suit jacket. He looked good in khaki. "Are we done here?" he asked. I nodded. "Let me walk you down to your car."

Since I was leaving, and he was leaving, I just nodded. We took the elevator to the basement parking garage. We had first level reserved spaces. "Goodnight," I said. "Thanks again for the card, flowers and candy. That was really sweet of you."

He stood behind my car as I walked to the driver's door. There was a folded piece of paper tucked under the rubber strip. I snatched it out, annoyed. Solicitations appeared fairly regularly tucked beneath the windshield wiper for local businesses. I sort of scrunched it up and was going to throw it into the car when I got in when Dr. Fox said, "Maybe you should look at that."

"It's just an ad," I replied. My eyes met his and something about the way he looked, sort of anxious, made me smooth out the paper and then unfold it. It was not a flyer but a handwritten note that simply read, 'Please join me for dinner tonight, Drew.' My hand was suddenly shaking. "Oh," I said aloud.

"We have reservations for six-thirty. If we leave now we'll just make it in time," he said. "Please, Charlotte, will you have dinner with me?"

"Is this part of Secretary's Day?" I asked. "Because, really, you have done too much for me as it is."

"No, it's not for Secretary's Day. This is…" He paused, struggling to find the word he wanted. "This is, uh, personal. Not work related."

My heart gave a bit of a jog in my breast. He was asking me out to dinner on a personal level. This was a…holy smoke! This was a date! My arms beaded up with goosebumps. "All right." I tried to be nonchalant about refolding the note and tucking it into my bag but my hands were still shaking. He must have noticed that by now. "Are you driving?" He nodded.

Conversation petered out to practically nil during the drive as neither one of us was used to being with the other after working hours, but whenever our eyes met across the center console of his Lexus sedan we smiled at one another, albeit somewhat awkwardly. "You do like Italian, don't you?' he asked as he shut the car off. We had reached the restaurant and parked.

"Yes. I love spaghetti and meatballs." I glanced down at the pale yellow dress I was wearing and its matching cardigan.

He gave me a wry smile, knowing exactly what I was thinking. "I've never seen you with so much as a crumb on your clothes," he said, "whereas, you are forever taking my jackets, ties and shirts to the cleaners."

"I'm a little nervous this evening," I replied.

"We'll muddle through," he assured me. "I mean, we've spent quite a bit of time together these past five years. You probably know more about me then I know about you though. We'll fill in some blanks maybe?" I nodded.

We were seated in a booth practically hidden from its neighbors and the nearby tables by large potted ferns and strands of twinkly white lights. There was soft Italian music playing in the background, a candle flickering in a jar on the table. He asked if I drank wine. I said I would have one glass, not to waste his money buying a whole bottle.

I declined an appetizer. I was still feeling nervous, my stomach all fluttery. We ordered salads. He ordered chicken parmesan with penne pasta. I ordered shells with meatballs in sauce to be on the safe side. He ordered a red wine to go with the meal, a glass apiece. We were served warm breadsticks and our water glasses were filled.

"Where are you from originally?" he asked after toying with a breadsticks for a few moments.

"I grew up on Cape Cod, actually. In Yarmouth."

"That must have been nice."

I wrinkled my nose. "Too many tourists clogging the roads and beaches. My family always vacationed in Maine, believe it or not."

"At the beach?"

"No, Sebago Lake. My parents had a summer cottage there."

"So the ocean girl vacationed in Maine at a lake." I nodded. "You're very fair-skinned."

"I have to slather on the sunscreen, the maximum SPF."

"Does skin cancer run in your family?"

I shook my head. "No, it doesn't, but don't ask me medical questions, okay? I'll feel like you're examining me rather than dating me."

"Sorry, bad habit." He broke the breadstick in two, looked at both halves, and then bit the end off one and chewed it thoughtfully. "What do you like to do outside of work?"

"I read a lot. I paint sometimes, when I have time."

"Paint? Do you mean acrylics? Or oils?"

"Water colors. I like the delicacy of the colors and how they can be washed out to just a mere hint of color." He nodded. "Do you have any hobbies? Besides golf?"

"Golf is strategy and exercise. I'm a woodcarver. That's my hobby." He held up his hands and I noticed some scars in his palms, a few shiny nicks on the backs of his hands. "From my early days. I don't maim myself as often anymore."

"What sort of things do you carve?"

"Oh, whatever—small animals, ducks, birds of prey, flowers, objects."

I was thinking. He had a nice peregrine falcon wood carving on a shelf in his office. I'd looked at it a number of times since it had appeared on the bookcase about three years ago. "Did you carve the falcon in your office?" He nodded. "You're very good then." He shrugged, pink staining his cheeks again.

"I'm boring," he said, setting the remainder of the breadstick down on his napkin. "That's the gist of things." He sipped some water. "Women find me incredibly boring." He nearly spilled the water setting the glass down and I realized he was just as nervous as I was. "I'll be upfront and honest with you. I don't go nightclubbing. I seldom attend parties. I'm not a very good host when it comes to having people over. I travel a little, but I don't go out carousing every night when I'm in a foreign country. I like to see the sites, visit museums, cathedrals, look at the architecture, visit bookshops and antiques marketplaces. I like antiques."

"Okay. Well, I can put your mind at ease about some things. I'm not a party girl. I prefer a quiet life. I occasionally wouldn't mind having family or a few close friends over for a cookout. I feel most at ease in small groups. I live modestly, but I'd like to travel someday. I like going to museums, too, because I'm interested in art. Books are my thing. I own a lot of books, more than my landlord should legally allow." He smiled at that. "I have a few antiques, but my space is limited where I live, due to my books."

"I have a library in my house," he said and my eyes must have lit up at that revelation because he relaxed a bit. As he was about to ask me something else our server appeared with our salads. I liked ranch dressing. He liked vinegar and oil. That was fine. I didn't like couples who did everything identically as if they were clones of one another. I found that disturbing. People should have differences. It made life more interesting.

"What kind of music do you like?" I asked.

"Classical, easy listening. Cultural." He looked almost embarrassed that he didn't like heavy metal, rock, and rap.

"Me, too. I have never listened to the radio in my car. I only play CDs of my choosing. Radio chatter is just so banal and insulting. Commercials are annoying."

"Well said!"

We ate our salads. Then he started talking a bit about his ex-wives. After a few minutes of trying to explain what had gone wrong in his previous marriages I held up my hand. "Shh! You surely didn't invite me to dinner to talk about Ashley and Olivia. I'm not interested in them. I am interested in you, so let's stick to that subject, okay?"

"Yes, sorry. You're right. I just…"

"We all have histories. Sometimes it's best to close the book on the past and start writing a new book that will take you into the future."

"You're right," he agreed. "You're absolutely right." He ate a few more bites of salad. "I've been doing some thinking lately."

"About the future?"

"Well, yes. But what I meant is, I've been finding myself thinking about you. Well, actually, I was thinking about the type of woman I really want and need in my life, so I started listing attributes on a notepad on my desk at home. As I was listing them I realized that I had you held up as the ideal woman and I was listing attributes you possess. I found myself wondering where on earth I would ever find someone like you. And the other day it occurred to me that I knew exactly where to find that woman. She was right there in my office quietly and efficiently keeping me on track every day, keeping me going without expecting anything in return."

"Well, I do expect a paycheck," I admitted.

"Yes, for the work you do, but not for the kind and thoughtful things you do every day, the things that make all the difference in my life. I feel that at times I've taken advantage of your good heart."

"No, you haven't."

"You're really a very lovely young lady. You aren't seeing anyone are you? Irina told me you weren't when I asked her last week."

"No, I'm not seeing anyone. My boyfriends have all turned out to be disasters of one sort or another. I really haven't been looking again."

"Would you be interested in exploring a relationship with me, on a personal level?"

He looked so worried that I would thank him for a nice dinner and tell him I preferred things to remain as they had been. "I'm here, aren't I?" And before he could say anything I plunged on. "Look, you'd better take your tie off before your dinner comes. Roll it up and stuff it in your coat pocket. Take your coat off, too. A shirt costs less to dry clean. No, better yet, give me your tie. It won't get so crushed in my bag and I'll give it back to you in the car." He was laughing now. "I'm serious. Italian restaurants are notorious for staining clothes."

"Are you sure it's the restaurant and not the patrons themselves who stain the clothes?"

"It could be a combination of the two," I conceded as he unknotted his tie, pulling it off over his head and handing it to me across the table. I finished untying it, quickly rolled it up and stuffed it into my bag. He removed his suit coat and hung it on the hook at the corner of the booth. Then he rolled up his shirt sleeves. He had nice hands. His arms glistened with golden hairs in the light from the lamp hanging above the table.

"You make me smile, and laugh," he said.

"Laughter is good medicine," I pointed out. "Did you know that's the absolute truth? It really is good for you to laugh?"

"Yes, I read an article on that recently." Our salad plates were whisked away and our entrees placed before us. The server set a glass of wine down to the left of our plates. When he had vanished, Dr. Fox lifted his glass. "May I offer a toast to my lovely, charming and sweet dining companion. You are not just the best secretary a doctor could ask for. You are much, much more and I apologize for not realizing this years ago."

"I wasn't ready for you to have that kind of realization years ago."

"Are you ready now?" he inquired quietly.

"Yes, I am." I looked across the table into his hazel eyes. He was six years older than me, not an impossible number to work with. He was a decent man. I had not discerned a whiff of scandal associated with his name in the five years I'd worked for him. He hadn't been able to keep his first two wives because they were looking for a glamorous lifestyle and he was not that sort of man. He liked a quieter life. So did I. I think we were pretty compatible in areas that mattered, so far. This was just our first date. "I'm not jumping into bed with you tonight," I said, just blurting it out since it was on my mind.

He was slicing his chicken. His eyes rose to meet mine. "Good, because my house is a mess at the moment, and your place sounds too crowded with books. We'll hold off on that until, well, I may need to hire a cleaning woman."

"How about, when you invite me over for a cookout in a couple of weeks, you know, some steaks on the grill, potato salad, corn on the cob, that sort of thing? You can invite me to come at say two o'clock and we can do some stage setting for the rest of the night together? I actually like doing laundry, putting clean linens on beds, fluffing pillows."

"I couldn't possibly expect you to wash my bed sheets so we can make love in a clean bed!"

"Well, when you test drive a car do you avoid every pothole or divot in the road? Do you steer around puddles, go easy on the cornering, never press the gas pedal a little harder than the sales associate is comfortable with?" He shook his head. "We need to see how well we work together to accomplish goals. We need to test drive our relationship. I don't want a cleaning woman thrown into the equation. Two is company, three's a crowd. I don't want someone else laundering our sheets. That's how rumors start."

He understood what I was saying. "All right. It won't be a pigsty by any means, but if you want to wash the sheets then you may do so. I can run the vacuum around or dust."

"That would be nice. Then after dinner, we can appreciate the fruits of our housekeeping labors at our leisure."

He was grinning now. I wasn't just good at painting on water color paper. I could paint a pretty picture in his imagination as well. "You see how happy you make me?" he asked.

"I do now."

"I only hope I can make you as happy as you make me."

I ate a bite of meatball. "You surprised me today with your thoughtful gestures. I didn't know what to think at first. But now I see you were just practicing, trying to see how I would react to the unexpected."

"I really didn't know there was such a thing as Secretary's Day. I heard about it at the club and that started the wheels turning."

I nodded. "Do you make good money?" He cocked an eyebrow at that. "It really doesn't matter, because I have a decent salary for a secretary. I could support you, but you might have to sell pencils on the street corner to afford country club dues and greens fees."

"Charlotte, really!" he cried and then he laughed. "I make an indecent amount of money. I no longer have to pay alimony. I never fathered any children so there're no child support payments, no college tuition monies to be set aside." He made a gesture. "Not yet anyway. I mean…I have nothing against children. My former wives were on birth control. They didn't want to be tied down with babies. They didn't even want to discuss the subject." He looked a bit uneasy. "Do you like children?"

"Of course I do. I have three brothers and a sister, all older than me. I have seven nephews and six nieces. I'm afraid if we have the families over to dinner that the place will be overrun with kids."

"Then we should have one or two ourselves or we'll feel like underachievers in the heir department."

"One or two would be fine, but I think a year or two of being able to live together, to solidify the relationship before introducing children into the circle of our lives would be practical."

"I agree. I just don't want to be forty and a first time father."

"Thirty-five or thirty-six isn't too old to be a first time dad, is it? I mean, you'd only be fifty-four when the first one graduates from high school and goes off to med school."

"Only if they really want to go to med school. If they want to study art I would not say no." I smiled. "Look at us, already talking about the future and it's only our first date."

"What about you? Brothers and sisters?"

"A younger brother and three sisters, one older, the other two younger. My older sister, Marie, is a doctor, an oncologist. My next youngest sister is a graphics artist. You and Penny might get along well, seeing as you're both creative people. Deborah works at a travel agency. She's married, has two small children, but her marriage is unstable. Mark is sort of a ne'er do well. Being the baby of the family he's never felt he could live up to any of the rest of us. He's currently in counseling."

"No one has a perfect family. If they say they do, they're lying."

"I have a good family."

"Me, too."

We finished our dinner, ordered plain cheesecake with a sprinkle of nutmeg and whipped cream for dessert, and coffee. Although it was almost nine o'clock by the time we were back in his car it seemed like we'd been together only a few minutes. "We'll have to do this again soon," he said. "Go out, have dinner, talk." I nodded in agreement. "Charlotte," he said. I turned my head and looked at him in the light from the dashboard. He smiled. "I like your name."

"I've noticed."

"You can call me Drew."

"I will, but not at work. I'm hopelessly old school. I think it would be disrespectful to call you Drew in front of patients and Irina. You're a doctor. You went to school for years to earn that title. I am not going to call you Drew at work, sorry. Just can't do it."

"I understand." He pulled out into light traffic, heading back downtown to the office where my car was still in the parking garage. "Not even in private in my office with the door shut?"

"I'd have to think about that…Drew." His first name on my tongue felt a bit strange but he smiled. "I actually like the name Andrew. How come you don't?"

"My father's name is Andrew. I just prefer Drew." Now I understood. He wanted his own identity.

"All right. I'll call you Drew outside the office." I looked out at the passing scenery, thinking. It had been a very nice night out and I hoped we'd be doing this again soon. We seemed to get along well. He seemed happy. I knew I was happy.

All too soon he was pulling up behind my car in the garage. "Well, here you are, safely delivered to your vehicle."

"I really had a very nice day, and evening. Thank you." I reached for the door handle but paused, turned my head and my eyes met his. "I'd like to kiss you goodnight, if you wouldn't think that was inappropriate."

"I was thinking the same thing. I don't think it would be inappropriate at all."

He leaned toward me. I leaned toward him. Our lips met. One goodnight kiss turned into several very nice kisses. I was reluctant to pull away but knew I had to. I could hear a guard's footsteps approaching down the nearby ramp, probably sent down to investigate the car just sitting there. "I have to go," I whispered.

"Maybe we can go to the new exhibit at the college art gallery this weekend?"

"That sounds great."

"And dinner after? Your choice of restaurant."

"Oh, I like Samuel's."

"Samuel's it will be then. Goodnight, Charlotte."

I opened the door and got out as the guard came around the corner. "Goodnight, Doctor," I said, swinging the door shut.

"Everything all right, Miss?" asked the guard.

"Yes, Dr. Fox and I had dinner and he brought me back to my car. I need to get home now. Tomorrow will be another busy day."

"Oh, now I know who you are. Charlotte, isn't it? Dr. Fox talks about you all the time. Best damn secretary in the building, he says. Took you out tonight for dinner to show you his appreciation on Secretary's Day, did he? Nice guy, he is. Well, I'll make sure you get on your way home safely."

"Thanks. Have a good night."

"Yeah, ought to be a quiet one. Wednesdays usually are."

I reached into my bag for my keys and came up with Drew's necktie. The guard cocked an eyebrow at me. Even though I felt heat flame in my cheeks I shrugged. "Guess I won't be dropping the boss's dry cleaning off on my way home tonight. The cleaner closes at six."

"There's always tomorrow," he replied.

I got into my car and was on my way home a few moments later. On the drive, I draped Drew's tie around my neck, the smell of his cologne teasing my nose. He always smelled so good. I was tempted to keep his necktie but then the realization that if things continued to go well with us I would soon have the man himself, not just his tie, to hold close occurred to me. That thought made me shiver and grin.

If we got married I wondered where we would honeymoon. That thought was prompted by my passing Palmer Travel. He'd said he liked to travel a little, but it seemed he had me calling the travel agency quite often. As I was sitting waiting at the next red light for the light to change a fragment of our conversation popped into my head. He had mentioned he had a sister named Deborah who was a travel agent. She was the sister whose marriage was in trouble. Was she the Deborah Yardley he was talking to? It must be. He was clearly concerned about her and keeping in touch like a good big brother would. That said a lot about his character, too.

A short time later, at home, snuggled in my bed, his tie draped over my headboard, I hugged my pillow and smiled. My previous four Secretary's Days working for Dr. Fox had been unmemorable but this one…I didn't think I would ever forget it.

A SPECIAL VALENTINE

I was glad that I worked in a school that still allowed the children to exchange Valentines on the fourteenth of February. I liked my first grade class and thought I was pretty lucky to have twenty-eight boys and girls I really enjoyed teaching. Oh, a couple of them were a challenge at times but around the various holidays they all seemed more eager and focused on the planned special events than they were on teasing and tormenting one another. My room mother, Mrs. Douglas, was bringing a variety of chocolate and vanilla cupcakes that were approved by the parents and school nutritionist. They contained nothing that the children were allergic to or could not eat. We did not have any gluten free diets to worry about, no chocolate allergies. Candy Kisses had also been okayed. So cupcakes and Kisses were going to be served. The children had been busy earlier in the week designing valentine decorations that I had spent an hour and a half after school yesterday hanging up all around the room. I had heart-shaped stickers to hand out. And the kids had made their Valentine mailboxes from whatever box or container they had been able to bring from home, or if they couldn't get one, I'd had some on hand. These had been decorated with all sorts of materials—pieces of fabric, lace, ribbon, sequins, flat-backed jewels, stickers, paint, construction paper, tissue paper and whatever else I had been able to scrounge from various sources. Most of them were very colorful and creative. I had made my own mailbox from a cylindrical oatmeal container I had covered with shiny red wrapping paper and then decorated with white lace, pink ribbons and a string of tiny plastic pearls.

I don't care how old or grown-up you are, the excitement of receiving a valentine stays with you all of your life. I always enjoyed the valentines that I got from the kids. I had a scrapbook I'd started back when I was a student teacher. I'd been teaching first grade now for five years. My scrapbook had lots of room for more Valentines still.

I walked around the classroom, fussing with this and that, making sure everything was perfect before the children came in from recess. Mrs. Douglas had set up the snacks on a side table. She had gotten some juice from the cafeteria and brought some small, red, plastic cups. She was a miracle worker.

Every desk had a mailbox on it, and I had already distributed my Valentines and stickers in them, each envelope personally addressed. The students had been told to bring twenty-seven Valentines in plain envelopes. The Valentines had to be signed with their first name only. They could bring a teacher Valentine and one for Mrs. Douglas if they wanted to but it was not mandatory. Mrs. Douglas had a pink paper-covered shoebox on her snack table with a slot in the top.

The bell rang and I hurried to get my coat. "Here we go," I said to her as I headed out the door and she smiled.

I slipped on my coat and went to meet my class outside to lead them back into the building to their lockers and then to the classroom. I liked how all their cheeks were rosy from being out in the cold. I handed out a few tissues to those with runny noses from the cold air as they passed by, hopefully saving a few coat sleeves from being used for nose wiping in the process. Little Sarah's glasses fogged over and she nearly collided with Gregory as she flailed about as if she had gone blind. I grasped her hand and said,

"This way. Let's walk in a straight line." I guided her to her locker and by then two dots had cleared in the center of her lenses giving her an owlish look, bright blue irises peering through the remaining fog. She grinned at me and I smiled back. "Okay, boys and girls! Let's get our coats, hats and gloves off and neatly put back into our lockers. Andrew, stop that! Put your scarf in your locker, please!"

Somehow I got them all back into the classroom and into their seats, although they could hardly sit still. "Miss Vance?" cried Rebekah, her arm up, hand waving to get my attention.

"Yes, Rebekah?"

"I brought you a valentine!"

"Thank you. Now, I want you all to take out your cards. We're going to start with A row. Everyone in A row is to place a card in a mailbox. Go row by row please. Do not hurry. We have plenty of time. Please do not miss anyone, and that includes your fellow students in your own row. Please do not put a valentine in your own mailbox or you may be short a card for someone else. Also, please do not open your mailbox until all cards have been delivered and I tell you it's time to open your mailbox. After cards are all delivered we're going to start with F row. F row will be first to visit Mrs. Douglas at the snack table. Please take one cupcake, four Kisses and a cup of juice if you want some and then return to your seat. Does everyone understand what they're to do? First we deliver cards, then we get our snacks, and then we can eat and open our valentines." They nodded, squirming in their seats in anticipation. "All right then, A row, let's deliver the mail!" I said.

I watched them as carefully as I could, redirecting attention back to the task at hand if necessary. I was happy to see little white envelopes being dropped into Mrs. Douglas's pink mailbox and heard a few get deposited into my cylindrical red box behind me.

The distribution of the cards went well. Then F row went up for their snacks. One cup of juice was spilled but Mrs. Douglas quickly sopped up the spill with paper towels with no rebuke to the child who had knocked it over. Accidents happen.

When the last student in A row had gotten his snack and was back in his seat I gave a nod to the opening of mailboxes and their valentines. I helped myself to a vanilla cupcake with pink icing and then sat at my desk. "Open your cards, Miss Vance!" Kyle called from row C seat four. He was a husky boy with a blonde bottle brush haircut and brown eyes. He grinned at me. "I put one in there for you!"

"That was very nice of you, Kyle. Thank you."

"I gave you one, too!"

"Me, too!"

"Let me open them and then I will thank all of you." I pulled my mailbox over and popped the plastic lid in which I had cut a wide slot to make it easy for the kids to drop their cards in. I dumped the white envelopes out onto my desk and set the mailbox aside. There were quite a few small white envelopes and one larger cream colored heavier weight envelope. Someone's mother had probably purchased a single card for teacher. Maybe her child had messed up printing their name on the teacher card included in most boxed valentines for children to exchange at school.

I opened the cards and smiled. I loved looking at them and reading the often amusing things they said. I had a few duplicates but was surprised by the overall variety. I looked around to make sure everyone was still busy opening and looking at their cards, and then picked up the cream-colored envelope. I had to use my plastic letter opener to unseal it. I pulled out the card. It had a big red embossed heart on the front pierced by Cupid's arrow. It simply read—"Valentine" on the front. I opened the card and tiny white, red and pink foil hearts spilled out, most of them onto the desk but a few into my lap. Then I noticed that someone had glued a piece of ivory paper over the verse inside the card and hand-printed a message themselves. The message read, "Diane, please be my valentine forevermore. Will you marry me? Love, Jeremy." I gasped and looked up— and there he stood beside Mrs. Douglas who was looking at me with a huge smile on her face and tears in her eyes. And then I noticed all the children were absolutely silent and carefully watching me.

Jeremy came to the desk and held his hand out, taking mine. I stood up, still in a daze, not quite believing that this was happening. He led me to the open area in front of my desk and then got down on one knee, reached into his jacket pocket and produced a small, dark blue velvet box. "Miss Vance, will you marry me?" he asked, opening the box to reveal a beautiful diamond ring.

I glanced around the room at all the eager, expectant faces before returning my gaze to meet his warm brown eyes. "Yes, I will marry you," I replied, and my classroom broke into raucous cheers. Jeremy slipped the ring onto my finger and then stood up. "Does anyone want to see my pretty ring?" I asked. There was a rush of chairs being shoved back and a flurry of footsteps as I was swarmed by my students. I got hugs from all of them. Jeremy got quick hugs from the girls, handshakes from the boys and a few cocky winks as well.

Then, over the PA system came an announcement from the office. "Teachers, students, I am pleased to announce that Miss Vance has said 'yes'." Throughout the building I heard cheering coming from every classroom. Nearly all the children in grades two through five had had some exposure to me from first grade on. "Congratulations to Vice Principal Chandler and Miss Vance!"

"Aren't you going to kiss her?" asked Kyle.

"I'm not allowed to kiss Miss Vance in school," he replied. "But I can assure you that I will kiss her later when I take her to dinner tonight." That seemed to satisfy them. He smiled at me, squeezed my hand. "Very nice party, Miss Vance. I'm glad Mrs. Douglas invited me. Happy Valentine's Day everyone!" he said as he waved from the doorway.

"Happy Valentine's Day, Mr. Chandler!" they chorused, grinning and giving him thumbs up signs.

Mrs. Douglas began to clean up the snack table. I instructed the children to throw their envelopes into the recycle bin. Sarah stopped at my desk on the way back to hers. "Yes?" I asked.

She came around my desk and motioned for me to lean down so she could whisper in my ear. "The whole school knew about it," she whispered. "We did good keeping it a secret, didn't we?"

I smiled at her. "Yes, you all did a very good job keeping it a secret. Thank you. It was a wonderful Valentine's Day surprise." She returned to her seat, blushing and pleased with herself. "Thank you for the lovely, funny and sweet valentines. I'm going to tape them all into my scrapbook so I can look at them for many years to come." I looked at the ring and smiled. "And thank you, all of you, for keeping Mr. Chandler's secret. I can't believe the entire school knew about this and I never even heard a whisper about it!"

That night, as we enjoyed our candlelight dinner, I shook my head. "How on earth did you ever manage to pull this off?" I asked, still amazed that he had proposed to me in front of my class, and that the entire school had known he was going to do it.

"I got John's permission first, then Mrs. Priest who's friends with Mrs. Douglas told her and they hatched the Valentine's Day plan. The day you were out because you were in the ER after falling on the ice and badly spraining your wrist Mrs. Douglas and I talked to the class about the plan and made them all promise to keep it a secret from you. Word got out on the playground, as I thought it might, but incredibly they all kept it a secret. Mrs. Priest told the other teachers and pretty soon the entire school knew about it while you remained totally in the dark." He grinned and laughed. "We pulled it off! I can't believe it but the whole school kept the secret!"

"Well, my kids are never going to forget this Valentine's Day, that's for sure!"

"It doesn't hurt to let kids know there's still a little romance left in this world." He lifted his wine glass. I lifted mine and we touch them together across the table and then sipped our champagne. "I love you," he said.

"I love you, too, but I think we should get married in the summer. I'd love to have my class attend, but I think having twenty-eight kids, plus our own young relatives, running around at the reception might be somewhat distracting."

"Think about it and then let me know the date you choose and I'll clear my calendar."

I tossed a roll at him. "You'll clear your calendar!" I cried.

"We got engaged today," he told the waitress who had just arrived with our dinners.

"Congratulations! There're a lot of couples celebrating anniversaries and engagements here tonight. Good luck to you guys!"

I looked around as Jeremy dug into his steak dinner. It wasn't hard to spot the older couples celebrating their anniversaries. The seniors held hands across the table and weren't talking, just gazing at one another, remembering all their years together. The middle-agers were talking about their kids and home projects.

The thirty-somethings were smiling and talking, occasionally checking their cellphones. The twenty-somethings and teenagers were busy texting and taking pictures. I plucked my cellphone from my purse and Jeremy rolled his eyes. "Don't take my picture," he said. He was thirty-two years old to my twenty-eight.

"I'm not. I'm just updating my facebook status from in a relationship to engaged."

"Have you called your mother yet?"

"I did. Right after school I was on the phone with her. She's thrilled! I'm posting this now because I'm sure she hasn't had time to call all the relatives and they'd want to know because if someone doesn't tell them before tomorrow their noses will be out of joint." I finished sending the status update and then looked him in the eye as I shut my phone off. "I am *not* taking any calls tonight," I said. He got my message, reached into his jacket pocket, took out his own phone and did the same; he shut it off.

"Dessert here, or at my place?" he asked.

"I thought it would be nice to have dessert at my place."

And then we both laughed. We had actually been living together for a month now, only the school didn't know about it yet. Hardly anyone knew. And we'd continue to keep that fact quiet for now. We had plans to pool our savings to put a down payment on a nice condo we had already looked at. That would be our address when we were a married couple.

"Eat your dinner," he urged. "I'm hungry for dessert. It's my favorite."

I suppressed a grin as I picked up my fork and began eating. "Mine too," I said. "I like dessert."

He winked, and my heartbeat quickened. He really was my forever valentine, and I knew I would never forget this Valentine's Day either!

LOCKOUT RESCUE

Jennifer Shelton felt a sense of satisfaction as she cleared the last bit of snow from the trunk of her car. Smiling, she tapped the snow brush against the side of the driver's side rear tire to knock the remaining clumps of snow from the bristles before reaching for the rear driver's side door handle. Frowning, she looked at the handle. It was locked. She moved to the driver's door and lifted that handle fully expecting it to open but it too was locked. "Oh, fudge!" she said, bending to peer through the window at her beagle puppy in his carrier on the back seat. The puppy regarded her happily through warm brown eyes. "The doors are locked," she said to the puppy as a frisson of panic shot through her chest. The car was locked and running. She didn't have a lot of gas as she meant to stop at the gas station today on her way to the vet's since she'd gotten out of work late last night and just wanted to come straight home with the snow coming down like it had been. "Great," she muttered, standing up straight and looking at her neighbor's snow-covered cars and the empty slots where some of them had already left for the day. Her mind buzzed through her limited options.

Setting the snow brush down on the roof of her car she patted her coat pockets and smiled. Luckily she had been on the phone with the vet as she'd carried the puppy to the car ten minutes ago. She'd heaved her bag onto the front passenger seat and then stowed the carrier on the back seat. The snow brush had been on the floor in the back and she'd grabbed that as she'd backed out of the car and swung the door shut, disconnecting the call simultaneously before stashing the phone in her pocket and pulling on her glove again. She'd closed the door and that was when the front driver's door had most likely latched shut. She hadn't thought the car would lock itself while running, but evidently it had.

Removing her glove, she paged through her contacts list. Her parents were in Florida and would have been useless anyway as they lived eighty miles away when they were in Vermont. Her closest friend was in the hospital having her baby today. She'd gotten the text message last night saying she was heading to the hospital and would let her know when the baby had arrived. Her co-workers had all been talking about going skiing yesterday. She had forgotten to renew her AAA membership. Grimacing, she tapped in 9-1-1, not her best choice by far, but she was cold, the car was going to run out of gas and the puppy would freeze if she just stood there.

"What's the nature of your emergency, please?" asked a dispassionate female voice.

"I've locked my keys in my car. My car is running and my puppy is locked inside."

"Ma'am, this line is for emergencies only. Please hang up and call the fire department's non-emergency line. That number is…." And here she rattled off a series of numbers before abruptly hanging up.

Jennifer repeated the numbers she had heard three times and then typed that number in. "Bob's Tire Shop. Yes, we still have snow tires on sale," said a man's voice. He sounded somewhat harried and distracted.

"I'm sorry. I'm trying to reach the fire department," she said.

"Keep tryin', honey," he replied before hanging up.

"Well, of all the….!" Inside the car, the puppy woofed. Jennifer blinked tears of frustration from her eyes and tried a variation of the number she thought the dispatcher had given her, transposing the last two digits.

"Yo, this is Aaron, how can I help you?"

"Is this the fire department?' she asked tentatively.

"You on fire, sweetie? I can hose you down, put that fire out."

"Oh, my God," she said, disconnecting the call. She stamped her cold feet as she stared at the traitorous phone. Then she gave it one more try.

"Dave's All Power. Can I help you?" He, at least, sounded competent and friendly.

"Hi. I hate to bother you, but I'm at my wit's end."

"What's the problem?" he asked. "Maybe I can help you."

"It's stupid, but I've locked my keys in my car. It's running. My puppy's sick and he's in his carrier in the car. I can't reach the fire department. The 9-1-1 dispatcher gave me a wrong number! I'm desperate! Do you have the number?"

There was a long silence and then he said. "Are you here in Abington?"

"Abington? No, I'm in Prescott!"

"Oh, well, hold on, let me get on the computer and see if I can Google the fire department number over there."

"I'd really, really appreciate that," she said. She switched hands, burying her cold hand deep into her pocket. She heard the murmur of voices in the background. Then the phone slipped from her hand and fell in the snow. "Damn it!" she said aloud, crouching down to grab the phone and brush it off on her coat. "Hello?" There was a moment of panic when she heard nothing and then he was back on the line.

"Hey, where about are you in Prescott?" he asked. "Reason I ask is we got a guy who works here who lives out that way. He's a volunteer firefighter in Dana. He knows how to open cars with a slim-jim thingy. I think he carries one around in his truck. I can give him a jingle, see if he can run over and lend you a hand."

"Oh, that would be too much trouble for him!"

"Naw, he won't mind. He's a good guy. Likes helping people out. Give me your address and I'll send him over."

"But what if you call him and he says he can't come?"

"I'm going to call him on my cellphone while I have you on this line."

"Oh, all right. I'm at Willow Park condos on Winding Hill Road on the southwest side of town off route 11."

"Okay, hang on. Let me get him on the other phone."

Jennifer paced around the parking lot as he called his employee in Dana. She could hear a muted conversation, a bit of a cajoling tone then a louder, "Thanks, Billy! I owe you!" He was soon back on her line. "He's on his way. Said it would take him about fifteen minutes, depending on traffic. Watch for a black pickup truck."

"Oh, thank you so much! I really appreciate your help! I am freezing out here!"

"No problem, little lady. Bake us some brownies some time or something."

"I will! I promise!"

She disconnected the call and continued to pace, occasionally pausing to bend, tap on the window and talk to the puppy who had vomited in his cage. "Oh, ewww!" she said, wrinkling her nose. Her car would reek as she had the heat blasting in there to keep him warm.

It took Billy twenty-two minutes to arrive and her car had stalled by then. She was probably out of gas now, another dilemma. The black pickup came slowly through the lot. She waved. He slowed down, rolled to a stop and lowered the driver's window. "You the lock out girl?"

"Yes, that's me."

"Okay, let me get out of the way. I'll be right with you." He glanced at her car. "It's not running."

"I think I'm out of gas." He shook his head as he rolled the window back up, and then parked several spaces away where there was a clear area. He got out, rummaging around behind the driver's seat, grabbing something else before elbowing the driver's door shut and turning toward her. She stared at him, incredulous. He had stopped for coffee! He was going to drink hot coffee while she stood around half-frozen, her feet going numb even with boots on!

"Here, I figured you'd be an ice cube by now," he said, holding out the cup. "Don't know how you like your coffee so I got you hot chocolate. Everybody likes cocoa, right?"

"I would drink hot lemon juice right now, I'm so cold!" she replied, giving him a grateful smile. "Thank you so much!" She felt guilty now for thinking he was selfish and rude.

He gave her a wry smile before bending to peer into the car. "Hey, little fella. Have you reunited with your mistress in a jiff." He stood up, "Looks like he puked."

"He's sick. I'm trying to get him to the vet."

"What's his name?" he asked as he removed his glove and worked the thin strip of metal with the angled cut-outs down between the window glass and the rubber guard.

"Derby." He didn't say anything to that as he concentrated on breaking into her car. It gave her a few minutes to observe her rescuer. He was tall, lean in faded blue jeans that fit him very nicely, a red and navy blue ski jacket, navy blue watch cap. Sandy brown hair stuck out from beneath his cap and over his coat collar where it curled and looked slightly damp, as if he was not long from a steamy shower. Fleetingly her imagination placed him behind fogged over pebbled glass and she liked the outline she saw. Yummy! Then she noticed that he was looking at her expectantly and she blushed hotly. "Sorry," she said. "Did you say something?"

"I asked where the nearest gas station is," he said as he opened the door. "You're going to need some gas." He wrinkled his nose. "Poor puppy!"

"He's been throwing up since six o'clock this morning."

He stood looking at her for several long moments and then said, "Look, let's go get a clean towel. We'll change the one in the carrier, wipe his feet off, and then throw him in the truck. I'll get you both to the vet. We'll get some gas on the way back for your car."

"Oh, really, I can't put you out any more than I already have."

"How are you going to get to the vet on an empty tank?" He had amazing hazel eyes. And he had a point. "Go on, don't leave him standing in puppy puke."

She grabbed her bag, turned the car off, pulled the keys out of the ignition, and then hurried up the walk to her back door and let herself in. He had grabbed the carrier and followed her. "I just have to run upstairs for a clean towel," she said.

"We'll wait here." He set the carrier down on the granite counter.

Jennifer ran upstairs and was back soon with a clean bath towel. She opened the carrier door. He lifted the squirming puppy out and held him while she washed his feet with wet paper towels, then grabbed the messy towel and threw it into the sink. Folding the clean towel, she laid it in the carrier and he put the puppy back inside of it. He was smiling because Derby had been vigorously licking his scruffy jaw. "He likes you," she said.

"He's cute, but he's not my type," Billy replied. "Let's go."

They went back outside . The truck had an extended cab so he put the carrier in the back, positioned so that the puppy could see both of them in the front seats, and then got behind the wheel. Jennifer gave him directions to the vet's office. "I really appreciate this," she said. "Are you losing time at work?"

"No. I have the day off. My brother's getting married this afternoon."

"And you're wasting time helping me?"

He shrugged. "All I have to do is put on a suit. No big deal." He glanced at her from the corner of his eye. "How's the cocoa?"

"Hot," she replied and saw the corner of his mouth curve up. He put on sunglasses as they were heading into the sun. He looked positively roguish, like a ski bum. "Are you the best man?" she asked.

"Hardly," he replied. "My brother is actually my step-brother and we never really got along well. It's a token invitation. I'm going only because my mother will be hurt if I don't show up."

"Oh. It doesn't sound like you'll be having a fun afternoon."

"Nope. My life has not been much fun lately. Found out three weeks ago my girlfriend was running around behind my back with my best friend Greg. Threw her ass out. Last night she calls me wanting to come back because she found out Greg's cheating on her. She played the, 'Oh you need a date for your brother's wedding' card. I told her I was going stag, have a nice life, goodbye." He tapped his fingers on the steering wheel, clearly still agitated by the breakup and the girl's audacity. "Sorry. Didn't mean to dump that on you."

"It's okay. I'm a good listener."

He nodded. "What's your name? Dave never said."

"I don't think I told him. It's Jennifer."

They were stopped at a red light. He turned his head, lowered his sunglasses and peered at her closely over the top of them. "You look nothing like a Jennifer. You look like a Lydia." He gave her a quick wink before resettling his sunglasses and moving with the traffic as the light changed.

"Why do you say that?"

"Lydia seems like a mysterious name to me. Dark. With your black curls and dark eyes you look mysterious."

"No one's ever told me I look mysterious before."

"Well, you do. Do you have witches and sorceresses in your family tree?"

"No, but there's a horse thief, a counterfeiter, and a candy maker," she replied.

"Hmm, that candy maker sounds very suspicious to me."

She laughed. "Are you a volunteer police officer, too?"

He laughed. "No. I read a lot of books. Mysteries. Sci-Fi Fantasy. Books about police and firefighters."

"And you work full time at Dave's All Power?"

"How'd you know…oh, right. You called there and talked to Dave. Yeah, I sell ATVs, dirt bikes, tractors, lawn tractors, all sorts of stuff. And I repair it all too."

"You sound like a pretty handy guy."

He shrugged. "What do you do?" he asked.

"I'm a paralegal downtown."

"A not-quite lawyer?"

"Yeah."

"Okay, that's pretty cool, I guess."

"No, you think it's boring. I can tell."

"No, not really. What do you do for fun? Do you ski? Ice skate? Go sledding? You know, like Flexible Flyer sleds, or the big kid ones like Polaris or Arctic Cats? Do you play hockey?"

She laughed at that. "I am not a good skater, but I can ski. I haven't been sledding in years!" She glanced back at Derby. He was sitting in his carrier watching them. "I've never been on a snowmobile." She looked at Billy. "Do you play hockey?"

"Yeah. You should come to a game sometime. I play for Dave's. We have a game coming up." He turned into the vet's lot and parked. "Do you even like hockey?"

"Of course I do. I used to watch it all the time with my Dad. I like baseball and basketball too. But I am *not* a football girl."

"No sacks and tight ends for you?' She flushed and he grinned as he tossed his sunglasses onto the dashboard. "Let's get little Derby in for his sick visit." He carried the carrier in for her.

She thought he'd wait out in the waiting room when Derby was called in but he carried the puppy in and he stayed. They sat side by side as the vet technician weighed Derby and then took his temperature. Jennifer answered some questions. "Dr. Fontaine will be in shortly."

Billy held Derby, rubbing his ears, letting him lick his jaw again, cradling him in one arm, tickling the puppy under his chin. Derby was relishing all the attention. "I'm not a vet but I think you're going to be okay, fella," he said quietly. He looked at her. "What are you doing this afternoon?"

"Um…laundry?"

"That sounds boring. Why don't you come with me to this damn wedding? When I responded two months ago I said I was bringing Michele. That's *not* happening. I hate going to weddings alone."

"I thought you wanted to go stag."

"No, I just told Michele that because I'm not taking her. She had her shot at me. It's over. I've moved on. I don't want to look like a loser at his wedding." He kissed the top of Derby's head as the door opened and the vet came in.

"Hi," said the vet, glancing down at the chart. "Looks like little Derby has both his Mom and his Dad with him today. He's been having some vomiting? When did it start?"

"About six o'clock this morning."

"How often has he been vomiting?"

"Well, it's slowed down. He threw up three times and since then it's been just yellowish and foamy."

The vet nodded and then looked up, his eyes meeting her worried gaze. "Has he eaten anything he shouldn't have? Candy? Cigarette butt? Bacon fat?"

"Uh, no. Nothing like that. Just his usual puppy chow."

The vet looked at Billy. "Anything you're aware of?" he asked him.

"No. He chewed on a dirty sweat sock and then my sneaker for a bit but I don't think he swallowed anything." She looked at him, her eyebrows raised. He shrugged. "Just puppy chow. We're very careful, watch him like a hawk."

"Don't let him chew on your sneaker anymore. He could bite off a piece and choke on it."

"Okay. I'll throw them in the closet when we get home."

The vet turned to Jennifer. "It looks like gastroenteritis to me. Puppies get it. Their digestive systems are still developing. He might have simply eaten too much. I'll take him in the back and try to get a little stool sample and a urine sample. You didn't bring any of the vomitus with you?'

"No, he threw up in his carrier but we couldn't stand the smell of it so we cleaned it."

"It's okay. Light diet today. Buy a little boneless chicken breast and boil it. Chop it up fine. Mix in a bit of boiled white rice. Let him have a little water. Tomorrow he'll be feeling better."

"Doc, we have a wedding to go to this afternoon. It's at three o'clock. We should be home by seven at the very latest as neither one of us drinks or cares much for dancing. We don't want to leave the Derb alone for long. You think he'll be okay for four hours, or should we skip the wedding and stay home with him?" Billy asked.

"Do you have a gate? Can you confine him in the kitchen or bathroom? Put his bed there, his food and water and a few toys?"

"We can do that," Billy replied. He looked at me, "Right, Jen?"

"Um, sure. I, uh...we have a gate." The vet took Derby into the back. "I don't know what to wear to this wedding," she said.

"Wear that little black dress."

She started. "How do you...?"

He chuckled at her expression. "I *don't* know. I just heard that every girl has a little black dress in her closet."

"Have you ever been arrested?" she asked.

"No, but I got a speeding ticket once. I was responding to a fire. Didn't have my light flashing."

"Did he tear up the ticket?"

"Nope. I paid the fine. No big deal. I didn't have my wallet at the time either with my ID in it. My bad."

"Have you ever been in a serious relationship?"

"Once or twice. They were no laughing matter." He cocked his head. "I like to have fun, okay? I don't mean crazy, stupid, malicious fun. I mean, I like to go to the movies. I like skiing, skating, going to games, out to breakfast in my pajamas, but not the holey ones, the good ones. I like to go on picnics. I like to go fishing. I hang out at the bookstore, maybe go to a concert now and then. I like to go to museums and amusement parks. I like going to the park and hiking around. I wish I had a dog but I can't have one. I live in a no pets allowed apartment. I'd run around on the grass and then lie down on a blanket and take a nap in the shade with my canine companion, and my girl. That kind of stuff. It's hard to do it alone though because then it's not so much fun."

"I see."

"My serious girlfriends wanted to go to clubs and dance and drink. I don't drink. My Dad was an alcoholic. Mom finally divorced him and then promptly married Frank who brought along Brandon who is a year older than me. Anyway, my serious girlfriends found me boring." He shrugged. "So, what do you like to do?"

"I like making popcorn and then eating it while watching a movie while I'm wearing my pajamas and sitting in the dark in my bed."

"Scary movies?"

"Um, no. Action and adventure, mystery, funny movies. And I like going to the lake. I can sail. My dad taught me. I can paddle a canoe, too. I like picnics, hiking. I like to go to the beach. I like to go to baseball games. I like skiing. I can cross country ski and downhill ski. I like going to the bookstore, too. I'm surprised I've never seen you there."

He nodded. "So, if Derby's okay to stay alone for a few hours, will you go with me to Brandon's wedding?"

"I really should do my laundry."

"I'll help you do your laundry tonight."

"Uh…that won't be necessary. I'll do it tomorrow morning."

"You're not going to breakfast with me in your pajamas?"

"No! Not tomorrow!"

"How about next Sunday morning then?"

"We'll see. Let's see how the wedding goes first."

"I chose the chicken for you."

"For Michele, you mean."

"Yeah, well, she wasn't a big red meat eater. But you can have my prime rib and I'll eat the chicken, if you don't like chicken."

"Is it chicken cordon bleu?" He nodded. "I'll eat that."

The vet returned with Derby who looked anxious to go home. He squirmed as the vet handed him to Billy who took him and cuddled him. "No parasites. Light diet today and tomorrow morning, and then ease him back into his regular diet. He should be fine. And keep the sneakers in the closet. He looks like a happy, healthy little fellow."

"Thanks, Dr. Fontaine."

"Gate him in the kitchen and he should be fine for a few hours. Enjoy the wedding."

Jennifer paid while Billy took Derby in his carrier out to the truck. When she came out he said, "We should have brought his lead. I think he needs to pee."

"Let me see if they have one I can borrow." She ran back inside and came out a few minutes later with a bright yellow leash. He clipped it to Derby's blue collar and walked him in the snowy designated dog walking area with the fake fire hydrant. After, Jennifer returned the leash, came out and climbed into the truck.

    Billy drove her home, carrying Derby in for her. They had stopped at a gas station on the way back and he'd filled his two gallon red plastic can. He poured the gas into her tank and then got into the car and started it. "All set. We'll need to fill it up later." She nodded as he hung her keys up on the hook beside the door on the kitchen wall. "I need to go get a few things done and then shoot home and get dressed for the big wedding. I'll be back around two-thirty?" She nodded. "Don't worry, you'll look beautiful in whatever you wear. It's not formal. It's casual, okay? I'm just wearing my regular dark suit." She nodded. "Thanks for agreeing to go with me."

    "You did me a huge favor. I owe you," she replied.

    "Dragging you to a wedding where there'll be no one but a bunch of strangers is an even huger favor then unlocking your car, taking your puppy to the vet and getting you a couple gallons of gas."

    "It'll all balance out in the long run," she replied.

    He smiled at that. "Okay then, see you this afternoon."

    Jennifer watched him go. He smiled, waved as he pulled away. She closed the door, her heart beating quickly. "Oh, my God, Derby! He's cute!" She scooped up the puppy and cuddled him. "So are you, sweetie pie!" She laughed as Derby licked her chin. "Let's go upstairs and see what we have in the closet that will go with his dark suit. We'll show his stepbrother that he's no loser."

    She smiled as she carried Derby up the stairs. Hadn't Billy said they'd get gas for her car later? Did that mean he planned to stay and visit for a while after they'd gotten home from the wedding? How long would he stay? "I'd better do a little cleaning," she said, glancing at her rumpled bed, the damp spots on the carpet where Derby had vomited and she had cleaned up the mess, her laundry thrown about. "I've been playing too much with you and not doing my housework!" She set him on the bed and then lay down beside him. He pounced on her, tail wagging. She laughed. He licked her face, her ear. "Oh, don't get me all dog slobber and drool!" she cried, pushing him over and tickling his belly gently. "You need to take a little nap so I can get some things done." A few minutes later his eyes were half-closed. She rubbed his nose. He heaved a huge sigh, and then he fell asleep.

It startled her when her cellphone rang at noon. Frowning, she saw it was Dave's All Power. "Hello?" she said.

"Hi, is this J. Shelton, the lockout girl?"

"Yes. Is this Dave?"

"Yes, it is. I was just wondering how things turned out? I tried calling Billy but he's not answering."

"He's getting ready for his stepbrother's wedding."

"Oh, right. Brandon's getting hitched today to one of Billy's exes. How's the puppy?"

"He's fine. Sleeping."

"Good. So everything worked out all right?"

"Yes, everything went great. Thanks so much for sending Billy over. My car ran out of gas so he bought me a couple gallons on the way back from the vet's."

"He took you to the vet?"

"Yes, I had no gas."

Dave chuckled. "He's a good guy."

"Yes, he is," she agreed. "I'm going to the wedding with him."

"You are! Well, he wasn't happy about having to go alone. That Brandon has always been trying to one-up him since he was a kid. I don't like him. Smarmy bastard." He paused. "So, you're going with Billy to this wedding?"

"Yes."

"Your boyfriend doesn't mind?"

"I don't have a boyfriend. He was killed in a bike accident six months ago."

"Oh, sorry," he said, sounding uncomfortable for touching on a tender topic. "I'm sorry to hear that."

She looked out the window at the snow and nodded. It was time to let Luke go. "Thanks. Billy told me about Michele. I guess we both need to move on, get past the past."

"Yeah."

"Thank you for being so kind, and for sending him over to help me out."

"Not a problem, sweetie. I hope things go well for you, for both of you. You sound like a nice girl. Glad your puppy'll be all right."

"I'll bake you some brownies and send them over with Billy."

"No, you bring them over in person. Billy'll bring you over on a Saturday if you ask him to."

"Okay. I'll do that then."

"Nice talking to you, J. Shelton."

"Jennifer."

"Jenny. Hope to see you soon."

"Maybe next Saturday?"

"Sounds like a plan. Dress warm as we've got a hockey game against Macro Auto Sales next Saturday night. After the game we're all going to Swanson's Diner for something to eat. They have a big room in the back."

Jennifer smiled. "Sounds good. Bye, Dave. And thanks so much. You're the best. I really mean that." She hung up, glanced over her shoulder at Derby still asleep in the middle of her unmade bed. "Maybe he's the one, Derby. Maybe he'll turn out to be the right one."

She tossed her phone onto the dresser and then opened her closet. No, not the little black dress. She would look too monochromatic. The red was too vampish. The bottle green was too slinky for a casual wedding. She pulled out the ultramarine blue dress. She'd bought it for her cousin's wedding last winter but had come down with the flu the day before and had stayed home in bed. She'd wear the blue. It would go well with his dark suit if it was black, charcoal or navy. She still had the shoes to match. Perfect! "I need a shower!" She hadn't taken one this morning.

Glancing at the clock she saw that it was after twelve-thirty already. Two hours. In two hours Billy would be back and she wanted to be ready. She had no doubt that they would making a striking couple. He was quite handsome and she had been told often enough that she was a pretty girl although she saw herself as merely ordinary, nothing special. But, from the way Billy had been looking at her all morning she could tell that he had liked what he was seeing. He'd probably gotten the same message from her. She hoped the impromptu wedding date would go well.

At two-thirty she was pacing the kitchen nervously. Derby was sitting on the rug in front of the sink watching her. When there was a knock on the door he stood up, tail wagging and barked. Jennifer opened the door and caught her breath. He was gorgeous! "For you," he said, handing her a small box from the florist shop. He had not taken his eyes off her yet. "Christ, you're beautiful," he said. Then he reached into his coat pocket and produced a sheepskin covered plush toy. "And this if for you, Derby." He squeezed it, making it squeak. Derby jumped up, begging for the toy. Billy tossed it up in the air and Derby tried to catch it, but it glanced off his nose. He snatched it up and carried it to the rug where he tackled it and bit it, making it squeak. "I think it's a hit," he said. "I like the dress. Nice color on you." He looked at her more closely. "I thought your eyes were brown, but they're really very dark blue." She nodded. He picked up her coat from the back of the kitchen chair and held it for her. She slipped her arms into the sleeves. He settled it onto her shoulders, lifting her hair out from where it had been trapped inside. She turned and he started buttoning the coat for her. She looked up into his face. He buttoned another button before his eyes rose and met hers.

"Dave called," she said.

"He called you? Here?" She nodded. He looked confused. "How does he know your number?"

"He must have gotten it from the business phone memory."

"What did he say?"

"He said you have a hockey game next Saturday night, which is perfect because I can bring the brownies that I'm baking for him and give them to him there."

"You're making him brownies? Do you know him?" he asked, looking and sounding even more confused.

"No. I've never met him. But he helped me out once and I am very grateful for what he did."

His eyes met hers again and he looked into them for several long moments. "So am I," he said. "Very grateful. I'll have to buy him a case of beer to go with those brownies." He gave her a quick wry grin. "We're going to sit with my mom and stepfather. Her name is Catherine O'Brien. His is Sean O'Brien. Brandon is Brandon O'Brien and he's marrying Bridget Maguire."

"What's your last name?" she asked.

"Grant. I'm William Grant. I'm only half Irish."

"Happy to know you, William Grant," she said.

"Happy to know you, Jennifer Shelton."

"I hope I don't prove an embarrassment to you."

"I don't think that's possible," he replied. "Ready to go?" She nodded. "I'll pin your corsage on when we get to the church. It's a purple orchid. I got my mom a pink one because I doubt my stepbrother or Bridget thought to get her something."

"Billy," she said, reaching out to touch his arm as he turned toward the door. He looked back at her. "The bride may think she's the luckiest girl today, but she's not. It's me. I'm the luckiest girl." That made him smile. She loved his smile. This one reached his eyes. She liked how a light danced in their depths. She gave his arm a squeeze and then looked down at Derby who had come to sit at their feet. "Be a good boy. We'll see you in a few hours. We'll play with you when we get home." She was glad she'd gotten all her housekeeping chores done.

Billy liked how that sounded. Home. Jennifer. Derby. *Home.* A new hope rose in his chest. He was twenty-six years old. He was ready for something good to happen in his life, and he had a strong gut feeling that it had started this morning when he'd gotten the call from Dave about a desperate young lady locked out of her car with a sick puppy locked inside it. He'd rescued her this morning, and now she was rescuing him by going to this wedding with him this afternoon. If this went well, then maybe this evening he'd be playing with Derby and maybe kissing and cuddling a bit with Jennifer. Maybe she would make popcorn and they'd watch a movie and Derby would snuggle down between them.

"Can you stay for a while tonight?" she asked. "Do you want to watch a movie or something? I can make popcorn."

He wondered if she could read his mind but then he realized that she couldn't, not really. "That would be great. I need to swing by my place and change out of the suit into something suitable for watching a movie in."

"Bring your pajamas," she said. "Not the holey ones, the good ones. The ones you wear out to breakfast." He cocked an eyebrow at her. She flushed. "I changed my mind. I do want to go to breakfast with you tomorrow."

He opened the door of his truck and helped her up into the passenger seat. His hazel eyes met hers as he seat-belted her in. "I'd better bring my boots then. I heard we're getting another five or so inches of snow."

"Oh." Something flickered in her face, and then she said, "Bring your slippers then. We'll stay in and I'll make waffles instead."

His heart soared. She saw the darkness slip away from his features. "Then we'll also have to stop and get some chocolate chip ice cream on the way home. I have to have ice cream when I have hot waffles."

"Me, too," she said.

"Have you been here all along?" he asked.

"Yes," she replied.

"I'm glad I finally found you then."

Me, too." And then he kissed her. Jennifer's shuttered heart unlocked, releasing Luke and welcoming William Grant. "I'm glad you found me, too." She pulled his face back to hers, kissing him and then said, "We'd better go."

"Yeah," he replied. "But we're definitely leaving before the dancing starts. I am not a dancer."

"Me neither," she confessed.

He nodded. "Do I have lipstick now?"

She laughed. "Yes, you do." She dug in her little bag for a tissue, wiped his mouth and chin.

He got behind the wheel, glanced toward the condo and said, "Be back soon, Derb!"

Jennifer looked at her car hunched in the snowy parking space. She'd have to go get gas, but it could probably wait until tomorrow. Maybe he'd go with her and they'd pick up something for dinner. She wondered what he liked to eat. She hadn't cooked for anyone but herself lately. She liked cooking. And baking, which was good because she had to bake those brownies for Dave. And then she thought she just might bake a batch of brownies for the emergency 9-1-1 dispatcher, too. After all, if she hadn't rattled off the number so fast and confused her then she might never have dialed Dave's All Power and met Billy.

She looked down at the round corsage box she held on her lap. There was another on the dashboard for his mother. He was the kind of man who made sure his mother had flowers to wear at her stepson's wedding. He was the kind of man who made sure his girl had flowers as well. Although they had just met and their relationship was just beginning to bud, she felt as if she had been waiting for Billy since she was a teenager. She smiled.

"Penny for your thoughts," he said.

"They're worth more than that."

He smiled.

She forgot it was the dead of winter. His smile made her feel warm all over.

DRAGON AND BUTTERFLY

Darach Blackstone glanced up through his black bangs as the office door of the **The Flyleaf**, the college arts and literary magazine, opened. Inwardly he groaned as the girl named Nova, a recent transfer from a northern California university, came in. She was a petite girl full of energy and far too perky for his taste. She looked at him, flashing him a cheerful smile. "Hi!" she said. "You're just the person I was hoping to see here!"

"Yeah, well, I'm done. I'm leaving." He shoved the artwork he'd been looking at back into the folder as he rose from his stool.

"It'll only take a second," she said, depositing an armful of folders on the work table across from where he'd been sitting.

"I have a class to get to," he muttered.

"Oh, please! One second?" Before he could reply she shrugged out of her fringed leather jacket, draping it across the stool on her side and then started sorting through the folders. "It's here someplace. Hold on. I'll find it in a minute."

"A minute is too long. I've gotta go." He was shaking his head when she looked up at him, her eyes meeting his. She had corn silk-blonde hair that was long with a bit of natural wave to it. It was baby fine and flyaway, always coming loose from the thick plait she wore it tied back in. Wisps of white-blonde hair stood out like an aura around her face. Her skin glowed. She was the kind of girl who would burn to a crisp in the sun at the beach. This afternoon there was a flush of color staining her cheeks. Her eyes were an incredible shade of pure blue, like a cloudless summer sky in late afternoon. "Please, just wait, okay? I want to show you something."

"I can't be late for class," he said, forcing himself to look away from her eyes. Her gaze had an unnerving effect on him. He couldn't stand her incessant perkiness, her sweetness and utter lightness of being. She was the easiest going girl he had ever encountered—uncomplicated, earnest, honest, real—and he could not tolerate her in the least. At least he knew where he stood with every other girl on campus. They found him dark, dangerous, brooding and desirable. They found his darkness and surliness sexy. He didn't lack for girls wanting to jump into bed with him, that was for sure. He just didn't give a damn about any of them after spending a few hours with them. They were shallow, addicted to their damn phones, obsessed with their clothes, hair, nails and make-up. Always tweeting and texting and sharing photos with their girlfriends about who they were seeing, who they'd slept with. He'd been pissed off to discover a former girlfriend had only rated him a 5 on a scale of 1 to 10 for hotness in bed. Since then he'd been more or less avoiding all girls, his ego wounded by some stupid bitch who had been drunk at a party and all over him. He'd walked by her twenty times since then and she'd acted like she didn't even know who he was. Screw that! "I have to go."

"No, look!" She pulled something from the folder and held it up as he passed. "Darach, you have to see this!" she called after him. "It's perfect for the magazine, for your dragon picture!"

He walked out, pulling the door closed behind him, shutting her away alone in the room where he hoped her annoying brightness would be snuffed out before he had to see her again. She was like an irritant against his skin. She inflamed his brain. "I need to quit the magazine," he muttered as he pounded down the stairs to the first floor.

Nova stared a moment at the closed door before slowly turning back to the table and laying the curious yet lovely poem about the fire breathing dragon that she had found among the literary submissions down on the table. Reaching across the table she pulled the folders of artwork over and began going through them, looking for the pen and ink drawing Darach had done of a fire breathing dragon. She found it in the third folder. "This is perfect," she murmured, smiling to herself. "They go together so naturally."

She set them aside together and then went to get a glass of water before turning on the computer to work on the magazine layout. She had been on her previous college's art and literary magazine staff freshman and sophomore year. In her junior year she had been editor. She was glad that Hawthorne-Ivory College had an art and literary magazine. The English Department professor who was the magazine's advisor, Professor Julianne Jameson, had been thrilled to accept her application to join the staff. She'd been put in charge of layout, which was something she had never done before. She was finding it challenging but fun.

She had been worried about not fitting in on campus here on the east coast but so far everyone she had met had been very welcoming and friendly toward her. Well, everyone except Darach. He was just one of those people who was always difficult to get along with, she supposed. There had been a few of his kind in California as well. Her philosophy was to treat everyone nicely, no matter what. If he didn't like her, so be it. She wasn't going to change anything about herself to try to please him. They could work together on the magazine and be civil to one another. It wasn't like she was interested in him at all. Being around him was like standing in the shadow of a tall skyscraper that blocked the sun. He was about a foot taller than her sixty-one inches, lean and sinewy. He played soccer, ran track and was on the fencing team. She'd been to the fencing meet last month. He fenced saber. It had been exhilarating to watch his bouts, but also nerve-wracking as she hadn't realized how brutal fencers could be with one another to try to score a point. She'd walked over to say hello to him after his bouts when he was sitting on the floor amid the team gear. He'd had his jacket off, was in knickers and a thin t-shirt. His arms had been like a kaleidoscope of colorful bruises from yellow to green to violet to deep purple. His hair had been damp and spikey from his running his long fingers up through it, pushing it back from his face. He'd looked up at her as if she was an annoying mosquito he wanted to swat away. All she could think to do was hand him the granola bar that had been in her jacket pocket at the time because he'd looked hungry. It was honey oat. He hadn't taken it, so she'd quickly crouched down, placing it on the floor beside him, murmuring, "You fence dramatically." He had not said one word to her so she'd walked away. At the exit she had turned her head, looking back at him over her shoulder. He'd been eating the granola bar, talking to a team mate. The rejection hadn't stung so bad knowing that he had needed the granola bar to refuel for his next bout.

    She worked on the layout for an hour and a half before her stomach reminded her that she needed to think about grabbing something to eat. She saved what she'd done, shut down the computer and then gathered up all the submissions materials and placed them all in the appropriate file cabinet drawer. She pulled on her brown leather jacket, zipping it. It was mid-October and when it grew dark early like this it could get chilly quickly.

    Slinging her leather pack over her shoulder, grabbing the book she had bought at the campus center bookstore, she turned off the lights and left the office, securing the door. Luckily the English

Department office was still open. She returned the key to Mrs. Taylor, the department secretary who smiled at her. "How's it going?" she asked.

"Slowly but surely. It should be an awesome issue when it's all put together," Nova replied.

"I can't wait to see what you're all doing. There's so much creativity on campus this year."

"There certainly is." she agreed. "Goodnight, Mrs, Taylor."

She was crossing a dark area of the campus when a voice said, "Hey, there's Miss Goody Two Shoes!" Nova knew immediately who it was and hoped he wasn't with his friends who were equally obnoxious, but he had to have been talking to someone, right? Not just talking at her about her?

"You know what they say about those California girls," replied his friend.

"I'd like to surf her waves."

"Hey! Wait up, Sunshine!"

"I have to get to the cafeteria. I'm meeting friends," she said, hoping her lie sounded convincing.

"They'll save you a seat," Brian Kent said as he fell into step beside her, kind of forcing her to move to the edge of the sidewalk. "What's you hurry, golden girl? You're always in such a rush. You flit around here like a butterfly, never landing in one place for long. I'd like to pin you down and get to know you better, if you get my meaning."

"I really can't talk to you right now," she said.

"Well, isn't that too bad. I guess we'll just have to make time in your busy schedule. It just so happens Joe and I have free time right now." He grabbed her arm and shoved her off the sidewalk.

"Hey!" she cried, stumbling, off balance on the grass. "Let go of me!"

"Be quiet!"

Before she could muster a scream a quiet, firm male voice said her name from someplace. "Nova," he said. "Let's go."

Brian spun around. He had a grip on her arm and twisted it in turning so fast. "What the hell do you want, Blackstone? You want a piece of this, pick a number. Joe and I have dibs on it."

"You'd better let go of her, Kent. And you, too, Thornton. Back off."

"She don't belong to you," Kent sneered.

"You're wrong about that," Darach replied in a cold voice. "You mess with my girl, you have me to deal with. Understand?"

"You ain't dating this ditzy bitch! Are you? We ain't never seen her with you."

"Do you need me to open your eyes for you?" Darach replied. "You'd better let go of her arm while you still have fingers you can bend of your own free will."

"Yeah, hey, all right. No harm done. We were just teasing her a little, you know, her still being a new kid on campus and all. We're cool. Come on, Joe." He and his friend hurried off.

Darach stood on the sidewalk watching them go. When they had vanished from sight around the side of Sutton Hall he turned his head and looked at Nova who seemed rooted to the shadowed grass near the stand of evergreens. "You might want to move your ass before someone else comes along with the same idea as those two had. Christ, Nova, the rule is you never walk anywhere on campus alone after dark." She did not move. He stood looking at her. She was so small. It occurred to him that those two fools could have easily overpowered her in the darkness provided by those evergreens. She'd never have been able to fight them off on her own. They could have had their way with her, even killed her and left her body there if they'd thought she might rat them out. Who knows how long it would have been before she'd gone from *missing student* to *murdered student's body found amid the firs*? "Nova, come over here. I'll walk you to wherever you need to go." He couldn't just leave her here to be victimized again. "You want to tell me what you found to go with the dragon drawing?" It was the only thing he could think of that they had in common, the magazine.

"A poem," she replied, her voice barely audible.

"Tell me about it. Where were you heading?"

"To dinner."

She was still not moving. "Are you all right? Did they hurt you?" he asked. He took a step off the sidewalk toward her. Even in the darkness he saw her shudder. "It's all right. I'm not going to hurt you." He took another step toward her. When he was two feet from her she flew at him. All he saw was her pale face, pale hair coming at him. He instinctively caught her in his arms, not knowing what else he could do. Her arms went around him and he felt that she was trembling. "It's okay," he said, patting her back. "It's okay." She nodded against his chest. "Come on, pull it together." She nodded again. "Okay?"

"Yes."

He let go of her. "Come on, then." He turned and she followed him to the sidewalk, fell into step beside him. "What are they serving in the caf tonight?" he asked, just to make conversation, to try to get her mind on something normal and ordinary.

"Um...American chop suey, I guess." She didn't sound like herself.

He grimaced. "I could go for some Chinese food." She didn't say anything. He risked a look at her, saw that she was walking with her head bent. He frowned. He had never seen her like this, so subdued, so down. The fright had taken the sparkle right out of her, and with a jolt he realized that he missed that about her. He'd had a bad fencing practice. John had really whacked him good a few times. He felt like he'd been beaten up and it had put him out of sorts. "Nova. What the hell kind of name is that anyway?" he asked. "Isn't a nova a star or something?"

"It's actually a Hopi name. It means butterfly," she replied, her voice sounding oddly dull, flat.

"Well, does the butterfly want to go grab some Chinese food with the dragon?" he asked, trying to make light of things. Trying to perk her up. It startled him when she raised her head and looked at him. There were tears in her eyes. Her face was wet. She had been crying and he hadn't even realized it! Those assholes! They'd scared her and made her cry! He felt a flash of anger with them but they were not his problem at the moment. Nova was his problem. He couldn't just let her go to her apartment, her room, curl up and cry herself sick over this. "Come on. We'll run into the dorm. I'll grab a quick shower. I just got out of fencing practice. It was brutal. You get ready to go and I'll come get you. We can walk down to the Silver Moon. You can have whatever your heart and stomach desire. My treat."

"You don't…"

"I know I don't, but I want to. Okay? Yes or no? Do you want to go? If not, I'll just have Ramen noodles and tuna fish." She wrinkled her nose at that. "I could use the company," he said. With another jolt he realized that what he'd said was true. He had distanced himself from the female population on campus the past few weeks. He was sick of their utter silliness, their shallowness. But he didn't have that sort of problem with Nova. He could tolerate her for one evening if it meant he wasn't alone and he was doing something to cheer her up, because if truth be told, it was rather unnerving having her so quiet beside him.

"All right. Thanks. That'll be...um, good."

They had upper class apartment/suites in the same building—Parkington Hall. Her apartment, shared with three other girls, was on the fourth floor. His apartment, shared with three other guys, was on the seventh floor. As she stepped off the elevator onto the fourth floor he said he'd come down and get her when he was ready and she nodded, told him her suite was four-oh-eight.

After his shower he stood studying his reflection in the still somewhat foggy mirror. He stroked his jaw. He should shave. Having such dark hair, his five o'clock shadow was very noticeable and it felt scratchy. Then he shook his head. He didn't want to shave again today, and it wasn't like he was going to kiss her or anything. He'd skip shaving, but he brushed his teeth and ran a comb through his black hair. He needed a haircut. Well, it wasn't like they were dating and he had to look good to meet her parents or anything.

Towel draped low around his hips, he crossed to his single bedroom to get dressed, choosing black jeans, a long-sleeved black t-shirt and black boots. Black was his signature color. He ran his fingers through his hair again after pulling on the shirt, grimaced because his hair had gotten messed up, but shrugged it off, grabbed his black leather jacket sliding his phone into one pocket, stuffing his wallet into his hip pocket. He then shoved the lanyard with his door key card and room key into his other coat pocket, slipped a little change into his front jeans pocket and headed to the main room where Tom and Luke were watching the evening news while eating leftover pizza. "Where you off to?" Tom asked, his cheek bulging with a huge bite.

"The Moon," he replied.

"Hey, bring us back some!"

"What do you want?"

"I don't care, do you?" Tom asked Luke who shook his head. "Just anything. Here!" He got up, digging in his pockets.

"Forget it. I'll get it this time," Darach said. "Later."

On the fourth floor he wiped his hand down the thigh of his jeans, looked at it a moment and then rapped on the door. It took about thirty seconds for her to come to the door. "Ready?" he asked. She nodded.

In the elevator he noticed she'd changed into brown corduroys. She had on her brown leather jacket with the fringe again, had added a paisley scarf. "Are you cold?"

"Um…a little." She shrugged. "Everyone thinks I'm from southern California but I'm not. I'm from northern California. Almost in Oregon. It gets cold there." She sounded a little defensive and annoyed.

"In New England we tend to think of all of California as a sunny and hot place, all beaches and desert."

"That's just plain crazy."

They didn't talk much as they walked down the hill to the village below the campus. There was a convenience store, a liquor store, a music store and then the Silver Moon, a little hole in the wall place before the bowling alley next door on the other side. He opened the door and they stepped into the too hot vestibule. He reached around her to open the inside door and they passed through into the narrow restaurant. It was sort of dim inside with red lanterns dangling in a row down the center of the room, red-shaded lamps over the tables in the booths along the right hand wall. There was a bar halfway down on the left wall, a row of tables for four ran down the center of the room and a couple tables for two on the left wall before the bar.

A short Chinese man in black, wide-legged pants and a red jacket trimmed with black appliques and black frogs smiled at them and bowed. "Two for dinner?"

"Yes," Darach replied.

"This way, please." He led them to a booth about halfway along the right wall.

Nova slid into the seat with her back to the door. Darach slid into the seat facing her. He shrugged out of his jacket. She left hers on for the time being, but unwound her scarf from around her neck, placing it on the seat beside her. Her pale hair was in a ponytail caught high up on the back of her head this evening. The blotchiness was gone from her face. She had beautiful skin, flawless. It looked soft and satiny. He was a tactile person, he liked textures. It was just part of who he was. He was an artist and he appreciated form, surfaces, angles, planes, perspectives, lines. She had a perfect face as well, perfectly symmetrical. Her nose fit her face. Her mouth was somewhat bow-shaped but she didn't have the fat, puffy lips girls strived for lately. They were terrific lips just the same. She didn't wear make-up, he realized as he studied her in the red glow of the lamp above the table. She was quite pretty, if truth be told. Why hadn't he noticed that before? With a start he realized that she was looking at him. "Uh, what do you feel like eating tonight?' he asked. The sort of girls he was used to would undoubtedly reply, 'You,' and give him a sultry glance or a slutty wink as they licked their lips. He was holding his breath waiting for Nova's reply.

"I like vegetable lo mein."

"Are you a vegan?"

She shook her head. "No. I eat meat. What do you feel like?" she asked.

"Steak teriyaki. Shrimp Rangoon. Chicken fingers. Beef fried rice." He couldn't help giving her a wry smile the way she was looking at him. "My suite mates will devour the leftovers. I don't plan on eating it all myself."

"Can we get sweet and sour chicken, too? I can help pay."

"Sure. And no, you're not paying. This is my treat, remember?" She nodded. "Don't argue."

The waiter came back. He ordered the food, and two Cokes, at her nod of agreement with his choice of beverage. He shook his head as the man walked toward the swinging doors at the back of the restaurant to place the order. "Did you see his face?"

"He probably thinks we only eat once a week," she said. He nodded, tapping his fingers on the table. He was nervous now, didn't know what to talk to her about. She looked around the restaurant. There were some delicate framed watercolors and typical Chinese restaurant gold-painted sculptural plaques on the walls. There was a dragon on the wall of their booth. Her eyes fell on that and she smiled. "He's supposed to look fierce, right? He looks like a pussycat compared to the dragon you drew."

Darach looked at the dragon on the wall and had to agree. It didn't look very fierce at all. "My dragon is Welsh," he said. "Different breed entirely from the Chinese dragon."

"How many different kinds of dragons are there?"

He shrugged. "Quite a few. A lot of cultures have dragons in them." He flipped his placemat over, patted his pockets without finding a pencil or pen. Nova realized he wanted to draw something and dug a pen out of her bag, passing it to him across the table.

"Fountain pen," he said after uncapping it. "You don't see too many people using fountain pens these days."

"I like how the ink flows so smoothly when I'm writing." The waiter brought a small silver tea pot, teacups without handles, noodles, small bowls of duck sauce and hot mustard. "Tea?" she asked.

He didn't ordinarily drink tea but nodded. She gracefully poured tea into both cups. He'd have dribbled it all over the table. That's why he usually didn't drink it anymore, the damn spouts leaked like sieves and it was embarrassing to spill tea all over the table. "Thanks," he said, then he popped some noodles into his mouth and began sketching on his placemat. "The snout of the Scottish dragon is this shape."

Nova sat watching him sketch, sipping her tea. She'd added a packet of sugar to hers and one to his. "The author of the dragon poem didn't include his or her name," she said.

"Probably wants to remain anonymous," he replied.

"It's very well written. It's…well, it's really very beautiful. A dragon chasing a butterfly. Very unusual imagery there, but I really love it. It's like they're playing together. But it's actually more that the dragon has fallen in love with the beautiful butterfly and he's courting her, right? Have you read it? Do you agree with that, or am I way off base? I know! I know!" she said, rolling her eyes. "I'm a hopeless romantic! Shoot me now!"

He chuffed a soft laugh. "Nothing wrong with that. I did read it, but I'm not sure what it's about. When I read it the first time it was more like the dragon is just utterly fascinated with the butterfly. He's mesmerized, curious and just can't figure it out. The butterfly is such a tiny thing, so delicate, graceful and beautiful. He's this great big, scaly, hulking, ugly thing. He's sort of in awe of the butterfly. I think the butterfly is a little frightened of him. One fiery breath and she's toast. One wrong sweep of his tail and she's just gone. Poof!" He raised his eyes, catching a thoughtful look on her face. She was looking beyond him, over his shoulder at the gold-painted scrollwork above the back of the booth.

Slowly her eyes came back to meet his. "I was just thinking that it would be awesome if you could draw a dragon and a butterfly for the cover of **The Flyleaf**. They could sort of be chasing one another and there could be cherry blossoms tumbling through the air around them!"

He opened his mouth to protest but it struck him that she was coming back to life, becoming more animated again. Her sparkle was reigniting. He didn't want to discourage her too much. "You don't think that's too cutesy?" he asked, his voice neutral.

"No! The magazine comes out in the spring. People flock to Washington, D.C. to see the cherry blossoms! Love is in the air in springtime! It would be perfect! Darach, you could do it, couldn't you?"

He could, but he certainly wouldn't want to put his name on anything so syrupy and girlish. The dragon would have to be less fierce, too. It was not his style or what he liked to draw, but looking at her, he thought he could do something like that. It would be a less dark and dense work, more open and lighter in feel. "Yeah, I suppose I could."

"Awesome! You're the most amazing artist!" She fell back in her seat smiling, her delicate pale hands around the china cup. "Sorry," she muttered after a few moments, sobering up. "I was gushing."

"Gush all you want. It doesn't hurt my ego any." She made a face at him and he gave her a wry smile. "Okay, if I do the cover art then you write the story. Forget the poem. It's weird."

"No, it's not!' she protested.

"It doesn't exactly go with what I'm envisioning for the cover. It has to be lighter in tone. The poem has tension because you don't know if he's going to end up squashing the butterfly or what. If you write a short story to go with the art it can be lighter- they fall in love and live happily ever after kind of thing. Girls eat that stuff up."

"Don't generalize. But I could probably do something like that. I can see the butterfly riding on the top of the dragon's head between his scowling brows. Or at the tip of his spikey tail, wings fluttering wildly in the dragon's slipstream."

"Why can't the butterfly just cling to his strong scaly chest and enjoy the ride?"

"Like she's pinned over his heart?"

He shrugged. "Sure, why not?"

"Okay. I'll figure it all out." She was silent for a full minute and then said, "But I think we need to keep your original dragon drawing and the poem in the magazine too. Kind of a running theme."

Before he could reply the waiter brought their plates and then returned a minute later with an array of food. He looked at the dragons Darach had sketched on his placemat and nodded. "Velly good!" he said, grinning and nodding. He put his hands up beside his head and began bobbing back and forth and up and down. "Chinese dragon dance like this!" Nova clapped her hands, smiling brightly, loving it. He bowed and walked away. The bartender chattered at him in Cantonese then clapped his hands and laughed. The waiter bowed again then disappeared into the kitchen.

Darach capped her fountain pen and handed it back to her. She put it away. "Don't ruin your placemat. I want to take it with me and pin it up on my bulletin board," she said as she finally removed her jacket.

"Here, we'd better swap placemats then. I can be a slob sometimes." They swapped placemats and then helped themselves to the food.

They didn't talk much as they ate. Nova sampled a small amount of everything. Darach ate much more because he was starving after all the fencing practice, and he hadn't had time for lunch. There was still a lot of food left when they were through. The waiter whisked it away to box it up. "When are you going to be in the magazine office again?" he asked as she sipped some Coke.

"Um, maybe tomorrow around three o'clock?"

He thought for a moment, reviewing his schedule. "No, can't do that. Look, do you want to come up for Ramen noodles and tuna fish tomorrow around six? I can do a few quick sketches tonight for the cover. You can pick the one you like best and then I can do a final version."

She had been going to ask him for the leftover vegetable lo mein to have for dinner tomorrow night but it was such an unexpected invitation she knew she shouldn't decline. Besides, maybe he had sketchbooks she could look through. She liked his style, his drawings. She wanted to see more. Maybe he'd show her if she asked him tomorrow? "Okay. That works for me."

Darach suddenly felt nervous. When was the last time they'd cleaned the suite? Did he have two cans of tuna? He knew he had plenty of noodles. She'd probably like a vegetable too. What about dessert? His stomach clenched as the waiter set down the boxed leftovers in a plastic bag, a tray with two fortunes cookies, and a tray with two hot, moist finger towels on it.

"I'll make chocolate chip cookies for you and your suite mates. Or would you prefer brownies?"

"Cookies," he replied without even having to stop to think about it. He hadn't had any homemade cookies since who knew when?

"Walnuts or no nuts?"

"Luke's got a nut allergy."

"No nuts, just chocolate chips then."

"Sounds good." Dessert dilemma solved, he passed her a fortune cookie then took the other. They opened the cellophane packets and cracked the cookies open. "Mine says 'Your prospects look brighter,'" he read from the slip.

Nova looked at hers, a slight frown creasing her brow, "Mine says, 'Behind the clouds the sun still shines.'" Her eyes rose to meet his. "I guess that's true enough. The sun never stops shining."

"No, it doesn't. Clouds blot its light from reaching earth sometimes, the rotation of the earth means we can't see it at night, but it doesn't mean it's not shining." He looked at her. He'd thought her light had been extinguished this evening when he'd come across those morons harassing her. He'd been afraid they had doused her inner glow, but they hadn't. They'd cast a cloud across her but the cloud had lifted and she was shining once again. "The sun always shines."

"It's faithful like that," she said, popping the cookie into her mouth.

"Good ol' sol."

He paid the check, got his change. They put their jackets on and left the restaurant. "Brr!" she said, shivering.

"Fall is definitely here."

"I love how the trees change color. I love the smell of wood smoke. Autumn is so beautiful with all the fiery colors and the bright blue sky and fluffy clouds! I like scarecrows."

"Scarecrows? Really?"

"Straw-stuffed human effigies. They look so content just dangling there from poles in the fields. Dancing on pumpkins." She laughed. She had a sweet laugh. It made him smile. "I can just see a scarecrow slipping off his pole at night, putting on pumpkin shoes and dancing in the light of a big, orange harvest moon!"

"There's another story for you. You have such a vivid imagination."

"My mind never shuts off. I'm like this receiver that just keeps picking up signals."

He suddenly wanted to hug her. "Show me how a scarecrow would dance with pumpkin shoes on," he urged.

She didn't hesitate, didn't have to stop to think about it. Even though there were people around she jogged a few steps ahead, turned and began doing a strange but joyful dance, lifting her knees up high and hopping around, flopping her arms all over. "Like this! You have to use your imagination to hear the hollow thump-thump-thump of the pumpkins striking the ground with every step! It's sort of like the beating of a drum!"

A guy pushed himself away from the wall of the music store and began imitating her. "What are we doing?" he asked. "What kind of dance is this?"

"A scarecrow dance! We're wearing pumpkin shoes!" she replied with a grin. The guy laughed and continued dancing. His friends began supplying the beat. Several girls who'd been coming down the sidewalk joined in the dance.

Darach stood watching them, shaking his head. He thought he might feel embarrassed having her dance like that on a public sidewalk but no one seemed to be giving it a second thought. They were all getting into it! "I have to go!" she said cheerfully to her fellow dancers. They waved her off, kept on dancing. "That was crazy, but fun!" she said as they continued up the sidewalk toward the campus.

"Yeah, it was crazy all right. But you looked like you were having fun."

"I was. But, well, were you having any fun?"

"Yeah, I'm having fun just being with you," he found himself answering. And that was the truth of it. She was a carefree spirit, buoyant and light. She was radiant. People reacted to her as if touched by some special glow that lit them from within. He felt illuminated walking beside her up the hill, as if he was glowing from within.

"I'm so glad you asked me to join you for dinner. I feel so much better now, Thank you, Darach."

"No problem."

All too soon they were back at Parkington Hall. They were quiet in the elevator but as she moved to step off on the fourth floor he stopped her, asked for her cellphone number. He blocked the door from closing as he dug his phone out of jacket pocket and added her number to his contacts list. He gave her his number and she put it into her phone. "See you tomorrow at six?"

"I'll be up," she said. "Thanks again."

"You're okay?"

"I'm fine. Really. Bye." She waved, turned and headed down the hallway.

He stepped back into the elevator car and continued up to his floor. Tom, Luke and Nate grabbed the bag out of his hand, spreading the containers out on the counter almost as soon as he was through the door. "What the hell is this?" Nate asked.

Darach glanced at the open container and said, "That's not for you guys. Put it in the fridge for me, okay? I'm having a guest for dinner tomorrow. We're going to finish that."

"What is it?" Nate repeated.

"Vegetable lo mein."

"You dating a vegan?"

"I'm not dating anyone. It's just a girl from the art and literary magazine coming over. We need to get some stuff done. Professor Jameson is expecting a mock-up next week."

"A girl? You invited a girl over? I thought you were practicing celibacy these days."

"I'm not sleeping with her!" Darach said, annoyed by their thinking that.

"Who is it? Anyone we know?"

"I don't know. Do you know Nova?"

"California girl Nova? That Nova?"

"How the hell many Novas are going to school here?" he snapped, irritated now.

"Only the one. She's cute. A little weird but, damn, she's adorable, eh?"

"You're not hitting that?" Tom asked. "Are you crazy? Do you need a doctor? A therapist?"

Darach rolled his eyes, stalking off to his room and slamming the door. His suite mates looked at one another, smirking and nodding.

Nova was at the door at six the following evening. Luke leapt up to open the door before Darach could even move. "Hey, Nova, welcome to the Dragon's Lair." He stepped back so that she could enter.

"What've you got there?"

"Cookies," she replied. "For you guys."

"All right! I'll take those!" He took the plate from her hands.

"Don't you guys have someplace to go?" Darach asked.

"Oh, they don't have to go. I brought six more cans of tuna fish and more noodles. We can cook enough for everyone, right?"

"I *like* this girl!" Luke said, grinning.

"Come on, I'll show you around the kitchen," Nate said jumping up, leading her around the counter and into the kitchen. "There're five of us. We'll need the big pot to cook all those noodles. Tom, you start opening and draining the tuna fish."

"Don't forget Darach wouldn't let us touch that vegetable stuff last night. We need to throw that in a bowl and nuke it in the microwave!"

Nova glanced over her shoulder at Darach who was slumped on the couch in the sitting area just watching his suite mates as if he had never seen them before. She gave him a quick grin before she was steered to the cabinet with the dishes and told to set places at the counter on both sides, they'd find enough seats when the food was ready. Nate told her where to find the flatware.

In a relatively short time dinner was ready and they all gathered at the counter. Nova was placed between Nate and Luke. Tom and Darach sat on the opposite side of the counter in the kitchen, Darach on his task chair that he'd wheeled out from his room. Nate and Tom had beer, Darach had root beer, Luke had fruit juice and Nova had milk. They polished off the noodles, the tuna and even the vegetable lo mein, Nova having convinced Darach's suite mates to try it. Luke jumped up to grab the plate of cookies and they had those for dessert. Nova and Nate washed the dishes, laughing about something Darach couldn't make out. He felt a bit out of sorts and hoped they weren't laughing about him. She was his guest and they were monopolizing her. He'd hardly gotten to say one word to her since she'd walked through the door.

Nova slung the damp dish towel over Nate's shoulder as she turned from the sink. "You guys are going to have to excuse us now. Darach and I have some stuff to do for the magazine tonight."

He got up. "Leave the door open!" Tom called as they retreated to Darach's room. In response, he slammed the door shut, which only made them catcall and whistle for a little bit before they settled down in front of the TV to watch the basketball game.

"You have to excuse them. They're not used to being around girls."

She smiled as she threw herself down on his bed, hauling her tote bag up and rummaging through it. "They're harmless."

"Just add enough alcohol and you'll change your mind about them quick enough." He grabbed a sketchbook from his cluttered desk, came and sat down on the bed, leaning back against the wall it was against.

"I did a little mock-up at four o'clock this afternoon. It needs work, nothing is set in stone." He nodded, took the pages from her and looked through them. She had a talent for putting things together in a way so that it all flowed smoothly. In the center she had placed the dragon and butterfly poem opposite the original dragon picture that he had submitted. His eyes came up to meet hers. She had been watching him. He picked up his sketchbook and tossed it onto her lap. "I did three quick sketches. Tell me which one you like best." He went back to looking over the rest of the mock-up.

Nova turned the sketchbook right side up on her lap and looked at the first sketch. It immediately struck her as not quite right. The lines were too tight, too tense. She turned the page. This attempt was better. She liked it but still it wasn't quite right. She turned to the next attempt and simply said, "Oh!"

He looked up. "What?" He'd been deliberately ignoring her, not wanting to see her reaction to the sketches, but now he was curious by her somewhat breathless cry of surprise. She had the pad tilted toward her so he couldn't see which one she was looking at.

"This one is perfect," she said, her voice sounding a bit strangled. "It's absolutely right." She turned the sketchbook, raised her head.

He could not look away from her face. Tears were streaming down her cheeks. Why the hell was she crying? What had he done? "Nova…"

"Darach, this is so beautiful," she said. She took one hand off the sketchbook to brush tears from her cheek. "I'm sorry! I just cry when I see something that touches me inside. It's just me." She shook her head.

She had responded to his sketch with tears. His art had touched her on some deep inner level. "Oh," he said.

"I feel it…here," she said, laying her hand over her heart. "He loves the butterfly so much! It's right there in his eyes, in his expression. And the butterfly loves him! Look at how playful she's being, pulling her wings back like that, almost doing a backwards somersault in mid-air. It's such a joyful movement!" She took an unsteady breath. "I don't know how you can capture movement in a static drawing like this! It just boggles my mind!" She absently turned to the next page. Before she got too close of a look at it he tore the pad from her hands.

"There are only three," he said. "So, the third one is the one you want me to do in ink for the cover then?"

"Let me see that," she said, holding her hand out.

"You're here to pick the cover art," he reminded her.

"Darach, let me see that. Please."

He got up off the bed taking the sketchbook with him. He paced up and down the narrow aisle between his bed and his desk. She remained seated on his bed, one leg dangling, the other curled beneath her. "Fine," he finally muttered, almost hurling it back at her.

She caught it awkwardly, watching him warily as he turned and stalked back toward the closed door. As he reached for the door knob she said, "No, don't," her voice very quiet. It was not a command. It was a soft request for him not to open the door. He stood there gripping the door knob, unable to let go of it, his escape just a matter of giving it a quick twist, tugging open the door and walking through the doorway into the hall.

For almost too long a time she was silent as she studied the fourth drawing he'd made. He didn't know why he had done it, but he had, and she had glimpsed it and was now looking at it for an uncomfortable length of time. His muscles, his stomach were clenched in an internal cringe. He felt tense as he waited for her to grab her things, shove him aside in disgust and stalk out. The echo of the door slamming in her wake was already an auditory foreshadow in his ears. "I'm sorry," he heard himself say, his voice low.

Nova had gotten up off the bed and was standing behind him. "Why?" she asked. "I mean, you don't even like me, right? Every time we've been alone together in the **Flyleaf** office it's like you couldn't wait to get out of there, to get away from me. So, what would possess you to draw such a thing? I don't understand."

He struggled with his answer, not really understanding what had happened to him, what had possessed him. Finally he said, "I wrote the poem." She did not say anything to that. "It's about me and you." Still she remained silent. "Damn it, Nova!" he cried. "I'm the big bad beast and you're this beautiful, bright butterfly! I don't want to…"

"Hurt me?" she supplied quietly.

"You can do better for yourself."

"Don't you think that maybe I should be the one to decide who and what is best for me?" She glanced back at the sketchbook lying on his bed. He had drawn his own face on the dragon, hers on the butterfly. They were face to face, gazing into one another's eyes and it was obvious that they were about to kiss. The scale was outrageous- a huge dragon, a tiny butterfly but he had imbued it with so much feeling, so much emotion one didn't even notice. All one felt was the ache of love needing to be fulfilled between the two. "Is that how you really feel about me?" she asked.

"You drove me crazy when you first walked through the door. But…something's changed. Yesterday it all changed."

"I grew on you?"

"You grew on me."

"Like a fungus?"

He chuffed out his breath. "No, of course not. You grew on me like buttercups and bluebells." He slowly released his grip on the door knob. "You just got to me. You filled me up with warm fuzzies, damn you!" She laughed. He turned around and his eyes met hers. "You are too damn irresistible, do you know that?"

She shrugged. "People find me annoying."

"*I* found you annoying!" he said, and then he shook his head. "But all of a sudden, I don't find you annoying at all. I think…Jesus, Nova! I think I fell in love with you yesterday!"

"Oh, it's probably just a crush. You'll get over it. It'll pass. You'll get over me."

He put his hands on her shoulders and pulled her closer. "No, I don't think I will. I'm never going to get over you." He looked down into her incredible blue eyes for a long moment. "Can I kiss you now?"

"Yes, I was hoping that you would," she replied.

And so the dragon claimed the butterfly for his very own with one sweet kiss as the cherry blossoms spun and tumbled in the air around them. The End

Excerpt from *Heart of the Dragon Lost in Spring* by Nova Paris, **The Flyleaf, Vol. 45, Spring,** Hawthorne-Ivory University Press, pg. 5.

NINE INNINGS

"You're late, Cooper!" Andrew Jacobs shouted as the locker room door banged open and a tall, lean young man with below-collar length, naturally wavy, dark blonde hair entered, his equipment bags in both hands, baseball cap backwards on his head, mirror-lensed sunglasses still in place. He was unshaven, dressed in greasy work pants, work boots and a dark t-shirt that hid the grease stains well.

"Lost track of time makin' out with your old lady in the back of the Rolls," Noah Cooper retorted as he made his way through the crowded room to his assigned locker. He dumped his bags on the floor and began stripping down, hanging his dirty work clothes in the open locker. "She's a bitch," he muttered.

"I hope you're talking about my wife, and not the car," Jacobs said, causing a ripple of laughter to circle the room.

Noah gave a wry grin as he shrugged, crouching down to unzip one of the bags. He tugged out his uniform. "Great chassis on her," he said, "but she's showing her age." He caught the twitch of a muscle in Jacob's jaw which signaled his willingness to joke around was over. "You want the truth, I found floor rot in the rear passenger area." His boss grimaced. "Sorry I was late. I was trying to assess how much work is going to be involved in fixing it."

"Bad, is it?"

"It ain't pretty." He stood up, pulling his jersey on over his head. "Henry is in mourning."

"I'll bet." He sighed. "All right, get your damn pants on and then get your ass out there. You'd better be on your game tonight."

"I'm always on my game."

"I mean on the field, not in the bar afterwards!" Jacobs called over his shoulder as he banged out of the locker room.

"So whatta we gotta do, replace the whole freakin' floor?" Silvio Calabrese asked as he leaned against his locker watching Noah finish dressing.

"Yeah. Felt ok under the carpet but they'd laid sheet metal over the rot and no one picked up on it." Noah sat on the bench, putting on his cleats. Sam spit on the floor. "Hey, stop that! Christ, that's disgusting!" He stood up after grabbing his gear bag. "Come on, we'd better get our asses out there."

"Hey, Cooper! Your girlfriend's out there!" Lucas Benjamin called from the doorway.

"Great," Noah groaned. The girl Lucas was referring to was not his real girlfriend, it was the redhead with the camera from the Bristol Star Record. She seemed to be at every game and he couldn't count the number of times he'd turned his head and caught the camera pointed at him. Granted she had caught some incredible shots of him firing the ball to Mike Thomas at second base for an out, or sprawled and stretching to get the out at home plate. She was good at what she did, shooting sports pictures for the newspaper, but she did seem to be a bit obsessed with him in particular. She was on the young side for him, too slim and boyish in figure, although she was probably pretty enough. He'd never really seen her at close range. He wasn't that interested in her though, he had more than enough females in the girlfriend department. He and his brother Jesse, despite growing up on a farm, had always had girls chasing after them. His brother had found the right one for him last year and it had been a bit of a shock since the girl had been engaged to someone else when he'd met her, and she was from one of the wealthiest families in the area as was her former fiancé. How she'd fallen in love with Jesse was a mystery to Noah since Jesse had chosen to stay on the farm while Noah had chosen to get the hell out when the getting was good.

He came up into the dugout and walked along the bench to sit beside pitcher Mason Hewes. "Hey," he said.

"Hey. Was wondering when you'd bother to show up."

"How does Kelp look?"

Hewes screwed up his face. "I don't see a win in our immediate future."

Noah shook his head. "Don't be so negative. You've got the best catcher in the league. I do my homework. Just stop being so damn arrogant and give me the pitch I want and we may make a miracle happen tonight."

Hewes snorted and then spit. "You're so damn cocksure of yourself sometimes, Cooper, it scares me. I don't know if you're brilliant or a freakin' idiot."

"I'm probably somewhere between the two extremes, but I've been playing baseball my whole life. I'm just better at observing other players than you are. You see a guy twitch you think he's looking for a fast ball. I see he's got jock itch and can't wait to do something about it. He just wants you to throw the damn ball already. He doesn't care what you pitch him. He's going to swing at it. I give you the pitch he's most likely to miss."

"Yeah, I know," Hewes admitted. He looked up and surveyed the crowd. "More people tonight."

"Weather's gorgeous."

"There's you're little red-haired stalker."

Noah looked up, his dark eyes searching for and easily finding the bright coppery hair of Evedan Renfield. She was talking to the photographer from Portsmouth, Carl Harte. Harte was a sleazy pig in Noah's opinion and it didn't look like she was happy about having been cornered by the man. He was probably hitting on her. He'd go after his own daughter's best friend if he thought he could get away with it. It gave Noah a cold sensation in the pit of his stomach seeing Harte with Evedan but he didn't have time to think about why it should bother him so much. It was really no concern of his.

He finished putting on his catcher's gear, grabbed his mask and headed out onto the field as his team was announced. They were the Mechanics playing for O'Toole's Antique & Vintage Auto Restorations. Tonight they were playing the Depot Dawgs from the big box home and garden chain distribution center in nearby Castleton. He did a few stretches and squats behind home plate and then stood up to talk to Tim Bayer the home plate umpire. "I want a good game tonight," Tim said.

"We always play a good game," he replied, reaching up to pull his mask down into place. As he did so he caught Evedan with her camera raised, huge lens in place. She was aiming at him. He suppressed the urge to flip her off, scowled at her instead and then went into his crouch. "Freakin' crazy redhead," he muttered, vaguely wondering exactly how many pictures she had of him on her computer. It was kind of unnerving. What in the world did she do with them? He shook his head. It was too distracting to think about. He needed to get his head into the game. He needed to give a sign to Hewes and get this game rolling.

It was slow going at first. There were a few single base hits but many more outs. The Mechanics scored the first run in the bottom of the fifth. The Dawgs then scored three runs at the top of the sixth. Noah was getting pissed and called a time out to go to the mound to have a few words with Hewes. "What the hell is wrong with you? Just pitch what I tell you to pitch and stop shakin' me off!"

"You see Harte last inning?"

"What? What the hell does he have to do with anything?"

"He was all over your girlfriend like flies on shit. She was rattled."

Noah couldn't help it. His eyes moved to where Evedan had been standing but she was no longer there. Harte was and he didn't look happy. He raised his camera and shot a picture off toward his left. Noah shifted his gaze and found Evedan had moved closer to the dugout. Her expression was hard to read as she wasn't looking his way. He looked toward Harte again and glared at the man. He didn't like men who groped females for any reason, especially in public. "Asshole," he muttered.

"Give me something I like and let's get this inning over with," Hewes said.

"It's not about what you like, it's about the pitch that's going to make him freeze or make him swing and miss. Stop thinking you know it all. You don't."

"And you do?"

"I know more than you do. I study these guys."

"He's calling you back."

"Just throw him what I tell you to throw him," Noah hissed as he turned and made his way back behind home plate.

"Have a little tiff with your sweetheart?" Devin Jones asked, looking back and down at Noah.

"Shut the hell up," Noah replied.

Hewes surprised him by giving a curt nod, and he threw the sweet curveball Noah asked for. Jones took a mighty swing at it, and missed. "Strike one!"

The game ground on. The Mechanics scored one in the bottom of the sixth, two more in the seventh and one in the eighth but they still trailed the Dawgs going into the ninth inning. Noah swatted a mosquito that was dive bombing his ear. He caught Jacobs' signal from the dugout. Jacobs wanted the Dawgs shut down. Easier said than done tonight. They were smokin' hot. The Mechanics were struggling.

He called for a time out and went to talk to Hewes again. "I hate being called a loser," he said.

"You are what you are. Tiger can't change his stripes."

"Don't make this personal."

"You were hitting on my kid sister the other night at Pagan's."

"Shit," Noah said. "How many damn sister's you got?"

"Six."

"Why didn't she say something?"

"She thinks you're hot."

Noah rolled his eyes. "I didn't touch her."

"Yeah, I know. And she's pissed about that."

"And you're pissed because…?"

"You attract girls like iron filings to a magnet. What's your damn secret?"

"I take a shower once in a while," he replied as he turned back toward home plate. "And I try not to scratch myself in public."

The Mechanics pulled off a win with a grand slam by short stop Sam Bannon with two outs on the board. They swarmed out of the dugout to wait for him to make his round of the bases and met him behind home plate, pounding the crap out of him in the traditional victory beating. Sam was good natured about it. Enrique Delgado had taken down three players the first time he'd been met at home plate, not quite understanding what was going on. His cousin Juan Santiago had finally grabbed him and rapidly explained to him in Spanish that he wasn't supposed to beat the shit out of his teammates like that. He'd been fine since then. Noah had gone home with some good bruises on the rare occasions he managed to score the winning run.

The shower facilities at Bristol Park were primitive and temperamental. Noah's showerhead fitfully spritzed out water that varied from lukewarm to bone chilling cold. "Invigorating!" he said, stepping aside after rinsing off so Jake Lyons could have his shower.

"What the hell!" shouted Jake as Noah walked away, towel wrapped low around his hips.

He stood talking to Mike Thomas at his locker for a while. Mike had just opened a microbrewery with his brother-in-law and Noah was interested in how that was working out for them. He hardly ever saw Mike at work as Mike worked in the paint and detailing area. Noah worked in the body work area. They were two of the last players in the locker room when Jacobs flashed the lights. "Come on, fellas! Get dressed, kiss each other goodnight and get the hell out of here! The custodian wants to clean up and get home to his little woman! You're holding him up!"

It was not quite full dark yet, a mellow moon beaming down from a nearly cloudless sky. Noah headed to his truck, eyes uplifted to the sky where stars twinkled. They weren't as bright as they were at the farm where there were no streetlights or other ambient light sources to interfere with their own luminescence. It was one thing he missed about Freemont, those clear unobstructed views of the stars.

He slung his gear bag and his duffle bag into the back of the truck. He'd have to wash his uniform tonight when he got home so it would be clean for tomorrow. He rubbed his shoulder where a foul tip had struck him. Luckily the padding had protected him but his shoulder had still taken a jolt. "Icy Hot," he said aloud. "Maybe an ice pack tonight for a while. And a cold beer." He nodded as he unlocked the driver's door and opened it. He was just getting in when he heard an angry female voice shout, "Leave me alone!" He stopped. There was something in the tone of her voice that pricked his senses, put him on instant alert. Someone somewhere was bothering the girl. He slid back out of the truck and searched the parking lot. Part of the lot was obscured from where he was by evergreens. "Don't you dare touch me again!"

"Hey!" he shouted, heading toward the trees at an easy run. The girl screamed something. "Hey!" he shouted more loudly, breaking into a full out run. He came around the stand of evergreens into the secluded section of the lot and spotted a man struggling to put a young woman into a dark-colored SUV. He caught a glimpse of a dark rectangular bag lying on its side beside a small light-colored sedan. "Hey! Stop! Let her go!"

The man realized that someone was coming. He shoved the girl away hard, causing her to go sprawling onto the asphalt. He quickly climbed into the SUV, slammed the door shut, started the vehicle and peeled away, tires squealing. Noah ran a few yards giving chase, trying to get the license plate number but the guy hadn't turned on the lights yet. "Damn it!"

He turned back and jogged to the girl who was now on her hands and knees. She seemed to have had the wind knocked out of her by the hard fall. When he reached her he was stunned to discover that it was Evedan Renfield whom he'd just come to the rescue of. "Hey! You all right?" he asked.

"I've been better," she replied. "But thanks for asking."

"Who was that? Harte?" He bent down. "Come on, let's get you up on your feet." He helped her up. "Are you hurt?" He turned her toward him. There was an abrasion on her left cheek from where she'd hit the ground and she'd bitten her lip, dark drops of blood dribbling down her chin. "What was he trying to do? Kidnap you?"

"He was just not taking no for an answer and he got mad. I don't know what he had in mind."

"You should call the cops." She shook her head. "He was trying to force you into his car! He could have driven you someplace, raped you, left you for dead!"

She looked at him and then looked away. "I just want to go home." She headed toward the small sedan.

Noah noticed she was limping a bit. "Evedan, hold on." He caught up to her at the car, bent and picked up her camera bag. "You really should report him. He's dangerous. He grabbed you during the game."

"You saw that?" she asked.

"No, but I heard about it from Hewes. He saw him do it."

"He's just a jerk." She was looking around. "Damn!"

"What?"

"I lost my keys."

"Did you drop them?"

"I guess."

"Hold on." He went and got his truck although he didn't like leaving her alone and out of his sight although it was just a minute or so that he couldn't see her. He drove into the smaller lot and jumped out, leaving the headlights on. It still took them a few minutes to find her keys over toward where Harte had been parked. At her car he noticed her hand was shaking so much her keys were jangling. She hit the panic button instead of the unlock button, setting off her car alarm. "Why didn't you hit the damn panic button when he grabbed you?" Noah shouted over the noise.

"I didn't think of it!" She got the alarm turned off and slid into the driver's seat of the Toyota. Noah handed her the camera bag.

"I'm going to follow you home and make sure you get inside safely."

"You don't...."

"I do have to. I just saved your ass from a pervert. I'm duty-bound to make sure you get home safely."

"All right," she relented.

"No fancy maneuvers to try to shake me off your tail. It won't work." She grabbed a tissue from the passenger seat and held it against her bleeding lip.

"Stop it. It hurts when I smile."

"Drive carefully. I'll be right behind you." She nodded. "Put your seatbelt on."

"I will."

He closed the door but didn't walk back to his truck until she had buckled up. He didn't have time to be following her home but he was revved up now on adrenalin, and he was more than angry with Harte for what he'd just done to her. She was no match for a burly man like that. She was damn lucky he'd heard her and not just jumped into his truck and driven off.

Evedan lived at Meadowlark Manor, an apartment complex with units that were all designed to look like different style cottages all attached together in staggered rows. "It's like a maze in here," he complained as he got out of his truck.

She stood on the curb and looked at him. "I'm home. You can go. I think I can get inside on my own."

"Does he know where you live?" She shrugged, but frowned, not certain if he did or did not. "I'm walking you to the door at least," he said, joining her on the curb. She turned and walked across the grassy strip to the sidewalk and up the walk to her kitchen door. She lived in a unit that resembled a carpenter's gothic style cottage. Her roofline was sharply pitched. The peak was decorated with intricate gingerbread scrollwork. The siding was vertical, painted schoolhouse red with blue trim. Her windows were arched at the top. "Do you live with a guy named Hansel?" he asked as they reached the door.

"No." She unlocked the door. "You can go now."

He stood looking at her. "You're in a big hurry to get rid of me for a girl who's spent two years shooting thousands of pictures of me."

"I've been shooting pictures for the sports pages for three years."

"Three years?" He shrugged. "So, invite me in."

"What for?"

"Offer me a cup of coffee."

"Wouldn't you rather have a cold beer or something? You just played several hours of baseball in the heat. Gatorade, maybe?"

"Do you have beer?"

"Some."

"Then I accept." She looked almost confused by how she had invited him in but went inside, flipping on the lights. Noah followed her in. She set her camera bag down on the counter then went to the stove and stood there unmoving. "Are you okay?' he asked, his voice quiet. "Evedan?" He unlaced his work boots and took them off because they were greasy and he didn't want to track grime across her sparkling clean floor. "Hey, Evedan!" He crossed the room. She was hugging herself and he could see goosebumps on her arms. "Here we go," he said. "Come on, let it out." She raised her hands, covered her face and sobbed, shuddering hard. "You're home safe. It's okay."

"He wouldn't leave me alone! I kept telling him to stop, to go away, to not touch me again and he wouldn't listen! He would *not* stop!"

"Come here," he said softly, touching her shoulder. She turned toward him after a moment and he took her in his arms and held her. She was probably going to get grease on her pastel tank top but right now it didn't matter. If she did he'd offer her some money to buy a new one. "You need to invest in some pepper spray. Believe me, that stuff works. I got blasted once, by mistake, of course. I don't molest girls but the guy I was sitting next to in a bar evidently did and the girl was pissed. She got him and then she hit me with it because she thought I was his buddy who'd also been bothering her. That guy was sitting on the jerk's other side." Evedan was shaking like a leaf. "This is just the aftermath of an adrenalin rush," he said, patting her back.

"Don't do that," she said.

"Do what?"

"Pat my back like that. I had one of those greasy burgers from the snack bar. My stomach's been queasy ever since." She uncovered her face and tilted her head back, looking up into his face. Her eyes were raw-rimmed and her nose was running. He noticed she had hazel eyes, warm brown with flecks and dashes of gold and green in the iris. She also had a very faint smattering of freckles across the bridge of her nose. The rest of her skin was flawless. Her bitten lip was still dribbling a bit of blood.

"Damn, you look like shit," he said and something shifted inside him, catching him off guard, putting him off balance. She stared at him a long moment and then he grinned. She smiled. "You really need to go wash your face. You're a mess."

"Don't be an idiot," she said, slipping her arms around him. "I feel like I'm going to fall on the floor if I try to walk away right now."

"I have that effect on girls." She turned her head, rested her cheek against his upper chest. "I'm filthy from work."

"You smell like my Dad's garage."

"Yeah, well, these are the clothes I wore all day at work. Sorry. I didn't know I'd be rescuing you and holding you like this after the game tonight." He was surprised by how much he liked the feel of her in his arms.

She was quiet, getting her emotions under control. Finally she pushed herself away from him. "I'm okay. You can let go of me now."

"Do you really have beer here?"

She nodded. "In the fridge. Help yourself. I need to go wash my face." There was a lavatory through the dining area and off the short hall leading to the living room.

Noah opened the refrigerator and found three bottles of microbrewery beer on the shelf. She had a wedge of cheese, a big bunch of grapes, a bottle of wine, a loaf of bread, some leftover chicken, a couple apples and half a small cake that looked as if it was from a birthday party. He grabbed a bottle of beer, closed the door and leaned against the counter. The interior of the apartment was sort of vintage cottage style to match the exterior. He could see into the dining area and noticed that she had some framed photos hung on the wall. He pushed away from the counter and wandered into the other area, flipping on the light so that he could see the pictures better.

She had them hanging in clusters, nature in one cluster, architecture in another, animals in a third and people in the fourth. If she had taken these photographs she had more talent then he'd given her credit for. He was nearly finished with the beer as he studied the pictures of people. He didn't recognize any of the people in them. As he turned to head back to the kitchen he saw a larger picture on the hall wall and it startled him because it was a picture of him. He walked over to it and stood looking at it. It had been taken at a game but he didn't know which one because there were no reference points. It was just a close-up shot of him in semi-profile—very stark but somehow also very powerful. His catcher's mask was raised and he was looking at something in the distance. His expression was unreadable. There was some dirt smudged across his cheek, and he was unshaven but that was not unusual. He was unshaven tonight as well. He shaved about every three days or whenever it started to bother him, or his current girlfriend. There was a cut across the bridge of his nose and suddenly he knew exactly when she'd taken this particular shot. It was last fall, during the finals. Greg French had hit him in the face with the bat by accident, so he claimed. The blow had caused the mask to cut him across the bridge of his nose. It had hurt like hell, made his eyes water, but his eyes were clear in the picture and the cut was healing so it was probably a day or two after the fact.

"Game four, final inning. The Mechanics were losing. You suddenly stood up and shoved your mask up and just stared off into space for a long time. Finally, the umpire hit you on the shoulder and you just pulled your mask down, crouched down and got back into the game," she said as she came up to him. "I don't know what you were thinking but it was like you were in another world, another place."

"Jesse had called me before the game and told me Mom had been taken to the hospital. I had this feeling that she was gone. I don't even remember this, but now that I see it, and you've told me when you shot it, I remember what it was. I think it was the moment she died because Jesse called again later that night to tell me she was gone. She died at eight past eight that night."

Evedan looked at him for a long moment. "I could look at the date and time stamp on the disk."

He shook his head. "No. You don't have to do that. I don't want to know." He went back to the kitchen. "You going to be all right now? I should get home. It's been a long day and I have to be up early in the morning."

"I'll be fine. Thanks for taking the time to rescue me and escort me home."

Noah put his boots back on, laced them loosely. "Stay away from that bastard, and call the cops if he bothers you again. Call them if he even looks at you." She nodded. "See you at the game then?"

"I won't be there tomorrow. I have to shoot a diving competition at Castleton College."

"Men's or women's?"

She rolled her eyes. "Women's."

"I wouldn't mind seeing that, but I've got to play." She shook her head. "See you whenever then."

"I'll be there on Thursday to cover the game against Exeter. See you then. Bye, Noah, and thanks again."

Saturday was cloudy and Noah got to the park early. He changed into shorts and a t-shirt, put on his sneakers and ran ten laps around the field. A few spectators were filing into the stands with each lap, and he saw Carl Harte along the fence talking to a field maintenance worker named Case. Evedan hadn't been at Thursday's game as she'd told him she'd be. Although he'd read the Bristol Star Wednesday and Thursday there hadn't been any pictures of the diving competition and he'd vaguely wondered about that. There hadn't been much of a write-up either and the byline was by John Landers, another sports writer and it had sounded like something that he'd cobbled together from reading other writer's pieces on the competition. Maybe Evedan had been more shaken up then he'd thought by the near abduction.

    He glanced at Harte again thinking that if he saw him bothering her tonight he'd vault right over that fence and take the guy out right then and there, teach him for not taking 'No' for an answer. Of course a move like that would get noticed and his girlfriend would be hard pressed to understand why he'd do such a thing, but he couldn't just stand by and let some guy treat a girl like that.

    "Noah!" It was Lucas Benjamin waving to him from the ramp leading to the locker rooms. He waved to let him know he was on his way in. Time to change as the other team was now on the field warming up and some of the guys on his own team were already standing outside the dugout doing stretches and talking. He glanced toward the area where the photographers stood but he still didn't see anyone with red hair. Frowning, he jogged to the ramp, thinking perhaps she was just dragging her heels about being in close proximity to Harte tonight. "Your girlfriend's late."

    "Knock it off. Kyla's going to be here watching the game and going out with us after. I don't want to hear you call Evedan my girlfriend in front of her."

    Lucas winked. "Gotcha! I'll keep it hush-hush."

Noah was annoyed. "Kyla's my girlfriend, my only one."

"Sure, if you say so I'll play along."

Noah resisted the urge to give Luke a quick hard sock in the jaw to shut him up. "Come on, Cooper! Even when you're early you're running late!" Jacobs bellowed.

"I'm comin'!" Noah snapped, tugging off his damp t-shirt, rummaging in his duffle bag for the clean white t-shirt he wore under his team jersey. He found it, shook it out, and then pulled it on. As his head emerged he saw Mason Hewes standing close to him. "What do you want?"

"That Jason Roman worries me. He's better then you are."

"What do you mean by that?" Noah demanded.

"He studies all the players, same as you, knows their weaknesses. Only he's been studying a few years longer than you. He's just better at letting his pitcher know what to throw and when."

"And you're worried?"

"Of course I'm worried! I have a reputation to uphold!"

"And what reputation would that be? The one where you never listen to anything your catcher tells you?" He changed into his uniform pants after pulling on his team orange socks. Their colors were teal and orange. Then he understood. "Maryann's in the stands tonight." It was a statement, not a question. Hewes and Maryann Golden had been having an affair off and on now for three years. Neither one was willing to leave their spouse so they had their ups and downs, and now was an up time since she was going to be at the game. Hewes didn't want to look bad in front of her. "You watch for the sign where I twitch my pinky twice and that's the one you throw. Shake off everything else. I'll mix it up, make you look like you're the one calling the shots. She'll think you're brilliant and she'll do whatever you ask tonight because you'll be her hero."

"Like I need to take advice from a guy who juggles a half dozen little tramps at a time."

"I don't know why you and everyone else think that. I don't. Kyla's out there, too. And I don't have a damn wife I have to worry about showing up and raining on my parade."

"It's all going to bite you in the ass one day," Hewes warned.

"Do I look like I have anything to be afraid of?" Noah retorted. "Kyla, only one. I've been thinking about taking her to look at rings, get an idea of what she wants."

"You can't afford that girl. She's champagne and caviar class."

"Not in the bedroom." He winked as he stood up from tying his cleats. "Come on Hewes, we've got a game to win. I think we both want to look good because we both want the same thing tonight."

They went out to the dugout. They were playing the Flyers from the aviation hangers in Franklin. Their team colors were sky blue and gray. "This is going to be a bitch," Mike Thomas muttered as he stared out at the field.

"Ah, c'mon, Mike," Enrique said, turning to punch his team mate on the shoulder. "A couple hours of ass-whuppin' and we can hit the bars and have some real fun."

Mike snorted. He tilted his head back and closed his eyes, blew out his breath. "Gilly asked me for a divorce last night. We really got into it this time. The kids were crying, her mother was screaming at me. The neighbors called the cops." He shook his head. "I slept at the Holiday Inn Express. I'm not going anywhere tonight."

"Sounds like you need a night out, my friend. Just come and have a beer or two. You don't have to stay. You're a part of this team. We're all going. You have to go, too."

"I don't know…"

"Ah. C'mon, man! We need you there."

"We'll see," Mike replied.

Noah leaned forward, turned his head and looked at him. "You going to be all right out there at second? If I hurl a scorcher at you for an out you're not going to stand there and take it like I'm tattooing your forehead, are you?"

"Might put me out of my misery if you beaned me, Coop."

"Don't even say that, man!" Enrique said, shaking his head and crossing himself.

Luke nudged Noah and nodded toward the photographer's area. "Notice anything?" he asked. Noah looked and it was more than obvious that Evedan was not there. John Landers was there representing the Star. "What's with that? He covers school sports."

"Maybe she's sick," Noah said, but he thought it was more likely that she was avoiding Harte.

The game started with the Flyers scoring five runs in the first off a shaky Hewes. Noah was pissed and when he had a chance he hauled him just into the ramp and got right in his face he was so mad at him. "Just throw the damn pitch I tell you to and stop being an asshole! You want to get laid tonight you'd better damn well get your head into the game or she's going to jump in her Beamer and leave you standing in a cloud of dust!"

"Feel better?" Jacobs asked as Noah came back to the bench.

"Remind me again why I put up with his shit," he muttered.

"There's that team spirit that's going to get us a win tonight," Jacobs said wryly.

"He's a fu….!" He cut himself off at the sight of Jacobs' narrowed eyes and hardened jaw. He himself was walking a thin line these days.

"Five bucks in the swear jar, Cooper. There're kids listening to that mouth of yours!" The money collected in the swear jar was donated at the end of the season to the Dana Farber Institute for cancer research to help kids.

Noah slumped on the bench and then realized that he was up at bat. He bit off another curse, grabbed his bat and jogged out to the batter's box. He got two quick strikes before he got himself focused. Two balls followed and then a foul ball to the third base line bleachers much to the delight of a teenaged boy who caught the ball with his bare hand and proudly presented it to the California-blonde girl seated beside him who kissed him in a way that made Noah hot under the collar. He shook his head, glad the ball hadn't hit a little kid in the head or a pregnant woman in the belly. They really needed to put some netting up along that line. He forced his attention back to the pitcher, set his stance and then an image of Harte trying to force Evedan into his SUV flashed through his mind and it provoked such a rush of anger that he wanted to hit the guy and knock his block off. Instead, he hit the ball with the force of his anger backing the swing. The ball cracked off the bat and soared toward the fence in left field. Behind him his teammates were shouting. He almost forgot to run, but then he was racing around the bases, chasing Delgado, Bannon and Lyons. A grand slam! A freakin' grand slam and Evedan wasn't there to see it. As he rounded third and headed for home he saw Kyla jumping up and down and that vision was enough to distract him from thoughts of the red-haired photographer who'd missed a great shot or two today already. He crossed home plate and was grabbed in a bear hug by Sam Bannon, picked up right off his feet and spun around. Lyons pounded him on the back. Delgado swatted him on the back of the head, knocking his batting helmet off. "You rock, Cooper!"

Jacobs merely swatted him on the butt as he passed by, the only sign of appreciation he was likely to get, but it was enough. The old man could be hard on all of them at times, but he cared about them, he cared about the team as a whole, and he cared about baseball.

The Mechanics squeaked a 10-9 win. The Flyers looked disgruntled by the upset win, declining an invitation to meet the Mechanics at Tully's Tavern.

"You were awesome, Noah!" Kyla said for the hundredth time as she squeezed his arm. "We aren't going to stay much longer, are we?" She moved her hand from his arm to his thigh under the table and that got his attention quickly.

"No. Just let me finish this one and we'll go."

"Hey, Coop! Your other girlfriend's on TV!" someone called from across the room.

Kyla stiffened beside him. He turned his head and there was a picture of Evedan, possibly her official press photo because her hair was shorter and she looked like a scared kid staring into the camera lens when the picture was shot. She was behind a serious-faced anchor. He frowned. Why was she on the news? Had she won some sort of award? Or…a cold fist gripped his heart. "Turn up the damn volume!" he shouted.

"Noah!" Kyla cried, feeling how tense he had become. "What's the matter with you? What does her disappearance have to do with you?"

"Disappearance?" He glanced briefly at Kyla who looked pissed off.

"It was all over the news at noontime. The Star reported her missing. She was supposed to cover some sort of swimming event the other day and never showed, and then hasn't shown up for work since. Her editor called the cops when he couldn't reach her at home or on her cell. She's probably run off with some guy or whatever."

"…Again, Miss Renfield has not been seen or heard from since this past Wednesday. A family member who was reached this morning told the Bristol News that Miss Renfield had not been in contact with her family recently but their not having heard from her for a few days is not unusual. They are, of course, concerned about her well-being and would like to know where she is. If anyone has any information regarding the disappearance of the Bristol Star Record's photojournalist Evedan Renfield please contact Detective Joseph Geary of the Bristol Police Department who is in charge of the investigation…"

"Holy shit," Noah said. "Move!" He shoved Juan Santiago who was sitting at the end of the bench seat of the booth. "I need to go."

"What's the matter with you?" Juan asked as he stood up so that Noah could get out. Kyla slid out in his wake.

"Noah! Hey! Where are you going?"

"I need to go to the police station."

Kyla caught his arm but he shook her off. "Why? God, you weren't with her after the game Tuesday night were you?" She saw by his face that he had been. "Damn you, Noah Cooper! God damn you to hell! You bastard!" She let go of him and veered away, angry. "I've had it with you!" she shouted at his back as he made his way through the crowded bar. "Do you hear me? I'm through with you!" She turned back to the bar in general. "Kyla Fontaine is a free woman! Who wants to help me celebrate with a drink?"

"C'mon over here, baby! I'll buy you a drink!"

Noah jumped up from the uncomfortable chair he'd been directed to sit in. He couldn't sit still as he waited for Detective Geary to arrive. "Been drinking, son?" asked the desk sergeant as he watched Noah pace.

"A couple of beers to celebrate the win," Noah replied.

The officer looked at him more closely then nodded. "Catcher, right? Cooper, isn't it?" Noah nodded. "My son plays for the department team. You know Joe Reynolds?"

"Yeah, I've met him. Third base, right?"

"That's him."

"Hell of an arm on him."

"Yeah, but he's starting to get some bursitis in the right shoulder. He's in PT for it."

"Kind of young for that."

The officer shrugged. "That's what I say, but what can you do." He looked up as someone entered the desk area behind him. "Hey, Joe, Noah Cooper thinks he might have some information for you on the Renfield case."

"That so? Give me a couple minutes and then bring him into my office. I'll talk to him there."

Noah was taken down a beige hallway to a room near the end. The detective's office wasn't very large. "Hey," he said as he entered.

Joseph Geary was perhaps in his early-fifties, sandy blonde hair worn a bit too long, starting to thin on top. He had blue-grey eyes, a bit pouchy underneath as if he'd been losing sleep lately. There was a dense five o'clock shadow on his jaw and he scratched at it with his knuckles as he nodded at Noah and motioned for him to take a seat. He leaned across his cluttered desk to shake Noah's hand. "I'm the detective in charge. Her parents insisted. Phil says you have something for me on the Renfield girl? She's been at the games shooting for the Star." Noah nodded. "And she was there Tuesday. We have witnesses, and she downloaded her pictures onto her home computer, sent a few she was considering using for her write-up to her office email. She printed out an 8x10 shot of you, in fact. It was on her desk at her home." He picked up a 9x12 envelope from his desk and slid the picture out, handing it across to Noah who took it and grimaced as he saw a close-up of himself glaring into the camera. "You didn't look too pleased."

"I guess not."

"Were you angry with her?"

"No, not really. Just annoyed somewhat. She's always shooting pictures of me. I don't know why."

"Do you have or have you ever had a relationship of a personal nature with Miss Renfield?"

"No."

"No? Her apartment has pictures of you all over the walls."

"I only know about the one in the hall on the first floor outside the lav. It was a great shot but it brought back some unhappy memories when I saw it."

"When did you see it?"

"Tuesday night."

Detective Geary straightened up in his chair and gave Noah a long speculative look. "I guess we're going to be having a much deeper, lengthier conversation then I thought. Can I get you some coffee? You been out celebrating the win tonight?"

"I had a couple beers at Tully's. I'm not drunk. I've been eating, too. A couple bacon cheeseburgers, fries, nachos, some chocolate cake. But coffee sounds good if it's no trouble."

"I'm not supposed to do it but I'll send the nearest patrol car to the donut shop for real coffee, not this piss-water we brew in the break room." He excused himself and left the room for more than a few minutes. He returned with another officer who sat in the only other chair in the small office with a pad and pen. Detective Geary took a digital voice recorder from his desk. "Do you mind if I record our conversation? Officer Perry's going to be taking some notes also, but the recorder keeps everything in perspective, and I don't forget anything important if I have a recording. It'll be transcripted tomorrow and included in the case file."

"I don't care. If it helps you find her then what's the big deal?"

The interview began with the detective asking Noah his name, date of birth, address, and a few other personal questions. He was then asked how he knew Evedan Renfield, how long he'd known her, what his exact relationship with her was. "I don't exactly know how to answer that one," Noah said. "I mean, I know who she is and she knows who I am and we've exchanged a few words over the three years I've been playing ball for O'Toole's but we really don't know one another or run in the same circles."

"Tell me about Tuesday evening." Noah told him how he'd seen Evedan where the photographers were allowed to stand. He related how she seemed upset and possibly angry with Harte and how she had moved out of the area after a while. He didn't know the exact time frame as he'd been playing ball but guessed at the innings using that as a framework for the detective. "Now tell me how you ended up at her apartment that night."

"I was late to the game so had to park way the hell out in the main lot. I guess she and Harte were also running late because they were both evidently parked in the small auxiliary lot that's partially blocked from view of the main lot by that stand of evergreens. I was talking to a couple of the guys and it was getting late. My truck was practically the only vehicle left in the main lot. I threw my gear in the back, unlocked the door and was just getting in when I heard a girl's voice from a distance. She sounded mad, upset, a little scared. I thought it was, you know, a lover's quarrel or something going on in the other lot. It's darker over there and I figured a couple kids were parking, getting into it and she decided she wasn't going to go as far as he wanted to go. I wasn't too willing to get involved but then it dawned on me it was Evedan. She'd shouted at me a couple times to get my attention so she could get a shot she wanted so I know her voice enough to recognize it. Then she screamed and I knew there was trouble. I ran to see what the hell was going on."

"And what did you see?"

"I came around the trees and I saw a man trying to force her into a dark-colored SUV. I ran past her car. Her camera bag was on the ground near the driver's door, on its side like she'd dropped it. I yelled and just took off toward the SUV. She was struggling. The guy suddenly heard me coming or saw me and he spun her around and shoved her face first onto the ground, jumped into the SUV and flew out of the lot. He didn't have the lights on and I couldn't make out the plate. I tried chasing him but he was going like a bat out of hell, and I was worried about her, so I went back to help her."

"Was she hurt?"

"Some abrasions on her face, the heels of her hands and her knees. She might have bruises on her upper arms and wrists. I noticed some red marks there when we were in her kitchen."

"Okay, you're with her in the parking lot. It's dark. What did she say? Did she tell you who it was?"

"Yeah, she said it was Carl Harte. He'd been bothering her earlier and he evidently started in again in the parking lot."

"She positively identified Harte as her assailant?"

"Yeah."

"How was she emotionally?"

"Upset, mad. Sort of incredulous that he'd try something like that. When she got home I think she was scared."

"Okay, now, what did you do next in the parking lot?"

"Got her back to her car. It was locked. She'd dropped her keys. It was dark, so I ran back, got my truck and drove around so we could use the headlights to light up the area. We found her keys and she was just going to go home. I told her she should call the police but she didn't want to do that. We argued a bit about it but she wouldn't budge, so I said I was going to follow her back to her place to make sure she got there safely and she agreed to that. That's what I did. I followed her home and when we got there she seemed okay but I knew it was going to hit her hard once she was alone, and I also wanted to make sure no one was waiting for her inside."

"Rather noble of you seeing you don't really have much of a relationship with her."

"I may have grown up on a farm but my mother taught me manners. You don't leave a lady in distress alone until you're sure she's going to be all right. I also wanted to try to talk her into calling the police and reporting him again." He rubbed his nose. "And it's not like I don't care about her or anything. I see her around at all the games. She's kind of hard to miss with that red hair."

"But she refused to call the police?"

"Yeah. She sort of had goosebumps and then she started crying and shaking. Shock, or the aftermath of a huge adrenalin rush. I held her for a little bit to try to help calm her down, and then she went to wash her face. I looked at some pictures she had on her dining room walls and then saw the picture she has of me on the wall outside the lav. Turns out she took it the day my mom died. I didn't know she was gone, but I had a weird feeling that day during the game. I just sensed she was gone. I don't remember standing up and staring off into space like that, but I guess I did because she was there and saw it happen and took a picture."

"Close to your mother were you?"

Noah shrugged. "She was my mom. Jesse and I mostly spent our time outside helping Dad. He was a real bastard, used to beat the shit out of us. Never had a nice thing to say to us. Mom sort of made things easier at times, but she was afraid of him at times, too. He drank a lot, could get ugly and mean in a heartbeat. Jesse was good about getting in between me and Dad and taking the abuse." He looked away and was quiet for a few moments. "I guess I owe him for that now that I think about it."

"Is there anything else you can add? How did she seem when you left her Tuesday night?"

"She told me she had to shoot a swim meet at Castleton College Wednesday night but she'd be at the game Thursday evening. She seemed okay when I left. I didn't see any dark SUVs lurking suspiciously in the complex as I left."

"Are you in a relationship?" Geary asked.

"I've been pretty steady with Kyla Fontaine for about a year or so. I look at and flirt with girls when I go out after games but I've basically been faithful to Kyla for at least the last seven months. I've been kicking around the idea of taking her ring shopping, but after tonight, I'm not so sure I'll go that route."

"Why's that?"

"I think she just broke up with me before I came here."

"Why do you think that?"

"She said so, announced it to everyone in the bar and was offering herself to whoever would buy her a drink as I left. I guess I never noticed how jealous and possessive she was before. I never really even talked to Evedan before except to say 'hey' until Tuesday night. Kyla just seems to think every girl I look at or talk to I sleep with."

"And that's not true."

"Hell no! Christ, I'd be a dead man by now if I lived like that! I get up at the crack of dawn, go to work, do hard physical labor all day, grab something to eat and go play baseball during the summer, hockey in the winter. I sub in basketball when needed. I go out a couple nights but I'm not out late because I have to be up early and sober for work. On weekends I play ball and do yard work and there're some remodeling projects I've got going at the house, too. I don't have time to fool around!"

"You live here in Bristol?"

"On Cottage Street. I bought that run down Craftsman bungalow where that elderly couple were found dead a couple years ago."

"The Talbots. I remember, sad story, that one."

"It's a great little house but it'd been badly neglected. It's a labor of love."

"I love those little Craftsman houses. Great woodwork in them. Maybe one day I could stop by and you can show me around. Might be interested in looking into buying one when I retire if one comes up on the MLS."

"Sure, come on over whenever. Sundays I'm usually home doing stuff around the place."

Geary nodded. "Is there anything else you remember about that night?"

Noah shook his head. "No. I was with her probably less than an hour total." He shrugged then said, "Oh, I drank a bottle of beer while I was there. Microbrewery." He frowned. "I think it was from the Bristol Fields Brewery."

"Any significance in that" Geary asked as he reached for his digital recorder. "I've sampled it at Octoberfest last fall. Not bad. Couple of local guys started it, didn't they?"

"Yeah, actually it's Mike Thomas our second baseman who went in with his brother-in-law Dave Fields."

Geary's hand hovered above the recorder and his bloodshot eyes met Noah's across the desk. He withdrew his hand. "Really? That's interesting. Did she have a beer with you?"

"No. She didn't drink anything."

"You notice a lot of alcohol in her apartment?"

"No. She had three bottles of Bristol beer in her refrigerator and an opened bottle of wine. I didn't see anything else, nothing that would indicate she drinks much."

"She doesn't drink at all, except she had some wine at her birthday party last Sunday night. Her sister Gildan said Evedan took the rest of the wine and cake home with her. It was a small party at Gildan's house. Just three or four people. Evedan said she'd use the wine for cooking." He leaned back in his chair, raising his arms, bending his elbows and cradling the back of his head in his folded hands. "So why would a young lady who doesn't drink have three bottles of beer in her refrigerator?"

"Maybe she keeps them in case people drop by," Noah theorized.

"Or maybe someone gave them to her when they stopped by to visit? What do you know about this Mike Thomas?"

"Not much. He works in the paint and detail department. He's good. Um…he and his wife are splitting up. She asked him for a divorce. Guess they had a nasty fight and the cops were called. He's staying at the Holiday Inn Express. He was pretty bummed out about it tonight. He didn't go out with us to celebrate the victory."

"He ever show any interest in Miss Renfield?" Geary asked.

Noah shrugged. "I don't know. Not that I heard or saw. You'd have to ask someone in his department, but I really doubt it. He seemed devastated about Gilly asking for the divorce."

Geary put his arms down, reached for the recorder and switched it off. He rose to his feet. "Thank you for coming down tonight and providing us with this information. Any little bit we can gather will help us find her."

"Harte was at the game tonight."

"Was he there Thursday evening?"

"Yeah."

"Did you notice what kind of mood he was in?"

"No, not really. I just glanced at him a couple times."

Noah took another shower when he got home, a long hot shower to relax his muscles. He didn't have to work tomorrow. He'd planned on taking Kyla ring shopping but now she was pissed at him and maybe this time they wouldn't be able to repair the rift. He sighed. It was probably for the best, because if absolute truth be told, he'd begun to notice some things about her that bothered him, like her possessiveness and jealousy. He didn't want to be married to a girl who would suspect him of cheating on her if he so much as glanced at another female. He was a man after all and men liked to look. It didn't mean he was going to chase them or anything. He admired the female form in its infinite varieties.

And if the real honest to God truth be told, he'd felt something he hadn't expected to feel when he'd had Evedan Renfield in his arms Tuesday night. He'd felt an undeniable attraction to her. He'd thought maybe it had been due to his masculine instinct to protect the female of his species, an inherent trait most men carried but suppressed these days with women barking and snapping at you if you tried to do anything for them, and bitching and sniping if you didn't do what they might expect. It was confusing to be a man these days. But that night Evedan had needed him and he hadn't failed her. The whole thing had created a bond between them, at least that's how he felt anyway. He didn't have a clue how she felt, but she did have all those pictures of him around her apartment.

He shut off the water, grabbed his towel and began toweling himself. Of course all those pictures could mean she was just obsessive about him for some reason. Maybe she was a little crazy, but he didn't think so. She'd been scared, sure, but she'd had him alone in her apartment and she hadn't gone all psycho-bitch weird on him, hadn't said or done anything suggestive or to indicate that she had a weird sexual obsession thing going on. She'd just seemed like a sweet, scared young lady who was grateful he'd come to her rescue during a dicey situation that could have turned out badly for her.

He used the blow dryer on his hair, and then got into bed, turning out the lights. He lay awake for a while running Tuesday night over and over again in his head but there was nothing more that he could think of that might help the police find her. He sighed, closed his eyes and waited for sleep to overtake him.

"Noah! I need you!" Noah moaned, stirring in his sleep. "Noah!" He started to come up out of sleep but was reluctant to leave the dream he was having about Evedan. He had her in his bed and he thought she was speaking to him in the dream but her voice seemed to be coming from outside the dream in some strange manner, as if from a distance.

"Evedan?"

He looked down at her face against the pillow in the dream and her eyes were closed. Her face was covered with scratches and bruises. There was a bloody gash on her temple that her hair was glued to. Her nose had bled but the blood was dry and crusty. Blood had trickled from the corner of her mouth and down her neck. She was dirty and there were leaves and debris caught in her hair. The pillow beneath her head was now a tangle of leaves and twigs as if she was lying on the ground. He could smell stagnant water, motor oil, gasoline. He could hear crickets chirping and bull frogs croaking. An airplane droned in the distance. And suddenly her eyes fluttered open and she looked straight into his eyes. "Find me, Noah. Please, find me!" she said, her voice weak, desperate.

Noah came up out of sleep with a gasp and sat bolt upright. Her presence had seemed so real in his bedroom that he expected to see her beside him in bed, or lying on the floor, but she was not there. He got up out of bed and walked to the window, pulling the curtains aside and looking out. The neighborhood was quiet. The only light that he could see was in the bedroom of old man Foster three houses down on the opposite side of the road. He'd slept with the light on ever since his wife had passed away in the bed beside him three months ago. He was afraid she would haunt him and didn't want to be alone in the dark if she did. Noah couldn't understand his fear because they had been a very loving couple, but he guessed Lloyd Foster had just been watching too many paranormal programs on TV and had spooked himself.

His eyes traveled up to the sky and he saw the red lights of a private jet high in the sky. Businessmen traveled at all hours of the day and night out of Castleton Airport if they couldn't get flight clearance in Portsmouth. He started to look away but then he stopped. The sound of the plane reached him faintly and it gave him goosebumps. It sounded exactly like the plane he had heard in his dream. His skin felt electrified and Evedan's voice echoed in his memory, "Find me!"

He knew in his heart that she was alive. She was still alive, but she was badly hurt. And she was desperate to be found. She was reaching out to him because he has rescued her once before. And she knew he could hear her because she had captured the moment his mother's spirit had come to him to whisper goodbye during the final inning of the fourth game of the playoffs last fall. She knew he could tune into things like that. "Holy shit," he said aloud, letting the curtain fall.

He pulled on his clothes and hurried downstairs, flipping on the light in the den. He grabbed the road atlas off the desk. He'd brought it in from the truck last night although he didn't know why he'd done it, but now he knew. He needed the Castleton road map to find her.

In the kitchen he opened the book to the double-page spread of Castleton's roads. He knew she'd been headed to the college to shoot the swim meet. He knew where she lived, where she worked. He studied the map, trying to figure out which route she'd most likely taken. He went back to the den, grabbed a highlighter and brought it back to the kitchen where he highlighted the possibly routes she had driven. He didn't know if she had made it to the college or not. Geary hadn't said. The police must have questioned people who had been at the swim meet. They must know.

He grabbed the phone and called the police station. "I need to talk to Detective Geary. Yeah, I know he's not there. This is

Noah Cooper. I came down earlier and he came in to talk to me about Evedan Renfield. I need to know if she made it to the college Wednesday evening to shoot the swim meet." He scowled. The desk officer didn't have that information and couldn't provide it to him even if he did have it because it was an ongoing investigation and the public couldn't have that information yet. "I need to talk to Geary now. It's important. Please, here's my cellphone number. Have him call me. It's urgent."

He hung up, grabbed the map book and his keys and went out. It was three-thirty seven in the morning. The desk sergeant probably thought he was a nut case. Only nut cases called and demanded classified information at this hour. He growled with frustration. He needed to know if she had made it to the college or not.

He had just crossed the Castleton line when his phone rang. He glanced at the screen, saw it was Geary. "Hey."

"What's going on?" Geary grumbled, not sounding at all happy to have been woken up.

"Did she make it to the college or not? Did anyone see her there?"

"I can't tell you that. But you can tell me why you need to know if she did or not."

"I know this is going to sound crazy but I just had a dream that wasn't like a real dream. I saw her where she is right now and she needs me to find her."

"Jesus Christ, Cooper! You have a freakin' erotic dream and you call my desk sergeant and have him wake me up in the middle of the night?"

"When my mother passed I heard her say goodbye as if she was standing right in front of me! Evedan knows that because she snapped that picture of me the exact moment it was happening on the field last fall! She got through to me tonight because I was thinking about her, I was tuned into her! She's hurt, she's lying in the woods or something. She's weak and scared." There was silence at the other end of the connection. "She doesn't look beat up. She looks like she's been in an accident, somehow managed to get herself out of the car. She's banged up, scratched, and covered in dirt and debris like twigs and leaves and stuff! She's dying and I have to find her! Right now! So tell me if she made it to the damn college or not!"

"Yeah, she did. People saw her there."

"Then somehow she went off the road on her way home. I'm going to start looking for her."

"Cooper, listen, you came to her rescue the other night. You've still got some feelings going on about that. You had a dream tonight. That's all. It's wishful thinking. Chances are, and I hate to say this, but it's been over 72 hours since she disappeared. She's probably already dead if someone grabbed her. It's just a matter of time before we find her body in a shallow grave in the woods someplace. And if she had an accident and she's been laying out in the woods or something for three days without food and water..." His voice cracked.

"I could smell water. Not fresh but it's near her. She could be drinking it."

Geary sighed. "I'm not going to convince you to go home and go back to bed, am I?"

"No! She needs me to find her and damn it, I'm going to look for her for however long it takes to find her!"

Geary was silent again for a long time and then he said, "There was an accident on the main road between here and there late Wednesday night. The road was shut down for a few hours due to fatalities and the vehicles involved blocking both lanes. There were detours set up that night. She'd have had to have taken a detour to get back to Bristol. If she wasn't familiar with the roads maybe she could have had an accident. Or maybe someone in a hurry to get home drove her off the road. I don't know. People were being detoured down Jackson Road which is mostly farmland but there are some areas of woods and some deep drainage ditches running alongside it. The other route was less direct and that was South Exeter Road and then Fairlane Street to High Street to Bristol Township Road. That one's trickier but it probably would have brought her out closer to where she lives."

"I'll try that route first then."

"I still think you're wishful thinkin' this, Cooper."

"If I am then I'm not wasting anyone's time but my own."

"Look, you find anything at all you call me and I'll contact Castleton PD. I don't want you calling them and sounding like a nut case. Let me be the go between."

"Fine, whatever."

Geary gave him his private cellphone number. "Good luck, son."

Noah had been creeping up and down all the roads of the detour five times at least and now the roads were busier with people going to church. He went into town because he was starving, found a Dunkin Donuts shop and went in, ordering an egg and sausage bagel and coffee. He sat at a small table and ate, staring out the window. He was sipping coffee when he saw a tow truck go by. On the back of the tow truck was a really battered small tan sedan. It looked as if it had tumbled down a mountain. The driver's door was strapped shut. He thought whoever had been in that car was a goner for sure. And then he nearly choked on his coffee. He had followed that little tan sedan last Tuesday night hadn't he?

Jumping up he ran outside, got into his truck and impatiently waited for several cars to slowly go by before he could pull out and follow the tow truck. Three miles down the road it pulled into a garage and stopped. Noah pulled in behind it and was out of his truck and headed toward the driver's door as the middle-aged driver slowly eased himself out. The man gave him a scowl. "What do you want?"

"I'm from Bristol and I'm looking for a tan Toyota Corolla that may have gone off the road late Wednesday night here in Castleton."

"This here's a Toyota, or what's left of one anyway. Just pulled it up out of the woods. Kid found it yesterday afternoon while hunting for newts. Was in a kind of swampy area off Bristol Township Road just past Wilson's place."

"Is there a camera bag inside?"

"Nope. Nothing inside you can see. Probably some damn fool kids stole it, took it for a joy ride and then ran it off the road. Crazy idiots. Probably blocked the gas pedal and let it go. They've done it before. Farm kids with nothing better to do during the summer."

Noah walked around behind and read the license plate. A chill rolled down his spine. It was Evedan's. He knew her license plate by heart from having followed her. "No, a girl was driving this, a girl from Bristol who works for the Bristol Star Record. She came up here to cover the swim meet at the college."

"Don't know nothin' about that. If she was, you'll probably find her in the morgue, or the hospital. No one would have survived this wreck."

"Where exactly is Wilson's place?"

"Oh, I can't say for sure. You ain't from around here?"

"No, but I have a map in my truck. You could give me a general idea where you found the car."

The man shrugged. "Yeah, sure. Make it quick. I don't usually work Sundays but wanted to grab the car before the kid and his friends got the bright idea to torch it." Noah got the map book and the man studied it for a good long while. Noah was growing impatient. Finally the man said, "This is Arms Brook. Wilson's property runs alongside it. On this side there's a curve. You can't miss it. The car was down in the woods off the curve. On the outside of the curve, you know what I mean?"

"Yeah. I do. Thanks."

"Look, you think there's a body out there someplace?"

"Could be. She's missing."

"Poor kid. Probably some car came around the corner wide on her side and ran her off the road. Night time it's dark in that area. If you ain't familiar with the road it comes up on you quick. Always accidents there. DPW can't keep the guardrails in good repair there. All bent over, or missing in places. Winched the car up through a gap in the rails, You'll see the place easy enough."

Noah thanked him and got back into his truck. He punched in Geary's number. The phone was answered on the second ring. "What have you got?" Geary growled.

"Her car was just pulled out of the woods on Bristol Township Road. It went off the road on a sharp curve. It looks like it rolled over a few times. It's totaled. Nothing was in the car. I'm going out there now to look for her."

"You sure it's her car?"

"Tan Corolla." He recited the plate number and heard Geary curse softly. "It's hers."

"Yeah. Damn it! I'll call Castleton PD, tell them you're out there looking for her. They'll get some searchers to help comb the area. I'm going to drive out. If we find her I'll make the arrangements to bring her body home to Bristol, contact her family and all that." He paused and then said, "You find her you don't touch her. We'll have to take pictures and document the scene. Call me."

"If she's alive I am going to touch her. I'm going to be right there with her," Noah said.

"If she's alive…I like your optimism, Cooper."

"Yeah, well, I guess I'm a glass half full kind of guy. And she was alive early this morning when she called to me. I'm not going to think otherwise at this point."

"Call me. I'll have this cell with me."

Noah disconnected the call and slid the phone into his pocket. He was almost to Bristol Township Road. His heart was pounding hard and he felt a bit lightheaded. He knew he had to calm down and stay focused, watch for the curve, the muddy drag marks and tire tracks of the tow truck and the Toyota being dragged up onto the road.

He skidded to a stop when he found the area, eased his truck off the road, careful not to get too close to the ditch. "Okay, Evie, where are you, baby?" he said as he slid down the ditch into a stream of murky water. He saw where the car had landed and shuddered. There were crushed and broken plants and small saplings where the car had tumbled, broken glass, pieces of broken taillights, a side view mirror. "Evedan!" he called. He stopped and studied the ground, turning to look back up the path of destruction. Then he looked ahead at where the car must have come to rest. The driver's door had been sprung. The roof had been crushed, but he knew that she'd had her seatbelt on. He was sure she was the kind of girl who always wore her seatbelt. She'd have been in the car still, hurt bad, but still in her seat, the airbag deployed from the initial impact.

He skidded down to the place where the car had come to rest. He could smell gasoline, oil, radiator fluid. And he saw another dark fluid here and there in smears, blood. It was dried in places, pooled in others. And there was a faint trail, as if she had managed to wriggle out of the crushed vehicle and drag herself away. She was probably afraid of the car bursting into flame. How far had she managed to get though? "Evedan!"

He swept aside sumac branches and stumbled over something fairly substantial. Pushing leaves aside he found her camera bag. She had dragged it along with her as far as she could but it had gotten tangled in some roots. He tugged it free and continued.

A little farther on he saw her bare foot, pale and stained with dried blood sticking out from beneath some bushes. "Evedan!" He dropped the bag and started tearing at the branches under which she lay. She became visible little by little and his heart began to ache. Her clothes were torn, bloodstained. Her leg was obviously broken in two places. Finally he uncovered her face and his heart plummeted. She was so still, so pale. Her eyes were closed. He dropped down onto his knees on the spongy ground, brushing ants off her cheek and lips. "Evedan?" There were maggots squirming on many of her wounds and he nearly vomited. "Jesus Christ," he muttered. "Jesus fu…"

"No…ah."

His eyes shifted back to her face. Her lip had cracked and a trickle of blood was leaking from the corner. "Evie?" He lifted her eyelid and felt the flutter of it against his finger as she tried to close it against the light. "You're still alive," he said, letting her eye close. He sat back on his heels and pulled out his phone. He still had a decent signal. "I found her. She's not in good shape but she's alive. Get some help here fast!"

"You're sure she's alive?" Geary asked gruffly.

"I'm positive, but she won't be if you don't get her some help here pronto!" he fairly shouted into the phone. His hand was shaking. He felt so helpless. He didn't know what to do for her. He sat on the damp ground beside her after breaking some branches away and held her pale, clammy hand.

It seemed to take forever but in fact it was less than ten minutes before he heard paramedics, police officers and firefighters crashing down into the ravine. A red-faced Geary, huffing and puffing from his quick descent grabbed Noah and hauled him away. "Let them take care of her, son," he said. "You've done more than your share here already."

"She's got goddam maggots all over her!" Noah said, and then he turned away and vomited violently. Geary patted his shoulder.

"They're eating the dead flesh around the edges of the wounds. They'll clean her up at the hospital. She probably isn't even aware of them. Don't tell her all the gross and disgusting details if she lives through this. She's going to have enough to deal with getting her health back. You got me?" Noah nodded. Geary threw his arm around him. "You goddam optimistic son-of-a-bitch," he said, his voice thick with emotion. "Good job, son. Damn good job."

Evedan was in critical condition due to her injuries, dehydration and exposure. She was isolated in ICU for several days and only family members were allowed brief visits. When her condition was upgraded to serious she was moved to a private room but still only family was allowed to see her. Noah was finally allowed to visit her when she was upgraded again to fair two weeks after her rescue from the ravine. "Noah!" she cried when he entered her room carrying a big bouquet of bright flowers and a dark gold-colored mohair bear dressed like a baseball player in a teal and orange uniform with the number 11 on the back. "Oh, my God! He's a teddy bear version of you!" She smiled up at him. "How did you pull this off?"

"I found the bear, my sister-in-law made the uniform. She's pretty talented that way." He laid the flowers at the foot of the bed. The nurse had said she'd find a vase for them. "How are you?"

"I might get to eat solid food tonight," she said.

"That's a good thing."

"How's the team doing?"

"Not bad. We're second in the league. We'll be going to the finals. You think you'll be there to take pictures when we do?"

"Of course."

He pulled up a chair and sat down beside the bed. "I had your cameras and lenses checked out. The case is well-padded and everything is in good shape. You won't have to replace anything. You got lucky there. Your car, however…" Tears flooded her eyes. "Oh, hey…don't cry." He reached over and brushed tears from her cheek. Her bruises were still pretty vivid. She had a puckered pink scar on her temple where they'd stitched her head wound. "Cars don't matter. They can be replaced. You, Copper Penny, can't be replaced."

"How did you ever find me?" she asked.

He shrugged. "I don't know."

She reached up, grasped his hand. "Noah…I was so scared I was going to die. I tried to sleep as much as I could, but then I guess I got kind of delirious. I couldn't tell if I was awake or unconscious or dreaming, or hallucinating. I ate ants! Oh, my God!" She shuddered. "And flies!" Tears filled her eyes again. "I guess I probably would have eaten dirt to stay alive if I had to!"

"Shh!" he said, squeezing her hand gently. "You have a strong survival instinct but it's over. You're getting real food tonight. Granted it's hospital food but it should be more palatable than ants and flies."

"Noah? I want to tell you something but I don't want you to think I'm crazy." She looked uneasy.

"I'm not going to think you're crazy."

"Yes, you will, but I want you to know this. I had a dream that I was lying in your bed. It was nighttime. I knew I was still in the ravine but I was also in your bed and I was calling to you and you woke up and you looked right at me. I asked you to find me…and you did!" Her face crumpled and she sobbed. "You found me!"

Noah leaned over the bed and she wrapped her arms around his neck, sobbing against his shoulder. "Shh, it's all right, Evie. It's all right." A nurse had braided her hair. He stroked her hair, caressed the back of her neck. "You're not crazy. You were there on the edge of a dream. You knew I'd hear you and come find you. You know more about me then I know about myself."

"Noah…"

He pushed her back, wiped tears off her face, found some tissues and gave them to her. "We'll talk about all this again. Now is not a good time. You need to heal. You need to get back up to speed. I have no doubt whatsoever that you'll do exactly that. None at all. You're going to be aiming your camera at me again before you know it."

"There's just something about you…"

"I can say the same about you. But we'll explore that when you're out of here, okay?" She nodded. "Right now, you just focus all your energy on healing. I'm not going anywhere. In fact, I found you a sweet '64 Mustang. It's in the garage at my house. I'll be working on it on weekends. I think you'll like it."

"You're restoring a car for me? A Mustang?" She looked incredulous.

"Yeah, it's my wedding present for you. But we're going to have to discuss that later too."

"Wedding present? I don't even have a boyfriend."

"You do now." He caressed her cheek gently. "If you want me."

"Are you serious?" Her heart began to beat more quickly as she looked at him. He really was gorgeous. She'd had a crush on him since she'd started shooting pictures of the amateur league baseball games three summers ago. She'd even shot pictures of him playing hockey the past two winters. But more than that, she'd sensed that there was something more to him and he'd proven to her that there was indeed something that set him apart from others.

"Evie, I think it's pretty damn clear to me now that you're the only girl for me." His dark eyes met hers. His heart ached with love for her, feelings he'd suppressed because he'd thought she was too young for him. "We've made it through one hell of a first inning. Do you want to forfeit? Or do you want to continue and see how this all plays out? Do you want me?"

"I have five hundred pictures of you." His left eyebrow elevated. "Of course I want you! I want to be in the game with you for the whole nine innings, Noah Cooper. "

"Extra innings, maybe?" She smiled. "So what do you say we seal that game plan with a kiss then?" She nodded. He moved his hand down under her bruised jaw, tilting her head slightly back. Their first kiss was proof enough that they were meant for one another. Noah didn't want it to end, and neither did she.

"You know, you should reconsider taking that first responder course, Cooper. You've got that mouth to mouth thing down pretty good," a gruff voice said.

Noah straightened up, turning his head to discover that Detective Geary had entered the room. He hadn't even heard him come in. Evie grinned. "Uncle Joe!"

"Good to see you again," Noah said, shaking the man's hand. He was a bit caught off guard to hear her call the detective 'uncle!' But now he understood why he'd been allowed to search for her, to persist when there seemed to be a bad outcome in the wings.

"Looks like you've got yourself one hell of a guy here, Evie."

"I certainly do, Uncle Joe. In fact, I know I do." She looked at Noah and wished she had her camera to capture the moment. It was the photographer in her, but she also thought he looked pretty damn gorgeous standing there beside her uncle for a man she never thought she'd see again as she lay so badly hurt in the underbrush of the ravine. She hadn't thought she'd ever have the chance to tell him how she felt about him. But he'd seen the photograph she'd shot of him when he'd heard his mother that day. Seeing it reflected in his own face, in his own eyes caught in that single frame of film had changed his life forever. He no longer doubted himself, his ability. Through her skill as a photographer Noah Cooper had finally found himself, and found the girl he was meant to be with forever too.

THE WEEPING ANGEL

I look up from the book I'm reading at the counter to the left of the door as the shopkeeper's bell jangles. A young man of about my own age, which is twenty-six, or perhaps a bit older, has entered the shop and stopped. He stands there holding a scrap of paper in his left hand as he looks around the shop as if trying to orient himself to his surroundings. A look of confusion on his face causes me to think someone has sent him on a mission to find a certain book and he has no clue where to even begin to look. Or perhaps he's just in the wrong place. "Hello," I say. "Welcome to *The Weeping Angel*. Is there something I can help you find?"

He turns his head, noticing me for the first time. I must have been nearly invisible the first time his eyes had turned my way. Clearly I'm not who he expected to see here. "Is this 961 Raven Lane?" he asks, sounding baffled.

"Yes, this is 961," I reply. I slip down off my high stool after turning my book face down on the counter. I don't like to leave books like that, open with pages spread as it stresses the binding, but I don't have a bookmark or anything else close at hand that I can tuck between the pages. "Are you looking for a particular book?" I ask as I come around from behind the counter, approaching him. He stands staring at me. I stand just five feet high and am petite I have flame-red hair, naturally curly that I wear in a thick plait, caramel-colored eyes. He's staring at me so intently it's enough to make me hesitate, to glance down at my shirt to assure myself all the buttons are fastened and no lacy bra is showing. The fly of my black jeans is zipped. It's not my clothing then. I begin to raise my eyes and that's when Legs, my spider decides to sprint up from my left hip diagonally across my torso to settle on the top of my right breast.

"D…d…don't mm..move!" he cries. "I'll gg…get it off you!" He starts to look around, almost wildly, for something he can use to brush the spider off of me.

"It's okay," I say. "This is just my pet tarantula, Legs. She's harmless." His face is rather ashen, his eyes wide. I recognize the signs of arachnophobia. "I'll just put her back in her tank, and then I'll help you, if I can."

"Th…that th…thing is huge!" His panicky stutter is kind of cute, but he's even cuter with his rather shaggy, surfer-dude ashy-blonde hair and smoky-gray eyes. His jaw is stubbled with white-blonde whiskers that glow in the light coming in through the front window. He's tall and lean, tanned, dressed in well-worn blue jeans and a navy blue t-shirt that is sculpted to his muscular upper torso. I feel way too short and way too pale compared to him. "Do you know an Amanda Franklin?" he asks as I place Legs back into her environment and close the grated lid securely.

"No, does she own a business on this street?" I ask. "Or live in one of the apartments above the shops?"

"Um, she runs a business. Maybe she owns it. I don't know. Well, actually, it's a massage parlor. I got the street number of her place from a buddy on the job site over on Pierce Avenue. He went there the other day."

"The job site? Do you mean the *demolition* site?" An old theater built around the turn of the century is being demolished to make way for a modern bank and financial complex. I find it disgusting how this city government blithely grants permits to demolish beautiful old and historic buildings so that ugly glass and concrete modern monstrosities can be erected. No one even tries to renovate or restore these old buildings anymore. "Let me see that." I snatch the paper from his hand and look at it, roll my eyes, turn it upside down and hand it back to him. "Your buddy's printing is atrocious! Maybe you should try looking for 196 Raven Lane. I think you were holding that upside down."

He glances down at the scrap of paper. "Oh," he says, and then he laughs, embarrassed by his mistake. "I'm clearly at the wrong address."

"Yes, obviously. However, I do sell massage oils, over there, in the gifts section, but I don't provide massages here. There's just a stockroom in the back." I look toward a section of books near the gift area. "I also sell books on massage techniques, if you're interested." I point toward that section.

"Really? They have books about massages?" His curiosity piqued, he wanders over to that section. I trail behind him, curious about him. He's running his fingertips across the spines, reading the titles. One catches his attention. "*Erotic Massages For Lovers*, this sounds interesting." It's a trade paperback. He pulls it down and starts flipping through the pages. I see his eyebrows rise. This book contains real photographs of consenting adults demonstrating the various techniques. "Damn!" he says, his eyes meeting mine briefly before he snaps the book shut and replaces it on the shelf. There is a bit of a flush in his tanned cheeks. "Is this an adult book shop?"

"No. I have a small children's section and a young adult section. This is the alternative therapies section. Not too many little kids wander over here, and they can't reach that shelf if they did." I point to the small label that says 'not suitable for ages under 18' as I cock my head slightly. "I thought you were interested in a massage."

"Yeah, well, I am. But not *that* kind. I have some neck and shoulder pain. I've been doing a lot of heavy demo work, using a pry bar, reaching up over my head. Jack said I could probably find some relief by getting a massage to loosen up all the knots I have by the end of the day. He tried it the other day and told me it helped him."

"I see. Well, let me go look online to make sure he's actually given you the right address number. We can't have you getting lost again, going to another wrong business." I return to the counter. He slowly follows behind me.

As I'm Googling 196 Raven Lane he plucks a business card from the holder on the counter and studies it. "Is this you? Rowan Teaberry?"

"Yes, that's me."

He looks at the card again then looks at me. "Aren't you the girl they arrested for trying to block the demolition crew from entering the theater two months ago?"

"That would be me," I acknowledge. It's a matter of public record so it's pointless to lie or deny it.

"You're a gutsy girl," he says, and surprisingly I detect admiration in his tone. "You must have a strong passion for old buildings."

"Yes, I do." I could easily launch into my speech about the importance of preserving important buildings from this city's past but I restrain myself. I mentally kick my soap box aside and hold my tongue.

He laughs a bit. "Truth be told, it's breaking my heart tearing the Persian Garden apart. That place has been neglected over the past three decades but there're still a lot of beautiful features inside—architectural details, a marble fountain, elaborate moldings, wrought ironwork, plaster friezes." His eyes meet mine again as I look up at him. I sense a passion in him for old buildings similar to mine. He's gained a whole new dimension in my regard. "Maybe I should have been camped out on the sidewalk with you that day."

"If you care so much about old buildings why on earth do you work on a wrecking crew?" I query.

"I got laid off from my former construction job during the new construction slow down last year. I needed the job. I need the money. It's work. I'm trying to save up to start my own renovation and restoration business. I have a small inheritance from my Dad's estate that I'm trying not to touch. I've been adding to it. I'm getting closer to having what I need for start-up costs. That's my dream, my long term goal, actually, having my own business, doing the kind of work I want to do."

"And that would be renovation and restoration work?" I want to be sure I understand him correctly.

"Yeah. I want to renovate and restore old houses. Have you ever been down Juniper Avenue?" I nod. It's one of my favorite streets in this city. It's where all the leading merchants and wealthy founders of this city built their mansions in the 1800s. "Some of those places are in dire need of TLC. That's the kind of work I want to do."

I look away, back at the monitor. I could gaze into the amazing depths of his smoky-gray eyes for hours. I could listen to him talk about what is obviously his passion—old houses, for hours as well. He's got the kind of voice that will convince a loan officer of his sincerity and integrity so that he will go to bat for him and convince the bank to back his business prospectus. He's got the drive and ambition to make a success of his business and himself. "Here's the place you're looking for. Magic Fingers Massage. It's at 196 Raven Lane."

"Raven Lane is pretty long then if I'm at 961."

I nod. "It's probably the longest lane in the United States. It used to be the town farm road. Where these buildings stand now there used to be nothing but fields divided into plots. The road was dirt and well-rutted. There are some pictures of the city when it was more rural in some of the local history books on the shelf."

"I might have to come back one day when I have more free time. I'm on my lunch hour right now. Are you open on weekends?"

"Yes. Nine to three on Saturdays, twelve to four on Sundays." He nods. "You are at the wrong end of the road unfortunately."

He sighs, slips my business card into the pocket of his t-shirt. "Why is the name of your book shop *The Weeping Angel*?" he asks.

I point to a framed five by seven photograph hanging on the brick column behind where I sit. He walks around the counter to take a closer look at it. The photograph is of a Victorian era marble angel with drooping wings who has draped herself across a grave marker. She is clearly mourning over the grave, the loss of life of its occupant. It's a beautiful work, exquisitely detailed right down to the lines in her feathers. "I like old stuff. One of my favorite things to do on weekends is traipse through old cemeteries and photograph the interesting tombstones and monuments. I guess the word for what I am is taphophile. That's someone who does exactly that, admires old cemetery monuments, collects the sayings on old tombstones, the epitaphs, and just likes cemeteries in general."

"Interesting," he replies. "Sounds a bit morbid though."

"It's not really. I mean, there's a lot of great art in old cemeteries. And some of the old epitaphs on the graves are rather amusing. Our ancestors had a sense of humor."

I think for sure he's going to walk out the door now and head down the street to *Magic Fingers*, but he just nods and then starts wandering around the shop. I let him poke around. "Do you have any books on cemetery art?" he asks.

"None in stock at the moment. I can probably order one if you're interested."

"Do you have a collection of grave monument photos?"

"Yes, I have a few albums full. I've been doing this since I was a teenager."

"You do this on weekends?"

"I like to go in the fall," I reply. "When the trees have changed."

"You go by yourself?" he asks.

"Why do you want to know?" I'm starting to get a little nervous with all these questions he's asking.

"I'm asking because maybe I'd like to go and check out a few cemeteries in the future. I go by Bridge Street Cemetery all the time on my way home. There're some old mausoleums there. There're marble but they're kind of grungy and mossy now. They're beautiful but kind of spooky looking."

"Oh, I've been there. I know the ones you mean, down at the back where the ground drops off to the river below?"

"Those're the ones."

"I have some pictures of them upstairs."

He stops at the table where I have a coffee urn set up, pours himself a cup of coffee, adds two sugar packets and some non-dairy creamer. He stirs his coffee thoughtfully, lost in thought. I wonder what he's thinking about. He goes back into the ranks of bookshelves as the door opens and Mrs. Greany enters. She's a regular, a real sweetheart, living two blocks over in senior housing. She's one of my historical romance readers.

"Hello, dearie," she greets me with a smile and a twinkle in her blue eyes. "Got anything new I might find interesting?"

"As a matter of fact I do, Mrs. Greany. I have two books here you might enjoy. One is about a Scottish laird who decides he's going to take a very unwilling chieftain's daughter as his bride and the other is set in old Ireland. It's the story of a highwayman who falls in love with the beautiful daughter of a tavern owner."

"Sounds delightful! I'll take them. You always have excellent taste in books and know what your customers will enjoy most!"

"You don't have to buy them, you know."

"Oh, I know, but I trust you, Rowan. You're such a good girl! I wish I had a grandson you could marry but they're all too old for you and the great-grandsons are all too old for you, too!" She chuckles.

"Are you seeing anyone?" I ask her as I ring up the sale.

She glances around but does not see the young man at the back of the shop, and smiles slyly. "I have my eye on that Jonas Tucker! Oh, he's a character, that one! And such a dandy! Wears an ascot to breakfast every morning!"

"He sounds very dashing," I say.

"Oh, he is, and such a talker! He's got stories to regale the ladies with, he has! I'd invite him to my room for tea but I'm afraid he'll get fresh and I'll have to slap his face!"

She is ninety-two years old and has a lot of sparkle left in her. "Then you should meet him in the common room a few times and see how it goes before you invite him to your room," I advise.

"He's only eighty-five. He might think I'm a tiger if I invite him upstairs."

I smile. "Cougar," I say. "A woman who prefers the company of younger men is called a cougar."

"Reow!" she says, making a swiping motion with her arthritis crippled hand. "That's me! I'm a wild cat, I am!"

"You certainly aren't a domestic cat!"

She stuffs her books into her ladybug tote bag. "I'll see you next Tuesday!" she says as she toddles to the door and back out into the sunshine. I go to the window to watch her, to make sure she gets across the street safely.

"Maybe you can help me," my only other customer says. I'm not exactly sure where he is when he speaks, so I have to go searching for him. "I'm thinking I might want to give someone a gift."

"Well, what are his or her interests?"

"Historic preservation. Architecture. Romance."

"Romance?"

"Yeah, you know, that kind of stuff where boy meets girl, girl meets boy and sparks fly sort of story. The kind with the happily ever after ending." He grins. "The kind of books that you just sold to that old lady.

"She's something else, isn't she?" He's obviously overheard our conversation and found it amusing. "I do have a selection of historical romances. Maybe one of them will be appropriate?"

"Show me where they are." I lead him to that section. It's a rather large section as I have a lot of customers who avidly read romance. He takes the books down one at a time, glances at the covers with their long-haired, half-naked, muscular heroes and their fiery, amply endowed and beautiful heroines then puts them back. "My grandmother refers to these as bodice rippers."

"That's pretty much an accurate description, although I prefer to call them seven dollar dates."

He laughs. "My sister reads this stuff. Maybe I need to see the books you have on architecture or local history." I take him to the local history section.

Two more customers come in. I recognize them as secretaries from a law firm a block south of me. They're also regulars. I know them only as Phyllis and Margie. They're middle-aged and they make a beeline to Romance. I return to the counter and open the mail that was delivered at eleven o'clock. It's been sitting there awaiting my attention. The UPS truck pulls up out front. Bob delivers a stack of three cartons, dropping them beside the counter. He grabs a cup of coffee before leaving.

I'm checking in some new romances when Margie comes to the counter. "Are those new ones?" she asks.

"Yes, hot off the press."

"Can I peek?"

I haven't even finished checking them in yet, but I trust this supplier so I nod and let her look. She soon squeals with delight, grabbing a book and clutching it to her breast with a look of rapture on her face. "I have been waiting for this to come out for *ages*!" she cries. "Phyllis! She's just gotten it in! Hurry! There're only five copies left!"

Phyllis comes quickly over and snatches her copy. I ring up their purchases and they leave, excitedly talking about what the book will be like. I finish checking in that carton and then go to put the books on the shelf. They'll be flying out the door as soon as word gets out that I have them.

While I'm in the racks I make my way over to local history where my wrong street number visitor is quietly looking through a book on the old part of the city down here near the waterfront. He looks at me when he senses me close by. "Here're some pictures of the Persian Garden when it was first opened in 1901." He tilts the book so I can see. "Look, I'm working at removing this molding now." He points to the molding around some niches containing huge potted plants.

"Are they trashing everything?" I ask, feeling sick to my stomach at the thought of all that destruction going on.

"No, actually we're setting a lot of stuff aside for a salvage firm who'll come and take it to their yard. They'll sell it to designers looking for interesting pieces for new construction, or renovators looking for old architectural items for their projects. Sometimes museum curators even go and poke around to see if there's something they want to add to their collections. Stuff we demo out gets recycled, repurposed."

"I'm glad to hear that."

"Look at this," he says, flipping back a number of pages. "You'll find this interesting." He locates the page he wants and turns the book to show me the picture. "This is Raven Lane around 1888. If you look really close right here," he says, pointing to a building near the convergant point of this particular perspective of the street, "you'll recognize this building."

I look and sure enough I do recognize this building where I work and also live. The dormers on the third floor are quite distinctive as no other building on this street has front facing attic windows like this. "Wow," I say, impressed that he's found the picture and noticed such tiny detail in the distance.

"Have you ever done any research to see what kind of businesses have been in this location previously?"

"No. I did find a lot of old advertising from the previous business that was here for thirty years before I took over the space. It was a stationer's shop, and he also sold cameras and film. The shop sat empty for two years before I rented it. I liked the space, and the apartment was available too, making it really convenient to live and work in the same building."

"I bought a farm house on the outskirts of the city. It's a real fixer upper. I got it dirt cheap and have been working on it for two years. I live in the downstairs rooms. I'm still working on the second floor. I've gutted it. I want to put in a big master bedroom and master bath, two guest bedrooms and another full bath. Downstairs I have five rooms done. I'm using the study as my bedroom. There's a bathroom with a shower off of it. I converted a shed to make that room. The kitchen has a massive fieldstone fireplace in it with a Dutch oven and a warming box." He suddenly laughs self-consciously. "You're probably not interested in all that."

"No, I like that you bought a rundown old farmhouse and that you're fixing it up. Someone else might have bought the property, razed the house and built a new house. I admire you for investing money, time and physical labor in restoring and renovating a house. Maybe someday I'll have enough money to buy a little cottage I can fix up where I can grow some flowers and vegetables."

"Would that make you happy?" he asks.

I nod. "I think so. I'm a simple girl."

He closes the book, looks at its cover for a long moment and then asks, "What's the name of the oldest restaurant in this city?"

I shrug, but the wheels are turning in my head as I flip through a mental Rolodex of names. "I suppose that would be

Samuel's over on Water Street. It's been there a long time. It's located in an old warehouse on the docks that's original to the city. It dates from the late 1700's. It's a long low brick building with a loft they've converted so people can dine up there with all these massive hand hewn beams over their heads. They've managed to preserve as much of the original features as possible, like the old block and tackle, old pulleys and hooks, exposed beams and brickwork. The bar is made from a slab of wood they found in the loft. It's been polished so much over the years that it glows. It's beautiful."

"Do you and your husband go there often?"

I shake my head. "I'm not married." I flex my naked left hand at my side.

"Well then, does your boyfriend take you there on special occasions?"

"I'm not in a relationship at the moment. I have eaten there three times with friends though."

"Why aren't you in a relationship? You're a pretty girl."

I really don't want to discuss my personal history with him, but I answer anyway. The shop is empty today. "My last boyfriend turned out to be a lazy, controlling jerk who assumed I would support him for the rest of his life while he slept late every morning and then sat in a bar all afternoon getting drunk." I look away, the bitter disillusionment of that relationship still stinging. "I finally woke up and realized there was no way that it was ever going to work out."

"That's not an easy thing to do. I've had a few less than ideal relationships myself." He starts to put the book he's holding back on the shelf, hesitates then takes it back down again. "I might get this book." I head back to the counter. I have two more cartons to check in, and my inventory to work on today. "Why don't I take you to Samuel's Saturday night?"

"Who are you talking to?" I'm back at the front of the shop. I'm not sure he's actually going to buy a book today even though he's said he is.

"I'm talking to you." He's followed me back to the front where he lays the book on the counter.

"I don't even know your name," I point out.

"My name is Adam. Adam Hawthorn."

I stop and slowly turn around from where I've set carton number two on the back counter in preparation of opening it. "That's pretty cool," I say. "We both have trees in our names."

He thinks about that. "Oh, right! Rowan, Teaberry and Hawthorn." He smiles. "That sounds like a great business name, but I would just call it Rowan and Hawthorn. It flows better that way." His eyes meet mine. "It sounds like a great partnership."

I wake up abruptly to the fact that he is coming on to me. He's letting me know he's interested. He's asked me out on a date and I am being as receptive as a brick wall! I begin chipping away at the wall. "If we go to Samuel's," I say as I ring up his purchase, "you'll leave your pry bar and sledgehammer in your tool box?"

"Yes."

"Promise?" He raises his right hand and makes cross my heart motions, index finger extended. He's got great hands, long fingers. My heart suddenly swells against the chains I've bound it in after letting it lead me too far into a bad relationship with Brian. I have been protecting myself against that kind of hurt again. Go slow, girl, I counsel myself, but I like this man. He and I have common ground we might be able to build a solid relationship on. We both have names with trees in them. If I wind up marrying him one day I could be Rowan Hawthorn! I like the sound of that. Whoa! Slow it down, there! I suddenly feel myself blushing.

"You said you live upstairs??" he asks.

"Yes, right above the shop," I reply, pointing up toward the original tin ceiling above my head.

He looks up, smiles at the ceiling above us. "I guess I won't have trouble finding you again." I nod. "This is a great old building. I can see why you've set up shop here." He takes my business card from his breast pocket. "How about six thirty on Saturday? I'll come and get you." I nod again. "Do you have another number other than the business phone?"

"Yes." I give him my cellphone number, watching to be sure he jots it down accurately. "Don't dial it wrong," I say.

He laughs. "I'm not usually dyslexic, and like you said, Jack's got really bad handwriting, but I'm not going to complain about it to him. Reading the number wrong led me here after all." He pulls out his wallet. It's old and worn, leather with some design work on it. It looks handmade. He sees me watching as he slips my card safely inside. "I made this in art class in high school. I was seventeen years old. It's eleven years old and I still can't replace it."

He's twenty-eight. I like that he's a couple years older than me. I like that he's gainfully employed. I like that he has dreams and goals. I like him— period. "Made to withstand the test of time."

He smiles at that, reopens his wallet and pulls out a card. It's for *Wrecking & Demo Pros,* the company he currently works for. He takes the pen from the counter top near the register, prints his name and his cellphone number clearly on the back of it and hands it to me. "I'll call you Friday night to confirm." I nod, tucking his card safely into my hip pocket. His eyes follow the direction my hand moves and I find him admiring my hip, my butt when I return my gaze to his face. I feel myself blush again, but haven't I been admiring him head-to-toe while following him around the shop? "How much do I owe you for the book?" I tell him and he pays me, accepts his change, shoving it into his front pocket as he looks up at the clock behind me and sighs. "I don't have time to go find 196. No massage for me today." He shrugs, looks over his shoulder toward the alternative therapies section then back at me. "Maybe I should buy one of those massage books. But it's probably not easy to give yourself a massage, especially if it's the back of your neck and shoulders you're trying to work the knots and stiffness out of. I'd probably have to find someone willing to give me a massage some night after work."

"Yes," I agree. "It sure sounds like you would benefit from one regularly. Massages can be very relaxing, too, but you generally do need someone who can give you one."

"I'll think about that book. I'll have to come back again when I have more time. I've got to get back to work. It was a pleasure meeting you by mistake." I smile. "I'll call you for sure on Friday, hopefully see you Saturday night."

"Sounds good to me. Remember, don't dial a wrong number!"

He grins and then waves as he steps outside onto the sidewalk. "I'll be damn sure I dial the right number! See you later, Rowan!"

I walk to the front window to watch him walk up the street. I watch for as long as I can see him. I feel as if he's carrying my heart away in his hip pocket, but I'm not too worried about that. I have a feeling that when I see him again this coming Saturday night he'll bring it back to me, all polished up and shiny bright, mended, and with the dents all hammered out—fully restored. In the meantime, I'll put that massage book that caught his interest in the back room on the layaway shelf. If things work out well between us, maybe I'll buy the book for him because I'm willing to learn new skills, and I have a feeling that he's a hands-on type of guy, one who might be interested in giving me a massage after work occasionally.

"Legs," I say to my pet spider as I return to the carton of books waiting for me to check in, "I just may have to find you a new home in the near future."

Susan Buffum

Cupid's Darts: A Sweet Hearts Collection

JACK CAMERON TAKES A BRIDE

"Not bad, you old dog," John "Jack" Cameron said to his reflection in the bathroom mirror. "Not bad at all, if I do say so myself. You're a lucky man, Jack! A lucky man!"

"Grandpa, who are you talking to in there? Are you almost done? I've gotta pee!"

He opened the door, peering out at his six-year old grandson James. "I was just talking to that handsome fella there in the mirror," he said. "Come on in lad, I just need to put my tie on straight."

"Isn't there any privacy in this house anymore," James grumbled as he scuttled past his grandfather.

"You'll have plenty of privacy pretty soon, laddie. Ol' Grandpa is moving to his new condo after the wedding and the honeymoon. Kelly will have her room back and you'll be back to sharing your room with Johnny-boy and Rex." Rex was their dog that was over at the accommodating neighbor's this morning so he'd be out of the way. John was James's twin brother.

"Do I have to keep my suit on all day?" James asked peevishly.

"You can take your jacket and tie off at the reception, roll up your sleeves, kick off your shoes. How many whiskies do you want?"

"Seven!" James replied.

"Ach, and I wouldn't be alive to see me lovely bride on our weddin' night! Your father would skin me alive."

"Naw, he'd just bash you in the eye and bend your arm up backwards until you cry uncle and promise never to give me whisky again." James flushed the toilet and then began struggling with the zipper of his new suit pants. "Damn zipper!" he muttered.

"Watch that salty tongue, boy-o. You don't want your sainted mother hearin' you cuss like a sailor."

"She says worse than that. When Daddy told her you were going to marry Mary Shea she said shit."

"Did she? In a good way or a bad way?"

"I don't know the difference," James said, shrugging. "Sorry."

"Never you mind about that. She was probably just taken aback by my finally proposin' to the woman after courtin' her for five years." He grunted a bit as he knelt down, being careful of his bad knee. "Let me take a look at that zipper before you hurt yourself." He had to dig out his pocketknife to use the blade to work the tab of the zipper out of the seam it had buried itself into. "There you go!" he said, sitting back on his heels.

"Dad! What on earth are you doing with that knife?" Bridget, the mother of James and his other grandchildren, cried from the doorway.

"Jesus, woman! You gave me half a fright shoutin' like that!" Young James darted around him and then past his mother who yelled after him to put his shoes and socks on, they were leaving in *five minutes* for the church. "Lad had trouble with his fly." He closed the knife, slipping it back into his trouser pocket before hauling himself to his feet. Turning, he looked at his daughter-in-law and smiled. "Aren't you a vision!" he cried, making her blush. "I always thought my Danny had chosen the belle of the ball when he brought you home to introduce you to his folks."

"None of that horseshit from you today, Jack Cameron," she said.

He laughed. "Blarney, darlin'."

"I'm only callin' it what it is and you know it," she replied.

"Crisp as an autumn apple and just as tart," he murmured, shaking his head.

"You'd best get yourself downstairs. The limo just arrived. Danny and I have to round up the kids and get them into the van and then we'll be along." She turned and shouted, "Hey!" at someone in a tone that would have brought the troops to attention were she in the army. "Go on! Off with you, old man!" she said, heading down the hallway in pursuit of someone who was evidently in trouble and about to pay for it.

"Don't you be skinnin' the hide off my grandkids, you red-haired witch!" he called as he started down the stairs. "Kelly, get the broom out! Your mother's on a tear! She'll be wantin' to ride it to the church, I dare say."

"Danny! Will you please get your father out the door and into the limo! For the love of God! What have you done to your dress Megan?"

"Dad, you'd better get the hell out of here before she starts biting heads off," Danny said as he met his father at the foot of the stairs. "She's a bit tense this morning," he confided.

"You don't say. I hadn't noticed." He paused to smooth his neatly barbered hair. "Is my tie on straight?"

"You look sharp, Dad." A series of thumps came from the upstairs hall. "Incoming!" Danny cried as the twins came barreling down the stairs.

"Who's ridin' with Grandpa in the half-mile-long car?" Jack asked as he stepped outside.

"I am!" James cried.

"Me, too!" cried Johnny.

"Don't you dare!" Bridget called from the top of the stairs, the baby in her arms in diaper, t-shirt and a single sock.

"Ah, honey, let 'em go. We have Kelly, Megan and the little one to worry about. Let Dad take the boys with him."

"The church will be in a shambles," she said, turning away. "It's his wedding. If the flowers are trampled and the candles are toppled and they set the church ablaze it's on his head, not mine!"

"He raised seven kids of his own, if you recall."

"He had your mother. He didn't do it singlehandedly."

Danny reached the landing. "Give me the baby."

She shook her head. "You don't want him, he's wet."

"Then take a moment to catch your breath. You've been flying around here like a screamin' banshee since you fell out of bed." She stilled and then slowly turned and gave him a look. "My bad. I hadn't noticed you were so close to the edge. Best sex we've ever had, though, wasn't it?"

He thought she was going to snap at him but after a moment she ducked her head, raising her bright blue eyes to give him a coy look through her lashes. "You didn't hear me complaining, did you?"

"I'll round up the girls and get them in the van. You get little Mickey dressed and we'll be on our way."

"Right." She went into the small bedroom that had served as their nursery since they'd bought the house.

Kelly had been three and Megan a year old then. Eight years they'd lived here already. Five kids. He'd never pictured himself having a large family when he was younger. He didn't mind. He was from a large family, and Bridget was as well. They had aunts, uncles, cousins, nieces and nephews galore. The church would be full of family today. The reception would be chaos with kids running around like wild warriors, but it would be fun. He was happy for his father, glad he wouldn't be spending the rest of his golden years alone, living with one son or daughter or another until he reached the end of his days. "Girls! Let's get the lead out!" he called as he went back downstairs.

"Do you, John Cameron, take Mary Shea to be your lawfully wedded wife…" the priest intoned.

"Hold on just a minute there, Father," Jack interrupted causing the priest to falter in the familiarity of his reading, having never been interrupted before during a ceremony.

"What is it, John?" he asked, worry evident in his expression. He was obviously concerned that Jack Cameron had suddenly developed cold feet, had changed his mind.

"I think my hearing aid battery has died. Can't hear a word you're saying. Do you mind very much if Mary and I switch sides so as I can hear you in my good ear. I don't want to be making any mistakes, it being a very important occasion we're here for today."

"The groom is always on the bride's right," the priest murmured.

"As he should be, I'm sure," Jack replied. "But I'm also sure the Lord will forgive me my human frailty and faulty battery and not mind my placing her on my right so that I may hear the lovely vows that I'll be recitin'. I'll be wantin' to say them correctly in His ear and hers."

"Ahem," said the priest, not quite sure what to do. He gazed out over the church full of expectant faces, family and friends of the couple before him. Finally he shrugged and nodded. Jack and Mary changed places.

"Remind me to have the driver stop at the pharmacy for a new battery," Jack murmured to Mary. "I'll not be wantin' to miss any of the sweet nothings you whisper in my ear tonight."

The exchanging of the vows continued without further interruption, if you didn't count the squalling of an infant in the seventh row, bride's side, and the sudden phlegmy coughing fit of an elderly man in the fifteenth row on the groom's side, followed by rather loud nose blowing that set forty-seven children giggling and twenty-four various parents shushing in unison. About half the church missed Mary saying, "I do," but no one missed the lip-lock Jack Cameron laid on her, accompanied by a rather bold ass grab, before God and the entire congregation. The priest mopped his brow before waving the happy couple away from his altar, glad to see them go. Of course he'd be making his appearance at the reception to bless the wedding feast and the happy couple, and not above accepting a whisky or two at the bar with Jack and a few of his cronies before the fruit cups were even brought out.

The photographer paled at the size of Jack and Mary's combined families. He had not thought to bring his panoramic lens with him. Finally, he decided he'd have to shoot a series of pictures and then Photo Shop the lot of them at the studio to manufacture one group shot. It was an arduous chore to get the children to stop squirming and making faces. He was glad that digital cameras had replaced film cameras. He'd have been wasting a dozen miles of film today. Instead, he'd be deleting hundreds of bad pictures to weed out the few good ones for the wedding album.

Jack's best man was Barney Kelleher, owner of O'Leary's Pub, O'Leary having died and Barney not having bothered to change the name to Kelleher's when he'd taken it over. Jack had bent many an elbow there throughout the years. He was a round-bellied man, quite jovial in nature with bushy salt and pepper eyebrows and a headful of unruly curls to match. His plump cheeks were flushed, his nose the color of an apple's blush. His brown eyes sparkled as he raised his glass to offer a toast to the bride and groom. "May their days together be long and full of health, happiness and harmony. May they be tolerant of one another's foibles and faults and rejoice in their shared pleasures and joys. May they always be surrounded by family and friends. And may the wedding bed be strong and sturdy for many a year to come! Ladies and gentlemen, to the bride and groom, *slainté*!" He gulped down his champagne, made a face and cried, "Jesus Christ Almighty, where's the bloody Jameson! This stuff is weak as piss-water!"

"Ah, sit the hell down, Barney, or they won't bring out the food!" called Seamus O'Connor who had been one of the ushers. He was eighty-three years old and in an assisted living facility but had been brought by his daughter Cathy and her long-suffering husband Liam. Seamus was a bit of a curmudgeonly fellow since developing dementia but he'd been Jack's brother Thomas's best friend. Thomas was gone now, cancer having claimed him over two years ago.

Bridget realized belatedly that they should have brought a stroller or something to put the baby in. Danny ended up cutting up her chicken cordon bleu and then all the kids meat into bite sized bits. His own meal was less than lukewarm by the time he resumed his seat in anticipation of a hot meal. He was sorely disappointed but tried not to let it show. James dripped gravy on his pants and Johnny dropped a pat of butter on his lap. Bridget just rolled her eyes and blew a wisp of red hair off her cheek. Kelly sat scowling at her scrod, having decided she would have preferred the beef instead. Danny ended up giving her half his prime rib and eating her cold fish that she had poked to pieces with her fork.

After the meal and the cutting of the cake, while they were waiting for the kitchen staff to portion out the cake and add a scoop of vanilla ice cream to the servings, all the granddaughters and grand nieces gathered on the dance floor. The musicians, with pipes, accordion, drums and guitars, played traditional Irish music and the girls danced, all of them having had lessons since before they were old enough to tie their dancing shoes themselves. Those few who had not had lessons were out there, as well, following the lead of their cousins. The girls kept their composure, their ramrod straight backs, their arms glued to their sides through the first two dances, but then the boys started running out onto the floor to dance, getting in their way and it all broke down to something resembling more of a war dance than anything else. But still the adults applauded and cheered when the last song concluded before calling their children back to the tables as the first servers emerged from the kitchen with their dessert laden trays.

Jack led his new bride out onto the dance floor for the first dance while most everyone else finished their desserts and sipped their tea and coffee, or stronger spirits of their choosing from the still open bar. It would become a cash bar at two o'clock. Jack's pockets were only so deep. The dance floor was ringed triple deep with relatives capturing the moment on their cellphone cameras. There would be a hundred or more video clips posted on social media within minutes so that family and friends across the country and back in Ireland who'd been unable to attend would feel like they were there themselves.

"I'm driving home," Bridget said as Danny returned to the table, his shirt sleeves rolled up to his elbows, his tie long gone, collar and top two buttons undone, face flushed, perspiring.

"Don't be a nag. Come dance with me. Put the damn baby down someplace and come dance with me. It's been years since we've cut a rug together."

"I believe I have rug burn on my arse to prove we were doin' somethin' on the bedroom carpet this mornin'," she replied.

"I suppose you could call that the matin' dance," he said, a gleam in his eye.

"Oh, go dance with Margaret. You know she's dying to partner with you."

He laughed. Margaret was the wallflower of the cousins. "She's a nun," he reminded her.

"So what? Is there some rule saying nuns can't dance at their uncle's wedding? Go on. No one else has the balls to ask her."

"Darlin', you shock me with that vulgar tongue!"

"That's not what you said this morning," she replied, slanting him a look. "Go on. Just ask her."

Three minutes later he was waltzing Sister Ann around the dance floor, all the cousins backing away to the perimeter to give them room. Plain Jane Margaret, known as Sister Ann these past eighteen years, was flushed and smiling, thrilled to have been asked to dance by her handsome cousin Danny whose entire bag of marbles she'd won off him when they were kids. She'd come to the house before she'd gone to take her vows, bringing a leather bag she'd kept the marbles in, telling him she thought he might like to have them back so he could play against his sons one day. The bag of marbles was in his sock drawer, way at the back. The boys liked to play video games with their dad and he was teaching them to golf.

High spirits reigned during the remainder of the reception. A few tempers flared over old issues but there were enough cooler heads present to intervene before fisticuffs broke out. Parents with small children who had grown restless and fussy began to depart. Bridget was looking done in by three. Kelly was bored. Megan was dancing with her cousins Ashley, Jennifer and Quinn, grabbing the full skirts of their fancy dresses and flipping them side to side like French cancan dancers to the delight of the band they were performing in front of. James and Johnny were sprawled on the floor, James half asleep with his head on the diaper bag, Johnny counting kernels of corn that had fallen on the floor under the tables. "We need to get going before they all crash," she said.

"Dad and Mary are about ready to take off."

"You guys decorate the limo?"

"Nope, guy wouldn't let us near it. Only thing in it are the roses Jack bought for her. When you were socializing with the ladies a few of us ran over to the hotel and paid the manager to let us into the bridal suite. We delivered their luggage, short-sheeted the bed, tucked *The Joy of Sex* under one pillow, a few toys for them to enjoy under the other, batteries included." He winked at her. "Used shaving cream to leave a few words of advice on the bathroom mirror and shower stall door."

"You're so bad, Daniel Cameron!"

"Not all bad. We left them a bottle of good champagne and a tin of biscuits to sustain them."

"Very thoughtful of you."

"Looks like they're ready to go. Let's go see them off on their honeymoon and then get our brood home, and hopefully to bed early tonight. Daddy wants to play 'remember our honeymoon?' with Momma tonight."

"Was that just a brief refresher this morning then?"

"It got me thinkin'," he replied, and then he winked at her, helped her up out of her chair. "I didn't do so bad for myself askin' you to marry me all those many years ago."

She cocked a red brow at him, giving him a look, shaking her head. "Twelve and a half years we've been married and you can't remember how long."

"Why keep count?" he answered. "What do years matter? It's moments that count. Every moment I'm with you is a blessing, an honor, a privilege but, most importantly, a pleasure."

"You're as full of it as your father," she said, but she softened it with a smile. He adored her smile. It lightened his heart.

Jack Cameron opened the door to the bridal suite and then turned to his bride who waited behind him in the hotel corridor. "I wish I was a younger man and could lift you in my arms and carry you across the threshold, but at my age I'm liable to rupture myself and that would delay our honeymoon."

"I have two good legs. I can walk into that room on my own steam."

He stepped aside, made a sweeping bow and murmured, "Milady." She entered the room and stopped. He nearly collided with her as he followed. "Ah, I see the boy-os have been at work here while we were celebratin' at the hall." He shook his head. "How many of them were yours and how many of them were mine?" he wondered aloud.

"Does it matter?" she asked, turning to him, putting her arms up around his neck, pulling him down for a kiss. "They're all way too old to spank or make stand in the corner."

"I think I'd like to get out of this monkey suit and into something more comfortable. My t-shirt and boxers come to mind."

"Did you bring your medication?"

He slipped his hand into his jacket pocket, pulling out a prescription vial. "Damned insurance doesn't cover this. Danny and Bridget dipped into the kids' college fund to buy us ten little blue diamonds of delight."

"Oh, Jack! You shouldn't have let them do that!"

"They asked what I wanted for a wedding gift. We don't need anything, except a little help in getting a rise out of the old monster. The spirit is willing but the flesh is startin' to show its age."

"Oh, you!"

"Do you have plans for an hour from now?" he asked, shaking the bottle, a twinkle in his eye.

"Go on, take one."

"I limited my drinking, you'll have noticed."

"I did notice."

He nodded toward the champagne bottle in the silver cooler. "That's for later while basking in the afterglow of wedded bliss."

"You go take your pill. I need to take these shoes off and put my feet up for a half hour or so." She went and sat down on the edge of the bed, easing her feet from her constricting pumps. Reaching over to plump the pillow she heard a rattle and peeked beneath. "Good Lord!" she cried.

Jack came quickly from the bathroom. "What's wrong?"

"Just look for yourself!" she cried.

He looked, and then he laughed. "Those damn kids!" He went round the bed and looked beneath the other pillow, drawing out the book, turning it so she could see the cover. The color in her cheeks deepened as he flipped the pages. "You think at their age they'd have realized by now that we're the ones who invented sex."

"They meant well."

He turned the book back around, looking through it, pausing to consider before shaking his head. "That would throw my back out and we'd miss our cruise. However, this looks interesting."

"Put that book away! Let's just do it impromptu style. Who needs death defying yoga positions?"

"Now you're talking my language. We don't need a manual! We're old pros at this stuff."

"But not with one another."

He nodded. "We had good partners the first time around, didn't we Mary? God bless them both."

"Yes, God bless them. And now I've got you."

"And you're all mine now."

"Is that pill starting to work already?" she asked, looking surprised.

"Naw, can't be. This must be the natural reaction of a man starting his honeymoon with his lovely bride." He crawled onto the bed, and she shrieked in mock outrage as he reached for her. "Want to see what this old boy's got in him still?"

"Let me freshen up first."

"Ah, hell, Mary, it may be gone before you get back. You're fresh enough for me."

"Not as fresh as you, Jack Cameron!' she retorted.

"But you married me anyway," he pointed out.

She sighed, fell back into his arms. "Yes, I did, didn't I? Well, let's give it a whirl, you old goat."

"Baaa!" he said and she laughed. "Damn it, but I love you, woman," he growled.

"Love you, too," she replied. "Now, enough chitchat. Let's do this!"

Jack Cameron obeyed her command and was glad of it. He'd had a good first marriage. He'd loved his wife, the mother of his children. But she was gone these nearly six years now and he wasn't so old that he was ready for the retirement home and a rocking chair. He was glad he'd found Mary in grief counseling. He hadn't wanted to go but Danny and Brian, his eldest son, had insisted. An invitation for coffee after a counseling session had led to the discovery of mutual likes, compatibility. It had taken him a year to decide to ask her out on a real date. She'd declined twice, but agreed the third time he'd asked. She was a real lady. And now here they were, a married couple starting their honeymoon. He was a lucky man. A lucky man indeed, even if his family had just doubled in size. "The boys left a message on the bathroom mirror reminding us to practice safe sex," he said.

"I feel safe. Don't you?"

"Quite safe," he said. "Safe in the arms and embrace of my beautiful lady."

"You have a gilded tongue."

"The other message was on the shower stall. It said to wear rubber-soled shoes so we wouldn't slip and fall when showering after sex."

"Well then, let's take a bath after we've had our fill. We wouldn't want to worry the children."

"Excellent idea, my dear. I believe I saw some candles they'd left for us. We'll bring the champagne. I'll wash your back. You can wash my front." She swatted him but she was smiling.

"Happy wedding day, my darlin'." In response, she drew him down to her. He knew what to do from there.

Susan Buffum

THE WINDOW WASHER

Every three months the company that owned the building where the business that I worked for leased office space hired a window washing service. Our office space was on the nineteenth floor overlooking busy Butler Avenue which was four lanes wide and lined with similar skyscrapers, all modern and faced with floor to ceiling glass windows. To me it was as if we were working in vertical fishbowls—tall, rectangular aquariums filled with human life forms darting and dodging around obstacles like desks and cubicle walls, chairs and copier machines, that obstructed our meandering paths throughout the day. Instead of aquarium plants we had the obligatory ficus trees here and there in large decorative pots.

I had been promoted from a cubicle to a corner office with walls and a door. It was quite spacious. Too spacious, actually. My desk and chair, visitor's chair and console table looked almost child-size in the large space. I had a ficus tree in the corner where the north and east windows met at a steel beam. It occasionally shed some leaves. I benefited from the sunlight in the morning but in the afternoon it could get somewhat gloomy as the sun passed over the building and hit the other side. The floor was covered in generic beige Berber carpeting. There was a wine stain near the desk from the previous occupant. It looked as if the custodial staff had tried every known method to get it out but they'd only succeeded in bleaching the red to a washed out pink in the process.

I was sitting at my desk typing a report around one o'clock when the clatter of the scaffold used by the window washers disturbed me. It had always made me nervous to see these men working so high off the ground, but there was this one guy who was really very cute. I guess he'd noticed me too, because we always waved and smiled when we saw one another. I turned in my chair and saw a grumpy looking middle-aged man peering in at me. He had an unlit cigar butt tucked into the corner of his mouth that he was working at as if trying to coax it to life. The other man had his back to the window, adjusting something on the scaffold that was swaying a bit. It was a little windy out today. This man had a bright green bandana sticking out of his back pocket and I smiled, which sort of startled the grumpy man because he nearly dropped his cigar. He said something to the younger man who straightened up, turned around and peered through the glass. My heart did a skip-beat thing like it always did now when I saw him. He grinned and waved. I smiled and waved back. He said something to the grumpy man who cocked an eyebrow at me and then shrugged.

They began washing the east window. I watched them for a few moments and then went, somewhat distractedly, back to my report. I could watch green bandana guy all day and never be bored. He was unshaven today, and hadn't had a haircut in a while as dark blonde curls spilled out from under his white cap and over his coverall collar. I could sense them moving behind me, up and down, back and forth, washing the great expanse of glass.

Suddenly there was a quick double rap on the window and I turned. Green bandana guy had written something on a piece of paper and was holding it against the clean glass. The print was small so I had to get up and walk to the window to read what he'd written. "Will U have dinner with me Sat. PM?" it said. I raised my eyes until they met his. He had gorgeous, dark brown eyes. My heart was beating faster now. I held up my finger to tell him to wait, as if he was going to turn around and walk away from the window nineteen floors above the sidewalk. His co-worker was sort of scowling, impatient to move down a floor to the next window.

    I grabbed a pad of paper from my desk drawer and quickly wrote, "Yes, call me 2nite," and then my phone number. I went back to the window, held the pad up to the glass so he could read my response. He grinned, nodded. Then he wrote something on his paper and turned it back to face me. "What's UR name?"

    I wrote "Mia. What's URs?" on my pad and turned it so he could read it.

    He scrawled, "Joe." Then he motioned for me to hold the pad back up. I did. He dug out his cellphone from his front pocket and I watched him add my name and number to his contacts list. He gave me a thumbs up sign and then quickly wrote, "U will have my # when I call U 2nite." I nodded. His coworker said something to him and he rolled his eyes, hastily wrote, "Later!" then turned and went to one end of the scaffold while his coworker went to the other end. They began to sink down toward the eighteenth floor window below mine. As his head reached near floor height he glanced up at me and winked. I stepped back from the window thinking maybe he could see up my skirt and blushed even though I realized he really couldn't see anything but my lower legs.

    I returned to my desk and sat staring at my unfinished report. Joe. Handsome, sexy Joe. He would be calling me tonight! I hoped he was as nice as he seemed to be. It certainly was not the conventional way to meet a man but sometimes unusual could work out. I'd have to wait and see.

I managed to concentrate on my work and got the report done and sent to my boss. I heaved a sigh of relief. I was a little on the young side for this job in a lot of people's opinion but I had the education and qualifications needed, plus I could write a decent unbiased report and Mr. Bacon appreciated that.

I was putting on my jacket when there was a knock on the door. "Come in!" I called.

Margie stuck her head around the door. "Heading home?" she asked. I nodded. "This came for you about a half hour or so ago. I didn't have a chance to deliver it until now. It's kind of weird." She shrugged and brought her hand up. My eyes must have widened when I saw the neatly folded bright green bandana that she was holding out to me. "I think there's something, a paper of some kind, folded up inside it. It's definitely not an interoffice message!"

"I guess not! Thanks for bringing it to me." She looked at me for a moment and then left, anxious to head home. I looked at the bandana for a few seconds before unfolding it. There was a piece of paper inside as she had said. I lifted that out, tucked the bandana into my jacket pocket to free up my other hand and then unfolded the paper. He had written me a note of some length:

Hi Mia,

I just want to tell you that I'm glad I finally got up the nerve to communicate with you today. You're the prettiest girl on the 19th floor— in the entire building in fact! I've seen you around up there for the past three years and was surprised to find you in the corner office, obviously your office, today. I'd hoped to see you but didn't expect you to have been promoted! Congratulations! I hope you still want me to call you tonight- at seven? Maybe you don't want to go out with a lowly window washer? But you gave me your number, so then again, maybe you do?

Anyway, my name is Joe Waterman. My Dad owns the company I work for. One day it'll most likely be mine. My older brother just quit and moved to Oregon to work for his girlfriend's father. Dad's pissed, but I'll make him realize he's still got me and I've settled down since my college days.

Looking forward to talking to you tonight. I know your voice is going to be as beautiful as you are!

Yours, Joe

I smiled, refolded the note and slipped it into my bag. I was glad he sounded like an ordinary guy, not a fruitcake. I dug my cellphone out and checked to make sure that it was on and charged. I certainly didn't want to miss the call from the cute guy I had been admiring for three years from behind the big glass windows of the nineteenth floor. I was glad that he'd noticed me through the light tinting and had finally found a way to communicate with me.

I could hardly wait until seven o'clock!

THE BIG LEMON

"We have to stop meeting like this." I looked around recognizing Vince from the dealership where I'd bought my car, now less-than-affectionately known as The Big Lemon. Vince was the mechanic who came out to the counter to tell me what he'd done to the car every time I took it in. As he described the work he'd done, I saw dollar signs in front of my eyes. "How's the car treating you these days?"

"It's sitting out there in the parking lot devising some new nefarious plot to dent my bank account again," I replied.

"Yeah, it's due. What's it been? Two months since you brought it in last?"

"More or less."

"Buy you a coffee?" he offered. Before I could reply he gave me a sheepish grin and said, "Seeing as I'm the guy whose pockets you've been lining with so many visits to the service department."

"Well, in that case, you can buy me a large regular coffee with a shot of mocha and two sugars.'

"You want whipped cream on that?"

"Sure, why not?" He moved to stand beside me which made the woman directly behind me scowl at us. I ignored her. "You have grease on your jaw," I said.

"Where?"

"Here," I said, touching my fingertip to his scruffy jaw. His whiskers made my fingertip tingle.

"I thought I'd gotten it all off." He moved to the counter, ordered my coffee, his own and then he ordered two blueberry muffins. He glanced at me to gauge my reaction to that. If he was hungry, he was hungry. He could eat whatever he wanted to, even though a muffin did sound good. I hadn't had time for lunch today. "Let's go grab that table in the corner," he said.

I followed him to the indicated table. I'd thought he was just buying me a coffee and then we'd both go our separate ways. He dropped down wearily into a chair. I sat down opposite him. He pushed my coffee across the table to me and then slid a muffin over as well, jumped up and went to grab some extra napkins. "You bought me a muffin?" I asked when he came back.

"Sure. You look hungry. Wouldn't be right my sitting here across from you shoving a muffin in my mouth while you sat there, your stomach growling like a bear."

"Well, thanks."

"Melissa," he said. I glanced up at him. "See, I remember your name."

I pointed to his blue work shirt. "Vincent, but everyone calls you Vince, not Vinny."

"I refuse to be a Vinny. Christ! I'm an adult!"

"You could be a Vin."

"I could. That's French for wine, right?"

"Yes."

"You drink wine?"

"Sometimes, when I go out."

"You go out much?"

"Not lately. My car's been eating money like it has some obsessive-compulsive disorder."

"Crazy little OCD car." He broke his muffin into sections, ate a third of it. "You need to trade that lemon in."

"But I like my car."

He took a sip of his coffee, wincing. "Hot!" He set it down, ate another third of his muffin. "Admit it, you just keep that car because if you traded it in you wouldn't get to see me every couple of weeks."

I looked across the table at him. He was gorgeous. He did make my heart beat faster whenever I saw him coming to talk to me from the vast service area behind the counter. "I plead the fifth," I said, so as not to incriminate myself. He smiled. "I haven't finished reading all the magazines in your waiting area yet."

"Is that what keeps you coming back, the reading material?" He finished his muffin. I had taken two bites of mine so far. "Excuse me a minute." He went back to the counter, bought himself another muffin. "I missed lunch today. Had to change out a tranny. Once I start I hate to stop."

He broke this muffin into thirds as well. He had nice hands, long fingers. His fingernails had grease under them but they were neatly trimmed. He had a little scar on the back of his left hand. He noticed me looking. "Burned it on a hot muffler," he said.

"Ouch."

He studied me as I ate a bit more of my muffin, sipped my coffee. "You don't talk much," he said.

"Not on a first date."

He had deep dimples. His gray eyes had dancing lights in their depths. "This is pretty casual for a first date. If we had a real first date I'd take you over to the Towering Pines for a surf and turf dinner with a bottle of wine. And afterwards we'd go for a drive out into the country and stop someplace, get out and look up at the stars for a while, maybe see a shooting star. Then I'd take you home, walk you to your door, make sure you got safely inside."

"You wouldn't try to kiss me goodnight?"

"I've gotta be honest with you, Lissy, I would want to kiss you goodnight, but you'd better just send me home. I'm the kind of guy, one kiss leads to another, and then another. I'm a kiss junkie. I admit it. I must have a luscious lip fetish."

"At least you're honest and up front about your fetish."

"Knowing what you know about me, would you still go out with me, if I asked you?"

"Are you asking me?" My heart was skittering around like pebbles on ice. I'd gotten through a messy divorce a year and a half ago. Danny had emptied the bank account gambling. He'd made it look like I was to blame for his addiction. I'd had to pay the lawyer and court fees because he'd had no money. And then I'd bought The Big Lemon and it was bleeding my already severely anemic bank account now. It would be nice to go out.

"I guess I am."

I liked that he looked a bit nervous that I might decline. "I'll go out with you, but I'd really like to go to Butterfield's for a roast turkey dinner with all the trimmings." I hadn't been there since I was a teenager.

"Are you serious? I haven't been there in years! I never really think about it. Sure, turkey sounds good to me. How about Saturday night?"

"Okay. I live…"

He held up his hand. "I confess, I've memorized your address from the invoices. Sorry. I'm not a stalker. I was just curious to know where The Big Lemon was garaged between visits."

I laughed, "Oh, you've heard me call it that?"

"On a few occasions."

"Why don't you pick me up at five o'clock and we'll get there early, have dinner and dessert, and then maybe we can go for a drive in the country. I like it out by Tepper Lake."

"I actually live out there," he said. "I have a cottage on the lake."

"Really? I used to go swimming there all the time with my family. At the public beach. We'd have cookouts and spend the whole day there."

"I have a small private beach, a little dock, a canoe. I could paddle you around on the lake while we wait for the stars to come out."

"That sounds nice." It sounded rather romantic, in fact.

"Done deal then. I'll pick you up on Saturday at five." He stood up. I got up, grabbed my coffee and walked with him out to the parking lot. He went to my car, looking it all over, even getting down on the ground and peering beneath it. "Looks like it may be leaking a bit of coolant again. Can you bring it in on Monday? Drop it off on your way to work. I'll come get you and bring you to the service department to pick it up around five thirty?"

"Do you think you can fix it this time?"

"I'd better or there might not be a second date, right?"

"Um, if we count this as a first date and we go out to Butterfield's on Saturday, then technically that would make it a third date that would hang in the balance."

He took the keys from me, unlocked the car. I slid in behind the wheel. He leaned in, slid the key into the ignition. "Do you kiss on the first date?" he asked.

"No. I do kiss on the second date, however." He grinned as he backed the upper half of his body out of the car so that he was leaning down looking in at me. "Is that good enough for you, considering your luscious lip fetish?"

"That's fine with me. I'll make sure I have all the grease off me." I nodded. "Good seeing you outside the service department, Lissy. Drive carefully."

"See you Saturday." He closed the door. I started the car. He gave me a thumbs up sign, meaning the car sounded fine to his expert ear. I waved and pulled away, glancing at him in the rearview mirror. My God, he truly was a gorgeous man! I tore my eyes away from his receding image in the mirror, reached forward and patted the dashboard affectionately. "Thank you," I said to the car that had more or less played matchmaker. And then I grinned as I pulled out into traffic and headed home, anticipating Saturday evening, and Saturday night at the lake. I was long overdue for some real romance in my life and I thought, as I cruised along the busy street, that Vincent was just the guy who would see that I got everything on my wish list this time around.

COFFEE CONNECTION

It took Dillon four years to realize that I was the co-worker who made the coffee after lunch every day. No one else cared about making it, but they liked to complain if the carafe was empty. The way he found out it was me making the coffee is that he quit smoking. He used to go outside and have a butt or two after eating his lunch at his desk in his cubicle two rows over and one row back from mine. He came into the kitchenette and stopped dead, a look of astonishment on his face. I was pouring clear, cold water into the top of the commercial coffee brewer. "So it's you!" he said. Those were probably the first words that he'd spoken to me this year. "You make the coffee."

"Yes, that would be me," I replied. I set the empty carafe on the top warming burner, snapped the water compartment lid shut. "It'll be ready in less than ten minutes," I said.

"Good," he replied. "Excellent!" He nodded, his brown eyes traveling down to my name tag. God, he didn't even know my name after all these years we'd been working in the same office! "Ginger." His eyes returned to my face, meeting mine. I have green eyes, auburn hair, a smattering of freckles across the bridge of my nose, pale and barely noticeable. I'd lost fifteen pounds of what my mother called baby fat since New Year's. I had five more to go to reach my goal. "My neighbor had a dog named Ginger when I was growing up. It was a cocker spaniel." My eyebrows shot up under my bangs. Was he saying I reminded him of a dog? He saw the look on my face and his cheeks turned pink as he rushed to say, "Not that you look like a dog. You don't look like a dog at all. You look like a human being."

"Well, I'm glad you didn't say I looked like a robot or an alien or something."

"No, no, really. You look like a girl." He went to the cabinet to get a cup. We had quite a collection of vendor logo mugs. He chose one, nearly dropped it. I caught my breath as I watched him sort of juggle the cup as if he was a circus performer all the while looking a bit panicky. Somehow he managed to not drop it. He set it on the counter, wiped his sweaty hands on the thighs of his dark pants. I gave him a quiet bit of applause. His flush deepened but he grinned wryly at me. "And for my next act…well, I could tap dance for you."

"Could you?"

"My mom insisted I take dance lessons. It was a waste of money, if you ask me. Two left feet." He nodded toward the mug on the counter. "And two left hands." I smiled. He shrugged, and then smiled. "You want some coffee? I hear it's pretty good. Girl who makes it must have some magic in her to make office coffee taste decent. I can highly recommend it."

"Maybe I will. I usually drink tea though."

"Oh. Do you want some tea instead?"

"No, I'll have coffee today, if you're serving."

"I am," he said, "but maybe you want to take down your own mug? Must have accidentally buttered my fingers this morning instead of the toast."

"You're funny," I said as I moved around him to open the cabinet to choose a mug.

"I'm Dillon," he said.

"Yes, I know."

"You do?"

"Um, yes. You've been here about the same number of years that I've been here."

"Have you?" He frowned slightly. "Four years? Where do you sit?"

"A couple of rows over from you."

He made a face. "I don't get out much."

"Neither do I, but I pass your cubicle every day on the way to mine."

"Turn around, maybe I'll recognize you from the back." I turned. "Ah, yes. Ponytail girl. You sometimes tie a bow at the end. Three times in the past two months you've tied the bow at the top."

My heart leapt at that. So, he had seen me, and he had been noticing me if he could spit out a detail like that. He was right! "Yes, very observant of you. You must have eyes in the back of your head because when I go by you have your back to me."

"Not always. Yesterday you wore a blue skirt and a light blue blouse with a purple and blue sweater." He lifted the carafe from the burner since the brewing cycle had ended and filled our mugs. I added sugar to mine, two teaspoons, cocked an eyebrow at him. He held up two fingers and I put sugar in his mug too. He got out the half and half. We both liked our coffee light and sweet.

I took my mug, he took his. "Cheers," I said.

"Did you eat yet?" he asked.

"I had a chicken salad sandwich at my desk."

"I haven't had chicken salad in ages. I had bologna." He rolled his eyes. "Boring!"

"Want me to make you a chicken salad sandwich tomorrow? I'm trying to use up some leftover chicken. I love roast chicken but you can't find one small enough for just one person."

"No, you'd have to have a roasted chick and people would picket any store that sold little chicks to single people who just wanted a little chicken." I laughed. He was so funny! "Yeah, I'd like that. Thanks for offering. You bring the sandwiches, I'll bring the chips."

"Sounds like a plan."

"Can I walk you to your cubicle?' he asked as the sound of our co-workers coming back from lunch reached our ears.

"Yes, that would be nice." Of course he had no idea which cubicle was mine. I showed him. He leaned against the half wall. I sat down, set my coffee down on the coaster just above my keyboard.

"Well, now that I know where you live I may stop by to visit you once in a while, if you wouldn't mind?"

"No, that would be nice. I'd like that. It gets lonely just sitting here by myself day after day."

"Same over there in my cubicle." He pushed himself away from the wall, lifted his mug in salute to me and nearly sloshed coffee on his orange sherbet-colored shirt. He winked at me. "I'm really not a klutz, I just play one in the office." I laughed. "Look, I get off at five. You?"

"Oh, by some coincidence I'm free to leave at five myself."

"Suppose we meet by the elevators and I'll ride with you down to the parking garage."

"All right. I'm on level 3B."

He nodded. "2A for me, your car must be on the way." I nodded.

"Dillon! No loitering!" called someone further down the aisle. "Get back to work!"

He leaned into my cubicle. "You know John? He thinks he's the boss of me!"

"He *is* the boss of me," I murmured.

"Then I'd better do as he says because I guess he's the boss of me, too. See you at five, Ginger. Thanks for the coffee!" He headed back toward his aisle.

I spun in my chair to face my computer monitor, grinning, hugging myself. Dillon Reed had finally spoken to me! He was so funny and nice, just like I'd hoped he'd be! Some cute guys could be such jerks!

From two rows over I heard a now familiar raised voice say, "Yes, this *is* office coffee. I highly recommend it. I know the brewer personally. She's brilliant!"

I grinned as I logged back onto my computer and then reluctantly turned my attention back to my work. Five o'clock wouldn't come fast enough!

THE UNDERTAKER'S DAUGHTER

Eamon McCleary stood in the parking lot beside the sprawling brick Victorian mansion staring at the round tower at the front corner with its conical witch's hat roof. How many times had he ridden his bike past this house as a boy on his way to elementary school and then middle school? It must number over a thousand, he figured. And after middle school he'd passed this house in the bus for a couple years until he'd gotten his first car at sixteen and a half, and then he'd driven by Mooney & Sons Funeral Parlor, laughing about the old 'haunted house' and the creepy people who ran it all the while hoping to catch a glimpse of old man Colm Mooney's son Declan's youngest daughter, Eve, she of the flamed-red hair and the penchant for wearing black. Her older sister Arlene, who had raven curls and deep brown eyes that looked purple in certain light, had been a year ahead of him in high school, the unattainable beauty queen lusted after by every red-blooded male in the school. Eve was two years behind him. He remembered now how cruel they'd all been to her, taunting and teasing her mercilessly about being the angel of death, a ghoul, a dark spirit, a ghost girl haunting the school, forever in the shadow of her more popular sister. She'd been a somber, solitary girl who'd often sought refuge in the school's library, burying her nose in a book and ignoring them all. Now, Eamon wondered if they would find Arlene inside. He knew she'd gone to South Carolina but heard a rumor that she was divorced and had come back to Hadleigh Falls with a little girl of her own. Or would he have to deal with the old man, Colm, who was hard of hearing and had a close affinity with the bottle? Or maybe Declan was back from Ireland now? There was another son, a bachelor, handsome devil, never married. What was his name? "Dad? What's Declan's brother's name?" he asked as his father slowly got out of the pick-up truck.

"What?" Jack McCleary asked, squinting at his son. He'd forgotten his glasses back at the house.

"Declan's brother, the dandy. What's his name?"

"Nolan. I believe his name is Nolan."

Eamon nodded. "Right. I remember now. You ready for this?"

"Are any of us ever ready to make funeral arrangements for our loved ones?" his father replied. "Christ, I never thought she'd go before me." He left unsaid that he'd never discussed her wishes with his late wife Mary although he'd been quite vocal about his own wishes. He'd told her he wanted a traditional Irish wake, with a bottle of Jameson on a silver salver and dozens of shot glasses for the mourners to fill, to offer his corpse a last toast. He wanted a piper, a drummer and a fiddler to play, not in the room, but perhaps in the hall so that they didn't drown out the conversation of those in the viewing room. He wanted to be buried in his Sunday suit, but Eamon was to loosen his tie and unbutton his collar before the casket was closed, and place his old Red Sox baseball cap on his head. He'd never asked Mary what she wanted and now he deeply regretted that fact. They weren't old yet, after all. And now he felt like a ship caught in the doldrums, no wind in his sails. Dead in the water. Dead in his aching heart, lost, his compass gone.

"I know," Eamon agreed. His mother had always seemed so vital, so full of life and good cheer. She had always been busy doing something—cleaning, cooking, baking, laundry, gardening, sewing, singing with the church choir, involved in clubs and social activities. "Let's go get this over with. We'll stop at O'Brien's on the way home for a beer, okay?"

"Yeah, okay."

They walked up the path to the front porch and paused at the double doors, unsure if they should ring the old fashioned doorbell or just walk in. Finally, Eamon grasped the ornate brass door knob and pushed the door open. They stepped into a vestibule with a gilt table to one side on which stood a huge potted Boston fern. There was an oval gilt-framed mirror hanging on the wall above the fern. On the opposite wall was an old-fashioned brass lamp. He opened the interior door that had a window through which they could see the reception hall beyond, the impressive free-standing staircase curving up to the second floor.

They stepped into the hall, quietly closing the door behind them. It was as silent as a tomb. Jack removed his baseball cap and held it nervously before him, twisting it around and around as his eyes searched the hall, taking in the grand Victorian decor. His eyes skimmed over the viewing room to the left, and the one to the right. He didn't want to think about Mary lying in an open casket in either one of those rooms. He cleared his throat, trying to move the knot he felt there.

Footsteps approaching from the rear of the house made them both look in that direction. Eamon felt his heart thud hard once. It was Arlene and she was as beautiful as he remembered. "Hello," she said. "May I help you?"

"Um, my mother was brought here last night?" Eamon said, feeling like a tongue-tied teenager. He was twenty-six now, which made Arlene twenty-seven. "McCleary? Mary McCleary? She passed away at the hospital yesterday evening."

"Yes, Mrs. McCleary. I believe Sean is bringing her over now."

"I want a nice funeral for her," Jack said, his voice gruff with emotion.

"Of course you do, Mr. McCleary. Shall we go to the consultation room where we can talk about what Mary would like." She led them down the broad hall with its maroon, navy, green and gold patterned carpet to a room that had probably been the informal dining room back in the day. "Please, sit down. Would you like coffee? Tea? Water?"

"Dad? Coffee?" Eamon asked. His father nodded. "Regular coffee, two sugars and a splash of cream. I'll have a glass of water, if it's not any trouble."

"It's no trouble. Why don't you and your father look through the selection of memorial cards. There are a variety of images and verses to choose from. Your family members, friends and acquaintances will like having a small memento of Mary's funeral." She slid two black binders across the table. "Take your time. I'll get your coffee and water." She left the room.

Jack glanced at his son, saw he'd been watching the young woman leave the room. "You went to school with her, didn't you?"

Eamon nodded. "She was a year ahead of me. Ran off with some college guy, got married down south, had a kid, got divorced and moved back north."

"Damn beautiful girl, she is." He pulled a binder closer and began paging slowly through it. "I don't know what your mother would want."

"She liked flowers," Eamon said. "Pick one with pretty flowers on it. She had a lot of friends in the Garden Club." He slid the other binder over and began flipping the pages. This one had all sorts of verses in it. He grimaced. How was he ever going to choose a verse? His father wouldn't be able to make up his mind either.

They heard the front door open and then close, heard rapid footsteps in the hallway. A child was complaining about something and another female, somewhat older, was trying to soothe her but not being very successful. "Go tell your mother, then, if you think I'm bein' mean. See what she has to say about it." Footsteps stomped off past the room they were in. Slower footsteps started to pass by the room a few moments later, but stopped.

Eamon looked up as another young woman entered the room. This one was dressed all in black— black jeans, black sandals and a black tank top under a short-sleeved black blouse that was untucked. Her flame-red hair was in a thick plait hanging straight down her back. She had the same pale skin she'd had in high school, only now Eamon noticed how perfect it was. Not a freckle or blemish marred her complexion. She stood in the doorway looking at him through eyes the color of a stormy sea, sort of bluish gray with flecks of green. "I'm sorry. I didn't realize you were here. Is Arlene helping you?"

"Yes, thanks," Eamon replied.

She shifted her eyes from him to his father who was surreptitiously wiping a tear from his cheek. For a long moment she studied Jack McCleary before she came into the room, grabbed a box of tissues from the windowsill and set it on the table within his reach. "I took the call yesterday," she said. "I'm very sorry for your loss Mr. McCleary. Mrs. McCleary was a wonderful woman. She'd given me so much advice over the past few years. I'm truly going to miss her. I promise you, we will do our best by her."

"You knew my mother?" Eamon asked, trying to fathom how on earth Eve knew her.

"Yes. I knew her from the Garden Club. Danny and I decided a few years ago to restore the formal garden. I joined the Garden Club and they were a huge help to us. I didn't want it so formal as to be intimidatin' to the mourners who might want to walk the paths and reflect awhile. Your mother sat with me and helped me plan the whole thing. Really, if you have the time, you should both go out back and walk through the garden. Your mother's spirit can be felt along every path. It's elegant and lovely but not fussy and over done." Both men were staring at her. "She never mentioned helpin' plan this garden?" They shook their heads. "Oh."

Arlene came back into the room with a tray on which there was a cup of coffee and a glass of water with a few ice cubes in it. "Oh, there you are. Sorcha has gone up to her room. Would you mind running up and keeping an eye on her. She's ready to apologize for her misbehavior."

"I have things to do," Eve said. "So I can only go up for a few minutes." Her eyes met Eamon's as his father was staring at Arlene. "I'll take care of your mother. We'll need something to dress her in, a favorite dress or pant suit. And if you could bring me a recent picture of her, that would be helpful." He nodded. "Again, I'm very sorry for your loss. Please excuse me."

Eamon couldn't believe she was the same girl. Well, he could, but he was surprised just the same. She still dressed all in black, she still had the eye-catching red hair and she was still tall and slender, but she was not the somber-clad, strange girl he remembered. Thinking back he couldn't recall ever hearing her speak. She had a nice voice with a hint of an Irish accent.

"Have you chosen a card and a verse yet?" Arlene asked, a hint of impatience underlying her words as her sister excused herself and left the room.

"No, there're too many choices. Look, Eve knew my mother. Dad and I would like something with a floral design. Do you think she could pick a card and verse for us?"

"Usually the bereaved do their own choosing…" she began, but he interrupted.

"I understand that, but Eve was a member of the Garden Club with my mother. Mom helped her design the garden here. I think she'd know better than Dad and me what Mom would have liked to help people remember her by."

"Are you all right with Eve choosing the card and verse?" she asked Mr.McCleary. There was a bit of a peeved undertone in her voice but Jack didn't seem to notice.

He nodded. "That's fine. I can't pick. I don't know what Mary would have liked."

"Shall we go and look at the caskets now? There are lovely models in a variety of price ranges."

This was difficult, choosing a casket on a tight budget. Mary McCleary had only been forty-eight years old. Jack was fifty-two. Neither one of them had been thinking about dying or funerals, putting money aside for this. Eamon had some savings he was going to use to help his father, but they would probably have to finance part of the funeral, if the funeral home did such a thing. He cleared his throat and asked if they had a payment plan. Arlene was straight forward about it. They did have a plan with a monthly payment option. They would discuss that after the selecting of the casket.

Jack picked a metal casket with simple floral chrome trim work, a white satin lining. They returned to the consultation room to discuss the service, church, cemetery, burial service and financing. They were midway through when Eve returned, now wearing a simple black dress, black stockings and low-heeled black shoes. She had tied a black ribbon in a bow at the end of her thick plait. "I hate to interrupt, but Sorcha needs her mother."

"She can wait."

"I'm afraid not, sorry." Eve looked at her sister and it was clear that she'd had enough of her niece for one morning. Arlene did not look happy with her. "I can finish up here."

"Don't you have work to do downstairs?" Arlene asked.

"Sean's not back yet." Eve slipped into a chair and pulled her sister's notebook over, picked up the pen. "Have we discussed the obituary yet?' she asked Mr. McCleary.

Arlene left the room, her back stiff, her stride angry. Eamon looked from the doorway back to Eve and was surprised to find she was looking at him. Their eyes met. "No, we haven't talked about the obit yet," he said.

"Do you have any brothers or sisters? I'm sorry I don't remember that."

"Don't be. You probably wouldn't have known him. I have a brother Patrick. He's still in college."

"Single?"

"Yes, he is."

"Um, I meant you? Are you single or are you married now?"

"No, I'm not married."

"Is there a girlfriend you would want to mention who was close to your mother?"

"No. Just Dad, Patrick, and me. Mom's parents are still alive, Edward and Mary Maguire. And Mom had three sisters and two brothers who are all married, and a bunch of nieces and nephews. And her grandmother's still alive. And Dad's got two sisters and four brothers, and their families."

Eve smiled at him. "Can you name them all?" she asked.

He glanced at his father who was gazing out the window, lost in his own thoughts. "I hope you have enough ink in that pen," he replied.

"I'm sure I do. I'll start with your father. When were they married?" He answered her questions, glad to have the distraction of trying to remember everyone they should mention. Then she asked about his mother's other activities, any jobs she may have had. "Any pets?" she asked.

"Mom has…um, had a parakeet named Jo-Jo. She let it fly around the house. It would sit on her shoulder and watch her sew."

"Should we mention her parakeet then?"

"Dad? Should we mention Jo-Jo in the obituary?" he asked.

"The damn bird? Why would you want to mention that crazy damn bird?'

"Because Jo-Jo was Mom's buddy," he replied. "You know she loved him."

Mr. McCleary waved his hand dismissively. "Do whatever you want. Your aunt's going to take the bird. I don't want to deal with it."

"You can mention her pet parakeet." Eve nodded. "Do you need a down payment right now?"

"No. Can you manage it tomorrow? You'll need to bring me the clothes and a photograph. You can bring a check then."

"Do you need underwear too?" He realized it was a stupid question as soon as he'd asked it.

"Yes," Eve replied in no different a tone than what she had been using, which was very quiet and gentle. "Is your mother still wearing her rings? Or did they remove them in the hospital and give them to your father? She had pierced ears, didn't she?"

Eamon shrugged. "Dad? Did they give you Mom's rings?" His father shook his head.

"Are we leaving her rings on or would you like them back?" she asked.

"You want Mom's rings?" His father began to weep. "It's your call. You gave them to her."

"Leave 'em on her for the funeral but, if you can take them off before you close the casket and give 'em to me after that'd be good."

"Yes, of course." She jotted a note. "And the earrings?"

"I think she had gold-colored studs in," Eamon said.

"You can bring the little gold shamrock studs she liked to wear on St. Patrick's Day. She can take them with her. I want the wedding band and the diamond, but, I think…I think I want her to keep the claddagh ring. Just move it from her right hand to the left after you take off the other rings. She can take that one with her."

"You sure Dad?"

"I'm sure. I bought it for her in Dublin. It was before you were born. I always wanted to take her back to Ireland but we never got there. I want her to take the ring with her."

"All right." He nodded and Eve jotted another note.

"I think this is all we need for now," she said. Her eyes met Eamon's for a moment, then she looked down at the notebook.

"Can I ask you something?" he asked.

Her eyes rose to meet his again. "Yes, of course."

"I get the impression that you're the one who'll be…that you're the…the, uh…"

"Embalmer?" He nodded. "Yes, that's what I went to college for. It's what my family has done for generations. My father had no sons so I chose to follow in his footsteps. Arlene wanted nothing to do with the family business. She went to South Carolina, but now that she's back, she handles this side of things, the arrangements."

"You're good at it, too," he said.

"I suppose I am. I've been doing it longer than she has. I started working here when I was in middle school. Not on the public side of things, downstairs with my father, mostly keeping things neat and orderly, ordering supplies, observing and learning. At funerals I greeted mourners, lined up the procession vehicles, put the little purple flags on the cars. One day I hope to inherit the business from my father." She stood up. He rose and nudged his father who got to his feet as well. "Everyone in school was right about me," she said.

Eamon shook his head. "No, everyone in school was dead wrong about you, no pun intended. I'm sorry if I ever said or did anything that made you think I thought you were weird."

"I don't believe you ever did," she said as she followed them out into the hall. "If I remember correctly you played baseball and basketball and were pretty popular with the girls. I don't think I remember you ever even noticing me."

Eamon opened the door so his father could pass through into the vestibule. He paused and looked at her. "I saw you in the hallways, in the library, sometimes in the cafeteria. You were the only girl in school with red hair. I mean, this shade of red. You were hard to miss. I did notice you." He was surprised by the flush of color that stained her cheeks at that. "You were just too young back then."

"Thanks for putting it that way." In that moment he saw a flash of the lonely girl she had been, might still be for all he knew, but then she was again professional. "When you bring the clothing for your mom tomorrow you can leave it with Arlene. I might not be here. Sometimes I go with Sean, but I think tomorrow I'll probably be at St. Mary's talking to Father John about the service for your mother. Ask your father about hymns later, if there were any that your mother favored. If so, call and let Arlene know. If not, then I can choose." He nodded. "You do want Father John to come here for the wake and for the service before we take her to the church?" He nodded again. "And burial will be at St. Mary's Cemetery? I'll take a walk with Father and we'll pick a lovely site for her. You'll be wantin' room for your father beside her? How about yourself and Patrick?"

"No, just Dad. He'll want to be buried beside her. Pat and I will probably get married some day and we'll want to be beside our wives, not our parents."

"I'll find them a lovely double plot."

"Thanks, Eve. I don't think Dad would be able to handle all of that. He and I appreciate it."

He followed his father out onto the porch, down the walk and into the parking lot to the truck. As he got behind the wheel he glanced over at the house. Although Arlene was gorgeous, he'd noticed today that she didn't have the quiet, gentle nature of her younger sister. She seemed to not want to deal with her own daughter, who sounded a bit like a brat with her whining about whatever it had been. And Arlene had seemed annoyed that they hadn't been able to choose a verse or picture for the memorial cards. It had all been a bit overwhelming for them. Eve, however, had been patient and kind, thoughtful and understanding. She was, in fact, the ideal undertaker, mortician—whatever she was. And he knew, because of her relationship with his mother, that she would take good care of his mom. Mary McCleary was in good, capable hands and that was a comfort to him. Weird Eve Mooney, Looney Mooney as they'd called her back then, had been a revelation to him today. She was the consummate professional, born to take her place at Mooney and Sons, to keep the business in the family. He had a whole new respect for her. "How about a Reuben and a couple of beers?" he asked his father. "I can only have one beer, I have to get to work later, but you can have two."

"You're buying, I hope? I got a funeral to pay for that I can't afford."

"Of course I am. And don't worry about it, Dad. I'll do what I can to help you out."

"I'll have to use what's left of Pat's tuition money," his father fretted as Eamon pulled out and headed downtown.

"No. I'll cover the down payment. After the funeral we'll go to the bank, see if you can get a loan for the rest of it. I'll co-sign on it. We'll get it paid off. Pat can finish college. We'll pay the loan off together, okay?"

"I don't want you having to pay for your mother's funeral. I should do that."

"I know that, but you guys put me through college, and Mom would want Pat to finish and get his degree. I'm doing all right at work. We're family, Dad. You can pay me back when you can if you want to, although I'm not asking you to. We have to do what we have to do right now. We'll worry about the rest later on, okay?"

"You're a good son, Eamon. Your mom was very proud of you."

It was quarter past ten when Eamon entered the funeral home with a shopping bag containing his mother's clothes. He'd spent the night at his parent's house and this morning he and his father had opened his mother's closet and chosen the dress she had bought to wear out to dinner when she and Jack had celebrated their twenty-eighth anniversary last year. It was in soft shades of purple, one of her favorite colors. He'd let his father select the undergarments while he found the matching shoes among a myriad of shoeboxes stacked on the closet floor, and then the shamrock studs in her jewelry box.

The hall was quiet. He paused, cleared his throat. A few moments passed before Arlene came from the consultation room. "Hi, Eamon. Did you bring the clothes for your mother?" she asked.

"Yes. I think everything is here. And I have a recent picture. This was taken on Valentine's Day."

"Is this how she was currently wearing her hair?"

"Yes."

"Did she wear make-up?"

"Um…" He had to think about it. "Not really. Just a little lipstick. She was naturally pretty."

"Of course." She took the bag from him. "How are you doing? I haven't seen you since high school. You played sports, didn't you?" He nodded. "Are you married?"

Obviously she hadn't read the obituary her sister must have written by now. "No."

"Haven't found the right one yet?"

"No, not yet."

"I thought I had but you know what they say, hindsight is twenty-twenty. I was way too young. I should have stayed here in Hadleigh Falls but I'd wanted to see the world back then. I got married, had a little girl, but it just didn't work out. Now here I am, back where I started from. Do you ever see anyone from high school?"

"A group of us meet in the park every Sunday afternoon to play some softball for fun. Do you remember Tim Rafferty? Kevin O'Shaunessey? Brendan Shea?"

"I remember Brendan. Dark hair, tall, dimples?"

"Yeah, that's him."

"Is he married?"

"No. Kevin and Tim are, and Frank Coulter. You should bring your daughter to the park and catch a game some Sunday."

"Maybe I will. Sorcha's so bored here. I was, too, at her age. Actually, I was all along and that's part of the reason I left. Eve, on the other hand, has lived and breathed funerals since she was born, I swear!"

"Is she here today?" he asked. He saw her react to his question as if he'd annoyed her by asking about her sister. "The reason I'm asking is she mentioned that my mother had helped her plan and design the garden here. I'd like to see it."

"Oh, she's out there now doing the weeding and whatnot, I suppose…" She was interrupted by the door opening. "Just go around back and you'll find the garden easily enough. She's out there somewhere. Please excuse me," she said quickly, then set the bag with the clothing down against the wall and went to greet the sad-faced middle-aged couple who had just entered.

Eamon waited in the hall until they had passed by on the way to the consultation room before he went back outside. The parking area was at the side of the house. He walked through the lot and around to the back. There was a carriage house where the funeral livery vehicles were parked, and an additional building to house the rest of the fleet of vehicles. A small bronze sign pointed the way to the Tranquility Garden along a brick path. A hose snaked across the lawn from the rear of the house into the garden.

The garden was entered through a brick archway in the brick wall that surrounded it. There were brick paths to left and right with gentle curves. He could hear the shushing of a fountain someplace toward the center of the garden. He chose the right path and began walking past beds of colorful flowers and shrubs. His mother probably could reel off the names of every flower and shrub, every ornamental tree that he passed, but he'd never paid too much attention to things like that. He liked to see them, thought they were pretty, but he'd never been to a garden show and really had never been in a garden like this in his life. Lush and beautiful would describe it. He saw colorful butterflies everywhere, and birds sang in the trees. It was tranquil here. There were marble benches for sitting and reflecting, pools with lotuses in them, or with koi.

He found the fountain. It was of an angel with her hands spread as if welcoming a weary soul to kick off their shoes and step into the fountain. Her expression was both serene and benevolent. It was warm enough today to do that, but there was also a certain heaviness in the air that promised a thunderstorm in a few hours, by evening at the latest.

He was standing there looking into the fountain, having tossed a few coins in, when Eve came up beside him. "Hi," she said.

He turned his head and looked at her. Today, she was not dressed in black, not completely. She had on brown work boots, skinny blue jeans and a black t-shirt that was tucked in. She really was very slender. She had a straw hat on to shield her face from the sun and had just removed grubby gardening gloves. "Arlene told me you were out here."

"Have you come to be alone with your mom's spirit?" she asked.

"I'm here hoping you have time to show me the garden."

She nodded, tossed her gloves into the tool carrier she had set down on the path. "Why don't we start at the back and work our way forward. There's this corner that I absolutely love. It's all evergreens. It's the shadiest spot, very peaceful. It's like a little glade in the middle of a forest. The fir and cedar are natural to the grounds. I guess, when the house was built there was nothing but woodlands behind it. When they designed the original garden they left this back corner natural. Your mother came here to see what I was talking about, and she helped me clear out a lot of undergrowth, and told me which trees had to go to open it up some." She glanced at him sideways. "Am I talking too much?"

"No. I spent the night with Dad when I got out of work. The house felt so empty without Mom there. Then we had to go through her closet. That wasn't easy. I kept expecting her to yell at us to stop pawing through all her stuff and go find something constructive to do." Eve smiled. "I was missing her."

"She's everywhere here," she said quietly. "See that wrought iron bench? She found it, called me and told me to come and get it quickly before someone else grabbed it. She was over in Prescott at an estate sale. Luckily, Danny was here. He has a truck. We flew over there and snagged it for thirty dollars and here it sits looking like it's been here all along."

"Who's Danny?" he asked.

She shrugged. "He's sort of the handyman, yardman, all around jack of all trades here. And he drives the flower car. Uncle Nolan found him begging on a traffic island, offered him a job. Guess his father had lost his job, couldn't support him, and kicked him out. Danny was half-starved and half-frozen when Uncle Nolan brought him here. That was three years ago. Now he's part of the family. He lives in the gardener's cottage."

"Do you still live in the house?" he asked.

"I have the apartment over the carriage house. When Arlene moved home I moved out there. I love my sister and my niece, but I do not love living with them." They had reached the center of the evergreen glade. The air was cool and spicy-scented from the cedar. "Isn't it amazing here?"

"It's like being in the middle of the woods," he acknowledged. "You wouldn't know there was a mansion over there."

They moved on to other areas of the garden and in each one she had something to tell him about his mother. Mrs. McCleary had come over to help Eve plant and they had been caught in a sudden downpour and been up to their wrists in mud. She said all they could do was sit back on their heels and laugh. He found it hard to picture his mother drenched, muddy and laughing about it, but the way Eve talked he could understand how his mother would have loved being with her. They had obviously shared a passion for gardening. He was surprised his mother had never mentioned coming here to the Mooney's, but then again, he hadn't lived at home since he'd graduated from high school except for summers when he was home from college working summer jobs. And then he'd landed his job upon graduation from college and lived in a studio apartment until he could afford the condo where he lived now. He hadn't really been home all that much, but he had talked to his parents on the phone regularly.

It was nearly noon by the time they reached the brick arch entrance. "I hate to be rude, but I have to get cleaned up. I'm meeting Father John at one-thirty. Are there any favorite hymns you want me to mention to him?"

"*Ave Maria* was one of Mom's favorites."

"I'll ask him to include it."

"Thanks." He hesitated. "I know this will sound weird, but I need to ask. Mom made it here all right?"

"Yes. I took care of her myself late yesterday afternoon. You, your father and your brother should come a half hour early tomorrow afternoon for the wake. That will give you time to visit with her privately. If there are any early arriving mourners we can keep the doors to the viewing room closed until you're ready.

Please know that there is no rush, no right or wrong amount of time that you are allowed to grieve in private. Our job is to guide you through the wake and service, but you let us know how long you need."

He nodded. "Eve," he said and she slowly straightened up with her gardening tool carrier in her hand. She had set it down on the grass while they'd been talking. Her eyes met his. They were in shadow under the brim of her hat, looked more gray than blue. "In case I forget to tell you I want to say thank you now for all you've done, are doing and will be doing for me, my father, brother and family."

"You're welcome, Eamon. It's not easy to lose a parent when they're still so young. My mother died when I was fourteen. That's why high school was so difficult for me. Arlene was older, it didn't really impact her life too much as she's always been more independent, and she's always been popular. I was close to my mom and it really left me in a bad place, even though I grew up in a funeral home surrounded by death, grief and mourning. It hits you hardest when it's someone you love and you aren't ready to let go of."

"I guess I didn't think about that. I don't remember hearing that your mother died."

"She died in Ireland and was buried there with her family. It wasn't common knowledge here."

"Were you living there?"

She nodded. "Yes. I lived there for over a year. Mom left Dad, went home to Ireland and took me with her. Arlene was halfway through high school and wanted to stay here with Dad. When Mom died, Dad came for the funeral, had a huge fight with my maternal grandparents and brought me back here." She shrugged. "And here I am today, the heir to the Mooney empire."

He followed her through the arch. "I want to go with you," he said.

"Go with me?" She gave him a strange look. "Where?"

"To the church and to the cemetery."

"Oh, um…well…I thought you'd be thinking about a reception for after the service."

"My Aunt Kathleen is taking care of that. I guess it'll be at the country club, a buffet."

She hesitated, thinking it over and then nodded. "If you don't mind waiting for me you can come with me. Why don't you come up with me. You can have some lemonade or something while I get cleaned up."

She stored the gardening equipment in a lean-to shed attached to the back of the carriage house, and then led him up an exterior enclosed rear staircase to the second floor. The apartment was fairly good sized, three rooms— a living room with dining area, a kitchen and a large bedroom with a bath that opened from the hall and the bedroom. She asked him if he was hungry. He said he wasn't, not wanting to trouble her but she shook her head at him. "Why don't you make us some turkey and tomato sandwiches. I'm going to take a quick shower and put on clean clothes. We'll have time to eat before we have to be at the rectory."

"I should probably swing by my place and change my clothes."

She looked him up and down and nodded. He had on faded, worn jeans and a brown t-shirt with a couple of spots on it. "Okay. I'll be as quick as I can. Can you find your way around my vast kitchen?"

"I'll manage."

"I'll leave you to it then."

She left the kitchen. He opened a few drawers and cupboards to familiarize himself with where things were, then tackled the refrigerator. She ate yogurt and a lot of fresh vegetables. She had some cheddar cheese. He found the deli turkey, roasted in natural juices, no salt added. There was a loaf of light rye bread on the counter. He found a small cutting board, grabbed a tomato from the fridge and a slicing knife from the knife block. It felt good to have something definitive to accomplish. He'd felt rather aimless since his mother's passing. He needed to keep busy right now and not dwell on it.

He heard the shower running. He was folding slices of turkey on the bread when a sudden image of Eve naked in the shower popped into his head, causing his hand to falter. "Holy shit," he said aloud, looking around guiltily as if the room was full of witnesses who could read his mind. "What the hell!"

He jumped when he heard the apartment door open. A little girl walked into the kitchen and stopped dead, staring at him. "Who are you?" she demanded, folding her arms and giving him a look that would have been threatening if she was not seven or eight years old.

"Eamon. You must be Sorcha."

She cocked a dark brow at him. She looked like her mother. "Are you Aunt Eve's boyfriend?" she asked. "Where is she?" She looked around and obviously heard the shower running. Her head whipped back around and she pinned him with a scowl of disapproval. "Did you just have sex with her?"

"No!" he said, sounding way too defensive even to his own ears.

"I'm going to tell my mother and she will be all over Aunt Eve for this!"

"I'm not her boyfriend," he said.

"Oh, puh-lease!" Sorcha said. "I may look like a child but I'm quite grown up. I know all about that stuff."

"Your family is handling my mother's funeral."

Her eyes widened. "When?"

"The wake is tomorrow, funeral the day after."

"And you're here fooling around with my aunt while your *mother* is just over there in the house dead? OMG! What is this world coming to!"

"Sorcha? Is that you?" Eve opened the bathroom door. She had a towel wrapped around her torso. "What are you doing here?"

"I'm speaking with your luh-vah."

"My what?" Eve came to the kitchen doorway. "Oh, you mean Eamon? Eamon is going with me to see Father John and then to help pick out a plot for his mother."

"Please go put some clothes on! I am quite scandalized by your behavior, Aunt Eve!"

"Oh, I'm sure you are. Your mother lets you watch way too much reality TV. It shows. Go back to the house and stop barging in here uninvited. I've had quite enough of you for today."

"Mother says…"

"I don't care what your mother says!" Eve snapped. "Take your nasty little imagination and leave."

"Grandpa wants to see you when you're available," Sorcha said as she gave Eamon one last long look before turning on her heel and stalking out of the apartment. They heard her clattering down the stairs.

Eve shook her head. "That child is just utterly disturbing," she said. "Carry on with the sandwich making. I'll be right out."

Eamon shook his head. When he was growing up little girls of that tender age did not even know what sex was never mind waltz into someone's apartment and accused people of doing it.

The world was becoming a troubling place, corrupted and in moral decline. He flushed because hadn't he just been picturing Eve naked in the shower just before he'd been accused of being her lover? "Damn, I'm as bad as the kid," he muttered.

Eve came to the kitchen dressed in black slacks and a black blouse, flat-heeled black shoes. Her hair was in a neat thick plait down her back. "I apologize for my rude little niece. She's just like her mother."

"She's something else. Why does your sister let her watch that trash on TV?"

"She parks her in front of the TV so she doesn't have to deal with her. She's creating a horrible little monster."

They carried their plates and glasses to the dining area, sat down and began eating. "There's something for that old adage that children should be seen and not heard." Eve nodded. "Do you need to see your father before we go?"

"No. I know what he wants. It's already taken care of. He'll figure that out for himself."

They left the dishes in the sink. Eve said she would drive. She had a black Toyota Camry, a hybrid. He hadn't experienced driving in a hybrid until now, found the silence of the car at stops eerie and a bit unnerving. He directed her to his condo. He lived at Whisper Lake Condos just down the road from the lake. She stayed in the car with the air conditioner running while he ran inside to change into black jeans and a navy blue polo shirt and black boots. He ran a comb through his longish dark blonde hair, checked his teeth and then rejoined her.

Father John's secretary greeted them at the rectory before leading them to the priest's office. "Please sit down and make yourselves comfortable. Father was a bit delayed on a call this morning and is just finishing his lunch. He'll be with you very shortly. Can I get you anything? Water? Lemonade? Iced tea? Ginger ale?"

"We're fine," Eamon replied.

Father John was in his early sixties, a slim man of average height. His hair was dark, turning salt and pepper but still thick and with a bit of a wave to it. He had blue eyes and a kind face. "Eve, always good to see you. You look as lovely as ever." He turned to Eamon. "Eamon, I am so sorry to learn of Mary's passing. I called your father this morning and spoke to him for quite a while . I didn't know you were coming over with Eve."

"I hadn't planned on it, but then I decided I wanted to come."

They discussed the service and the hymns and came to an agreement. Eamon said his Aunt Bridget would do one of the readings and his Uncle James another. With that settled, the priest took out a map of the cemetery and unrolled it on a side table. "I studied this last night and have marked a few locations where double plots are available. There is one here in the older section, and two here in the newer section and finally one here in the newest section. Why don't we take a walk over and have a look at them."

They left the rectory, passed in front of the huge church and then into the cemetery on the other side of it. Eamon was grateful for the tall trees that provided some shade. It took a while to walk through the extensive grounds and view the four plot locations. When they had seen all of them they returned to the rectory. Mrs. Steward served them raspberry iced tea and iced oatmeal cookies. "I think the plot in the old section would be best. There's that beautiful cedar nearby and it's quiet there and up on a bit of a rise. I think she'd like it there."

"A nice choice. I'll get Gerald and Barney busy. I'll contact Graves and Toomey Monuments down the road and arrange for the vault installation. Your father can pick the headstone after the funeral, decide what he wants on it." Eamon nodded. "Again, young man, I am very sorry for your loss. Mary was a remarkable woman, very generous and warm in both heart and spirit. The Ladies Guild will certainly miss her presence here, as will the choir. And I'll miss those peach cobblers she'd always contribute to the end of summer bake sale."

Eamon and Eve left the rectory, walking back to her car. "I never thought about how many people my mother interacted with in town."

"She was quite an active woman. Very vibrant and full of energy."

He was mostly silent on the drive back to Mooney's. Eve was quiet too. Occasionally he glanced at her. She was a pretty girl in her own right. He wondered why he'd never noticed that before. She shared a few features with Arlene. He thought Arlene looked like her father as she had his coloring. He didn't think he'd ever seen Mrs. Mooney. Eve probably resembled her mother more. "Did you like Ireland?' he asked.

"Yes. I miss it. I'll probably go there this fall for a week to visit my grandparents, aunt, uncles and cousins there."

"By yourself?"

She nodded. "My father's not on good terms with them. They feel he neglected my mother, should have realized something was wrong with her as he was closest to her. They feel their arguing and fighting caused her stress which made her sicker. I don't know what to think. I don't really want to be in the middle of their disagreement, so I try to remain neutral. I mean, how could my father had known my mother had ovarian cancer? She didn't look or act sick before we left for Ireland. It just, within a years' time, took her." She gnawed on her lower lip.

"Same with my mother. We didn't know there was something wrong until it was too late to do anything to stop it."

"Cancer is horrible! There's so much of it these days, so many kinds. It takes too many people too soon and leaves a lot of grief in its relentless wake."

He shook his head. "I never thought, back in high school, that I'd be driving around with you having this conversation."

She gave a soft little laugh. "I could see the athletic fields from the second floor of the library. I used to sit up there with a book, but sometimes I'd watch the baseball team practice. I like baseball. You played left field and sometimes third base." He nodded, surprised by this information, that she had watched him play baseball. "Even weird girls have fantasies about normal, happy lives."

"You're not happy?"

"Oh, I'm all right. I like what I do."

He heard the loneliness, though, in her voice. He understood that. He'd dated a number of girls but his relationships just hadn't clicked. None of them had been *the* girl. "I like what I do," he said.

She gave a half smile as she glanced at him from the corner of her eye. "What do you do?" she asked.

"I'm a civil engineer."

"Oh."

"I'm working on the site of the new middle school right now." She nodded. "That doesn't excite you, does it?"

"I haven't got a clue what a civil engineer does so it's kind of hard to get excited about somethin' one doesn't know a thing about. I mean, right now, the site is nothin' more than a big dirt lot."

"That's right, it is. We go in and look at the land, the water tables beneath it, the drainage and things like that. We have to okay the site and the construction plans and make sure there'll be no problems once construction starts on the site. We do a lot of testing and measurements."

"I guess we wouldn't want the new school to fall down or suddenly split in half or fall into an underground lake or anythin'."

"Okay, you don't find it very interesting."

"No, I do. I'm sure you have a lot of stories you could tell me that would fill in all the blanks in my brain about civil engineerin'. I could tell you a lot of stories about embalmin' and funerary science. It might gross you out if you have a weak constitution or if blood makes you squeamish."

"You could probably, very easily, give me nightmares."
She turned into the funeral home lot. "Oh, definitely!"
"Maybe we shouldn't talk about work too much."
"What else is there?"
"Do you go to the lake? Do you sail? Fish? Water ski? Swim? Build sand castles?"

She laughed. "Some of those, but not all. Do you ski? Snowmobile? Skate? Play hockey? Cross country ski?"

"Some of those, but not all." They looked at one another and grinned.

"Okay, this isn't good. We shouldn't be grinnin' like Cheshire cats. I'm supposed to remain sober and be a comfortin' presence to you."

He let the grin fade. "You are a comforting presence to me," he said. "More than you know." He got out of the car. Eve slid out from behind the wheel. "Thanks for letting me go with you. We'll be here tomorrow at three for the afternoon calling hours. I'm taking Dad and Patrick to the Towering Pines for dinner and then we'll be back at six-thirty for the seven o'clock calling hours."

'I'll see you tomorrow then." She watched him walk to his truck. He waved as he pulled away. She raised her hand in a brief wave and then headed toward the funeral home's rear entrance.

It was Declan Mooney who greeted father and sons the following afternoon. He shook hands with all three of the McCleary men and apologized for not being available until now. "Mary is in the Trinity Room, if you'd like to go in. Father John called to assure us he was on the way and should be here soon. He thought you might like a private prayer with him before we open the doors and allow the mourners in."

"Does she look like my mom?" Patrick asked. He was twenty-two, would be graduating in the fall as he'd been stricken with mononucleosis his junior year and lost an entire half year due to being very ill. He was pale this afternoon and looking uneasy in his dark suit. The McCleary's had all worn suits.

"I believe she does. Let's go in, shall we?" He slid the pocket door on the right open and then went into the room. The room was full of flower arrangements, plants and a couple of stained glass memory lamps set on a set of risers and illuminated. Jack McCleary wept at the sight of his beloved wife in her casket. He went and knelt at the casket, bowing his head. Eamon stood behind him, his hand lightly on his father's shoulder. Patrick stared at his mother for several long moments, then tore his eyes away, looking around the room at the flowers, all the rows of chairs. "I'll leave you alone with her. Father John should be here shortly. If you need anything I'll just be out in the hall. There's water, tissues and mints on the table there. Those chairs are for the three of you and the rows behind for close relatives." He slipped out into the hall, sliding the door shut.

All too soon it seemed the doors were opened and the stream of mourners came through. Eamon's hand began to feel numb from all the handshakes. He soon reeked of a myriad perfumes. The line seemed endless. He began to sweat. Many people stayed but some just passed through to pay their respects before heading home for dinner.

It was a relief to get out into the fresh air, even though it was a sultry evening. Eamon drove them to the Towering Pines and they were promptly seated. They explained they needed to get back to the funeral home for six-thirty. Their server took their orders and made sure they got their food promptly. She was very nice and it came as a jolt to realize she was flirting with him.

"She likes you," Patrick whispered.

"I don't date waitresses. I wouldn't know where to leave the tip." Patrick laughed and their father glared at him. "Sorry, Pop."

"Your mother's dead. We're burying her tomorrow," Jack said.

"Yes, but Mom's Irish. Do you honestly think she'd want us sitting here sobbing into our beer?"

"Mom enjoyed life, Dad," Patrick said. "If she were here she'd be telling Eamon just where he could leave the tip."

"You know that's true," Eamon said.

"Show some respect for your mother."

"We are. We always have."

Eamon paid for dinner. The waitress's name was Tanya. She'd written in in bold ink across the top of his receipt. It wasn't until he was folding it that he noticed she'd written her phone number on the reverse side. Outside he showed it to his brother. "She's a bold one," he said.

"I wonder how many guys she's picked up by doing that?"

"A self-serving server," muttered Mr. McCleary.

Colm Mooney was present upon their return. He shook hands with each of them and expressed his sympathy. They thanked him for all that his family had done for Mary McCleary. Arlene was also there in a dark blue dress, and two other younger men, one of whom Eamon figured out was Danny as he was close in age to Patrick. He heard the other one called Sean by Colm. Eve was not there as far as Eamon could tell. There were already a lot of mourners gathering for the later calling hours.

He excused himself, asked Arlene where the rest room was. She led him down the hallway. "I've bumped the air conditioning up," she said. "It was getting rather close in here."

"I don't think I ever want to smell another carnation or lily," he said.

"It can be overpowering, can't it? At least you don't seem to be allergic. We get some terribly allergic people here and have to wrap the arrangements in cellophane to keep the scent down." She indicated a pair of doors in an alcove. "The rest rooms are there."

He nodded, found the men's room and slipped inside. He wanted to take off his jacket, loosen his tie, unbutton his collar. Maybe in an hour he could do that. After washing his hands he stood looking at his reflection. His face was a bit flushed from the heat. He was perspiring. His hair was starting to get damp around his face and at the nape of his neck. He grimaced. He probably should have shaved again before coming over here but he hadn't thought of that. Golden stubble glinted along his jaw. "This will all be over tomorrow," he told his reflection. "You can get through this."

He came out of the men's room and stepped into the hall. The sound of murmuring voices reached him from the front of the house. He knew that he should get back, but there were two female voices toward the rear of the house he could also hear. They were arguing, doing a fairly decent job of keeping their voices down, but he could hear the bitterness in both their voices. He was pretty sure it was Arlene and Eve he was hearing.

"Sorcha's a liar and you know it! I don't know why you let her get away with everythin' all the time! I am not sleepin' with Eamon McCleary! To be accused of such a thing by a child, no less, and to have you, a grown woman, believe I would do such a thing when the man is grievin' the loss of his own mother is outrageous and unforgivable!"

"Sorcha said you were in just a towel and he was in your kitchen making sandwiches. You must have been going at him for quite a while to work up such an appetite! Oh, you've got Dad fooled with your following his footsteps routine, but you've not got me fooled! Not for one instant! You're nothing but a whore!"

"I cannot believe you, of all people, are standin' here callin' me names! Which one of us was seducin' the boys all through high school and then runnin' off with a college boy and gettin' herself pregnant, makin' him marry her and then makin' his life so miserable he couldn't stand the sight of her and divorced her? You know damn well I've never even had a boyfriend! Not after what that…that…oh, I can't even say what I think he was, did to me when I was in eighth grade!"

"Little sluts get exactly what they deserve when they flirt so shamelessly with their math teachers!"

"I never flirted with anyone!" Eve cried hotly. Arlene began to say something more but Eve cut her off. "I'm not goin' to stand here listenin' to you insult me. I've put up with your meanness toward me my whole life. It was a blessin' when you ran off with Tom and it's been nothin' but a damn curse since you came back with your vile little spawn who's your spittin' image right down to her nasty, mean-spirited disposition! If you want me out of here then you've certainly done an excellent job of gettin' your message across! I only regret that my leavin' will hurt Granddad and Dad the most because you certainly are no great asset to this business!"

"And you think that you are?"

"This is what I went to college for! This is what I want to do for a livin'! But I can't do it here if you and Sorcha are goin' to be livin' here makin' my life utter misery! I've been nothin' but miserable since the day I was raped but I'll tell you this—I have a fierce dedication to this business that you entirely lack! My path was to bring this business into the future. Your path is obviouslyto destroy everything that this family has worked their bloody arses off for for generations! Well, I'll leave you to it then! And don't you dare come cryin' to me with your wretched brat in tow when Mooney and Sons closes its doors!"

Eamon heard a door close firmly. He heard Arlene mutter, "Bitch!" He had gotten quite an earful, and shouldn't have been eavesdropping. He hurried to join his father and brother to greet the mourners who were lined up out the door.

It was very late by the time the last mourner left. They were all tired as they headed home. Tomorrow morning would come too soon.

Eve was present the next morning, dressed in her simple black dress, her red hair in a French braid. Sean and Danny were out in the parking lot with two other men getting the cars into the right position for the funeral procession. Eve was just inside the door and had greeted them when they'd arrived. She'd glanced briefly at Eamon and then looked away. He wondered if she knew he'd overheard her argument with Arlene last night but couldn't understand how she possibly could have known.

Declan, Nolan and Colm Mooney were also very visible. This was a huge funeral so the entire family was working, except for Arlene who didn't seem to be there. Maybe she was watching her daughter upstairs?

Father John arrived and led the brief service. Out on the lawn a lone piper began to play and Eamon felt the sting of tears at the back of his eyes. It was then that he caught sight of Eve. She stood weeping openly in the hallway, dabbing at her cheeks with crumpled tissues. He'd been to a few funerals in his life and had never seen any of the funeral home staff cry. It touched him that she was crying for his mother, the loss of his mother. And then he realized that Eve had lost her own mother, that she had been brought back to the States and had then been sexually assaulted by an eighth grade teacher. She'd had no adult female in the house to comfort her and counsel her. His mother had formed a bond with her, and Eve had obviously been close to her to be so affected by her death. He wondered how close they had actually been, and how his mother had kept it so quiet. Perhaps his mother had been a surrogate mother to Eve? He had to fight the urge to go out into the hall and comfort her.

She was not there later. The mourners were asked to pay their final respects and go to their cars. It took quite a while to clear the room. When it was just the three McCleary men Nolan said, "It's time to say your final goodbyes. Take as much time as you need. If there is any token or memento you wish to place in the casket with her do so now. When you're ready, just come through and we'll bring her out shortly."

Eamon saw that his mother still had her rings on. He wanted to go and look for Eve to remind her that his father wanted the wedding band and diamond, wanted the claddagh ring moved to her left hand. However, they had explained what they wanted and he had to trust that their wishes would be carried out. He bent and kissed his mother's cold cheek. "Goodbye, Mom. I love you." He turned and walked quickly away, blinking tears from his eyes.

Jack McCleary sobbed. He placed Mary's personal rosary over her hands. Patrick put a china figurine his mother had cherished near her shoulder. Then they walked to the pocket doors, slid one open and stepped out into the hall. Declan nodded and led them out to the limousine. Father John was riding with them. "So many family members and friends have gathered to say goodbye to our Mary," he said.

About ten minutes later the rear door opened and Eve slipped in, taking the last jump seat. "We'll be leavin' in a minute," she said. She leaned over and gave Mr. McCleary a small shimmery drawstring cloth bag. "Your wife's weddin' and engagement rings. I've done as you've asked. She's wearin' the claddagh on her left ring finger now."

He grabbed her pale hand and squeezed it. "Thank you, darlin' girl," he said.

She settled back in the jump seat, her hands folded on her lap. She did not look at them.

Eamon found himself studying her as the limousine slowly began to move forward. Her eyelashes were golden red and swept against her cheeks when she blinked. Her lower lip was bitten nearly raw. Two tears trickled down her cheeks to her jaw. She did not move to brush them off her face. He took a folded tissue from his pocket, leaned forward and blotted her tears. She turned her head toward the window and still would not look at him. He sat back. Father John caught his eye. He had not failed to notice that gesture, Eamon drying her tears. He looked at Eve, then back at Eamon and gave a slight nod as if giving his approval. Eamon felt an odd sensation in his chest. Had the priest just told him he approved of his developing a relationship with Eve? Or had he just simply been acknowledging a kind gesture?

"She looked like she did the day I married her," Jack said, startling them all. "You did a wonderful job, young lady. She looked as if she were sleeping. Thank you."

"You're welcome," Eve said, her voice quiet.

"Your father and grandfather should be very proud of you."

"They are quite proud of this young woman," Father John said.

Eamon saw that this was making Eve uncomfortable. "Did my cousin Sarah talk to you about playing her violin to accompany *Ave Maria*?" he asked the priest.

"Yes. I've given her permission to play up in the back choir balcony. No organ, just the violin."

The service was beautiful. Eamon occasionally glanced over at the Mooney family and their employees who were seated at the far side of the church in the front two pews. He noticed Arlene was not present, that Eve was sitting between her father and her grandfather. He saw Colm Mooney pass her his handkerchief as Sarah accompanied a soloist who sang *Ave Maria*. It was beautiful, gave him goosebumps.

Many mourners walked to the cemetery, leaving their cars in the church lot and on the street. The McCleary's rode in the limousine behind the hearse and flower car. Eve was in the jump seat again. Father John leaned over and whispered in her ear and she nodded. She still seemed to be struggling with her emotions.

At the cemetery she quickly got out and went to join her father. Father John saw Eamon watching her. He came up to him. "This is a difficult funeral for her. She was still young when she lost her own mother. Your mother was very good to Eve. They had a grand time with the Tranquility Garden project. Mary would come and talk to Moira Steward about gardening over tea. I overheard them discussing Eve often. Your mother was quite fond of her, thought of her as the daughter she never had. Took her under her wing and brought the girl out of her dark protective shell giving her the chance to blossom, which she has. Did you know Eve in school?"

"I more or less knew about her and occasionally saw her skulking about, never looking at anyone."

"She was a wounded fledgling. Your mother nurtured her, encouraged her. That's why our Eve is having such a hard time today. She's lost another mother."

"I'm fresh out of mothers or else I'd give her one more," Eamon said.

"It's not a mother that she needs now, young man," he said. "I'm afraid I must go conduct this service. Let's join your father and brother, shall we and see your mother off on her journey to join our Heavenly Father." Eamon nodded and followed him to the grave.

Eve rode in the hearse back to Mooney's and then disappeared. The McCleary's shook hands with the Mooney men, then walked to their vehicles. Patrick had driven his father. Eamon had come in his truck. His brother left, heading to the reception. Eamon hesitated, stood at the driver's door looking toward the carriage house. Danny had already changed clothes and was preparing to wash the livery vehicles. It was quiet and peaceful after so many people being around him all morning.

On a sudden urge he pocketed his keys and walked toward the garden. "Do you mind if I walk in the garden a bit?" he asked Danny.

"No, go right ahead. That was some big funeral. You probably need a bit of peace and quiet before going to the reception. That's what the garden's here for. Take your time."

Eamon nodded, strode up the path and entered the peaceful garden. He took a deep breath of the scented air and then headed toward the evergreen glade at the rear corner. It would be shady and cooler there. He'd left his jacket in the truck, had loosened his tie, unbuttoned his collar and cuffs, rolled up his sleeves. His shirt was stuck to his back. The sun had been merciless in the cemetery.

As he entered the glade he found Eve who was sitting on the wrought iron bench, elbows on her knees, face in her hands crying. She didn't even seem aware of his presence. He thought about turning around, leaving her to grieve in private, but then thought that she was grieving the loss of his mother, and they had that sense of profound loss in common. He walked to the bench and sat down beside her. Her head came up and he caught a glimpse of her face and it wrenched his heart. He found himself putting his arm around her, pulling her close, pressing her head to his chest. "Go ahead," he said quietly. "You can't hold it inside forever."

She cried hard for another five or so minutes before she raggedly said, "You should be at the reception."

"I should, but I'm not ready to go there yet. I wanted some time to myself."

"I should go then."

"No. Stay here with me."

"I'm such a wreck," she said miserably. "I don't have any tissues."

He dug some out of his pants pocket, kind of ragged but usable. She blew her nose, dried her eyes. There seemed to be a hollowness about her now that her tears had subsided. "I never realized just how generous my mother was," he said. "To me she was always just my mom. She fed me, kept me clean and healthy, made me eat my spinach and peas, rewarded me with cookies and brownies, took my picture way to many times for my liking, put Band-Aids on my cuts, gave me hugs when I brought home good report cards, made me clean my room. She did all the mom stuff so easily I barely even noticed what she was doing. When I was sick she made me toast. She cut it up into little squares. She brought me ginger ale and chicken soup. She read to me until I was in middle school, every night. Not kid's books. She read classics, adventure stories. She took me and Pat to the movies on Saturday afternoons while Dad watched sports on TV or washed the cars and mowed the lawn. I took her for granted every day. I thought she'd always be there."

"Did you tell her you loved her?" Eve asked.

"Yeah, I did. When I called her I always told her I loved her before hanging up. When I went over for dinner I'd kiss her goodbye at the door, thank her for a delicious dinner and then tell her I loved her. I don't know now if that was enough."

"You were her son. I'm sure it was. So many people never tell their parents they love them. Not until it's too late. I see it all the time. Don't tear yourself up thinkin' you should have said it more often. You said it enough to let her know how you felt about her."

"Did you tell your mother you loved her?" he asked. She nodded, biting her lower lip as her eyes brimmed with fresh tears. "Can I ask you something?" She nodded. "Did you tell my mother that you loved her?" The sound she made nearly broke his heart, but she nodded. "Father John told me my mother thought of you as a daughter. That's quite an honor, in my opinion."

"Oh, Eamon!" She stood up and walked fifteen feet or so away. Again she seemed to be struggling with her emotions. He saw her hands clench and unclench. He sat silently, giving her time. Finally she said, "I loved my mom but I wasn't happy when she left Dad and took me with her. She broke my family in half and tried to make me not like my Dad and my sister. I loved Ireland. I loved living with my grandparents, but I wasn't happy inside. Then she got sick and died and my father came and took me home. I was a mess thinkin' I somehow had contributed to my mother's early death, although now I understand that wasn't so. I didn't know back then. I was unhappy. I went to school after bein' away and it was like I didn't belong there anymore. I struggled with algebra. My math teacher offered to tutor me. We're raised to respect teachers and trust them. He preyed on me because I was vulnerable and young and miserable. And then, one afternoon, he asked me to take a walk in the woods behind the school with him after a gruelin' session tacklin' more advanced math that had left me discouraged. He raped me in the woods. I tried to fight him but he hit me and had his hand around my throat so I could hardly breathe. I was terrified. I guess he choked me enough to make me pass out. I woke up alone, mostly naked, in pain, horrified and only partially understandin' what he'd done to me. I pulled on my clothes and ran home. I didn't tell anyone then. I told Arlene later and she was no comfort to me. She accused me of leadin' him on."

"Is that what's led to all the animosity between you and her?" he asked.

"Yes." She turned back and returned to the bench. "I hated myself in high school. For most of it anyway. Until I met your mother. She changed my life. She took me under her wing and fed me little bites of goodness until I was quite full up with it." She smiled, her eyes teary again. "I can't begin to tell you how much I loved her after I'd gotten used to being mothered again."

"Then you have every right to mourn her the same as I do."

"I don't want to be intruding on your own mourning."

"Eve, it sounds to me like my mom made you a part of the family. What right do I have to deny you your right to grieve her?" He stood up. "Do you have another funeral today?"

"No. There's a wake tonight. It'll be small because it's an elderly man who died in a nursing home. Only one son and a few friends."

"Then, why don't you come to the reception with me."

"Oh, I couldn't!"

"I'd like you to come with me." She was shaking her head. "Eve, I'm asking you to come with me because it will make me feel better about going if you're with me." She looked at him, struggling with the fact that she was the undertaker who had handled his mother's funeral and undertakers did not attend the reception, but she had also had a personal relationship with the deceased and the deceased's son was asking her to accompany him to the reception to celebrate Mary McCleary's life, a woman who had been like a mother to her. "Please," he said.

She took a breath and he thought she was going to say no, but she said, "I'd like that. But do you think it will be all right with your father? Your brother?"

""I don't think they'll mind."

Most people did not recognize Eve as being part of the funeral home staff. Quite a few of them thought she was Eamon's girlfriend and told her they were happy he'd finally found a nice girl, that despite the sadness of the day and loss of his mother, he looked happy. Father John was still present and he had not been that surprised to see her come through the door with Eamon. He'd merely said, "We were wondering where Eamon had gotten himself off to. Was he persuading you to come?"

"Not at first. He wanted some quiet time in the garden but he found me there. I was rather a mess. We talked and he asked me to come here with him."

"He's a good man, Eve. I've known him since he was a baby. I baptized him. I've watched him grow up. May I be so bold as to suggest, if he asks to see you again, that you agree?" She looked caught off guard. Color stained her cheeks. "I believe there's some mutual interest?"

"We shouldn't be talkin' about this here."

"All I'm asking you to do, lass, is to find the courage to pursue what your heart desires. Don't be afraid. Trust the Lord who guides your path. Perhaps He directed you to Mary McCleary when you needed her most in your life. He gave you a second mother. And now, maybe He hasn't given you a brother, maybe He's given you something else that you have wanted— someone who wants you."

"I don't know."

"Why don't we see what happens. Just promise me, young lady, you will not reconstruct those walls and barriers Mary helped you to knock down."

Eamon came across the room carrying three glasses of ginger ale. He gave one to the priest, one to Eve and kept the third for himself. "Do you have a ride home, Father?" he asked. "I'll be going by the church on the way back to Mooney's to drop Eve off."

"Thank you for the offer, Eamon, but Mrs. Steward's taking me back. I believe we'll be going shortly. Just bear in mind, my door is always open to you any time of the day or night." He looked at Eve, "That goes for you as well, my dear."

They went through the buffet and then sat with Jack McCleary and Mary's sister Anne and her husband. "I'm afraid Eamon hasn't introduced us yet," Anne said. She resembled her sister somewhat. "I'm Mary's sister Anne Roarke and this is my husband Liam. And you are?"

"I'm Eve."

"Have you been with Eamon long?"

She floundered. Eamon swallowed and said, "I've known Eve since high school. I lost track of her for a few years but recently met her again."

"How nice. She's a lovely girl, Eamon. Did Mary know her?"

"Yes."

"Your sister helped me plan the garden at my home. She and I spent over two years working on it, and then she helped me with the plantin'. I guess I can rightly call her my gardenin' mentor."

"Oh, I swear Mary was born with a green thumb! Me, I can't keep a weed alive!"

Eamon relaxed. Eve was going to be fine with his aunt. Anne had noticed Eve's Irish accent and asked if she'd lived in Ireland at all, or visited the country. When she learned Eve had lived in Galway they were suddenly sitting with their heads together as Anne had just gone to Galway with Liam in May.

Jack McCleary watched Eve and Anne for a bit and then he looked at his eldest son. "Did I miss something?"

"No," Eamon replied. "You knew Mom and Eve were working on the garden project, didn't you?"

"Yeah, I knew. Mary talked quite a bit about the Mooney girl. I'd just never met her, put two and two together. Pretty girl, though not as lovely as her sister."

"I think she's beautiful," Eamon said. "Can I buy you a beer, Dad?" He went to the bar, bought drinks for the table. He chose a Bailey's Irish cream for Eve, beer for himself, his father and Liam and a margarita for his aunt. "A toast to Mary McCleary, a loving wife, an amazing mother, an awesome sister and sister-in-law and a wonderful friend."

"Here! Here!"

At three-thirty the reception had pretty much broken up. Eamon asked, "Are you ready to go?" She nodded. They said goodbye to his family members who were still present. His Aunt Anne told Eve not to be a stranger.

They walked outside into the sultry heat, got into his truck. He started it, started the air conditioner but didn't pull out yet. "Does it bother you that everyone thinks you're my girl?' he asked.

"No," she replied.

He adjusted the vents. "Look, I was thinking I'd like to go to the lake, maybe take a boat out for a bit later. You ever go sailing as the sun starts to set?"

"No."

"Do you think you'd like to go with me?"

"Today?" she asked, sounding surprised.

"Yeah. I was thinking I'd go home, change, and then go to the lake, swim for a bit, take a boat out for a while and maybe watch the sun set."

"That sounds nice." She turned her head and looked at him, then said, "I think I'd like that, but we'd have to stop someplace to get some sunscreen. I tend to burn."

"There's a drug store on the way back to your place. We can stop there."

"Do you want think we should pack a picnic supper?"

"That's probably a good idea. I'm not hungry right now, but if we swim awhile and then take the boat out then I'll most likely be hungry later. Why don't we grab the cooler and some ice packs at my place then pick up some grinders at Paulie's Deli on the way back through town, and some cold drinks, some bottled water?"

"Can we get whoopee pies at Paulie's?"

He nodded. "Sure. How many do you think you can eat?"

She laughed. "Just one!"

She went into his condo because it was too hot to sit in the truck while he changed and got the cooler ready. She was impressed by how neat and clean his place was. "Do you really live here?" she asked.

"Uh, yeah. I spend most of my time upstairs. The second bedroom is my den. You notice I didn't invite you upstairs. It's a mess."

She leaned against the counter as he ran down to the basement for the cooler, came back up and then dug ice packs out of the freezer. "Maybe you can straighten up the upstairs before you invite me over again," she suggested.

"You think you might want to come back?" he asked.

"Maybe."

He liked her response even although it had been sort of noncommittal. She was at least going to think about it, and that's the best that he could hope for today, anyway.

They stopped at the deli and the drug store to pick up what they needed and then went up her apartment. He sat in the living room while she changed into her bathing suit, shorts and a tank top. As they came back down the exterior stairs they encountered Sorcha who scowled at Eamon. "What are you doing here? The funeral is over."

"That's none of your business," Eve replied.

"You said he wasn't your boyfriend!" she cried accusingly.

"If it's any of your business, which it most certainly is not, I was in high school with Eamon. His bein' here should not be any of your concern. I do not need your permission, or your mother's, to spend time with a friend."

"Are you going to kiss him?" Sorcha demanded.

"I don't know. I can't predict the future. I haven't got the sight."

"You're being very rude to me!" She followed them to the truck. "Where are you going?"

"To the lake."

She looked as if the fact that there was a lake nearby was a complete surprise to her. "Can I go?"

Eamon replied, "Not this time. Maybe next weekend, if you stop harassing your aunt. If she tells me that you've behaved yourself then we'll take you to the lake, and maybe take you sailing. If you annoy her at all, the deal is off."

She looked at him incredulously at first, and then somewhat warily. "You'll take me with you next time?"

"There are certain conditions involved. If you stop pestering your aunt, yes, we will take you."

"Do you promise?"

"I promise."

Sorcha looked at Eve. "Just me? Not Mom?"

"Just you," she said.

"I can't go today?"

"No, not today. Eamon just buried his mother. His mother was my friend. We want to go watch the sun set and remember her. We won't be much fun. But next weekend, if you're good, we'll take you. You can swim and play with the other kids on the beach, and then Eamon will take us sailing. And maybe we'll have ice cream before comin' home."

"I've never been sailing."

Eve bent down and drew her niece into a hug. "I know you're bored and lonely. I'll take you shoppin' this comin' week for a bathin' suit and some beach toys, a life vest and everythin' you'll be needin' for a day at the beach, okay? Just you and me. We'll have lunch while we're out." Sorcha nodded. "I'll see you tomorrow and we'll make a list of all the things we'll need to get."

Sorcha nodded and then sadly watched them go. Eve commented that it was nice of him to offer to take her. "She's like you said, bored and lonely. Your sister probably never takes her anyplace."

"No, she's seeing someone, so she goes out and one of us has to watch Sorcha, so she's feeling housebound."

"You don't mind my offering to take her, do you?"

"No. She's been a plague to me, but I think, with your help, we can turn her around."

"Let's make her our project," he suggested. She agreed.

The sunset was gorgeous--all luminous shades of rosy pinks, lavenders, blues, golds and darker purples. Eve leaned against him, her head on his shoulder. She'd had a nice afternoon with him. He was a strong swimmer. She could swim, but not as good as he could. She liked having him slather on the sunscreen, laughed when he daubed it on the tip of her nose and her chin, smeared it across her cheeks and forehead like war paint. She rubbed some into his shoulders and back, down his arms. He noticed she hesitated before she touched his chest. He watched her massage the lotion into his skin. Her face was flushed from more than just the sun. He liked the feel of her hand on his skin. He liked being with her.

"Before the mosquitoes start eating us alive we should head back to the dock," he said.

"I'm starting to get cold, believe it or not."

"I think, despite the sunscreen, you might have got a bit of a burn." He adjusted the sail and headed them back to the dock where they'd rented the boat. "One day I'd like to buy my own sailboat," he told her.

"That would be nice, to have your own boat."

"Do you like sailing?" She nodded. "Do you think Sorcha will like it?"

"I think so. It'll be different."

"I think they have fireworks on Saturday nights. I'll rent the boat now for next Saturday so we'll be sure to get one. Bring a blanket in case she gets a burn and a chill when the sun sets. And we'll bring insect repellent. Let's not forget that!"

"Okay."

He bought her an ice cream cone at the stand on the road back toward town. They sat on the tailgate of his truck to eat their ice cream. Soon they were swatting at mosquitoes. "Time to get into the truck," he announced.

On the drive home she was quiet. He didn't try to initiate any conversation. It was good that they could be together and not feel a need to fill the silences. As they approached the funeral home she said, "Thanks for askin' me to go with you, Eamon. I had a nice afternoon and I really liked watchin' the sun set from the boat. It was beautiful."

He asked for her phone number, gave her his. "I'll call you this week and we'll firm up plans for Saturday. Keep me posted about your niece, whether or not she's behaving."

"I will. But I have a feelin' she'll be tryin' her best to be good. She's desperate to get out of the house, and I can't blame her. It's a funeral home. She's only half Mooney. It's probably not in her blood." She sighed. "It's not easy livin' in a funeral home. You can't go runnin' around much of the time as there're wakes and funerals goin' on downstairs and you can't be disturbin' people. You really can't go and play outdoors because, again, you'd be disturbin' people. She needs to get out into some open space and just be a child."

He nodded. "I guess I should be heading home." He had walked her to the base of the staircase up to her apartment.

"It's been a long day."

"It hasn't been as bad as I thought it would be. The morning was rough, but the rest of the day, it was very nice." She nodded. "Can I hug you?' he asked.

"If you'd like to."

"I think I'd like to. You've been a great comfort to me. I appreciate it."

"Are you goin' to have to tell all your relatives that I'm not really your girlfriend?" she asked.

"I was hoping I wouldn't have to. I was kind of thinking it might be nice if you really were my girlfriend. I just don't know how you'd feel about that."

She hesitated. "Are you askin' me to be?"

"I am." Her eyes met his in the starlight. "Do you think you're ready for somethin' like that?"

"Are you sure it's me you're wantin' and not Arlene?"

"Arlene's older than I am."

"By only a year, right?"

"And she's divorced, and I don't find her personality that attractive. I do, however, think you are the loveliest girl I have ever seen. I'm pretty sure you're the Mooney girl I want to be with."

"Then you can hug me," she said.

He took her in his arms and pulled her close, held her, but not too tightly. They stood together for a few long minutes, quietly, and then she tilted her face up to his. "Do you know what I think?" he asked.

"No, what do you think?"

"I think my mother intended to introduce us one day. I think, in the full game plan, she would have gotten us together somehow in the end."

She was quiet for a moment and then said, "It is the end for her, and here we are, so maybe this is what was meant to be." She moved her hand to touch his face. "I knew she was your mother but she only talked about you and your brother a little bit. She never mentioned if you had a girlfriend, or whether or not you were married. I wondered sometimes. I just assumed you were either seein' someone or were married. I mean, you were pretty popular in high school. All the girls adored you."

"*All* of them?" She nodded. He turned his head, his face into her hand, pressing his lips against her palm. She caught her breath. "Present company included?"

"Yes," she said, her voice barely audible.

"Since we can't go back in time I guess we'll just have to start here and move forward."

"Eamon?"

"Yes?"

"I think…I…I think…"

He shushed her, bending so his forehead touched hers. "Just come right out and say what you think," he said softly.

She drew in a breath and then said, "I think I'd like it if you kissed me goodnight."

"Was that so hard?"

She laughed softly. "No. Well…just a little. For me anyway."

"Tell you what. Why don't you kiss me first. You might feel better about it if you took the lead."

"I really haven't ever kissed anyone…a boyfriend, I mean. I've kissed my father goodnight, and my grandfathers and my uncles and so on."

"It's not that difficult. If you don't get it right the first time, we just make a few minor little adjustments to lip position and try again. There are no bad kisses. And first kisses with a boyfriend are generally some of the best kisses a girl can ever experience." He felt her relax a bit in his arms. "Whenever you're ready."

She nudged his head a bit so she could reach his mouth. Very softly, she touched her lips to his. His heart swelled in his breast. "Can I try again?" she whispered.

"They say practice makes perfect. Try as many times as you'd like."

"Will you tell me when I have it right?"

"I'll let you know." She kissed him tentatively a few more times, pulled back a bit to look at him for a few moments, then she put her hand behind his head and pulled his mouth to hers and kissed him like she had seen actresses kiss actors in the movies. She felt him react to her kisses and it awakened something inside her that quickened her heartbeat. "You got it right that time," he said. She grinned. "And on that note, I'd better go home."

"Goodnight, Eamon."

"Goodnight, Eve." He gave her a hug then let go of her and stepped away. "Hey, is there a funeral tomorrow?"

"At eleven."

"Are you free after that?"

"Um…" She thought quickly. "Call me at three, or is that too late?"

"No. I thought maybe we could go out to dinner, take a drive in the country and then I'd bring you home."

"All right. If a body comes in tomorrow I probably wouldn't do anything with it until Monday anyway."

Eamon thought it might take a little getting used to, dating a mortician, but he'd adjust. "I'll call you at three and probably see you around four thirty? Maybe we can go over to Dana to Grimaldi's for Italian?"

"Perfect! I'm dying…well not literally, for spaghetti and meatballs!"

"Italian it is then." He waved and then turned and headed for his truck.

There was a light on in a rear second floor window and he saw a small figure watching him as he crossed the parking area. He raised a hand and waved to Sorcha. She hesitated then waved back. She was a piece of work, that kid, but he thought, in time, he and Eve could help give her a real childhood. Her mother certainly wasn't all that interested in doing so.

As he headed home he glanced up at the twinkling stars. "Thanks, Mom," he said. "I think you were right. She's the one."

About the Author

Susan Buffum lives in western Massachusetts where she works as a medical secretary and writes as a hobby. She lives with her husband, John, and their daughter, Kelly, who also writes, in a mountainside home that they share with two literary cats—Revere and Riley Beans.

Susan is the author of a number of novels and story collections including *Miss Peculiar's Haunting Tales, Volume I-III, My Magical Life, The Subtlety of Light and Shadow, The Archetypes-First Generation, The Archetypes-Shockwaves, Talon: An Intimate Familiarity, Talon: A Sense of Familiarity, Love Me Knots, Auspicious Beginnings, Yuletide Stories, Always Christmas in My Heart, Together for the Holidays,* and *Life Skills.*

The author welcomes your comments and feedback at sebuffum415@gmail.com

Made in the USA
Charleston, SC
07 February 2016